SIMON *Says*

6.25.12

WILLIAM POE

This is a work of fiction. Names, characters, places, and incidents are the products of the author's imagination or are used fictitiously. Any resemblance to actual events, locales, or persons, living or dead, is entirely coincidental.

Copyright © 2012 William Poe
All rights reserved.

ISBN-13: 978-0615559575
ISBN-10: 0615559573

CHAPTER ONE

After ten years on a spiritual journey, I was again living in the same old house in Sibley, Arkansas, where I grew up. As I lay on the familiar four poster bed one afternoon, I recalled the time my childhood friend, Ernie, and I were caught fooling around during a sleepover. My mother told us that if we didn't behave ourselves, we would grow up to be homicidal. Even then, we knew the correct word was homosexual, but the situation was no laughing matter. Mother's eyes told us we were sinners. Our bodies told us a different story.

A few years later, when he started dating girls, Ernie and I had a falling out. He started acting as though we didn't know each other. I felt sucker punched every time I passed him in the hallway at school. I knew Ernie was in pain — the look in his eyes told me that. During the eleventh grade, he began abusing heroin and overdosed at age twenty-two. By then, I had converted to a fringe religion and was living in Chicago, but I managed to get back to Arkansas for the wake.

The last time I saw Ernie alive was at a party, just after I graduated high school. Drug abuse had given him a sallow appearance. Lying in his casket, I saw that death returned the innocent look I had wanted to recall. The pain was gone forever. When no one was looking, I bent over to kiss Ernie's lips. I felt him there with me.

Dating girls didn't turn out any better for me than it had for Ernie. I truly cared about one girl, but when she wanted to be intimate, I couldn't go through with it. The sense of failure, the feeling of shame, kept me from being comfortable around my friends. It was clear I wasn't like them.

During most of high school, I stayed at home and painted. Art had inspired me since I was six years old, when I first saw reproductions of works by Jackson Pollock and Willem Dekooning in our Funk & Wagnalls yearbook. I excised the images with a blade from my dad's razor. Precocious boy that I was, no one else in the family ever looked at the encyclopedia. Mom had no idea where I found the pictures taped to the wall beside my bed.

In my senior year, things began to change. The new art teacher was openly gay. I figured that out the moment I saw his plucked eyebrows and transparent fingernail polish. The teacher introduced me to the gay scene in Little Rock, such as it was at the time. Men gathered at parties hosted in turn by various friends. During a get together at the art teacher's house, I fell in love with Tony, a boy my age who attended high school on the other side of the county. Our relationship ended when he called one afternoon to tell me he had been saved by Jesus and that I was going to hell. I was only seventeen years old and took it hard. I raced my car up Lookout Drive in Little Rock and was ready to plunge off a cliff into the Arkansas River. At the last second, I stopped the car. Even so, a part of me was lost in the abyss that night.

Many friends who I had known since elementary school began smoking pot and dropping acid. Quite a few had quit school and never graduated. After my breakup with Tony, and for a year while I was at the local university, I became the biggest acid head among them. During one dramatic trip, I saw the face of God. A voice told me I was among the chosen, and that I should look to the clouds of heaven. A week later, I joined a religious group which, at the time, was known for the fact that its members lived communally, but which later became notorious for selling flowers on the street and for holding mass weddings, not to mention charges of brainwashing.

I listened to the group's lectures at the urging of a friend from the university. The theology attracted me, not least by offering high-minded justification for my self-loathing. The group's founder, Sun Myung Moon, and his wife, Hak Ja Han, were considered the embodiment of a God whose essence was both masculine and feminine. New members were instructed to remain celibate for at least three years until married in a mass ceremony to a spouse selected by Reverend Moon. Church elders still had to give permission before sex was allowed — even then, the first night was more ritual than love-making. Anything distorting the marriage relationship was Satanic by definition. Homosexuality was evil itself.

For a kid untrained in theology, the church's beliefs were heady stuff. I thought the ideas made sense, and found them far more compelling than what I had learned in Southern Baptist Sunday school. Those teachings had troubled me. I would ask questions, such as how God could ordain Jesus to die on the cross and then condemn those who killed him. I was told to quit letting the devil enter my heart. The new teachings, however, explained that the outcome had not been ordained — that Jesus should have lived and taken a wife. I felt vindicated.

Church members called themselves brothers and sisters, and referred to the group as "the Family." They weren't hollow terms. I'd never experienced such congenial relationships. Leaving the group after a decade of deeply shared experiences was a soul-wrenching experience.

People often ask "How did you get away?" but it wasn't like that. I was a trusted leader. Members respected the fact that I spent several years on the streets selling flowers before gaining positions of authority. In my last year with the group, I was a coordinator of legal affairs during a trial on tax evasion charges faced by Reverend Moon and a subordinate, who was my direct supervisor. As the trial progressed, I shuttled transcripts between the Federal courthouse in New York and attorneys working for the church in Los Angeles.

It had become obvious that no amount of prayer and fasting would change the fact that I was gay. As logical as the beliefs seemed, they had to be wrong. My adult life was built on sand that had slipped through the hourglass. I was not quite twenty-eight when I left.

In the old house that the Powell family had lived in for generations, I gazed out the window of my bedroom on the second floor and could see the swimming pool at Ernie's house. There he was, racing across the field on his way to visit me. Just as the apparition neared the base of the trellis, it vanished behind a haze of tears. The memory kindled a terrible longing to see Lyle, a hustler I had brought to my hotel room in Los Angeles during Reverend Moon's trial. Such things were forbidden, of course, but I took many liberties while working in Los Angeles.

Reverend Moon held a mass wedding ceremony while the trial was underway. I had already been matched to a Japanese woman named Masako.

We had gotten legally married so she could apply for a green card. The mass wedding made the marriage final in the eyes of the church. I should never have gone through with it — Lyle was waiting for me in the hotel room — but that is the virtue of denial. Surely, a last minute reprieve from heaven would transform me into a heterosexual.

Psychologists use the term cognitive dissonance to describe a person's ability to act sane while harboring internal contradictions. I couldn't do it. The divisions in my heart were pushing me over the edge. I wanted Lyle more than I desired the wife chosen by Reverend Moon. She was sweet, kind, and personable, but I wasn't physically attracted to her. The moment of decision had arrived.

I took my possessions from the room I occupied in the church's New York headquarters and returned to Sibley. When I got there, I realized that nothing had changed. I had simply been absent for a decade.

CHAPTER TWO

My mother, Vivian, was not well-educated, but she made up for her lack of book smarts through a keen intuition. Vivian would not have forgotten the incident with Ernie and me, but other than her misstatement at the time, she didn't mention it again. Ernie continued to spend the night every now and then, but Vivian never again came into my room unannounced. Did she actually think her admonition had set us straight, as it were, or did she just not care to know what might be going on when I closed the bedroom door for the night?

Even though I left my religion because I could no longer deny that I was gay, I could not imagine standing before Vivian and my father and saying, "Vivian, Lenny, I have something to tell you. I'm a homosexual. The main reason I joined that cult was to run away from myself. It took the prospect of married life to bring me back to my senses. I'm a mess. I'm addicted to drugs, and as a substitute for true love, I sleep with hustlers."

Telling them that I was dropping out of college to join a "religious commune" had been easier than it would be to admit to my current situation. I was as sure as I had been as a child that the world -- my parents, namely -- would reject me.

Lenny nearly died from shock when I told him I was leaving home. He'd been in and out of the hospital for years because of heart attacks. Finding out he had a queer son would be the final blow. It was clear how he felt. One night, Lenny almost kicked in the television when Liberace appeared as a guest on "Late Night with Johnny Carson". "That damn faggot is queer as a three dollar bill!" Lenny had shouted in disgust.

I could barely understand how much I needed Lenny's acceptance. He had wanted a son who worshipped him the same way he worshiped his own father. But growing up, we had never seen anything eye-to-eye.

As a little boy, I wondered why Lenny didn't play with me when other fathers were teaching their sons to catch baseballs. I probably would have resisted anyway, preferring to look at pictures in the encyclopedia, but Lenny never even tried to engage me. I recall only one time that he so much as put me on his knee. I must have been five. Lenny sang a song by Cowboy Copas that he remembered from a Grand Ole Opry radio broadcast. I don't recall the tune, only the smell of Lenny's Old Spice aftershave and the strong embrace of his muscular arms.

No matter how hard I tried to forget the many bad episodes between us, they'd surface at odd moments nonetheless. Simply hearing a dog barking down the street brought up one of the most painful memories of my childhood, one that involved Sparky -- the collie I got as a present when I was two years old.

I grew to be a skinny little boy who got picked on most of the time. When neighborhood bullies taunted me, my only defense was to retreat into our yard. Sparky's bared teeth told them not to follow.

One night, when I was ten and Sparky was eight, Vivian and Lenny went to a party at a cousin's house. Sparky started howling from the crawlspace under the porch. I got a flashlight, and despite my grandmother Mandy's scolding, shimmied through the dirt and cobwebs to find him. When he sensed my presence, Sparky began whimpering. He tried to find his way to the light, but kept bumping into support beams. Something had blinded him. I called out until he found his way to me. I wrapped my arms around his neck and led him into the house. Sparky's eyes were glassy and his stomach was swollen.

As she usually did when confronted with a difficult situation, Mandy began talking to herself and was of no help. I found the cousin's phone number scribbled on a note under a refrigerator magnet and dialed it myself.

"Sparky's sick," I cried when Lenny came on the line. "He's going to die!"

"Now, Bubby," Lenny said. "It's probably just something he ate."

"He's all swollen up!" I cried. "He's going to die! You have to come home."

"We can't leave just yet," Lenny insisted. "Sparky will be okay."

Mandy walked past while I was on the phone. She turned to the wall, and said, "No, I don't know why he's crying."

When Lenny hung up, I took Sparky into my arms and held him tight. "I love you, Sparky," I cried. A moment later, he was dead.

When he finally came home, Lenny told me that I should be a man and stop crying. He pulled Sparky from my arms and took his body to a spot near the barn. By the light of his Coleman lantern, he dug a hole and unceremoniously put Sparky in his grave.

Lenny thought it was ridiculous when, the next day, I planted an oak sapling on the soft earth where Sparky was buried. It is now the tallest tree on the property.

Vivian and Lenny came to New York when I was married to Masako in the mass wedding. Not long after that, the doctors told Lenny to take it easy because he was close to having another heart attack.

The doctor's words translated into further misery for Vivian. Already, she had become more nursemaid than wife. One afternoon, after I had come home, Vivian was outside raking sweet-gum balls into a pile before mowing the lawn. Lenny sat in a lawn chair, pointing out areas that she had missed.

I watched from behind the screen door before going outside, waiting for the right moment to rescue Vivian from Lenny's criticism.

"Hi, son," she said, taking a long overdue break.

Lenny growled, "You're not done yet, woman. Get to work."

"Not in front of Simon," Vivian said.

Lenny didn't realize that I was standing beside him until I placed a hand on his bony shoulder. Even then, it took a moment for him to recall that I had come home.

Vivian threw up her arms, exasperated by Lenny's forgetfulness. "Let's get you inside," she said, taking the oxygen tube from around his neck and helping him out of the lawn chair. "Will you take the tank?" she asked me.

When we got him settled into his recliner, Lenny fell asleep. Vivian set his oxygen tube in place.

"Will you help me upstairs?" Vivian asked.

She and Lenny had moved into a room on the ground floor, but most of her personal belongings were still in the upstairs master bedroom.

Vivian took my elbow. "It didn't used to be so hard," she said, pausing halfway up.

When we made it to the landing, she pointed to a small gash in one of the doors, about eight inches from the floor. The room had once belonged to my sister, Connie.

"Remember that?" Vivian asked.

"I was six, wasn't I?"

"That's right. You had just started school."

During a slumber party, Connie and her friends had locked themselves inside the room. I got mad when they wouldn't let me in, and hearing them whispering to each other, I lost control and kicked the door. More than thirty years later, the hole I made was still there.

CHAPTER THREE

Vivian worked at the local grocery store, starting out as a checkout clerk and eventually becoming the bookkeeper. She could have retired already, but work gave her an opportunity to escape being at Lenny's beck and call.

Before I came back home to Sibley, my sister Connie took care of Lenny while Vivian was at work, but now I took over. I stayed upstairs most of the day, coming down only to administer Lenny's medicine or check on the oxygen tank.

Lenny hated having the tube in his nose and never hooked it up properly when left to his own devices. One afternoon, I found him dozing in his chair. The tube hung loosely around his neck with the nosepiece dangling down his chest.

"You're supposed to use that oxygen all the time," I warned, lifting the tube.

"To hell with doctors," Lenny grumbled.

"Doctors or not, you don't look well. Did you take your pills?"

"Those horse pills would kill me for sure if I took them all," Lenny complained. "And what about that crap I'm supposed to drink? It smells so bad it would gag a maggot."

When I insisted, Lenny took the horse pills and swallowed the foul liquid medicine. As I repositioned the oxygen tube, a rosy hue came to his cheeks. He went back to watching his nature show on television without the smallest word of thanks.

Just after lunch – tuna fish straight from the can with a little mayonnaise, just the way he liked it – Lenny announced that he wanted to go out. He asked me to drive.

I was nervous about taking him out of the house, and made sure I had the doctor's phone number. Lenny first had me take him to a hardware store, where he purchased a band saw, a planer, and several canisters of caulk. He also picked out some lumber, which the owner of the store loaded into the Econoline van, a relic of Lenny's days as a plumber. Then, Lenny directed me a few miles down the road to a different store, where he bought rakes, hoes, a shovel, and a pickaxe, as well as a post-hole digger.

"What's all this for?" I asked on the way home.

"I'm going to set up a workshop," Lenny said. "The house needs repairs, and I want to fix the fence out by the barn. I'm going to buy a horse."

I was sure that Lenny had lost his mind.

"Did you go out, son?" Vivian asked when she returned from work. "It looks like the van's been moved."

"Lenny wanted to go shopping, so I drove him."

Vivian set down a sack of groceries and rushed to the den. "You didn't spend more money, did you?"

"What I do is my own business," Lenny fired back.

"Where did you go?" Vivian demanded to know.

Lenny remained silent.

"Where did you take him?" she asked, turning to me.

"He bought a bunch of tools and stuff." I hoped to avoid getting in the middle of the argument.

Vivian let out an exasperated sigh as she studied Lenny's expression. "You're hell-bent on breaking us, aren't you?"

Lenny drew his lips pencil-thin. His mouth twisted into a sardonic smile. "I can't take it with me," he said, "but I sure as hell ain't leaving it behind."

Vivian was beside herself, red-faced and ready to explode. "Just what do you expect me to do when you're gone?" she demanded.

But she knew the answer. Lenny didn't care what happened to her.

Vivian grabbed a dishtowel and held it to her eyes as she headed toward the bedroom. She slammed the door with enough force to shake plaster from the ceiling.

I raided the refrigerator for some of the tuna fish I had made earlier, and with a sandwich and can of Pepsi in hand, retreated to my room. I dug through the boxes I'd brought along, hoping to find a stash of cocaine that might have been overlooked.

No such luck.

Two days later, I took Lenny on another shopping spree. Though I protested, he told me to pull into a Mercury dealership, saying that I needed transportation. He wrote a check for the down payment on a charcoal gray Topaz and arranged for it to be delivered to the house.

"You need a car," Lenny said, "now that you're free again."

The turn of phrase made me feel as though I'd just been released from prison, which probably is how Lenny thought of my years in the church. I couldn't bring myself to protest too much. I did need a car.

On the way home, Lenny said we should stop by an auto repair shop where a friend of his worked. Lenny had met the man, a born-again Christian named Nathan, at a meeting of the anti-cult network that Connie and her husband, Derek, had helped to found. They had been active in all sorts of anti-cult groups during the years I belonged to the Unification Church. Connie basked in the sympathetic smiles she received when speaking from church pulpits about how her brother was "lost to Satan." She had hoped that I was leaving the Family because "Christ had opened my heart", as she put it. That would make her victory complete. But I reminded her that I never had been a Christian, that the closest I'd ever gotten was when I filled out a form in the back of an Edgar Cayce book to join the Association for Research and Enlightenment.

"You wait here, Bubby," Lenny said when I pulled into the parking lot of the repair shop. "I'll be right back."

I watched from the van while Lenny chatted at the garage door with Nathan, who'd gotten a metal folding chair out of the office for Lenny to sit on. The man's pompadour drooped over his forehead as he looked down at Lenny and nodded his head. He rubbed mechanic's grease from his hands with an orange chamois, and then took Lenny's hand and helped him up. They disappeared into the garage.

Soon, Lenny started walking toward the van. He'd been away from his oxygen for too long and was having a hard time catching his breath.

Nathan came running from the garage waving a hundred dollar bill. "Lenny, I can't accept this," he said, arriving at the passenger side window just after Lenny got in. "Don't make me beholden to you like this."

"Oh, hell," Lenny said with an air of self-satisfaction. "You and Louise need something extra, what with them babies on the way."

Nathan tried to force the money into Lenny's hand, but he wouldn't take it.

"Drive home, son," Lenny commanded.

Nathan stepped back as I put the van in gear.

"What was that about?" I asked.

"Nathan's wife is having twins," Lenny said, "and they can barely pay their bills. I wanted to do something."

It wasn't easy to keep my mouth shut. Nathan hadn't expected charity. I supposed that Nathan wanted nothing more than to save Lenny's soul. For all Connie's efforts, Lenny wasn't very religious.

Why didn't Lenny want to provide for Vivian? Maybe in his mind, she was little more than a servant – the one person he could treat badly and get away with it.

Just before we drove into the yard, Lenny said, "If you treat people right, Bubby, they'll be there when you need them."

Lenny might have realized how foolish his words sounded if he understood that everyone I had ever cared about had turned away. Lenny had no clue how little his gift of a car meant to me. I simply wanted to know that he loved me – me, his independent-minded gay son, not the fantasy offspring who was supposed to worship him.

When Vivian arrived home and I told her about the car, she didn't complain.

"Well, honey," she said, taking a skillet from the pantry as she began dinner preparations, "I'm glad Lenny did something for you."

She placed a frozen chicken in the sink and turned on the hot water to defrost it. Taking a break, she sat at the kitchen table, took off a shoe, and started massaging her arches.

"I hate to see you working so hard," I said.

"If your father's going to be so foolish, I don't have a choice," she said, pressing hard on the ball of her foot.

Lenny called out from his chair. Vivian rushed to the den. The oxygen tank was depleted.

"Will you get a new canister?" Vivian asked me as she placed a blood-pressure strap around Lenny's arm. Reading the result, she said, "His pressure is low."

We hooked up a new supply of oxygen, and Lenny perked up.

"What in hell ya'll staring at?" he asked. "I ain't dead yet."

"You looked pretty close," I told him.

Lenny waved us away. "Ya'll go away and let me rest."

Vivian went back to the kitchen. I followed.

"Lenny doesn't mean to make you feel bad," I said. But we both knew that was exactly what he meant to do.

A jar of pickles slipped through Vivian's hands, sending sweet midgets rolling over the linoleum.

"Damn!" Vivian cursed.

It might have been the second time in my life I'd heard her swear.

"That'll be the devil to try and get out of the cracks," Vivian said.

I found a mop and ran it over the floor while Vivian sat at the table. She was good at hiding her emotions, but the plaits forming on her pursed lips gave her away.

"If only he cared," she muttered, "even a little."

"That'll be the day," I said.

Vivian shot me a knowing glance.

"You remember that horse Lenny had?" Vivian asked. "You'd of thought he cared more about that animal than he did me."

I put my hands on each side of Vivian's head and kissed her forehead.

Lenny gave me a horse for Christmas one year, a pregnant mare named Bride. When the colt was old enough, Lenny decided to sell it. I was so hurt that I told him I'd never ride another horse. So the next day, Lenny sold Bride as well. He used the money to buy a pedigreed American saddle horse.

About a year later, the saddle horse cut its hoof on some old wire jutting from the ground near the corral. The wound became infected. Lenny thought he could treat it with store-bought salve and never called the veterinarian. The horse developed lockjaw. By the time Lenny was forced to ask for help, the veterinarian said the horse would need to stay on its feet if it was going to survive the night.

For twenty-four hours, Lenny stayed beside that horse. Vivian took him food and kept him supplied with coffee. I stood outside the corral, listening as Lenny brushed the horse's coat and whispered to it. "Good boy," he'd say. "You'll be okay."

"He didn't show that much concern when I had my gall bladder removed," Vivian said as I followed her back to the house after delivering Lenny a fresh cup of coffee.

"I did," I reminded her. "I stayed right by your side."

"That's right," Vivian smiled. "You didn't want to lose your mother, did you?"

The way she put it embarrassed me at the time, but she was right. I was terrified she might die.

Vivian and I were in the kitchen when Lenny ran through the back door at the end of his vigil.

"He died," Lenny said, tears forming in the corner of his eyes.

I was glad. Now he knew how it felt when Sparky died in my arms.

CHAPTER FOUR

As the days went by, responsibility for Lenny's care fell increasingly on me. Vivian was too exhausted and too distraught about the fact that she was almost out of money. I prepared Lenny's lunches, though mostly they consisted of soup that Vivian made in large pots and then froze in bags which could be put in the microwave. Lenny usually wanted to stay in the den and have me bring him a tray, but often I insisted that he sit with me at the kitchen table. Lenny would ramble, and I didn't pay a lot of attention most of the time.

One afternoon, he said, "I've tried to be good to people. Everyone loves me."

"Everybody but your son," I said, regretting it immediately.

The doctor had been very clear. The aneurysm on Lenny's aorta could rupture under the strain of too much emotion. I had snickered when I heard it, trying to recall a time, other than the death of his horse, when Lenny had been emotional. But this time, Lenny pressed a napkin to his eyes to dry his tears. I stood behind his chair and rubbed his shoulders.

"Don't cry," I said. "You're right. Everyone loves you."

"I was so young," Lenny sobbed. "I thought it was enough if I worked hard."

An encyclopedia of responses flooded my mind. I hugged Lenny, immediately recognizing the Old Spice cologne I'd smelled the one time he put me on his knee.

"It's the drugs," Lenny said, surprised at his own tears. "They're enough to make a grown man cry." He chuckled self-consciously.

Never having seen Lenny this way, my questions wouldn't stay put.

"Why didn't you want me around when I was little?" I asked. "What was wrong with me?"

I hoped my questions wouldn't set him off again, but I needed to know.

Lenny wiped his mouth with the tear-soaked napkin and gazed out the window. "When you joined that cult," he said, "I knew it was my fault. It killed me that you weren't going to finish school. That had been my own dream until the war hit and I had to enlist."

There was no hope. Lenny lived by his own mythologies. I had received a scholarship to a good college, but Lenny refused to help pay for the room and board. He claimed to be concerned that his health would deteriorate and that I needed to be close. He said I should go to the local college and live at home.

Ironically, I met members of the Unification Church at the college Lenny insisted I attend.

A week after the emotional outburst, Lenny asked me to take him out for a ride around the neighborhood. He knew every inch of the landscape and had a story to tell at every turn. Though I'd heard it hundreds of times, he related once again how marauders had hanged the family patriarch from an oak tree in the front yard, accusing him of sympathizing with the North – something that had caused my grandmother's blood pressure to rise every time she told me the story.

"There used to be black Powells in these parts. Did you know that?" Lenny asked.

It was an odd comment coming from a man who picketed Little Rock High School with gun-toting alumni during the crisis of 1957.

"Back when I was little," Lenny continued, "around 1930, my father drove me out to meet one of the former slaves. She'd been young at the time, but she remembered being a slave."

No wonder Lenny had such a hard heart. His father took him to meet someone the family used to think they owned! And this was the same man who Lenny considered a saint because he sacrificed for the Sibley community during the Great Depression. The man had a mercantile store and, supposedly, didn't call in the debts when farmers failed to pay on their accounts. The family slogan had been seared into my brain: Better one family suffers than for many to do without.

Lenny pointed out the location of the old store. Nothing remained on the spot but a monument put up by descendants of Sibley's pioneers. We stopped to read the names carved into it. Most were related to us, in one way or another.

On the way home, we drove up the dirt road to the family graveyard. The arched gate had fallen over in recent years, but the rusted letters still read Powell Cemetery.

"They're all here," Lenny said, his voice tinged with melancholy. He would be joining them soon, and he knew it.

"We should get home," I said. "Look at that sky."

A few clouds had gathered, but mostly I wanted to get Lenny home before his emotions flared up again.

I was in my room upstairs when I heard Vivian yell, "Bubby! Come quick!" I nearly flew to the ground floor, sure of what I would find.

Lenny was sprawled across the kitchen floor. Vivian was beside herself, screaming, "Lenny! Lenny!" as she bent over him.

Lenny's normally brown eyes had become steel gray. I called 911 and gave the operator our address.

"Don't die, Lenny!" Vivian kept repeating. "Not now, not like this."

I retrieved the oxygen tank and put the nosepiece in place, turning the knob to its highest setting. Lenny's breath returned and color flushed his cheeks.

The paramedics set up an I.V. drip when they arrived, and afterward said that my getting the oxygen probably saved his life. As they carried Lenny out on a gurney, I suggested that Vivian call Connie so she could meet us at the hospital. She dialed the number, but when Connie answered, Vivian lost her voice and I took the phone.

"Connie? It's Lenny. He's had a heart attack."

Connie called out Derek's name. "What about Mother? Is she all right?"

"She's following the paramedics outside," I said, and then asked them, "Where is he going?"

One of the men said, "Baptist," as he glanced at Vivian for confirmation.

"They're taking him to Baptist Hospital," I told Connie.

I rushed to change out of the shorts and tee-shirt I was wearing, and then ran to catch up with Vivian. She stood frozen beside her car, waiting for me. The ambulance had just pulled out of the driveway. We tailgated them to the hospital.

Lenny was taken to intensive care before we got to see him. One of the paramedics came over to Vivian. "We revived him three times on the way here," the man said.

Vivian grabbed my arm for support.

Connie and Derek arrived. Derek held the hand of their youngest daughter, Victoria, as she trotted hard to keep up.

Victoria leaped into my arms, asking, "When can I see papa?"

"We don't know," I said, brushing a lock of hair from her eyes.

"How is he?" Connie asked.

I took her aside, away from Vivian and Victoria. "It's a miracle he survived. The paramedic said his heart stopped a couple times during the trip."

"If Lenny dies, Vivian's going to take it hard."

"It's more a matter of *when*," I said. I didn't tell her that Lenny would have died at home if I hadn't gotten his oxygen.

A doctor came from behind some swinging doors. Vivian grilled him for information, pleading for him to let her see Lenny. Derek took Victoria to a sofa and sat her in his lap, while Connie and I coaxed Vivian to be calm. The doctor was adamant that it was too soon to know anything, and that Lenny needed to rest before receiving visitors.

Vivian refused to go home, despite the doctor's insistence. Connie and I decided to stay with her. Derek took Victoria home. He had to work the next day, and arranged for his sister to baby-sit Victoria as well as my oldest niece, Cheryl, who was at home, sick with the flu.

Connie and I called family members and friends to let them know that they should be prepared. Hearing us, Vivian went down the hall to sit near the doors to the intensive care unit. Connie telephoned Nathan and Louise, who planned to come to the hospital right away to be with Vivian. I had not realized they were such close friends.

Vivian and I were the first to see Lenny the next morning. His wrists were secured to the bed rails with cloth restraints. When I saw him clutch at the respirator tube extending down in his throat, I understood why.

Lenny glared at Vivian with unfocused eyes. Then, his midsection rose in a spasm just before he collapsed. Within seconds, a nurse rushed through the flimsy curtains separating Lenny's bed from the other patients.

"You'll have to leave now," she said.

I had to pull Vivian back to the waiting room. A few moments later, a doctor approached us.

"There isn't much I can do," he informed us. "Mr. Powell's arteries have deteriorated and his heart has lost too much muscle. He wouldn't survive another operation."

"My father didn't want to be put on a respirator," I said.

"Mr. Powell wouldn't make it twenty-four hours if we disconnected him," the doctor said. "But, if that is the case, we do have another option. An experimental drug has been effective in other cases such as this. It has to be administered directly through the aorta. We could remove the respirator and try that. The problem is that the medication is only safe for a week, otherwise it destroys the kidneys. The survival rate has not been good following withdrawal from the medicine."

"Are you saying the drug can help?" Vivian asked.

"There has been success, in the short term," the doctor told her.

"Go ahead, then," Vivian insisted.

The doctor had Vivian sign a release, and went to prepare the medication.

Lenny responded well. The hospital put him in a private room so that the family could be with him. The respirator tube was gone, replaced by an I.V. in Lenny's neck. The miracle drug was a yellow liquid that dripped slowly from a bottle hanging on a rod beside the bed. The effects were startling. Lenny's color was normal, his eyes were bright, and his mind was clear.

"How did I get here?" Lenny asked. His voice was hoarse after the removal of the respirator. When he spotted Vivian, he demanded she come to his bedside.

"Don't you remember?" I asked, intervening. It was clear that Lenny was about to blame Vivian for bringing him to the hospital. "You passed out in the kitchen. We thought you were a goner."

"How long?"

Connie went around to the other side of the bed and clasped his hand. "It's been three days," she said.

"They didn't put me on life support, did they?" Lenny said, glaring at Vivian, who was now standing near the foot of his bed.

"Call it what you like," I said, before Vivian could say anything. "That yellow medicine is keeping you alive." I reached for the dial controlling the drip. "I can disconnect it, if you want."

"Bubby!" Vivian screamed.

Connie brushed Lenny's graying hair with her fingers. "You old grump," she said. "Don't go upsetting everyone."

Fortunately, the doctor entered the room. "It's best to let him rest right now," he said. "The monitors are showing a rise in his blood pressure."

We left as two nurses scurried past us on their way to check the readings.

Lenny's room was on the twelfth floor and had a pleasant view of Pinnacle Mountain, a state park where I often went to drop acid with friends during my year of college prior to joining the church. I wondered what it would be like to drop acid again, a thought that at least distracted me from my current craving for cocaine.

Over the next few days, Lenny kept asking why he couldn't go home, saying that he felt healthy. He had to have suspected that the drip wasn't a cure, but he avoided the obvious question – what would happen when they took it out. The doctor only said that the medicine was helping him regain his strength.

I felt a much worse sense of doom than when I saw Lenny collapsed on the kitchen floor. That death felt inevitable, and natural. Lenny was now a fully conscious corpse, kept alive for a few extra days by scientific magic. Perhaps I should have used the opportunity to get closer to him, to view the situation as a last chance, but nothing about it felt real. I avoided being in the room with Lenny, spending most of the time in the waiting room reading whatever books were available in the hospital gift shop. For his part, Lenny never asked for me.

The night after the doctor removed the needle from Lenny's neck, it was my turn to sit with him. As the days had progressed, Lenny began having chest pains. The doctor added a morphine drip which caused Lenny to hallucinate. He was terrified when left alone, and could only fall asleep when one of us was sitting in the room.

Lenny hadn't made any sounds during the night, but in the morning he looked at me with horror in his eyes, and said, "Last night I thought there were snakes in my bed."

Saliva poured from the corner of his mouth as he spoke.

I thought about another time Lenny had seen things he couldn't explain. I was eighteen, just out of high school. Vivian, Lenny, and I went on a trip to Florida. I smoked a joint at every rest stop, and dropped a tab of acid before we arrived at our destination in Key West. On the return, Lenny wanted me to drive after he'd been at the wheel for over twelve hours. But I was fatigued from drug use. Instead, I talked to Lenny to help him stay awake.

"This is nuts," I confessed, not caring at all what Lenny would think about it. "I see giraffes running across the road."

Lenny's face darkened. "Hush up," he said, "I see them too."

When the nurse brought in a breakfast tray, Lenny was too weak to sit up without help. While I was feeding him, he began clawing at his forearm. I was afraid he'd make his arm start bleeding if he didn't stop. I signaled for a nurse, who increased his morphine.

Towards afternoon, Lenny's lungs filled with fluid and he began coughing up phlegm. Vivian and Connie took turns staying with him while I napped in the waiting room. They were so exhausted when nighttime arrived that I volunteered to sit with him again. I knew it would be our last hours together. All sorts of things ran through my mind – things I should say, questions I should ask. As it was, I made sure that Lenny got liquid through a straw when he smacked his lips and that I had a tissue ready when he coughed.

Vivian relieved me at sunrise. The first thing Lenny asked when she arrived was for her to help him with a bedpan. He'd clearly needed to go for a while. I tried not to let it bother me, but it would have made me feel closer to him if he'd told me what he needed – if only to get a nurse.

I went to the waiting room and collapsed on the couch. While I slept, Lenny's condition worsened. I awoke to find the waiting room full of aunts and uncles as well as Lenny's closest friends. Connie had called them when the doctor said he didn't think Lenny would make it another night.

Around dinnertime, a nurse came to say that Lenny would be passing soon. Vivian, Connie, and Derek went into the room. Without invitation, Nathan and Louise followed. I felt like telling them to get lost, but deferred to Vivian when she allowed them in.

Two nurses attended to Lenny, who sat in a nightshirt on the side of the bed.

"Oh, God," Lenny moaned, "don't let me die." He grabbed one of the nurses and pulled her to him, demanding that she do something.

The nurse took out a syringe and injected Lenny with a huge dose of morphine. She helped Lenny get back into bed, then, obviously concerned that we saw how much she had administered, said in a voice loud enough for everyone to hear, "It doesn't matter how much we give him."

I never felt so selfish. All that mattered to me was that Lenny would be gone and I'd never have another chance to know if he loved me. I went to a spot near the door where I couldn't see the deathbed drama. I leaned against the wall, folded my arms, and stared at the floor.

One of the nurses asked me if I was all right.

I wasn't. Not at all.

Nathan's voice rose above Lenny's moans. "You'll soon be in the bosom of Our Lord," he said. "Put your trust in Jesus."

I wanted to kick the fraud out of the room. To hell with Jesus. This is death. The end. Let my father go in peace, I wanted to shout. If Vivian hadn't been there, I would have.

Better to keep my torment to myself than for everyone else to suffer.

Lenny was flat on his back with a washrag on his forehead when I forced myself to stand at the foot of his bed. Derek was praying, having joined hands with Nathan and Louise.

Get the hell out of here, I yelled internally. Go somewhere else to address your fantasy god. This is reality! This is pain!

Connie dashed into the hallway, crying tears I could not find within myself.

Moments later, a doctor pronounced Lenny dead.

CHAPTER FIVE

At night, the still rural area around our home was alive with riotous cicadas, bellowing bullfrogs, and the snarl of an occasional bobcat. The barn, with its gray cedar planks and rusted tin roof, was home to a colony of bats. Most of our inherited property was gone, sold during the years when times were tough. Lenny ended up with ten acres, including a swamp and the stream that fed it.

Vivian had no idea where she stood financially, but she feared the worst, given Lenny's frivolous expenditures during his final days.

"Well, Vivian," said Derek, going over the finances one Saturday afternoon, and coming to a welcome conclusion, "I don't think you have to worry too much."

Vivian gazed out the window. "I remember when we came to this house," she said. "Lenny didn't care what I wanted. He said we were moving out here, and that was that."

"I know, mother," Connie said, taking Vivian's hand. "But he's gone now. You can do whatever you want."

Nevertheless, we all knew that Vivian would stay put. All the friends she had in Little Rock from the old days were dead or forgotten. And because of long-standing tradition, not to mention an old will governing disposition of the Sibley property, she couldn't sell the house.

After the funeral, I felt adrift. The best years of my adult life were gone, wasted on the misplaced pursuit of religious ideals. I was no further along than I had been at eighteen when an acid-induced revelation led me to follow a group that said it knew God's plan for humanity. It was just too bad, for me, that the core of that plan was to promote heterosexual marriage as the path to salvation.

All I could think about was getting high. My thoughts must have telegraphed a message to Los Angeles. I received a letter from Scott, a junior lawyer in the firm that worked on Reverend Moon's tax evasion case. The letter said that Lyle had gotten in touch with Sandra, the firm's secretary, and that they were living together! From the tone of his writing, Scott clearly found that humorous.

My blood boiled. Sandra, Scott, and I had gone out almost every night in Los Angeles during the year I shuttled transcripts. By that time, I had given up on trying to live a religiously devout life. I kept company with hustlers and hung out in gay bars. I knew the world would come crashing in on me, but drugs and alcohol helped me avoid thinking about it.

The day I received the letter, I set off in my Topaz toward Little Rock's gay disco, a place on Asher Avenue called Sergeant Preston's. Much had changed since I was a teenager and the only gay-friendly bar was after-hours at the Drummer's club in the Manning Hotel, which had long since been razed to make way for a convention center.

A drag show was getting underway as I found a seat in an open area at the back, where a stage had been built, illuminated by mosquito-repelling torches. I watched a few acts, breaking away between performers to refresh my gin and tonic. Rail-drinks were a quarter during the show. I was rip-roaring drunk by the third performer.

Drag shows are all about donning outrageous costumes and lip-synching to popular songs. One singer did a routine to the song "Daddy's Hands". As she belted out the mournful lyrics about a loving father, recently departed, the drag queen picked up a pair of rubber hands from behind a tombstone prop. "I remember daddy's hands", she sang, rubbing them against her phony breasts. "How I miss the touch of Daddy's hands".

The performance struck a nerve in my drunken mind. I went inside before she reached the end of the song. There were only a few people at the bar. About a dozen couples danced under the disco ball. I joined them, wheeling about more like a dervish than a disco dancer. Someone offered me a whiff of amyl nitrate – poppers. As my blood pressure spiked, the music became weirdly distorted. I began to feel nauseated and went out front to get some air. A stranger followed me.

"Hello," the man said. "You new in town?"

"Do you know everyone in Little Rock?" I asked.

"All but you," the man said, smiling broadly. "I'm Dean."

Dean appeared to be in his fifties, judging by the indistinct contour of his chin and receding hairline. His shirtsleeves were rolled up to the elbows and his shirttails tucked neatly into his jeans. A mat of thick hair filled the triangle at his open collar.

"My name's Simon."

Dean lit up a cigarette. "Want to get something to eat? I'm tired of this place."

"You aren't asking me on a date or something, are you? I'm not into older men. Not that you're old, exactly."

Dean took a leisurely puff from his cigarette. "It's all right, Simon. I just like getting to know people. Let's go to the Kettle and have a snack."

The twenty-four-hour Kettle Restaurant catered to gay men after midnight. Dean and I found a booth farthest from the jukebox, which was playing an anachronistic Frankie Avalon song. I ate quickly, mopping maple syrup from the plate with a final slab of potato pancake.

"You were drinking like you wanted to forget something," Dean said.

His directness caught me off guard. "Were you watching me?"

"You caught my eye, I won't deny it."

"My dad just died. I should be grieving, but I don't feel much of anything."

"So you drank to feel something? People usually do the opposite."

I smiled. Dean had an unusual openness about him.

"You must think I'm boring," I said, after relating to him the circumstances of my father's death, and explaining about the last ten years I spent in Hollywood.

"I find that we aren't so different."

"What do you mean?"

"I was a priest for a while, and then I became a college counselor for twenty years. My last stint was at Tulane. About five years ago, I faced the fact that I was gay. I haven't taken Communion since. I came back to Arkansas because there aren't many Catholics here. I didn't want to be reminded of my faith."

"That's a unique reason for living in Arkansas," I observed. "What do you do now?"

"Insurance. I'd like to find something better, but it doesn't sit well with people when you say you were a priest. They want to know what happened. Thirty years are missing from my résumé."

"I'm not sure which is worse: being an ex-priest or saying that you were in a cult."

"What would you do now if you could?" Dean asked, blowing cigarette smoke from the corner of his mouth.

"If I hadn't joined that group, my plan was to be an artist. It would be nice to start painting again. Do you think that's crazy?"

"Of course not. I think it's a wonderful goal."

"If my dad had thought that way, things might've been different."

"What did he have to do with your art?"

"Let's see, where to begin. As I recall, the first time I showed him a painting I'd done of my horse, he responded, 'Why in the hell are you fooling with such nonsense?' I must have been eleven. It was right after my mother got me an art kit for my birthday. Lenny got upset when he found out about the present. I remember him saying, 'No son of mine's going to be a faggot artist'. At least he got the faggot part right."

Dean signaled for the waitress to refill our coffee. After it arrived, he continued, "You father's gone now. He can't say anything like that ever again."

"That's one way to look at it, I suppose. But I keep feeling like I need his permission. That must sound crazy. Life was easier being in a cult. They told me to give up my art – just like my dad wanted me to do – but they said it was a sacrifice. 'Sacrificing my Isaac', they called it. To give up what we love in exchange for absolution."

Dean laughed. "Hey, don't get Catholic on me. Look Simon, I understand that this isn't a date, but you're welcome to come over to my house. I don't live far away. You can stay on the couch. It might be a good idea not to drive home tonight."

"Are you referring to my drunkenness, or my state of mind?"

"I've not met someone as interesting as you in a long time. You're welcome company."

"That's quite a come-on," I said. "All right, you talked me into it."

Dean lived in the Heights, a venerable neighborhood with houses that were stylish when first built in the 1920s, but now were mostly in need of repair. Dean's house was a modest brick structure with a screened-in porch, cozy and companionable – a good fit to Dean's personality.

I went straight for Dean's kitchen cabinets looking for alcohol and poured a glass of gin. The next thing I knew, I was laying on Dean's bed. My shoes dropped off. I felt my socks being tugged off my feet, then I was sitting up and my shirt was coming off. My belt loosened, and my jeans and underwear disappeared.

Details blurred in my memory the next morning, but the tale-tell soreness in my ass told me that Dean had seized his opportunity. He had kicked the covers off during the night and lay on his back beside me. I stared at his body, examining his hairy torso. Is that what Lenny had looked like, I wondered? In my whole life, I never saw Lenny naked, not even during the nights when he kept trying to pull off his hospital gown, screaming that his skin was on fire.

Dean made a breakfast of French toast and scrambled eggs. I felt calm and secure for the first time in a long while. Before I left, we exchanged phone numbers. Dean was my first new friend as I embarked on this unfamiliar journey. I considered it a good start.

CHAPTER SIX

The main question I had to answer was whether I would return to Los Angeles or stay in Arkansas. If I went back to California, I would have to face Sandra and the fact that Lyle was living with her. And then there was the availability of cocaine, which I wanted to give up. But in Arkansas, I would have limited freedom if I expected to remain in the closet to my family. Everything got back to Vivian through gossip at the grocery store, even if the events happened in Little Rock. Then there would be the constant attempts by Connie and Derek to convert me to Christianity.

I didn't have to deliberate for very long. The president of the church kept calling the house, insisting to speak to me. I wanted nothing to do with any part of my former religion, so I asked Vivian to lie for me. But when she said, "He's not here," her voice trembled. She was a terrible liar.

The man stopped calling after a while, and I forgot about it. Then, one day, I answered the phone. At first, I was greeted by silence, and then I recognized the church president's voice. We engaged in awkward small talk, but I knew what he wanted. As a church leader in San Francisco, I had purchased a three-story mansion. The seller had no idea that the church was behind the purchase. It was going to be used as a lecture center and dwelling for local members. The title to the property was in my name, and remained so – one of the many loose ends I had not wanted to think about.

"You're calling about the San Francisco property, I suppose. It's in my name, you know."

Dead silence.

"You intend to sign it over, don't you?" the president asked.

"Not for free," I said, the idea only then occurring to me. "You took a decade of my life. I deserve some sort of compensation."

The president began what sounded like a rehearsed argument, but realized right away that his words had no affect on me. "What would you consider fair?" he asked.

"How about twenty thousand dollars?" It was a miniscule amount compared to the actual value of the property, but I knew how the church operated and wasn't surprised when he balked even at that amount.

"That's not possible," the president responded.

"Oh, come on! The leaders of the fundraising teams skim money off the reported results every day of the week. Anyway, your problems aren't my concern any longer."

The president continued to argue, so I made it easier. "Let's settle on this. Pay me over time. After I've received the final installment, I'll sign the papers."

The president conferred with others in the background, barely covering the receiver to keep me from hearing.

"We'll have to dole it out over a six month period," the president said.

"Then we are in agreement."

For the president of the church, the experience on the telephone must have been like bargaining with the devil. I felt my head for any horns that might have sprouted during our conversation. A part of me felt that I was adding extortion to the long list of sins already charged to my cosmic account.

That afternoon, in a nostalgic mood, I poured over photographs. I had a dozen pictures signed by Reverend Moon as well as hundreds of images of members who'd been under my leadership. I'd forever miss those brothers and sisters. Lifting the lid on a cardboard box filled with books and pamphlets, I came upon the official picture taken when I was married to Masako at Madison Square Garden. Legally, and in the eyes of the church, we were still married.

By evening, my head swimming with memories, I wanted to get drunk, and decided to go back to Sergeant Preston's. By midnight, I was dancing with anyone who was willing to put up with my staggering. Pretty soon, the owner of the bar, Miss Phoebe, asked me to leave.

"You fucking sex-change!" I shouted. "Leave me alone."

A finger snap summoned the bouncer, who threw me out the front door. Several patrons applauded.

I stumbled through the parking lot, setting off car alarms as I pulled on random door handles. At some point, I must have found my own car, because suddenly I was zooming down the freeway. Then, I heard grinding noises and realized that sparks were flying over the hood. I managed to exit the highway, pulling into a twenty-four hour service station – a hangout for policeman stopping to get coffee.

Flashing lights and sirens started up from one of the cars. A voice rang out, "Step out of the car and place your hands on the roof!"

I opened the door and collapsed onto the pavement. The next thing I knew, I was in the police station drunk tank, yelling obscenities.

"Shut up," commanded a cop as he raked his nightstick across the bars. "With your blood alcohol, you ought to be dead. You might have killed someone. But you don't care, do you?"

"Is that a question?" I asked.

Another policeman approached. "Your mother's here to bail you out," he said.

Derek had also come. Passing in and out of consciousness, I wasn't sure what was going on as I was processed out of jail. I certainly didn't recall having telephoned anyone. Derek convinced the police to release the car, which had been towed after my arrest. Except for a bare rim – the source of all the sparks and noises – it was actually in good shape after putting on the spare. Derek drove me home in it as Vivian followed in her car. When we arrived, Derek supported my weight as he helped me get inside the house. I collapsed onto Lenny's recliner.

"What were you thinking?" Vivian asked, her voice piercing the haze.

"You don't want to know what I think," I said, more hurtfully that I meant for it to sound.

Vivian rushed into the dining room, sobbing.

"You need sleep," Derek said, sternly. "You shouldn't upset your mother more than you already have."

"Right, wouldn't want that. Not to poor, long-suffering Vivian." I turned my head toward where she was sitting. "Right Mom, let's pretend everything's fine. That's what we do in this family, isn't it?"

Derek took a position as though he were going to hit me. I kicked down the footrest of the chair and tried to stand. I managed to get to the stairs, but had to use the banister to drag myself up.

Vivian's voice carried all the way to my room. "Did you hear what he was saying?"

"That's the alcohol talking," Derek said.

"That's what you'd like to think!" I yelled before slamming the door.

Connie was waiting for me downstairs when I emerged the next day. I found her nursing a cup of coffee. "Vivian hasn't come out of her room all day," she said. "After what you did, I wonder if she'll ever come out."

"I was drunk, Connie. What do you want from me?"

"Is that your excuse?" She grabbed her cup with both hands.

"Should I try to apologize?"

"I wouldn't, Simon. Give her some time."

The church president called me that evening to say that the payment arrangements were being made.

"We need to get that property quitclaimed right away," he insisted. "We'll meet our obligations."

So he said, but I knew how he could justify screwing me over. I was now speaking as Satan, after all. Then an idea struck me. We could work out the contractual details through Scott and Sandra's boss, Maury Fender, after I returned to Los Angeles.

"How about arranging the transaction through Maury's office in Los Angeles?" I suggested.

The president agreed so readily, I wondered if he'd already considered it himself.

"I'm going to Los Angeles in a few days. How long to work things out?"

"A week, at most," he said. "But I hope you will consider what you're doing, Simon. This will affect your eternal life."

I was too hung over to argue. I simply told him to give it a rest.

Connie had been straining her ears to catch the conversation. "Are you going back to California?" she asked.

"It's where I belong," I said. "I've outgrown this town."

Connie emptied the pot of the coffee into her cup. I could almost hear what she wanted to say without her words – I wasn't acting as though I'd grown out of anything.

I left a message on Dean's answering machine, saying that I was leaving for California and that I'd stay in touch. By mid-morning, I was on the highway.

Though I should have waited to speak to Vivian, I simply left a note apologizing for my behavior and saying that I thought it best if I simply left town after the way I had acted.

For miles, I considered going back and saying I was sorry in person, but I never did.

CHAPTER SEVEN

Four days later, I was in Hollywood, after spending a night in Needles, California, hoping the weather would improve. It had been a slow drive with lots of snow and icy roads. From Needles, I drove straight through, all the way to Scott's house. He was drunk and barely realized I was there until I got him to drink a pot of coffee, and he took some pills he had stashed in his medicine cabinet. When he was somewhat lucid, I told him about the arrangement I had made with the church.

"Twenty-thousand," he slurred. "Why didn't you call me? I could have negotiated some real money."

Sure, I knew the money was a pittance compared to the years of my life given to the church, but that fact didn't stop me from feeling guilty for taking it. If couldn't justify the feeling to myself, how could I make sense of it to anyone else?

Scott had taken up smoking cigarettes again, having quit for a couple of years. We went onto the split-level deck. As he lit up, I looked out at the view of Hollywood. Sharing rent with two friends, Scott was able to live in a large house perched high in the Hollywood hills. It felt like a summer day as the sun's heat reflected off the redwood planks. I dipped my hand in the warm water of Scott's hot tub, installed at one end of the patio.

"Let's get in," Scott said, stripping down to his boxers. "Take off your clothes."

The hypnotic whir of the jets and the pressure from the waterspouts massaging my back made me doze off after the long drive. I was startled awake by Scott's voice. He had gotten out of the tub and was sitting on the edge of his bed, just inside the patio door.

"I've got drugs," he said with a wry smile. He had always been thin, but sitting there, he looked as though he hadn't eaten in a week.

I wrapped a towel around my waist and came inside, immediately spotting a mirror on the side table. Scott had laid out rails of cocaine and rolled up a dollar bill to use as a straw. After sucking drugs up his nose, he reared his head back and snorted to dislodge any cocaine stuck in his sinuses. He swallowed hard to push the drainage down his throat, and then, choking on his words, said, "Good shit, man."

He handed me the rolled up dollar bill and I snorted a line. The sting told me it had been cut with speed.

Scott increased the pressure from the hot tub jets and turned up the heat when we got back in. I could see that he was horny. The steam melted some cocaine stuck to the lining of my sinuses and I was hit by such a narcotic rush that I nearly passed out. Scott lifted his hips to the surface, making his erection look like a buoy in the turbulence. I watched transfixed as he grabbed himself, stood, and worked himself to climax. I ducked under the water to keep from getting sprayed.

"That is so rude," I said, irritated, grabbing a towel and throwing it at him.

He dabbed his body with an impish grin, and said, "Welcome back to Hollywood."

All was forgiven as we went back to snorting coke. Hours later, when it was gone, we got the bright idea to mellow out the experience with alcohol.

"Let's go to the bar," Scott suggested, devilishly adding, "I'll call Sandra so she and Lyle can meet us."

A voice inside shouted, "Don't", but of course, seeing Lyle, and figuring out what he was doing with Sandra, was the real reason I had come back.

"What about the Spotlight?" I suggested. I knew that Sandra hated the place, a low-life hustler bar in the middle of Hollywood, and it would make Lyle uncomfortable since he had once been a regular there.

Scott relished the idea; he loved intrigue. I went to the car to wait. When Scott came out of the house, he said, "They'll be there, or they won't. Sandra wouldn't commit to it."

I drove around until I found a well-lit parking place. That part of Hollywood was notorious for car thefts. We hurriedly walked to the bar, avoiding the coke dealers who seemed to appear out of thin air.

A burgundy curtain hung across the entrance to the Spotlight Lounge, a dense fabric with the texture of a rug. I pulled it back and welcomed Scott to scamper past. Coming from the artificial light of the street, it took a moment for my eyes to adjust. Soon enough, I was able to make out a few faces. I recognized several hustlers from the days when I was still a member of the church, living a double life – the period of time when I had picked up Lyle. The hustlers were skinny from doing speed, their thinness offering stark contrast to the girth of the paying customers. Both groups preferred that the bartender keep the lights low. The hustlers wanted the semi-darkness to mask their gaunt faces, and the dimness allowed the tricks to pretend they were not so wrinkled and overweight. The hustlers were not as young as they advertised, and the old men were older than they admitted.

Scott and I mounted stools at the far end of the bar. Three shirtless hustlers lurked nearby playing pinball. Each boy had a jailhouse tattoo, one a barely legible name – Mary or Mariah – and the other, a lopsided eight-ball.

We ordered drinks as a commotion began near the entrance. A hustler wolf whistled as Sandra pulled aside the curtain and stood silhouetted in the doorway. A taller figure appeared behind her, lifting the drape higher.

Scott threw back a shot of vodka and looked at me out of the corner of his eye. Sandra darted toward us. She wore a striking yellow dress with a patent leather belt at the waist. Her auburn hair caught the neon glow of a Budweiser sign on the wall. Lyle approached more cautiously. He had on a plain white shirt tucked neatly into the pair of tight-fitting Guess jeans that I had bought him not long before I left Hollywood.

"Don't be angry about Lyle," Sandra whispered as she kissed my ear. "I'll explain it all later."

"Come here, Lyle," I said, quietly.

Lyle's face contorted in a hangdog expression that made me want to forgive him on the spot.

"What was I supposed to do?" he said, pressing close so the others wouldn't hear. "Go back to the street?"

"I'm sorry, Lyle. As things turned out, I should have stayed with you instead of trying to go back to that group." Lyle barely knew anything about my experience in the church. I had not even explained what was going on when I left him in a motel room and flew to New York to marry Masako.

Lyle perched his foot on the lower rung of my barstool. He placed his cheek against my neck. The aroma of his silky blond hair brought back memories of our lovemaking. I ran my fingers through his hair and pulled him close. Lyle touched his forehead against mine and sighed.

Scott wailed, "Gag me! Get to drinking, you two. The night hasn't even started."

Sandra locked her arm in Scott's. They spoke a private toast and threw back shots of schnapps. Lyle broke away and went toward them, acting as though his only purpose was to get a cigarette from Sandra's pocketbook, but I noticed the glances they exchanged, even if I couldn't interpret what they were communicating.

Scott and Sandra licked salt off their hands after knocking down shots of straight tequila. As he got drunker, Scott started pawing a hustler at the pinball machine. I knew his routine. He'd take the boy to one of the junky dives along Hudson Avenue for a quickie and then take a taxi home. His roommates didn't want hustlers in the house. Too many possessions had walked out the door.

Lyle finished a third cigarette, crushing the butt on the rim of an empty beer bottle. He went to the jukebox and played a Metallica track, swaying his hips from side to side and jumping in the air as he strummed an air guitar. Twiggy, the portly bartender who had been there since the first day I walked in, set down five shot glasses, paid for by admirers of Lyle's ass, if not his performance. Lyle picked up the glasses, one to a finger, and came to sit beside me. Groans of disappointment rose from the men, who'd hoped to cop a feel, but at least expected a wink of recognition when Twiggy pointed them out. Lyle offered no acknowledgement at all.

Scott was now slobbering over a tall, raven-haired hustler, having been outbid for the pinball wizard. I pulled Scott away for a moment to the chagrin of the boy who'd yet to close the deal.

"We need drugs," I urged. "Alcohol just isn't cutting it."

"Give me five minutes," Scott said, "and then wait for me in the bathroom."

I told Lyle to stay put at the bar. "Drugs are on the way," I said.

Lyle smiled weakly. I wasn't sure if he was happy about it or not.

The urine stench of the Spotlight's bathroom overwhelmed upon entering and smelled even more rotten the longer one stayed inside. I was just about to quit waiting when Scott pushed through the swinging door. He opened a baggy-full of cocaine. His hand was so unsteady, I was afraid he'd drop it.

I took a dollar bill from my wallet, expertly folded it into a rectangular package, and scooped out a gram's worth. Scott rolled up the baggie and stuffed it into his pants.

At the bar, Lyle was talking to a middle-aged man who had taken my seat. They clicked bottles of Budweiser in a flirty sort of way. Lyle winked at me as I neared, rolling his eyes toward the ceiling to let me know he was simply humoring the guy.

"That's my seat," I said, nudging the man aside.

"And who the fuck are you?" the man growled.

"His lover, that's who."

The man laughed. "Fuck off. We're making arrangements." He took out his wallet and waved a hundred dollar bill in Lyle's face.

"Yeah, well, he's my boyfriend. So, *you* fuck off."

I pushed the man hard. He lost his balance and fell off the barstool. When he regained his composure, he grabbed the neck of Lyle's Budweiser and smashed it against the side of my head.

The bouncer, a brute with silver-studded knuckle gloves, tossed me through the curtained door. "Get your bleeding ass out of here," he said.

"I called an ambulance," someone said. Was it Scott's voice? Lyle's? The sound was hollow, as if spoken through a megaphone.

The next thing I knew, I was on the sidewalk in a pool of blood. My head hung off the curb behind a car whose driver was starting it up and placing it in gear. Tailpipe exhaust hit me in my eyes, already burning from the blood dripping across my face. Fortunately, the car pulled forward into the traffic without backing up.

"Simon, buddy," said a desperate voice. It was Lyle.

Sandra was there, too. Blood was spattered all over her yellow dress. She got on her knees beside me and patted down my shirt until she found the packet of coke.

"You don't need them finding this on you," she said. "I can't believe that bouncer threw you on the street!" Sandra took a towel she'd gotten from Twiggy and wiped the blood from my eyes. "That gorilla who hit you needs to be arrested! I'm calling the police. This is just terrible."

Lyle touched her arm and shook his head. "I don't think we want the police running a blood test on him," he cautioned.

Sandra looked at me sympathetically. "The ambulance is on the way, darling. That's what's important, getting you looked after."

Sirens pierced through the other noises of the street, growing louder and louder until the fluctuations in pitch became steady. Capable hands gently lifted my head and placed a foam collar around my neck. I strained to hear what was being said, but all I could catch were a few utterances. "Look at that ear," one of the paramedics said. Another commented, "He'll probably lose it." Suddenly, in a single motion, I was lifted onto a stretcher and seemed to soar through the back doors of the ambulance.

As we sped through Hollywood, I became aware of someone touching my hand. "You've got to stay awake, Mr. Powell."

I struggled to open my eyes. They felt as though they'd been stitched shut. A warm towel pressed against my eyes. I opened my mouth and stuck out my tongue, but no one gave me water.

"Do you have insurance?" someone asked.

I had the wherewithal to lie with a barely audible, yes.

The ambulance pulled into Hollywood Presbyterian. I was rushed to a bed behind white, gauzy curtains in the emergency room. Several doctors came to examine my ear. One commented, "Looks bad, but at least the pieces are all there."

More than anything, I needed liquid. I mouthed the word, water. A nurse brought over a cup with a straw and held it as I sipped.

"Has someone taken this man's blood pressure?" the nurse asked as she disappeared down the hall. A few moments later, she returned with a cart. I felt the pressure mount as the grip tightened on my upper arm. I flinched when the cold metal of the stethoscope touched the crook of my elbow. The nurse got her reading and rushed off, pulling the curtains closed around my bed before departing. Moments later, more low voices murmured around me.

"He might need a transfusion."

"Has anyone checked his insurance?"

"He doesn't have any. No card in his wallet."

"Why's he here, then?"

"Bandage him up. Send him to County."

The nurse who had given me the water and taken my blood pressure wrapped my head with surgical bandages. The smell of antiseptic began to replace the aroma of the dried blood.

"This might hurt a little," she said, "but I've got to pull tight to make sure you don't bleed out. We're sending you over to County Hospital."

The intensity of my rapidly beating heart drowned out all other sounds. No one had given me any pain medication. With each heartbeat, it felt as though a knife was sliding through my skull.

Orderlies strapped me onto a gurney and I was taken back to the emergency room. Paramedics loaded me, torpedo-like, into an older model ambulance. They shipped me to the pauper's hospital and put me in a noisy ward alongside a couple of Latino men with gunshot wounds. One stretcher had a body on it, covered with a white sheet. Rooms were in too much demand to use them for the dead waiting to be carted off to the morgue.

Hours passed and I began to worry that I had been forgotten. I yearned for a familiar face. Where was Lyle? Why hadn't Scott and Sandra shown up? Did they know where I'd been taken?

Someone took my arm and pressed two fingers into my wrist. It was a nurse. She unwound the gauze. When she reached the layers close to my head, her ministrations became more gentle and deliberate. "This might sting," she said. "There's a lot of caked blood. But I've got to get this off to see what I'm dealing with." When she lifted the final layer of cloth, she asked, "What time did this happen?"

I held up my left hand and showed all five fingers, then three.

"Eight o'clock last night?"

I wobbled my hand to indicate approximation.

"We need to sew this up right away. One piece is barely hanging on and it's not getting any blood. We wouldn't want you to go through life without an ear."

The words barely registered as fantasies of Vincent Van Gogh roamed through my thoughts.

The nurse went off to get a tray of sutures. "I've never worked on such a delicate job," she said on her return. "But there isn't anyone to do it at this time of morning. Do you want me to work on your ear?"

I gave her thumbs up, though I thought I was answering a question about getting morphine. The nurse cleaned the side of my head, applied a local anesthetic, and began to work. She carefully teased out pieces of ear from the mass of drying blood and puzzled them in a proper formation. A wall clock told me it was five in the morning.

"This is going to take a while," the nurse said. "Let me know if you feel any pain. I'll give you more anesthetic."

"Thanks," I said. It was the first word I'd been able to articulate.

An hour later, the nurse was done. "It was a lot like sewing a dress," she mused. "I make my own clothes. I know how to get a tight stitch."

I tried to smile, but wasn't sure how it came out.

"Now. Don't take off the bandages for at least three days. You should see your doctor about keeping the ear dressed. I've got prescriptions from the emergency room physician. It's for a painkiller and an antibiotic. You should start taking these right away."

The nurse brought a wheelchair into the room and rolled me to the front desk. I signed papers saying I would pay what I could. Then they released me. I'd lost a lot of blood and was so tired, I could barely make it to the pay phone. I dialed Scott.

After endless rings, someone picked up.

"Scott? Is that you?"

"No. It's Lyle," a sleepy voice responded. "Simon?"

"Yeah, it's me."

"Where in the hell are you? Those ambulance guys wouldn't say where they were taking you."

"Where's Scott?"

"He's here, asleep on the floor."

If they had been in the hot tub together, I'd have killed Scott.

"I've been worried about you," Lyle said.

His tone melted away my fear. There was genuine concern in his voice.

I let the receiver dangle while I found my keys and counted the money in my wallet. There was just enough to catch a taxi to Hudson Street where I'd parked the car.

"I'll get to my car and drive to Scott's. It should take an hour or so."

Lyle said something with his hand cupped over the receiver. "Sandra's here," he said, returning to the line. "She wants to come get you."

Sandra took the phone. "Honey! Thank God you're all right."

I began to cry.

"It's okay, sweetie," Sandra said gently. "Tell me where you are. I'll come get you. We can get your car later."

Sandra found me collapsed on a chair in the waiting room, surrounded by whole families piled atop each other asleep on the couches. I had hoped Lyle would come with her, but she was alone. She looked like a fifties vixen, wearing a man's shirt with the tails tied below her breasts and jeans rolled up four inches at the cuff.

"Nice to see you without bloody clothes," I said.

"I looked like Sissy Spacek in Carrie," Sandra laughed. "Scott loaned me these clothes. I was so worried about you, I just couldn't go home. I figured you would call Scott's, so I stayed on the couch."

"Did Scott and Lyle do all the drugs?"

"Don't worry about that right now," Sandra said, lightly touching my bandages. "Did they take care of your ear? Your head looked like it passed through a meat grinder."

"A nurse stitched me up."

Doctors and nurses scurried about the area as shifts changed from the night crew to the daytime doctors. The nurse who'd patched me up was signing out. I waved her over.

"I didn't properly thank you," I said.

The young woman, now in street attire instead of the white nurse's outfit, shook my hand. "Well, Mr. Powell, you can thank me by staying out of trouble. Let the Lord give you strength to stay away from alcohol."

"How'd you know?"

"Your breath," she said. "You're lucky not to have bled to death. The Lord saved you for a reason, that's for sure."

Before I could respond, she took off toward the exit. A man greeted her at the door and gave her a kiss. They disappeared into the morning light.

Sandra took my hand. "Simon, Lyle and I aren't sleeping together. I wanted to tell you last night."

"Scott told me you were living together, that you told people Lyle was your boyfriend."

"Oh honey, come on! You've seen my type. Smooth chests don't do it for me." She smiled, running her finger along her lower lip as she considered her type. "Lyle called after you left Hollywood. I let him stay with me in the Valley. He said you had spoiled him, and that he just couldn't go back to the street. He genuinely cares about you. He was very hurt when you walked out."

My drowsiness must have come off like disbelief.

"We didn't have sex," Sandra insisted. "Now that's that. I'm not going to say it again. Lyle cares for you. If he's what you want, go for it. The kid might even be able to love you someday."

"I'm sorry," I said, realizing that Sandra didn't think I believed her. "When I was in Arkansas, I missed him terribly. The news that he was with you tore me up. That's why I never called. I thought you two were a couple."

"Well, now you know the truth."

Sandra helped me to her Trans Am. Getting in, I bumped my head on the roof. Waves of pain shot along my arms.

On the way to Scott's, Sandra said, "Did I tell you that Mitsui's office contacted Maury?"

Mitsui was my boss during the final period of my church experience.

"Seems you are to get payments for some church property. Maury is drawing up the papers for you to sign."

"That's one of the reasons I came back."

"It will be the last thing Maury does for the church," Sandra said.

"What happened?"

"Mitsui accused you of spending money while you were out here. He blamed Maury for allowing it to happen. Like Maury was supposed to be your nanny or something. And...there's something else."

"What else?" Already, I was fuming that Mitsui would blame me for anything. He was the reason Reverend Moon went to jail. He'd forged documents to make it seem as though money held in Reverend Moon's name was made through fundraising, when in fact, Japanese church members had smuggled it into the country. The money had earned interest while sitting in the bank, and the taxes on it weren't paid. That was the crux of the prosecutor's case.

Sandra continued. "Maury told Mitsui that you were homosexual. That you were, in his old-fashioned term, 'catting around' Hollywood and that he couldn't stop you."

"The bastard!"

"Maury thought that exposing you as a homosexual who he had to deal with on behalf of the church would get him sympathy. The tactic didn't work. Mitsui's going to drop him. I mean, you're the second member who left the church after starting to work with Maury."

It was true. I'd taken over the responsibilities after Mitsui's first legal liaison met a woman in Los Angeles and left the church to live with her.

"Maury leveraged the situation. He said he would only help with the property transaction if they paid their outstanding bills."

"Any word on when I'll get the first installment? Now would be a good time."

"I think it will be soon. The church president wanted Maury to have you sign a paper saying you wouldn't use any information that you took from the church. But Maury convinced him that might provoke you."

"Damn right it would," I said. "I have documents that the IRS could use to take away their tax exemption."

"Let's get Lyle and go to my house. You two can use the bedroom that Lyle's been sleeping in."

"Sounds good to me."

"There's just one more thing I need to tell you," Sandra said. "Masako is in Los Angeles."

"What? How do you know?"

"She left the church, too. Mitsui thinks she's out here to find you. That's what he told Maury. It seems like every day, Maury hears either from Mitsui or the church president. I thought they hated each other."

"There's so much politics in that group, who knows what's going on these days."

"And who cares," Sandra confirmed.

"Do you know where Masako is living?"

"Maury knows. I can find out if you want."

I wished that Masako didn't mean anything to me, but she still did. I owed her an explanation for why we had to divorce.

CHAPTER EIGHT

During the first week at Sandra's, I was in such pain and so weak from loss of blood that I rarely got out of bed. Lyle spent most of his time watching television and swimming in the pool. At least we had a good time at night, even though I had to be careful about positioning. Every turn of my head brought agony.

When Sandra came home, she and Lyle prepared the evening meal. Knowing my appreciation for good red wines, Sandra made a point of stopping by Greenblatt's on Sunset Boulevard to pick up a good vintage when she got off work.

After dinner, Sandra took a nap, then dolled herself up and was on the road into Hollywood by eleven o'clock. She wouldn't return until sunrise. How she managed her job while keeping hours like that was a marvel.

Over dinner, Lyle and I were treated to the tawdry details of her previous night. Scott was often part of the narrative. Some nights, he met her at the Princess Lounge in Century City for happy hour, or he would start out the evening with her at Dan Tana's on Santa Monica Boulevard.

During my recuperation, Lyle never asked for drugs. He didn't even pilfer the codeine prescribed for me by the emergency room doctor. I hoped the dire experience might be a new start for us.

At the beginning of the third week, Sandra brought my first check from the church.

"Five thousand," she said. "Maury doesn't know you are at my house, but he knows that you are in Los Angeles and that we are in touch." She took a folder from her satchel. "You'll have to sign these to get more money." She placed an array of stapled copies of the deed on the coffee table.

Lyle sat beside me on the couch and pressed his knee against mine.

"And I have more news," Sandra said. "I found out about Masako."

At the mention of my wife's name, Lyle recoiled.

"She can't get any of this money, can she?" Lyle asked.

"No, Lyle. It's all ours."

"You're letting that group off too easy," he said. "You should have asked for a hundred grand."

"Yes, Lyle, you're probably right." The dark wing of a fallen angel brushed against my cheek as I uttered the statement.

After a month at Sandra's, I felt strong enough to drive. Sandra suggested that Lyle and I look for an apartment in the Belmont Shore area of Long Beach. Since first coming to Los Angeles, I had dreamed about living on the beach. Belmont shore was within the price range of my windfall.

We located a furnished apartment facing Ocean Boulevard, one block from a popular gay disco called Ripples. Each apartment had its own stairway leading to a second floor. The ground floor was comprised of garages. The stairs to my place rose sharply to a landing at the front door that offered a broad view of the beach.

The landing was just large enough for two chairs, and the concrete wall forming the porch was low enough to allow a good view when sitting down.

I was excited about living there, but when I asked how he liked it, Lyle only said, "Whatever." He preferred to live in closer proximity to Hollywood.

Though I was still tethered to the church because of the property and the fact that I was still married, I tried to imagine what it might be like if I actually got what I wanted. I had always known what that was, I had just set it aside when I joined the church.

One day I would be an artist. I had no illusions about bursting onto the art scene and making a name for myself. From the world's viewpoint, I was a college dropout who'd been brainwashed by a cult. I was nearing thirty, and should already be well underway on a career in painting.

The greatest sacrifice I had made when joining the church was to destroy every work of art I had done since the crayon drawings produced at Bible camp during summer vacation.

In the belief system of the Sun Myung Moon's religion, new members were expected to "sacrifice their Isaac," to give up whatever they held most dear. After I joined, I took my artwork to one of the abandoned bauxite mines that dot the landscape around Sibley and built a bonfire. I watched all my creations turn to embers. Yet I never truly let go. I remember thinking at the time, Somewhere in this universe, those paintings still exist.

If they were to exist again, I'd have to create them. I bought paint and canvases and let my earliest ideas guide me. I had always worked in an abstract vein, with washes of vibrant colors. Having turned the small dining room into a studio, I finished a few canvases and then began working on paper with India ink. Endless spirals invited the viewer to fall into a bottomless vortex. I was reminded of the "drawings" I had made as a child, using the sharpened end of an old broom handle to etch spirals in my sandbox.

Lyle told me I was losing my mind. "Why are you fucking doing that?" he challenged when I held up a drawing I'd just completed. The spirals wound so tightly at the center of the image that it darkened to pitch black. When I didn't answer, he said, "You need to get stoned."

In fact, I was beginning to feel like a fool. Lyle had simply stated the obvious. He lost all patience when I would pick up objects on the beach and begin painting them with enamels. Seas shells, pieces of driftwood, broken bottles – anything with a curious shape became a canvas.

In the back of my mind, I knew the freedom wasn't going to last; that the church money would eventually run out and I'd have to face some hard choices again. For the moment, though, I sustained myself by living out the fantasy of being an artist living with his lover on the beach.

Scott got too drunk every day to drive to Long Beach. I didn't hear from him for months. Then, one evening, he called to suggest that Lyle and I come to Hollywood and have dinner at Cyrano's Restaurant. Sandra would be there. Cyrano's had been our favorite restaurant on the Sunset Strip when I was paying for our nights out on the church expense account.

"Sandra's got another check for you," Scott said.

I went to Ripples and found Lyle playing pool in the back room. When I told him we were going to see Scott, he came alive. "We going to get high?"

I didn't say no.

Sandra was dressed glamorously, if somewhat austerely, in a black, low-cut dress. I'd never seen her wear diamond earrings. Silver bracelets dangled from both wrists. Scott was dressed in an ill-fitting suit, but at least he wore a tie – something required for Cyrano's. I got around the requirement by wearing a Nehru shirt. Lyle wore a turtleneck sweater I bought him for the occasion. If I had bought him a necktie, he would have hanged me with it.

"You're looking good!" Scott hooted. "Not you," he said when I took a little bow. "I mean Lyle-the-smile."

"Fuckin' drunk," Lyle said, scowling.

"Scotch?" the waiter asked Sandra, then turned to Lyle, raising his eyebrows.

"Same. With a water back," Lyle answered.

"Did you and Sandra come here while I was away?" I asked. "The waiter seems to know you."

He and Sandra exchanged glances.

When Sandra started to giggle, I said, "Maybe I don't want to know."

Sandra reached across the table and took my hand. "Lyle was my best defense against the maître d'. You know how she's always flirting with me."

In fact, the woman was standing near the door watching us even then.

"Let's drink," Scott said, raising his glass. "To the good times ahead, or else, time for good head."

Lyle downed the scotch and ordered another. He and Sandra began carrying on. Scott, drunker than I had realized, leaned close and pawed my arm. "Where you been," he slurred. "I've missed you."

"Waiter, can I have a barf bag?" Lyle blurted out.

"Fuck you," Scott countered.

Sandra added another dimension to the playfulness. "Give me a kiss," she said to me, puckering up and half-closing her eyes.

I was going to oblige her when Lyle kicked me under the table.

"I can't believe you two moved so far away, all the way to fuckin' Long Beach," Scott said, chewing on a morsel of escargot. No sooner had he asked than he forgot the question. He snapped his fingers to get the waiter's attention so he could order another drink. "So, what are you doing down there?" he asked me, picking up the thread of his thoughts.

"Painting," I said.

Scott sucked down the water at the bottom of his empty scotch glass. He struggled to recall what he had just asked. "Houses? Did they teach you to paint houses in the church?"

"He scribbles all day," Lyle said impatiently. "That's what he calls painting."

"It's art," I defended.

Sandra yawned.

"Okay, fuck you people."

"Well, I'd like to see your work," Scott said in a consoling tone. "You are always so 'au currant' – a hippie in high school, a cult member in the seventies, and now, an artist in the eighties. What a guy!"

"You'll see some day," I said conclusively.

For dessert, we had a choice between chocolate mousse and cherries jubilee. After placing our orders, Sandra took a long draw from her glass of scotch, and said, "I have to tell you something, Simon. Masako called Maury's office today."

A hush fell over the table. Scott and Sandra looked at Lyle. I rolled my empty espresso cup on the saucer.

"Does she want Maury to handle our divorce?" I said, breaking the silence.

"Maury won't say. Here's her address." Sandra handed me a slip of paper torn from the office message book. "That's the name of the restaurant where she's working."

My hand trembled as I took it.

Scott's face twisted deviously. "Call her now," he said.

"You're such a drama queen, Scott. This is serious. I can't talk to her until I'm ready."

Lyle took a cigarette from Sandra's pack of Pall Malls, lit it up with her gold lighter, and blew a stream of smoke from the corner of his mouth.

"You do want to divorce her, don't you?" Sandra asked. "I mean, now that you and Lyle are back together."

Lyle looked away to feign disinterest in the conversation.

Scott again insisted that I call her right then and there. Either I would do it, or he threatened to make a scene and get us kicked out of our favorite restaurant. In the end, I said I would. And Scott wasn't going to let me fake a conversation, so he stood beside me at the pay phone and watched me dial.

A man with a heavy Japanese accent answered. When I asked for Masako, he said to wait, that he'd get her.

When the timid voice came on the line, I choked up. "Masako?"

"Simon-san!" she said, anxiously. "You get message, finally! You get message. How you doing?"

"I'm okay, Masako. How are you?"

"Working this Japanese restaurant. Sometime baby-sit for Japanese couple. You not know?"

"I heard you left the church."

"I must see you, Simon-san. Please. Meet me restaurant. San Pedro Street, near Second. Yokohama Restaurant."

If Masako hadn't sounded so sweet, I might have said what I really needed to say – that it was over, you'll hear from my lawyer. But her voice melted my heart. She truly loved me, and I didn't want to turn my back on that.

"All right, Masako," I agreed, not for a minute considering the ramifications.

"What are you saying?" Scott prodded me.

I shooed him away.

"You come now?" Masako asked. "No phone at apartment. Only work phone."

"Not tonight. I will call again, though. I promise."

Before going back to the others, I told Scott I wanted cocaine.

"Finally! Here you get that windfall from the church and horde it all for yourself," he said. "How much do you want?"

"Let's get an eight-ball and go to Sandra's."

Scott managed to get some good stuff. Two days later, we were still up, talking.

CHAPTER NINE

Yokohama was an elegant restaurant with a Japanese bridge at the entrance that spanned an indoor pond stocked with koi. Speakers were concealed inside artificial logs that were inlaid with pots of flowering bromeliads. Koto music played in the background – mysterious and alluring.

Masako, dressed in a traditional kimono, spotted my dinner party at the hostess's station. She rushed over and took my hand.

I had called in advance to let Masako know that I planned to bring friends. Scott and Sandra hung on each others' arms, but Lyle's presence was harder to explain. Masako led us to a private room with a table low to the floor. Guests sat on pillows, allowing their feet to dangle in a pit under the table. I supposed it was a compromise with Asian style, which would have required patrons to sit uncomfortably cross-legged.

A few days had passed without drugs or alcohol. Lyle and I had been sunning ourselves on the beach, working on our tans, and talking. I had tried to explain about my life in the church, and confessed that I had left him to marry Masako.

"Sounds like a green-card wife," Lyle assessed. "You didn't fuck her, did you?"

"There's more to a marriage than fucking," I said. "I think I really do love her."

"You want kids, everyone does," Lyle said in a rare moment of astuteness. "You just think you love her. Forget it, Simon – you're gay."

Seeing Lyle and Masako together made me think. One attracted with warm feelings of companionship, but without a sexual charge; the other had an allure that was all about sex. Why couldn't they merge into one person? Then my life would be complete.

Every time Masako came to our table, Sandra seemed to intentionally pay me extra attention. At the same time, Scott would flirt with Lyle. Anyone watching the table would guess that Scott and Lyle were a couple and that I was on a date with Sandra. I wondered if that was the plan — to make Masako jealous in order to stir up trouble.

By the time dinner arrived, Masako's eyes began to display genuine fear. She must have realized that she didn't know why I had come, much less to have brought guests, and that I might have agreed to this meeting only to show her that I wasn't interested.

I encouraged Sandra to pay attention to Scott and leave me alone, but right at that moment, Scott and Lyle disappeared into the men's room. Masako, who had not made eye contact with me since bringing out the sukiyaki, returned with a fresh pot of green tea. Her hand was remarkably steady as she filled our cups.

"Get the fuck off my case," Lyle's voice resounded as he and Scott burst from the men's room. Lyle chased Scott over the bridge and out the front door.

What now? I thought as I quickly signed the charge slip that Masako had just returned to the table. I raced after them. Sandra grabbed her purse and followed.

Masako caught up with us at the exit. "Simon-san, what wrong?"

"Nothing," I said.

"Please don't go," Masako said, pulling on my sleeve.

"When do you get off work?" I asked.

"Midnight," Masako said, her expression heartbreakingly doleful.

"Wait for me out front."

Scott and Sandra were driving away in her Trans Am by the time I arrived on the scene.

"They're going to the Spotlight," Lyle said.

"What in the hell is going on?"

"Fuckin' Scott didn't want to give me a line unless I sucked his cock. The motherfucker."

"Let it pass," I said. "Scott's been a scumbag since I first met him."

"Fuck," Lyle said. "Scott might not score for us now that I've pissed him off."

"If we go find him," I said, "you have to swear you'll be good. I don't want to get us kicked out of the Spotlight, or get my other ear trashed by someone."

"Well, I ain't suckin' his dick."

"By now, Scott probably realizes he better give us a good deal to make up for what he tried to do back there."

At the Spotlight, the same bouncer who had thrown me out was on duty. I was sure I saw dried blood on his silver-spiked gloves. He paid no attention as I passed by him. He wouldn't even remember that a few weeks earlier, he had thrown me onto the sidewalk like so much Hollywood refuse.

I was relieved to see that Twiggy was bartending. He had a shot of Boodles gin poured before I'd even gotten to my seat.

"Something to steady your nerves," Twiggy said. "Someone told me you'd gotten killed, but lover, here you are." Twiggy weighed over three hundred pounds, but he maneuvered with the élan of a ballerina as he dealt with the drunken johns and needy tricks. "I didn't see who hit you that night, or I would've knocked him cold."

"You're a good friend, Twig," I said.

"Tonight, the gin's on the house." Twiggy tossed an air kiss in my direction.

The bar was crowded. I recognized most of the patrons, except for a couple of guys too old to be hustlers and too young to be tricks. Twiggy often cautioned about those types, always suspecting that they were vice cops. Serving alcohol to an underage patron or overhearing a hustler-john negotiation could mean a citation that would shut down the bar for two weeks.

Nervously, I ran my finger along the grooves where the slices of my ear had been pieced together as I followed Lyle into the back room. Scott and Sandra were sitting on stools at the wall behind the pool table. Scott hid behind Sandra when he saw us.

"Lyle told me about your proposition," I said. "That was a crappy way to behave. What are you going to do to make it up to us?"

Sandra took a sip from her glass of Chivas Regal. She placed a hand on my arm. With a giggle, she said, "I think Masako's cute."

I knocked her hand away.

"Oh, honey. This is Hollywood! Don't take things so seriously."

Lyle asked Scott to light a cigarette that he had bummed from a fellow making eyes at him. He sucked smoke into his nostrils as it poured from his mouth. "Tell him to make it right," Lyle said to me, cocking his head toward Scott.

"The call is already in," Scott said.

Lyle gave him a menacing look. "It'd better be good stuff!"

"Colombian Blue, ether-based. You won't believe it."

Lyle and Sandra knocked back shots as we waited. Scott and I drank Boodles, challenging each other to see who could hold the most alcohol. Scott usually won such contests. After three shots of the ninety percent gin, I nearly teetered off the barstool.

Someone put money in the jukebox and everyone sang along with the lyrics of the Spotlight theme song, "Life is a Cabaret".

Drinking made Lyle horny, even amorous. We were wrapped up in each other's arms when I noticed Scott talking to a man I didn't know. As soon as the guy left, Scott went straight to the men's room. Lyle stood watch as I followed.

As its name advertised, the powder had a bluish tint against the white paper that Scott unfolded.

"Like flakes of arctic snow," I marveled. "It's beautiful." I already had a dollar bill rolled up in anticipation of the moment.

Scott was right about the potency, too. The muscles in my throat tightened. For a moment, I lost my breath.

Cocaine acts like a truth serum. After two snorts, Scott felt compelled to offer a confession. "I was wrong to treat Lyle like a hustler."

The drug enticed me to forgive. I told him it was nothing, that everything was fine. Even though we stood next to a broken toilet seeping slimy water, the world was beautiful.

"Let's get back to the others," I said. "They should do some of this."

Toward midnight, a weird equilibrium established itself from the balance of cocaine and Boodles.

"I'm going back to see Masako," I told my companions.

Scott lightly knuckled my forehead. "Hello? Is anyone in there? What are you planning to do, bring her here?"

"Why not?" I said. "If she wants to be part of my life, she needs to know who I am."

Lyle was agreeable to anything at that point. "If you really love her, I won't stand in the way," he said.

I knew it was the cocaine talking, but I wanted to believe it anyway.

CHAPTER TEN

Masako was in front of the restaurant, clutching her purse. She had changed from the satin kimono to the type of demure street clothes worn by sisters in the church. Struck with a bout of paranoia, I thought maybe I was being set up – that Masako would try to lure me back into the group.

She got in the car when I leaned over to open the door. "Sorry about the trouble my friends caused," I said. My thick tongue made the words difficult to understand.

"You drunk?" Masako asked. "Maybe we park car. Take taxi."

I threw the car into gear and hit the accelerator, upset that she was challenging me. Masako fastened her seat belt and gripped the edges of her seat.

The drugs still held more sway than the alcohol, but I was beginning to feel woozy. The strobe-light effect of the streetlights had me mesmerized.

"I need to tell you something," I said as we pulled onto Cahuenga Boulevard in the last stretch of road before reaching the Spotlight. "I need to explain why I left the church."

Masako wasn't listening. Her eyes were fixed on the road. Twice, she reached for the steering wheel, nervous that I was about to veer into the wrong lane.

"The reason I left–" I paused as I remembered an event that happened in the church. A brother under my charge killed himself by jumping down an elevator shaft in the church's New York headquarters. He had admitted to me that he was homosexual, and after conferring with church leaders, we sent him to a psychologist. The man claimed that homosexuality was a mental illness that could be overcome through aversion therapy. After two weeks of it, Martin chose to kill himself. Masako would understand the comparison.

"I'm like Martin," I said. "Do you remember? The brother who jumped to his death?"

Masako didn't respond.

"Lyle is my lover. We live together."

Masako, not fully understanding my words, took my hand, and said, "All I want know – do you love me?"

My thoughts were in such a whirl that I didn't know how to respond.

"Where are we going?" Masako asked.

"Lyle and the others are waiting for us at a bar. Do you drink?"

"Sometimes I drink. I drink with you. But now you look at road. Drive safe."

The Spotlight was busier than when I left; the ratio of hustlers to tricks now weighed heavier on the hustler side of the equation. Soon, the competition would bring down the prices, men and boys would pair up and leave together, the hustlers calculating how much money they could get for putting out as little as possible, the tricks drunkenly expecting to have the time of their lives, but in the end finding themselves lonelier than ever.

Lyle had taken off his shirt and stuffed it through his belt. As Masako and I pressed through the crush of bodies, I thought I saw Scott's hand on Lyle's ass, but couldn't be sure.

A gang of hustlers was competing for Sandra's attention. All three were shirtless, older tricks with hairy chests – definitely Sandra's type.

Masako clenched my arm as I led her toward Lyle and Scott.

"You can sit here," Lyle said to Masako. "I was just going to the bathroom."

The jukebox was blaring so loudly, I hardly understood what Lyle said, but when he headed toward the rear of the bar followed by Scott, I knew exactly what was up. I wanted to follow them, but Masako had tightened her grip.

Twiggy was shocked to see me with Masako and came over as soon as he caught a break. Masako ordered a Mai Tai.

"Don't get much call for Mai Tais," Twiggy said. "But I do make a killer kamikaze."

"That good. I take kamikaze," Masako said.

Twiggy found a paper umbrella to put in the glass. "This makes it a little bit like a Mai Tai," he said.

Masako sipped her drink while I downed shots of Boodles. Soft Cell's "Tainted Love" started up on the jukebox. Every time the song came to its two word refrain, the entire bar seemed to join in. Tainted love, o-oh, tainted love.

The bouncer patrolled the crowd with a stance that signaled he was just waiting for the opportunity to bash in somebody's head. Masako watched his every movement.

"Why he wear dangerous gloves?" she asked.

"It's a dangerous place," I said, hoping the Spotlight would convince her that I wasn't anyone she wanted as a husband. "I come here a lot. I like danger."

"Me too," Masako said, casting a furtive glance at the bouncer.

Lyle watched Masako and me intently, the cocaine in his system dampening the sparks of jealousy. Scott kept his distance, playing darts with a hustler. But he kept one eye on us, waiting for, hoping for, an explosion of drama. Sandra was absorbed with the attentions of her admirers, hustlers who, she failed to realize, flocked near her because every trick's fantasy was to make it with a straight boy. Being seen with her would up their price in the waning minutes before last call.

Suddenly, Masako hopped off her barstool and raced out the door. I caught up just in time to find her retching on the sidewalk.

"She's wasted, dude," Lyle said, having followed us outside.

"Go in and get a wet rag, will you?"

Lyle quickly returned with a bar towel.

"Will you wait inside while I take her home? I think she's had enough excitement for one night."

"Yeah, Scott will keep me occupied," he said, intimating that they'd be doing drugs.

"I'll be back before the bar closes."

At that, Masako began pounding my chest with her fists.

"She needs a line of coke," Lyle said. "It'll make her horny. You might get some action when you take her home."

"It's not like that," I said. "You don't understand."

"Okay, dude. I just thought we'd have a hell of a time later if you came back smelling of pussy."

My disgusted look gave Lyle a good laugh.

"If you're not back when the bar closes," Lyle said, "I'll have Scott drop me off at Okie Dogs."

Okie Dogs was a hamburger stand on Santa Monica Boulevard where underage hustlers hung out. It was better than if he'd proposed waiting for me at Scott's house, considering that hot tub lure of the place.

I led a delirious Masako to the car, but as I opened the door, she demanded that we go back to the bar.

"Don't treat me like child!" she insisted. Trying to make doe eyes at me, she looked up and said, pathetically, "Don't you want me?" Then she passed out in my arms. With some difficulty, I got her securely into the car seat.

"What's your apartment number?" I asked, rousing her after I parked near the building where she lived.

"Second. Twenty-two," she muttered, stopping short of the complete number.

The building had a security door and I couldn't find the key in Masako's purse. I carried her to the intercom outside the front door and buzzed for the manager. A cranky Japanese man in a black robe let us in. He winced at the smell of the alcohol on Masako's breath.

"I thought she nice girl, not like that," he said. "You husband? She say she has husband was coming to town."

I nodded, and asked, "Her apartment's on the second floor?"

The old man eyed me suspiciously. "Second floor. Two twenty-three. Take elevator."

At her door, I again dug through Masako's purse while pivoting her on my hip. I finally managed to find her keys.

Masako locked her arms around my neck as I laid her on the bed. When I tried to pull away, she started wailing. "Please make love to me!" she cried.

"Don't," I said, pulling away.

The more Masako pleaded, the more I thought about Lyle. I was sure that he'd go home with Scott instead of waiting for me at Okie Dogs.

"Let me go," I demanded, wrenching free of Masako's grasp. "Lyle's waiting for me."

Masako flung her fists in the air. "I give you baby!" she argued. "What *he* give you?"

So, she understood all too well what was at stake and what was going on between Lyle and me.

As I headed for the door, Masako began unbuttoning her blouse. She tilted her head, eying me in a way she hoped would be seductive.

"It won't work, Masako," I said. "I should never have agreed to see you. I'm sorry." I closed the door, but couldn't make myself leave. This would be final, and I knew it. I leaned my forehead against her door.

Masako's wails echoed through the hallway as I raced down the stairs moments later.

As I began to drive away, Masako burst from the apartment building. I could see her in the rearview mirror, half-naked, trying to catch up with the car. I made a quick turn down a side street and meandered my way back to the Spotlight.

I pushed aside the noxious red curtain moments before last call. I didn't see Lyle, Scott, or Sandra anywhere. Twiggy was wiping down the counter.

"Twiggy," I hollered. "What happened to my friends?'

But he didn't have to tell me. Lyle had not gone to Okie Dogs; he would be with Scott and Sandra up in the hills at Scott's house. I could hear Lyle now – You went off with your wife, did you really expect me to wait at a hamburger stand until you came to your senses?

"Set me up, Twiggy," I said, holding out three fingers.

Twiggy set down a row of shot glasses.

After the last sour lime, the final lick of salt, and the penultimate last shot of Boodles, I sat up straight to allow my stomach to settle. A barechested wonder boy sat down beside me.

"Aren't you too young to be in a bar?" I asked.

The redhead grinned. I laid my face against his chest. He had an unwashed, sexy smell.

"Want to go home with me?" I asked.

The boy pulled away.

"I've got money, don't worry," I said, wrapping my finger through his belt loop and pulling him close. "Know where I can get some coke?"

"Sure," the boy said. "Let's go."

He led me to a particularly seedy area, just south of Sunset Boulevard.

"Give me your money, dude. The guy won't deal with no one but me."

"No way," I said. I was drunk, but not so intoxicated that I would trust money to a hustler. "I go with you or it's no deal."

I followed the boy to a ground floor apartment. A tough-looking man with a yellow bandana tied around his head opened the door. When he saw me, he whipped his arm behind his back and in a flash, I was facing a gun.

"Whoa, man!" the boy said. "He's cool."

The man motioned the boy inside, but put his hand against my shoulder when I tried to follow. "You wait here," he said.

Moments later, the boy returned, placing a couple of folded papers in my hand. "Give me the money. You can check it out in the car."

The dark hallway made me nervous. I did as asked.

We drove to Long Beach and snorted the coke well into a third day. It was the same Colombian Blue that Scott had scored, a drug so strong it neutralized the desire for sex while amplifying the need to talk. The redhead and I jabbered incessantly the entire time we were together. When the drugs ran out, we collapsed on the bed fully clothed.

All I could think when I woke up was that I had to have a drink of water. I stuck my head in kitchen sink and drank straight from the facet.

"Wake up, cutie," I said to my companion. As much as we had talked, we never exchanged names.

The redhead grumbled, but pulled himself up and got out of bed. He looked at his watch.

"Shit, man," he said. "I got to go. I was supposed to be home before morning. Where's that money you promised? Can you drive me back to Hollywood?" He looked out the window. "The beach? Fuck, where the hell are we?"

I was in no condition to drive, so I gave him extra money for a taxi. He left without saying another word. I ate pancakes soaked with molasses, and, still famished, devoured an entire loaf of bread.

I telephoned Maury's office and spoke to Sandra, hoping to find out what had happened. Lyle had not called the apartment since we parted.

"Honey, I've not seen Lyle or Scott since before I left the bar," she said. "Maury's really pissed that Scott hasn't come in. I called his house, but his roommate wouldn't tell me if he was there or not."

Sandra put me on hold for a moment. "Sorry – Maury was snooping around. I'll tell Scott you called when I hear from him. Um...you know, right, that Lyle left with him?"

"That's why I'm calling. I don't know anything. They weren't at the Spotlight when I came back. Lyle said he would be at Okie Dogs, but I didn't even look."

I left out the reason why.

"Don't be upset, love. I know I'm one to talk. But I got to know Lyle pretty well when you were in Arkansas. He's fond of you. But it's not love, and I think that's what you're expecting. Don't be mad at me, okay sweetie?"

"Never, Sandra. I'm not mad."

Visions of the redheaded boy's grin flashed through my thoughts.

"There's another thing," Sandra continued. "Masako's been calling here for two days. She insists on speaking with you. I told her I don't know your number, but she accused me of lying. What do you want me to tell her?"

"I wish *I* knew what to tell her," I said.

"She's going crazy, and she isn't going to stop calling."

"I hear you, Sandra. You know, Masako left the Church because of me."

"Well, that's her problem. She should have gotten hold of you first, not after."

"That's very eighties. It's hard for me to think that way. I feel responsible. Can we get together tonight? I need to talk to someone."

"Sure. How about the Princess Lounge? I was planning to go there after work."

Sandra was able to go from work to the gym, exercise, and then transform herself into a beauty queen with just few things she carried around in her bag. Sitting at the bar, she looked like a million bucks.

The Princess Lounge wasn't as crowded as usual. We managed to get a booth near the windows, overlooking an atrium garden.

When we were settled, Sandra said, "I heard from Scott just before I left the office. He's going to meet us here."

"Is Lyle with him?"

"I don't think so. He said he'd explain when he sees us."

Sandra placed an order from the Slavic waiter. "I'd love a White Russian," she said seductively, gazing up through her bangs.

I'd had a few shots of gin by the time Scott showed up. I thought I would want to slug him, but he had such a sheepish look on his face that I wondered what he had to say.

"I don't know where Lyle went," he said after giving Sandra a hug. "He came to the house with me. I thought you'd call or come by when you didn't find him at Okie Dogs."

"You could have left a message with Twiggy," I said.

"You're right. But I was drunk. I didn't think."

"So what happened? Or do I even want to know?"

"We sat around doing drugs, then it was morning, and then the day went by, and then it was night again. You know how it goes. When I realized I hadn't been to work in two days, I told Lyle we had to sleep. He blew up, accusing me of trying to get in his pants."

"Well, weren't you?"

"Come on, Simon. I won't deny I'm attracted to Lyle, but I was so high I couldn't even pee."

So if you hadn't been so high, and you could have peed, you would've made a move?

"Nothing happened! Okay? I went to bed. Lyle stayed in the front room on the couch."

"Then what?"

"He was gone when I finally woke up. None of my roommates knew anything. He was out of there by the time they got home. That's all I know."

The bar's pianist began an awful rendition of "Claire de lune". I wondered why a place as elegant as the Princess Lounge didn't hire a better performer.

When the shift changed, and the blond Slavic bartender was replaced with an efficient, but unattractive waiter, Sandra ordered Chivas Regal. Scott joined her. I started ordering Bombay Sapphire and tonic instead of straight shots.

"Lyle was my lover when I married Masako," I blurted out in a bout of drunken self-pity. "He's the reason I left the church." My emotions overflowed and I hugged both my companions. "You two know me better than anyone in this world."

"Oh, honey," Sandra offered. "You are so melodramatic." She threw back her hair and then took a sip from her glass of Chivas. A coy expression came over her face. "You know, I might have an idea where Lyle went. He told me about a girlfriend named Sandy. I think she lives in Anaheim. He's known her since high school. You know he never graduated, right?"

"Lyle never told me much about himself. When we got high, he would tell me the gross things tricks wanted him to do to them."

"E-ew," Sandra said, "not while I'm drinking."

"Anyway, he never mentioned a girlfriend."

"They had wanted to get married. But her father was a problem. He got a restraining order against Lyle.

This was a Lyle I didn't even know.

"Lyle wants to get back with Sandy," Sandra said.

"You're certainly not pulling any punches, are you?"

Sandra was such a forthright person when she drank.

"Never, sweetie. Life's too short."

I grabbed Scott and Sandra's arms. "It's the three S's," I said.

"The three S's?" Sandra laughed.

"Sounds nice, doesn't it? I just made it up."

"Let's get out of here," Scott said.

"Definitely. That's the worst Beethoven I've ever heard," I said. The pianist was attempting the Waldstein Sonata, but made it sound like a child pounding on the keys.

"Let's go to Long Beach," Scott suggested. "We haven't seen where you're living. And I want to view your art."

"Driving there and back, it makes me dizzy thinking about it," I said.

Sandra wasn't thrilled with the idea, either, but she agreed to the trip. "I'll follow you," she said.

Once we were in Long Beach, I pulled into the parking lot of The Beach House, a bar about halfway from my apartment and downtown. It was the closest thing we had to a hustler bar in Long Beach. Sandra stepped from her Trans Am and came over to Scott to take his arm. Her high heels were difficult to manage on the sandy walkway leading from the parking lot to the bar's entrance. "I'm so glad we stopped here," Sandra said. "I've heard about this place."

Scott and Sandra hit the dance floor while I sat at the bar. The more I drank, the more my mind dredged up images of Lyle with that girlfriend from high school. A cute blond guy came on to Scott and I saw him whisper something in Sandra's ear. She joined me at the bar. We had to yell to be heard over the charging sounds of the Oingo Boingo track blaring from the dance floor.

"Why doesn't Scott pay attention to me?" Sandra said, speaking with her lips to my ear.

"He's gay, Sandra. What do you expect?"

Sandra put her arm around me. "You don't know, do you?"

"Know what?"

"That Scott and I are having a thing."

"A thing?"

"You know. An affair."

"Scott would fuck anything, Sandra, don't you know that? I'm sorry. Maybe I'm being too direct. But seriously. He tried to make it with me the minute I was back in Hollywood."

Sandra giggled, "I'm not just 'anything'."

"I know, Sandra. You're gorgeous. Haven't I told you that before?"

"Tell me again." She put her head on my shoulder.

Drunk as I was, the smell of Sandra's perfume and the softness of her hair caused a slight stir, but only a slight one. The moment ended the second a young man in tight jeans walked past.

Around midnight, it was clear than none of us was in any shape to drive. We left the cars parked at the bar and made our way on foot toward my apartment, walking along the beach. The moonlight caused the saltwater minerals to fluoresce as waves washed across our path. Scott played tag with them, several times stumbling into the water. Sandra hung onto me for support, but I had little to provide.

"Wow, look at this incredible thing," I said, picking up a rock that was pockmarked in such a way that it appeared to have been drilled into from all angles.

"You are so weird," Scott said, tripping over a child's sandcastle from the day before.

"That's my apartment," I said, pointing. "There, at the corner."

"Who's that on the landing?" Sandra asked, peering hard through the darkness.

"Probably Lyle. The fucker knows I'll forgive anything he does."

"That's not Lyle," Scott said ominously. "I think it's Masako."

We stopped in our tracks.

The figure began to descend the stairs. The strange object fell out of my hand as I found myself face-to-face with my wife.

"Are you sleep with her?" Masako said, pointing at Sandra.

I was too high to take the question seriously. I started to laugh.

"You my husband," Masako said angrily.

Whatever tenderness I had harbored toward Masako completely vanished. I had not asked her to follow me after I left the church, much less to chase me to California.

"You better leave, Masako," I said flatly. My emotions were about to get the best of me, and I knew it. "Seriously, Masako. You better go."

Her eyes flared. "I your wife, Simon Powell!"

"This isn't make-believe," I said forcefully. "We're not following some crazy messiah any longer. This is the real world, and I didn't ask you to come here."

"I love you! That why I follow."

"Masako. Don't you get it? I like men."

Masako fell to the ground weeping.

Scott and Sandra had taken positions on the steps. Sandra's face was buried in her hands. Scott was staring at the ground.

"It's over, Masako. Just go. I'll give you a divorce. No argument."

Masako crawled forward and grabbed my leg. "Please love me! I be good wife."

I tried to pull away, but Masako locked her arms around my knees.

"Get away," I said, walking toward the steps, dragging Masako.

Scott and Sandra scurried to the landing. When I got to the bottom step, I pushed Masako away and ran to the door, key in hand. Scott, Sandra, and I rushed inside. I could hear Masako outside, whimpering, for at least an hour.

"I'm going back to The Beach House," I said when Masako finally left. "I don't have a drink in the house, and by god, I need one."

Sandra found the phone book in a kitchen drawer and looked up the number for a taxi.

"I was an idiot for letting things go so far with Masako," I said. "Why can't I just face the fact that I'm gay?"

"Right now," Scott said, "I'd call you a faggot."

Sandra had the taxi take us to the bar, then she and Scott headed off for Hollywood in her Trans Am. I sat in my Topaz and tried to decide what to do next. I didn't want to be alone, but by then, I didn't much feel like going inside to face loud music and people even drunker than me.

Cherry Park was the only place in Long Beach where I knew that hustlers hung out. After circling around several times, a boy appeared under a street lamp.

"What's your name?" I asked, pulling to a stop beside him.

"Joe," the boy said. "What are you into?"

"Nothing kinky. I just like to get my dick sucked."

"I can do that. How much you willing to pay?"

"Thirty bucks."

"Let's go." The boy hopped into the car and lit a cigarette. "You live in Long Beach, don't you?"

"Yeah. Belmont Shore, right on the beach."

"Thought I'd seen you before."

I pulled into my garage, and as I closed the door, I heard someone mumbling around the corner. Ripples' patrons often passed out on my street, but the voice I heard was a woman's.

"Listen," I said, as Joe and I walked toward the steps, "my ex-wife has been hanging around. I just wanted you to know in case she shows up."

We were at the bottom of the stairs before I saw Masako sitting halfway up. She was still weeping, her head buried in her knees.

"Ignore her," I whispered to Joe. We passed right by her on the steps. She didn't move.

I dead-bolted the lock, and heard Masako mumbling again. Only then did I realize she was quietly singing one of the church's Holy Songs.

"Come on, Joe," I said, leading him into the bedroom. "Let's get down to business."

I don't know how long Masako hung around. When I opened the door the next morning, she was gone. I gave Joe his money and sent him on his way. He disappeared down the street toward Ripples. I went out to the beach and found the pockmarked stone I had picked up on the beach the night before. I spent the morning painting it with silver enamel, filling in the craters with different primary colors.

I missed Lyle. It was hard to face the fact that he had left me for his high school sweetheart, but if I had run into my high school love, Tony, I'd have left anyone I was with at the time to get back together.

CHAPTER ELEVEN

Some weeks later, I received a registered letter from an attorney whose office was in Little Tokyo. Masako had filed for divorce. I signed the forms and mailed them back without hesitation.

When I eventually went to drug rehab, my counselor asked if I still believed that Reverend Moon was the messiah. I found it strangely difficult to answer at the time, remembering that when I had signed the divorce papers, I could not shake the feeling of having entered into a Faustian contract. According to the church's beliefs, by rejecting my marriage, I would end up in the lowest realm of Hell. Satan would once again become the Angel of Light, Lucifer, before the gates of Heaven opened for me.

Whatever I believed deep inside, while living in Long Beach, I pursued a hedonistic life of leisure. I sat on the landing in a lawn chair in the afternoons with a pair of binoculars and watched beautiful young men playing volleyball on the beach. Each night, I went to Ripple's and got drunk. Nearly always, I met someone to stumble home with when the bar closed. They invariably left the next morning and hardly said hello when I ran into them again. No one went to Ripples looking for a soul mate.

I continued toiling on the black drawings, calling the series "Spirals to Oblivion". No one would ever see them. Before I left Long Beach, I wadded them up and threw the heap into a trash bin along Ocean Boulevard. The works expressed what I felt at the time, but I didn't want them to become part of a legacy.

By the time the lease ran out on my apartment, I was penniless, having gone through every cent of my quitclaim windfall. Scott's place was crowded, with three people sharing rent and each taking a bedroom, but he allowed me to sleep on his couch. For all his goofing off, Scott had passed the California bar exam and become a lawyer. He encouraged me to get a real job rather than sell things on the street, which is what I had started to do for food money. He gave me the names of temporary placement agencies associated with motion picture companies, and I got a few gigs as a location sitter at homes in Beverly Hills. My car came in handy when I landed jobs serving as a gopher to production assistants.

Scott slowed down on his cocaine use after Maury complained that he was calling in sick too often. I didn't have money to buy coke during that period, but when offered a line, I rarely refused.

I took my meager and sporadic paychecks and spent most of the money at the Spotlight. Twiggy, sentimental and remembering how good I had been about tipping when I was flying high, set me up with a free drink for each one I bought. Having seen an endless parade of people come through the bar – one month on top of the world, penniless the next – he knew my fortunes would change.

Vivian urged me to return to Sibley, often saying that she wished I would go back to school. Her suggestions never registered with me. Hollywood allowed me to be anonymous, and that was what I wanted.

Connie never failed to tell me that I was in her prayers. "You should start going to church," she would say. "Jesus is the Savior, not that Korean anti-Christ." I would politely state that exposure to one group of true believers was enough for a lifetime. If anything, I felt the experience had inoculated me against religious thought.

One of Scott's roommates moved out right when a serious job opportunity presented itself.

"There's a chance I can get you set up with one of Maury's clients," Scott told me one night. "If you don't mind sweeping floors."

"What kind of job are you talking about?" I imagined myself in a white coat and bowtie like the fellow at the end of Peabody's Improbable History episodes from the Rocky and Bullwinkle cartoons.

"An Italian film distributor named Nicolò hired Maury to represent him in a case involving intellectual property rights. Something about video and whether non-theatrical clauses in old contracts cover those rights. I overheard him asking Maury if he knew someone who wanted a job organizing his warehouse."

As a regional fundraising leader in the church, I had managed dozens of warehouses, places where we kept the products that members sold. I knew what drudgery it could be: heavy lifting, ledger books, and lots of dust. My face must have shown that a job like that wasn't my idea of a good time.

"Come on," Scott encouraged. "It'll give you a steady income. And who knows, maybe it will lead to something bigger."

"Okay," I agreed. What choice was there? The ten-year gap in my resume had already become a problem at job interviews.

"I'll get Sandra to set up a meeting," Scott said.

"Sandra? Why not Maury?"

"Because he's so infatuated with her that he has to put a nitroglycerin pill under his tongue every time she walks toward him. Sandra will get you in the door, I guarantee it."

The next day, Sandra told me over the phone that she had told Nicolò I was experience in warehouse management.

"But Sandra," I said, "I don't know squat about the film business."

"Doesn't matter. From what I hear, his place is such a mess, he doesn't even know what he's got. You'll do fine."

"Maybe," I said.

Sandra gave me an address. "Got to go, sweetie. Maury's heading this way."

She had to be careful. Maury didn't want anyone talking to me.

Nicolò's office was on the Sunset Strip at the edge of Beverly Hills, in a stylish building from the 1920s. Standing in the reception area, I could see a long corridor with closed doors. In the other direction was a copy room stacked with six-drawer filing cabinets. A dark-haired fellow, who appeared to be in his twenties, worked feverishly at a computer terminal, apparently entering information from contracts spread out on his desk.

After a long wait, Nicolò appeared from one of the doors along the corridor and motioned for me to come inside. He was in his mid-fifties, overweight, and bald, with a large head and piercing gray eyes. His hand swallowed mine in its broad grip when he greeted me.

Ginger, his secretary, buzzed the intercom before we even started to talk. Someone was calling from Varese, the city in Lombard, Italy, where

Nicolò was born. I sat for the next thirty minutes listening to animated Italian. As he spoke, Nicolò seemed to study a print of the aging scholar by da Vinci that hung behind his desk. He waved his arm in my direction from time to time as if to say, not much longer.

When the phone call ended, Nicolò looked over the resume I had prepared. It listed the string of odd jobs I had held recently, naming several production companies and remaining vague about just how much of an assistant to an assistant I had been. It satisfied Nicolò that Sandra's endorsement of me was warranted. He took me to a large room at the end of the corridor.

"I cannot find a thing," Nicolò lamented, sweeping his arm through the air, as if to encompass the chaos within. "You see what I mean?"

The room was a jumble of cardboard boxes, each bursting at the seams. Film canisters and racks of three-quarter-inch videotapes were stacked floor to ceiling. Thousands of manila folders lay in dusty piles.

"You can make sense of this, yes?" Nicolò asked.

It would be a daunting task, but I had tackled worse during my days managing fundraising teams.

"My company is a small one. I cannot pay much," Nicolò said. "Two-fifty a week to begin."

"This could take months," I said. The man was offering me barely enough to survive.

Nicolò gestured toward the file folders. "Some of these are old contracts that need to be renegotiated. There is money in that. We can talk about a raise if you identify them."

I agreed to his terms. Nicolò shook my hand again. I followed him to the front desk. "Please help Mr. Simon fill out his employment papers," he said to the secretary.

"Hi Ginger. I'm Simon," I said, shaking her hand.

She wrote down my social security number and said she would pass it on to the bookkeeper, a man who only came to the office on Fridays.

Nicolò's salesperson, Patrick Day, arrived before sunrise to telex the European clients. He was the son of a pharmacist who worked at the Thrifty Drug Store on Rodeo Drive. His family lived in the Beverly Hills flatlands. In terms of local snobbery, one may as well live in Watts.

When trying to act sophisticated, Patrick always missed the mark. He wore earrings when they were not the fashion for men, and sported Italian-made shoes when sneakers were in vogue. His hair was slicked down when others strove for a look that said, I just woke up. But for Nicolò, Patrick had classic American looks, and that is why he was hired. Foreign buyers would first negotiate with Patrick, but only Nicolò could finalize a contract.

Sorting through the jumble of papers in his storage room, I learned a great deal about motion picture distribution. Before long, I had familiarized myself with representation agreements, the terms of contracts with video companies, and Nicolò's working relationship with custom brokers and video transfer labs as well as how to interpret letters of credit and other financial documents.

Nicolò got his start by marketing American cartoons dubbed in Italian. Eventually, he expanded to selling independent American films to Italian television. Most were low-budget and of very poor quality, but Nicolò had the finesse of a used-car salesman, bundling three awful films with one that promised a modicum of sales. Video had resurrected movies that for years had languished in vaults. People who thought they owned worthless film libraries suddenly found they possessed a potentially valuable commodity.

The advantage of film distributors was that they always made a profit, keeping twenty-five percent off the top, and deducting expenses from the remainder before giving the owners anything.

When I got the files organized, prioritizing the contracts according to their long and short term profitability, I asked Nicolò for a raise. His negotiating style was to promise anything and then claim he hadn't understood the agreement. He denied ever saying he would increase my salary if I made sense of his old contracts.

Unrelated to my demand for more money, Ginger resigned the next day. She wanted Nicolò to hire her away from the temporary agency that had placed her. He refused.

"Before you get another receptionist," I told Nicolò, "I have a proposal. Let me do Ginger's job. I'll continue to manage the inventory and also take care of the phones. Just up my salary to what she was getting. How about it?"

"Reception is a woman's job," Nicolò said. "Clients want to hear a female voice when they call."

"Think about the savings," I said. "We communicate with clients through telexes and faxes most of the time, anyway. Most of the phone calls are from your suppliers looking for money."

Nicolò rubbed his chin for a second, and then his eyes lit up. He thrust out his hand and we shook energetically. "You are right. Very correct," he said, gazing toward the ceiling, as if to get confirmation from above. "I do it."

"Things will be fine," I assured him. "You'll see."

As it happened, more of Nicolò's clients telephoned than he was remembering. Answering the phone would give me a chance to get to know them. I also wanted to connect with the producers who supplied his films. My goal was to take Patrick's job.

Patrick thought of me as the doofus who stacked boxes in the back room. He was appalled when Nicolò gave me Ginger's job. He had treated her as his personal secretary, but he couldn't bring himself to ask me to do anything.

When Nicolò agreed to buy a computer for the front desk so I could build an inventory system and create a phone log, Patrick nearly went through the roof. He struggled to get his work done on a computer that was so slow, it took minutes to save a large document. He challenged what I knew about computers in the first place, but by then, I had learned quite a bit from Scott, who had written a program to print legal forms, and had learned how to use a modem to connect to the courthouse to pick up the daily docket.

After a month, Patrick gave Nicolò an ultimatum: hire a receptionist and send me back to the inventory, or he was gone. Nicolò told him that he appreciated the sales he had made over the last two years and that he was sure he'd do well in the future. If he needed a reference, Nicolò would be happy to provide one.

It was the first real success since my glory days in the church leading hundreds of members and commanding millions of dollars. Despite the small size of Nicolò's company, I saw opportunity.

Nicolò quickly came to depend on me. Each day, I arrived earlier than Patrick had done to retrieve our telexes and check faxes. I dealt with most of the correspondence. Nicolò trusted my judgment, though he often penciled in changes when he signed contracts.

By autumn, I was ready for MIFED, an important market for selling independent films that was held in Milan, Italy. The annual event took place each year at the end of October. Most buyers were looking for theatrical releases, but some wanted video rights.

Nicolò placed an advertisement in the Hollywood Reporter's special issue. We had a poor offering, but the worldwide video market was hungry for any American film that had been shown in theaters. Though our most recent film was made over a decade before, each could claim having had a theatrical release.

I arranged tickets and made reservations at the Hotel Windsor in Milan. Nicolò had suggested the hotel since they catered to British and American guests and most of the employees spoke English.

The night before the event began, Nicolò introduced me to his cronies, a group of wealthy old men with white hair who all had gregarious personalities. Nicolò had known most of them since his youth. They showered him with affection. For me, the evening could not have been duller. After dinner, we toured piano bars, seemingly a popular form of entertainment in Milan. Not understanding either a word of the conversation or a lyric of the songs being sung, I drank nonstop – first wine, but then switching to "gin-tonic", as the Italian bartenders called it.

Sometime around dawn, after finally separating from his friends at a bar with the lousiest Barry Manilow imitator one could imagine, Nicolò took me to the Principe da Savoia, a palatial hotel where serious figures in the film industry gathered. Nicolò had nothing to offer these wheelers and dealers, but he liked to be seen there, hoping to gain a patina of legitimacy. Nicolò was the smallest of small potatoes, but everyone knew him. I had not realized until that trip that Nicolò had once been an actor.

It was a fascinating crowd. Everyone scrutinized everyone else's gestures, watching for the slightest hint that their bravado was bluff. Did they really have Robert De Niro lined up for a role in their new film, or were they fishing to see if an investor would be onboard if he was in their film?

Nicolò began telling people that he was in negotiations to distribute a film, currently in production. He came up with a title out of thin air, The Tragic Amazon. If I hadn't pulled him away, he would have signed letters of agreement for something that didn't exist and never would.

We arrived at the Windsor Hotel with only two hours before we had to be at the event. I could only have been asleep for an hour when Nicolò almost knocked down my door trying to rouse me. I dragged myself to the lobby for continental breakfast and cups of foamy cappuccino. Nicolò had the concierge hail a taxi.

MIFED was held in the largest convention center in Europe. By the time we arrived, Nicolò and I had fallen asleep. The taxi driver yelled several times before we woke up, wobbly as the hula girl glued to his dashboard. I'm not sure how much money Nicolò gave him, but it was far more than the cost of the trip. Nicolò's exhaustion was catching up with him.

At the main entrance, billboards announced the new films being screened. Some were enhanced with neon lights in hopes of catching the attention of buyers before they picked up their badges at the registration desk.

The offices were assigned according to an established pecking order. Those who had attended for many years got the best locations. New distributors got a booth.

For ten days, Nicolò and I spent most of our time in a medium-sized office negotiating contracts. Many buyers spoke neither Italian nor English. Nicolò's minimal command of French helped in some cases. Other times, I wasn't sure the clients understood what they were signing. Once, I saw Nicolò add a zero to the deal after the contract was signed, but prior to his giving the client their copy.

During slow periods, Nicolò roamed the halls to find people he recognized. Though I did most of the negotiating and greeted everyone who came by, to hear Nicolò talking to his cronies, one would think he was doing all the work. A wink from his friends, though, told me that his braggadocio didn't fool them.

One afternoon, Nicolò taped a "come back later" sign on our door and took me to lunch at an elegant restaurant deep in the heart of the convention center.

"I've ignored you for too long," Nicolò said, to my surprise. "I'm sorry about that."

After a few sentences, I understood his true motivation. He had noticed my lack of interest in making new sales. It had become clear that Nicolò was a crook, and I didn't want to be associated with his shady deal making.

"We are in the magnificent city of Milano," Nicolò said. "What would you like to do?"

I was sure I would never see the commission he had promised me. So this would be my only perk.

"What about going to La Scala?" I had loved opera since I was a child listening to Wagner's Das Rheingold on Sunday afternoons.

"No opera," Nicolò said glumly. "This is not the season."

"Surely there's something going on at La Scala," I said.

Nicolò promised to call and find out.

That evening, we took a cab from the convention center to the Teatro alla Scala. Flood lights shone on the baroque facade, enhancing its otherworldly grandeur. At the door, we learned that the evening's show – a concert including the Brahms violin concerto with Anna Sophie-Mutter performing – was sold out.

Undeterred, Nicolò led me to the performer's entrance. He scurried up some steps and spoke to an usher. The fellow stood his ground. Nicolò shook his head at the boy and took out his wallet, placing a bill in his hand. It appeared to be a £50,000 note – about forty dollars. The usher waved me up the stairs. Nicolò patted me on the back and said, "See you in the morning."

The usher pointed me up a small stairway only two feet wide. It led to the spectator's gallery – a space that abutted the ceiling, barely large enough for a pigeon to roost. Round wooden seats lowered from the walls, leaving about six inches between one's knees and a low railing. If a person were to become dizzy, he could plunge to his death without knowing what happened. But even these precarious seats were taken. I leaned against the door.

La Scala was magnificent with its elaborate gilt moldings, ornate boxes, rich burgundy curtains, and crystal chandeliers. The acoustics were stunning. I could hear the strings of Anna Sophie-Mutter's bow gliding over the strings beneath her delicate touch. The violin's dialogue with the orchestra was like that of an angel conversing with God. Ah, Brahms! My chest swelled with emotion. When the violin reached its highest register, I couldn't stop the tears. My journey to that moment seemed an unfathomable distance that stretched from hope to heartbreak, companionship to abject loneliness. I had been a naïve boy growing up in a town so remote from the modern world that the Civil War was as real as if it had happened last year. I had been the effeminate kid who everyone bullied, who fell into the snare of sexual complexities when he was just seven, lured by his best friend into "games" taught to him by the boy's lustful older brother. I'd dared to fall in love as a senior in high school, only to get my heart broken. I had attempted suicide before turning into a hippie, taking LSD, and believing that my mind had been opened to the wonders of the cosmos. Then, as a member of a despised cult, I had thought I could save the world, or at least rid myself from the shackles of homosexuality. What a mistake, to think I was abnormal because I desired the companionship of men. Self-deception had caused me to hurt innocent Masako and driven me to use drugs.

Why did I choose damaged hustlers such as Lyle instead of seeking mature love and affection?

After the performance ended, I waited until everyone had left the pigeon's roost. I peered over the railing at the darkened auditorium as workers began to remove the piano from the stage and others began vacuuming the aisles. I was ready to dive over the edge, to write a romantic ending to an otherwise meaningless life.

The usher who Nicolò had bribed approached me. In terribly broken English, he implored me to leave. "Please, you go now," he said, "Concerto. It is finish."

I smiled weakly and took a last look over the ledge. How inviting the red carpet seemed. My blood would hardly make a stain.

The usher grabbed me by the arm. "Please, sir."

Shaken by his touch and the concern in his voice, I ran down the stairs, crashed through the doors, and rushed toward the middle of the piazza. It was Friday night. Hordes of roller-skating young men were showing off for their girlfriends. Lovers sat close to each other on the benches. I spotted a bar at the edge of Piazza and went inside to find another type of oblivion.

The next morning, I awoke lying fully clothed on my bed at the Windsor with no recollection of how I got there.

CHAPTER TWELVE

Early in 1987, just before the American Film Market was held, I asked Nicolò to pay the commissions he had long promised. He had endless excuses about why he couldn't afford it. There was the cost of renovations to his house in Santa Monica. The private schools for his children had nearly broken him. He seemed to think I should care about these personal inconveniences. The man had no idea what a crummy apartment I called home; a tiny one bedroom on Poinsettia, between Hollywood Boulevard and Sunset, was all I could afford on the salary he gave me.

I let him think I was sorry I had asked.

The American Film Market, an event similar to MIFED, was held every year in Los Angeles. Halfway through it that year, while Nicolò was at lunch, a fellow came around handing out glossy flyers for a novelty video called Coed Jellorama, an hour of male and female semi-nude models slipping and sliding in a rubber-lined pool filled with squishy Jell-O. An audience of buxom women and beefcake men cheered from the sidelines. It was pure kitsch.

The producer introduced himself as Wally Freeze, a name he always repeated to make sure the person understood that it really was his name.

"My boss won't be interested," I said after reading the description on the back of the flyer. "He only deals with movies shot on film." I checked the hallway to make sure Nicolò wasn't on his way back. He probably wouldn't be interested, but I had a Japanese buyer in mind. "Perhaps I can do something for you," I told Wally. "Let's have dinner and talk about it." We arranged to meet later at the Hamburger Hamlet on Sunset Boulevard. Before leaving the office, Wally confessed that I was the first person who hadn't thrown his flyer in the trash.

At dinner, Wally explained that he had sold the U.S. license to a label called Bareback Video Sales. I held back a chuckle.

"But the international rights are free, correct?" I asked, taking out a legal pad and jotting down a letter of agreement.

Wally nodded.

"There's still a few days left in the market," I said. "Let me see what I can do for you on my own."

Overwhelmed with gratitude, Wally signed over all the remaining rights. He even agreed to let me have dibs on future productions as well as rights on a catalog of old films that he owned.

The next day, I spoke to Sugiyama-san, the Japanese client, and set up a meeting in his hotel room to screen Coed Jellorama. Sugiyama, who usually maintained a stern appearance, could barely contain his enthusiasm. I negotiated a contract for twenty thousand dollars, though later I realized I could have asked for much more.

Working behind Nicolò's back, I sold Coed Jellorama to Korea and Taiwan, and then to Australia, before the AFM was over. When the money arrived, I'd be a hundred thousand dollars richer.

Nicolò's stinginess became easier to tolerate. I needed access to his fax machine and telex, as well as the computer, and I saw no reason to buy all that equipment with my own money. Each day, after Nicolò went home, I stayed at the office to work on my contracts. Money became a consuming passion, the thrill heightened all the more because I was doing it at my boss's expense. I was fast becoming another Nicolò.

The long hours I kept didn't afford much time for any fun. By midsummer, I suggested that Nicolò get a new secretary since I was still answering the phones on top of everything else. Nicolò agreed. He wanted me to focus more on the contracts, believing that my efforts were all for his benefit.

I screened applicants sent by an employment agency, and eventually hired Clarice Smith, a jolly, overweight woman with a terrific personality. On the phone, Clarice spoke with a voice one might expect from the vixen in a film noir movie. She enjoyed it when clients visited. Clarice would put on her best phone voice and giggle at the disappointed reactions.

Clarice never suspected my nocturnal use of the facilities, or at least she never let on that she did. I appreciated her ability to keep Nicolò in check. No matter how upset he got, she was able to calm him down.

Toward the end of the year, just after our annual trip to MIFED, Nicolò hired a full-time accountant, letting it slip that he needed someone to work on "back taxes." He had run afoul of the I.R.S., a situation I knew a thing or two about from my work defending Reverend Moon against charges of tax fraud.

The accountant, Moe Dirksen, was recommended to Nicolò by one of his Italian friends, a man I felt sure had connections to organized crime. Moe was a disagreeable guy in his mid-fifties, always dressed shabbily in oversized suits that must have come from a thrift store. His steel gray hair was trimmed in a bowl cut. He showed up for work at exactly the same time every day, arriving by bus from his tenement apartment downtown. He invariably smelled of liquor and stale cigarettes.

Moe disliked me from the start. He distrusted computers and was unwilling to accept the printouts I gave him. He demanded that Nicolò have me transfer the figures into an old-fashioned ledger book. I refused.

"Just because you're from the Middle Ages doesn't mean I have to join you," I told him.

Moe glared at me fiercely.

The next morning, I was keying contract information into the computer when Nicolò came into my office. Moe followed two steps behind.

"Why are you being so uncooperative with Moe?" Nicolò asked.

"Uncooperative?! The man is illiterate." An overreaction to be sure, but I simply could not be bothered with Nicolò and his troubles. I was sure that Moe wanted the ledger so he could fudge the numbers and that Nicolò was complicit in the plan.

"Moe says you refused to show him the contracts. He thinks you're hiding something."

"If he can't read the printouts I give him, what's he good for?"

Moe stepped from behind Nicolò and approached my desk, arrogantly flicking cigar ashes over my keyboard.

"Did you see that?" I shouted.

Nicolò was dumbfounded.

"Apologize," I demanded, rising from my chair.

Moe shuffled to my side of the desk. He stood so close that his alcoholic's breath made me nauseous. He spat as he said, "What did you say, you snobby little bastard?"

"Get this maniac away from me," I said, looking toward an ashen-faced Nicolò.

Moe reached for the telephone and raised it above his head, primed and ready to crush my skull. I stooped just as the phone crashed against the wall.

Clarice was at the door as I ran toward her, followed by Moe. He tried to jab me with his burning cigar.

"Stop it, Moe!" Clarice shouted. She looked desperately at Nicolò. "Do something!"

Nicolò grabbed Moe by the coat. I made it to the stairs and stumbled onto the sidewalk. I thought about pressing charges, but figured it would cause more trouble than it was worth. I went to my car and drove to the Spotlight. I had to have a drink. After guzzling three beers, I felt calm enough to phone the office. Clarice answered.

"Is that asshole in jail?" I asked.

"He's in his office."

"Didn't Nicolò fire him?"

Clarice's voice betrayed her own exasperation. "After you left, Nicolò mumbled something about both of you being idiots. Then he went into his office and shut the door. He's been on the phone ever since."

"Tell Nicolò something for me, will you Clarice? Tell him that I need to take off the rest of the day."

"I think that's wise," Clarice said. "Nicolò's under a lot of stress. The I.R.S. is coming down pretty hard. Nicolò thinks Moe can get him out of it."

I wasn't sure if Clarice could truly be so naïve, or if she was being paid to look the other way.

The rest of the afternoon, I sat at the bar talking to Twiggy. We shared ideas about ways I could hurt Nicolò's business. Maybe I'd fax his clients and cancel the contracts, sneak in after hours and scramble his files, or even wipe the computer clean. Whatever I might do, it would have to wait until after I picked up my paycheck on Friday. I wasn't going to quit before getting every last cent he owed me.

On Thursday, Nicolò didn't come to the office. Moe was there when I arrived, but I went to my office and shut the door. I made backup disks of my private computer files. Then I copied Nicolò's files to a different set of floppies and put them in my desk drawer. I reformatted the hard disk to hide all evidence of my activities.

When Friday came, Nicolò acted as though nothing had happened. I waited until Clarice handed me my paycheck. During lunch, I went to Nicolò's bank and cashed it. Returning to the office, I marched in to see Nicolò and handed him my letter of resignation.

"You made your bed. Now lie in it, Nicolò."

He made a half-hearted attempt to dissuade me. "Simon, please. Let's work this out."

"Tell me one thing," I said. "Are you going to fire that crazy bookkeeper?"

"I can't," Nicolò said. He started to say more, but I walked out.

As I passed Clarice, she put her hands over her face. She knew this would be the end of Nicolò's business, and it was.

Nicolò didn't understand anything about computers and threw out the floppies I had left behind, not understanding that all his inventory information, contracts, and other business data were stored on them. He began to speak maliciously about me to anyone who would listen. But people knew him well enough, and his words had no impact on my reputation.

I never saw Clarice again, but I did run into Moe. I was shopping at a wholesale clothing store in downtown Los Angeles, a place that sold brand name suits for a hundred dollars. There was Moe leaning against a wall near the Jesus Saves rescue mission. He was tightly clutching a brown paper bag. I handed him a quarter, but he didn't recognize me.

CHAPTER THIRTEEN

To match my new status as an independent businessman, I moved into a house on Lookout Mountain Drive in Laurel Canyon, a split-level structure with hardwood floors in the cavernous living room that reminded me of an old-fashioned dance hall. The master bedroom had its own fireplace. I used the bedroom for my office and made the walk-in closet a storage vault for master videotapes. A balcony stretched across the front of the house and joined the master with the guest bedrooms. The patio behind the house had a hot tub at one end and a barbecue on the other. A steep hill planted with rare flowers from Indonesia rose behind the patio. An ancient avocado tree shaded the roof and raccoons made great sport of bombarding the roof with avocado seeds. At night, the raccoons raced through the limbs, leaping onto the roof and back into the tree as they played. I counted nine of them as I soaked in the hot tub one night.

Scott and Sandra called from time to time. On a few occasions, we got together at Dan Tana's or Cyrano's. They would catch me up news about their latest sexual conquests, and sometimes they wanted to share lines of coke with me. During that period, I refrained. I liked the high too much and was having a hard enough time balancing my desire to drink with my need to be focused on business. The entrepreneurial spirit of the 1980s had me clenched firmly in its teeth.

Wally had come up with a new video called Bel Air Babes, a soft-porn romp that was hardly more risqué than burlesque. It sold to every Asian market because it easily passed censorship panels, yet was titillating enough to find an audience. That one crummy video made me a small fortune.

No matter how busy I got, my day ended at the Spotlight. Sitting in the smoky darkness, listening to the eclectic jukebox, lost in an alcoholic haze, and usually hugging a shirtless hustler, time seemed to stand still. The owner, a retired law professor named Don, had long been a close acquaintance. Don allegedly had connections to Hollywood's crime underworld, but I figured the less I knew about that, the better.

One memorable night, after my seventh or eighth shot of Boodles, a fight broke out. That was not an unusual event at the Spotlight, of course, except that these weren't the usual lowlifes getting into a brawl. One was a fellow named Rudy Gutierrez, who I'd seen at the bar from time to time. At six feet four inches tall, he was the proverbial mountain of a man, an effect heightened by his weight of three hundred pounds. Rudy dwarfed his opponent, an ex-jockey named Tinker Bell, who he had pinned against the bar by the sheer force of his own body weight.

Don intervened, rising from his honored spot near the entrance to the bar and marching toward Rudy.

"Release that man or I'll eighty-six you for a year," Don said.

Rudy didn't budge. "Tell this motherfucker to apologize and you won't have to eighty-six me – I'll never come back. He apologizes, or I'm sticking to him like glue."

"Back off, Rudy," Don demanded. At this point, the spike-gloved bouncer was ready to clobber Rudy on Don's orders.

Rudy took a step back and flexed his hand into a fist. "Say it, fucker. Say you're sorry."

Tinker collapsed onto the floor. Rudy allowed him to drag himself to the bar.

"What do you want me to say, Rudy? I'm sorry I called you a fat queen! Okay, I'm sorry. You're not a queen. I mean, you're not fat. Hell, Rudy, I didn't mean anything!"

Rudy took a menacing step toward Tinker Bell.

Don stepped between them. "That's as good as you're going to get, Rudy. Come on. Let's play that round of liar's poker you promised." He walked Rudy to the bar and folded a dollar bill. "I call three nines. Call your numbers, Rudy."

A compulsive gambler, Rudy couldn't resist. He folded his bill and challenged with a bid of his own. He forgot all about his anger as he tricked Don into a round for the bar. Rudy was a master at liar's poker.

"That was quite a pillow fight," I said to Rudy just before last call.

Rudy stopped in his tracks. "Have we met?"

"I'm Simon, and you're Rudy the fat queen, right?"

Rudy almost tipped over my barstool as he pressed forward. "If you weren't rich, I'd rip you a new one." He set down shot glasses in front of us.

"But you are a fat queen, Rudy."

"Well, I am a queen," Rudy said, managing a curtsy as he demurely touched his index finger to his chin.

"What do you mean 'rich'?" I said after Rudy and I had downed the shots.

"Well, you have your own film company. You work alone. You live in a big Laurel Canyon house. I know it's got a hot tub with ceramic tiles. And you're about to go to Italy in a few weeks."

"I'm afraid to ask how you know all that."

Rudy smiled. "You make an impression on the boys. They tell Don everything, and he tells me." With that, Rudy twirled around, nimble for such a heavy person, and continued on his way back to a booth where two young men were waiting for him.

In time, I learned that Rudy was a well-known chef in Hollywood. Some of the biggest names in Hollywood hired him to cater private parties. The walls of Rudy's home were lined with photos of him standing next to celebrities. Many of the pictures were signed, often with reference to the delicious food he had prepared.

When I met him, Rudy was living in the servants' quarters at the estate of a wealthy director where he was the head chef. After our introduction at the expense of poor Tinker Bell, Rudy and I spent many hours at the Spotlight, ogling the hustlers, drinking to each other's health, and playing liar's poker with Don and the other members of the bar's inner circle.

One night, out of the blue, Rudy announced that he was moving back to Miami.

"I don't want to see you go," I told him. Rudy was fun and I would miss his company.

Rudy threw back a shot of Schnapps. "I was offered my old job back, working on a yacht."

"Old job? What happened to it before?"

Rudy twirled the empty shot glass on the bar. "I thought you knew why I left Miami."

"Someone told me you had a drug problem. But then, don't we all?"

"Honey, back then, I was Patti Paranoia. I smoked so much crack that I thought the police were always about to break through the door."

"Won't you get back into it if you go back?"

"I need the job."

"Really? I thought everyone wanted you as their chef."

Rudy fanned his fingers as he flipped his wrist. "I am a queen, honey. I got so mad at a cook who ruined my morning soufflé that I knocked him down and raked a cheese grater across his head."

"Didn't you have enough head cheese for your scrapple?"

Rudy tapped me playfully on the forehead. "Listen to you. Cute, and he has a sense of humor, too." He made huge doe eyes. "Where have you been all my life?"

"What would it take for you to stay?"

"What do you mean?"

"Look, I have money. Maybe I could give you a loan, or hire you as my own chef."

Rudy put his hands on his face. "That's the sweetest thing anyone's offered to do for me in a long time."

"What will it take, Rudy?"

"I have to move from the estate, and I have to get by until I find another gig, maybe in a restaurant. The celebrity circuit is off limits for a while."

"How much do you need?"

"Two thousand dollars," Rudy said.

"I'll have a cashier's check drawn up tomorrow. Pay me back when you can," I grabbed his ass, "or I'll take it out in trade."

Rudy hooked his fingers through the belt loops of his huge pants. "I'll pay you back with interest. And I'll fix you the most incredible meal you ever tasted. Just say when."

"Now, stop crying," I said, seeing that tears had begun to collect in the corners of his eyes. "The night is young, and so are they." I nodded at a couple of cuties playing darts.

The Spotlight had something for everyone, and no one went home alone – not even Rudy.

CHAPTER FOURTEEN

Several days later, I was sitting in my usual seat at the bar watching Rudy play liar's poker. It had been a slow night until a tall blond fellow walked in, stopping to say hello to Don before taking a seat at the bar. He was in the right age range, but didn't look like a hustler. If a hustler comes into the bar with a shirt on, it comes off in the first five minutes. Their jeans are strategically torn and the fly is nearly always unzipped at least a third of the way down.

The fellow staring at me had neatly parted hair, faded polyester trousers, and a long-sleeve shirt. A cowboy belt, with the name Thaddeus burned into the leather, stood out like a billboard saying, I'm not from around here. He wore a puka shell necklace, the kind of attire one might expect to see on a veteran of the disco era.

"Mind if I sit here?" the young man asked, pointing to a seat next to mine.

"Guess not," I said, figuring I could at least give him some advice on how to dress. "What's your name?"

"Thad," the blond said.

"Like Tad-pole," I laughed. "Tell me, Thad, do you have a big pole?"

He seemed genuinely embarrassed, another sign he hadn't been in Hollywood very long.

"What is your drink?" I asked. "Let me buy you one."

Thad leaned in close. "A slow comfortable screw against the wall."

"Twiggy," I called out. "This boy wants a screw."

But the drink was already prepared. "I knew you'd buy it for him," Twiggy said. "I've been telling him to say hello to you for weeks."

"I'm from Idaho," Thad volunteered. "Came to Los Angeles six months ago. You know the store around the block, Cinema Collectors?"

"Yeah, across from the Mark Twain Hotel. I know it."

"I do computer entry, inventory and stuff like that."

"Keeping track of the drugs? I've heard that the Mark Twain is heroin central."

"No silly, for Cinema Collectors. I stay at the Mark Twain. I work at Cinema Collectors."

"So, what tragedy brought you to Hollywood? And, by the way, it's not 'Los Angeles.' We call it LA."

Thad looked a bit puzzled. "Oh, like the song. 'I Love LA'."

"Exactly. Now you'll remember."

Thad took a long sip of his Sloe Comfortable Screw. His skin was so fair that it turned pink with the rise in his blood pressure.

"I don't get along with my family," Thad said, trying to explain why he came to Hollywood. "I'm supposed to inherit a fortune when I turn thirty. They're all jealous."

"That's a new one."

"It's true," Thad insisted.

"Sure. Why not?"

"It's important that you believe me."

"I don't believe anyone, about anything," I said. "Life has taught me to be skeptical."

"That's really tragic," Thad said as he ordered a second drink. As much as I enjoyed Thad's story and was drawn by his bright blue eyes, I had to get home. MIFED was coming up. This trip would be the first time that I would be attending as an independent distributor. I planned to slip out of the bar while Thad was in the restroom, lest he tempt me to take him back to my place. I told Twiggy to let Thad know that I'd see him another time.

But Thad was ahead of the game. He caught up with me outside. "You're too drunk to be driving," he said. "Let me call you a taxi. Leave your car parked where it is until tomorrow."

"Cabs around here cost too much," I protested.

"Then let me drive you home. I don't have to work tomorrow, and I didn't even finish that second drink."

Defeated, I handed him my car keys, but pulled them back when he reached to grab them. "Only if we stop for a bottle of wine at Greenblatt's Deli. It's on the way."

"I know where it is, right next door to Numbers."

"That would be the place." Numbers was an upscale version of the Spotlight. Same hustlers, but asking twice as much.

While Thad waited out front, double-parked, I ran inside to get a bottle of Italian Barolo. Driving up the hill into Laurel Canyon, I kept dozing off. Thad nudged me repeatedly, asking for directions.

"Beautiful place," Thad said as he helped me up the stairs to the front door. When we were inside, he went straight to the patio and switched on the lights. Two raccoons scampered up the hill.

"Turn that knob," I said, pointing to the wall.

The hot tub's jets began to whoosh and gurgle as I collapsed onto a lawn chair, but I wasn't too tired to say, "Let's see you get naked."

Thad had already begun to unfasten his turquoise decorated belt buckle. After taking off his shirt and exposing a smooth, tan torso, he unzipped his fly just enough to keep his jeans from falling off. He went into the living room and put a cassette in the tape deck, fast-forwarding to The Cars song "Shake It Up".

The bouncy New Wave tune blasted from the speakers, rattling the windows. Thad came back to the patio and continued his striptease. He was sexier than I thought he'd be – nipples high on his chest and close together, long torso with muscles that rippled slightly at his stomach. He raised his arms and wiggled so the heavy silver buckle would make his pants drop to the ground. The first thing I noticed was the lack of a tan line. I wondered where he was able to lie nude in the sun.

"Com'ere, banana dick," I slurred.

Thad slinked toward me, veering away just as he came within reach of my grasp, then stepping into the hot tub. I shucked off my clothes and got in beside him. The rush of hot water gave me a sudden migraine. I just made it out of the tub before throwing up.

"Sorry. I have to get to bed," I said. "You're sexy and all, but–" my voice trailed off as I stumbled toward the house.

I barely comprehended the fact that Thad was at my side, helping me get into bed. He toweled me dry and pulled up the covers. Then he climbed in and wrapped me in his embrace.

Despite the work to be done getting ready for MIFED, I met Thad at the Spotlight every night. We'd go to my house for a romp in the hot tub or a tumble in bed, and then I'd drive him to the Mark Twain. I wanted Thad to move in with me, but he thought we should date for a while. He was the first person I had met in Hollywood who used the word date.

I complied with Thad's wishes for two weeks, but then insisted that he move in. I hoped that I had found a genuine person who wasn't hustling me, but no matter what, I had fallen for him and was willing to take the risk.

Thad and I went to the Mark Twain and retrieved his meager possessions. He had a positive influence on me from the start. We stayed home most evenings listening to music and snuggling on the couch. At most, we drank wine. Sometimes we made an appearance at the Spotlight. Thad would order his Sloe Screw and I'd have a glass of Boodles. We'd sing along with the jukebox and gossip with Twiggy.

It was almost like having a real life.

CHAPTER FIFTEEN

Before I left for MIFED, Thad quit his job at Cinema Collectors. "Those guys were taking advantage of my talents," he complained. "And they weren't paying me shit."

That sounded like something a hustler might say. I considered the possibility that Thad might have been looking for a sugar daddy all along so that he wouldn't have to work a crummy job. Maybe I had blinded myself to his scheme. I forced such thoughts from my mind.

"You'll get a better job," I said. He didn't flinch at the implication that I expected him to continue working. I took that as a good sign.

The next day, I showed Thad a new computer I had bought. I figured that if he had an aptitude for computer work, he could help while I was in Italy. Thad was as smart as I expected. He knew much more about computers than the simple data entry that he had performed at Cinema Collectors.

A couple of hours before last call, we made an appearance at the Spotlight, taking a seat in a quiet booth near the entrance.

"You know, Thad," I said, thoughtfully. "You're the first normal person I've been with since I came to Hollywood."

Thad threw back a shot of Schnapps and grinned. "What makes you think I'm normal?"

Just before I was to leave town, Thad came home after having stopped in West Hollywood to pick up a Spartacus Gay Guide. We sat together on the couch and looked over the section about the gay scene in Milan.

"Since I'm not going, you have to tell me what the bars are like," Thad said. He opened the book to a page with pictures of swarthy Italian men. "There's even a hustler bar," he noted. "It's got a funny name, something like 'you eat me' bar."

"It says, Uiti Bar," I said, rolling my eyes. "I'd like to see what the gay bars are like. When I was in Milan before, I only saw heterosexual piano bars with my former boss and his friends."

"Sounds awful."

"Worse than awful." I poked Thad in the side. "So, you want me to check out a hustler bar? What if I meet a trick?"

"Then I want to hear about it."

"When in Rome, I suppose."

"Milan," Thad corrected.

The day before I was to leave, Wally telephoned with an unpleasant announcement. "Kathy wants to go with you," he said. "And that means Gus, too."

Gus was a crotchety old geezer who financed Wally's productions. Wally's eighteen-year old daughter, Kathy, had appeared in Bel-Air Babes, sitting naked on Gus' lap. Wally didn't have a problem when a relationship developed between them. I'd visited Gus's house in Bel Air. It was an inheritance from his father, who had been a chemical company magnate. The highlight of the visit was seeing one of only three copies of a rare print by E. M. Escher. At the time, I'd thought it a horrible waste for such a magnificent work to be in the hands of such a philistine. Gus had no appreciation for the art that had come down to him.

I scrambled for a reason to say that Gus and Kathy couldn't go with me, but since Wally's library was the bulk of what I had to sell, I couldn't protest too loudly.

"The hotels will be booked," I said, hoping that might put an end to it.

Wally said something to Gus, who was in the room with him. I could hear the old man grumbling in the background. His growl reminded me of Popeye in a bad mood.

"Make reservations at the best hotel in Milan. Surely there are suites available," Wally said. "Gus will pay."

"How about the plane tickets?"

"Gus will pay for those also. Let me know how much it will cost for the three of you."

I called my travel agent. She upgraded my seat on Alitalia Airlines to first class and got two more seats nearby. The Principe di Savoia was booked, but luckily, there were rooms at the Michelangelo, second only to the Principe in elegance.

Thad chauffeured us in my Topaz, which was packed to the gills with bags, mostly Kathy's. Gus was drunk. Security almost refused to let us through. If it weren't for the first class tickets, I don't think they would have.

Thad gave me a peck on the cheek in sight of Gus and Kathy, not to mention the rest of the world. I was horribly self-conscious about public displays of affection.

Fortunately, neither Gus nor Kathy cared about attending events at MIFED. The only reason Kathy wanted to visit Europe, as far as I could tell, was that she had never been. I don't even think she realized that we had flown across the ocean and were in a different part of the world. She and Gus had been making out under a blanket the whole trip.

Gus yawned at the idea of visiting Italy and seized every opportunity to denigrate Italians. Between the two of them, they exemplified everything Europeans hate about American tourists.

Some days, Gus and Kathy never left their hotel suite. By the time I came back from convention center, food trays often littered the hallway outside their door. When I knocked, they took forever to answer. Kathy usually greeted me, wrapped in a sheet she had pulled off the bed. I wanted to say, you could fuck just as well in LA, so why come all the way to Milan? But I reminded myself, yet again, that Gus was Wally's benefactor, and kept quiet.

MIFED was busy that year and I had a well-situated office that received a great deal of foot traffic. I arrived at seven in the morning and rarely left the market before it closed down at six. Then, I followed clients to their hotels for drinks, and hopefully to complete negotiations. A few sales slipped away due to my limited language skills. Had I been savvier, I would have hired a translator.

One evening, Nicolò was in the Principe bar when I showed up with a Spanish client who I had met while working for him. Nicolò was huddled with men who I recognized from my first trip to Italy. He made a point of gazing past me as if I wasn't there.

At about two o'clock in the morning, I went to the Michelangelo and was surprised to find Gus and Kathy heading toward the all-night restaurant in the lobby. They were almost sober and invited me to join them. Gus, who spoke Italian, ordered delectable dishes with names that had no English equivalent.

"How much money did you make today?" Gus asked, as if it meant anything to him. I had sold quite a few titles from Wally's library, but only mentioned one.

"Everyone likes Bel Air Babes. Kathy will be a fantasy in every part of the world, at the rate I'm going."

Kathy looked up from her plate of *formaggio* and sipped her glass of *barbaresco* without comprehending what I meant. I wondered if she even knew that she was in the video with everything exposed except what people couldn't see because she had her legs crossed on Gus's lap.

"I've sold to half of Europe and most of Asia. Now I'm working on South America."

Kathy whispered something in Gus's ear as her hand slipped under the table.

"That's right, dear," Gus said. "You're a fantasy to other people, but you're mine to touch."

I'd just have to gag all the way to the bank.

By the end of MIFED, I had written enough contracts to keep me busy until the American Film Market. If everyone paid, it would push my gross assets to several hundred thousand dollars. I figured a treat was in order, and decided to investigate Thad's you-eat-me bar.

Instead of going back to the hotel to change into casual clothes, I kept on my Christian Dior suit and hailed a taxi. I tried my best to articulate the Italian name, Uiti bar. The driver had no idea what I was saying, but following advice Nicolò had given me, I pronounced the words as flamboyantly as I could, something like Oo-EE-TEE-bahr, Por FaVOR-eh.

The taxi driver shook his hand in the air to indicate that he understood. We headed to an industrial section of town. As we got near our destination, the driver rattled off phrases that eluded me. The only word I understood was *finocchio* – Italian slang for queer.

"*Oui, je suis* gay," I said, wondering if he spoke French, as many Italians did. I knew a few phrases from my work with French members of the church.

The man muttered bitterly as he navigated a side street. He was so anxious to get away from the area that he nearly ripped off my arm as he gunned the engine after I handed his cash through the window.

I found myself alone on a cobblestone street with no one in sight. An incandescent light dangled over an anonymous door recessed into one of the buildings. A note above a buzzer had to say, Push to Enter, so I did.

A clanging noise echoed from inside the building. Within moments, a dark-haired youth opened the door and motioned for me to come inside. I followed him down a spiral staircase to a landing where an almost naked boy asked if I wanted to check my overcoat. The lad was exquisite in his net shirt that just reached the top of his jock strap. He flashed a toothy grin as I gawked.

Down another turn of the spiral stairway, we entered the main bar – a smallish room, more brightly lit than gay clubs in Hollywood. A row of booths ran opposite a long bar. Scattered about were small patio tables with hard benches where hustlers sat entertaining their tricks.

I found an empty barstool and tried to order a drink, not an easy task since the bartender didn't speak a word of English. He eventually understood "beer" and exclaimed, "Ah, *bira!*" proceeding to pour the house draft into a stein.

My poor command of French helped get across a pressing question – how much the boys charged.

"*Je voudrais le garçon. J'ai l'argent.*"

The bartender laughed as I opened my wallet and showed him my cash. He pointed to a £50,000 note. I laid a generous tip on the bar and put away my wallet. The bartender treated me to a shot of alcohol that tasted like licorice.

One cannot open one's wallet in a hustler bar without being noticed. A cute fellow approached and invited himself to sit next to me. He wasn't exactly what I was looking for – a little older than I typically preferred – but there was something to say for availability. Most of the guys were already deep in negotiations with prospective clients.

As was the style in Milan that season, the fellow wore tight jeans with short cuffs that exposed his white crew socks. His plaid shirt made him look somewhat like a lumberjack, but his brown derby contradicted the effect. His black hair was cut unevenly, as if a friend had trimmed it for him.

"What's your name?" I asked, hoping he spoke English.

"Yasha," the boy responded. "I am Yasha. You have name?"

"Simon. Do you speak English?"

"No really," Yasha said, then whispered in my ear. "I like sexy. You want I sex you?"

Without actually committing, I managed to communicate that I'd like to go to a different bar. Uiti Bar was interesting, but I wanted to experience more of the gay scene. Yasha led me up the spiral staircase. The jockstrap boy winked as he handed me my overcoat. He practically threw Yasha his coat, which was stashed under the counter. They obviously had some bad history between them.

Yasha whistled for a taxi passing on a distant street and directed the driver to take us to another part of Milan. We circled an ancient mausoleum, drove past the Sforza castle, and finally made it to a discotheque. It was larger than any club in Hollywood. The dance floor was a riot of purple and blue lights emanating from an array of neon fixtures that lined the walls. Lasers darted across the dance floor creating fantastic geometries.

We danced to the heavy throb of Michael Jackson's "Beat It". When it ended, I went to the bar and ordered a gin and tonic..

A George Michael song played next, "I Want Your Sex". Yasha sang along, misstating the words as "I want to sex". Suddenly, though, he had danced enough.

"We go," he said.

The cover charge had been the equivalent of fifty dollars. I was in no hurry to leave. Yasha pulled me into the bathroom and pushed me inside a stall. He plunged his tongue down my throat and rubbed his leg against the mounting pressure between my legs. He butted his forehead against mine and looked me in the eyes, the way Lyle had done when he wanted his way. "We go, daddy?" Yasha pleaded.

To a new disco it was.

I was so drunk that my awareness of our surroundings began to blur as Yasha took me to one club and then another. At some point, we were making out in the back of a taxi with our pants around our knees and my overcoat draped across our laps. Then we were at the Michelangelo.

Yasha kissed me on the ear as he took money from my wallet to pay the cab fare. We stumbled through the lobby toward the elevator. It seemed to take forever to get the key into the lock and open the door.

I collapsed on the bed while Yasha undressed. He had a chiseled body. I kept thinking of Donatello's David when I saw him standing before me in nothing but his bowler hat. Yasha tossed the hat on a chair, ripped off my clothes, and was on top of me. I drifted into a stupor.

Something startled me. My first reaction was to scream, but I couldn't move. My arms were stretched above my head and secured to the headboard with my knotted shirt. A sock was stuffed in my mouth. My legs were spread with my feet tied at the bottom of the bed. Yasha was sitting on top of me. When I struggled to turn over, he grabbed the back of my head.

"You wake for Yasha?" he said, pulling my head sideways so I could see him better. He puffed on a cigarette to get it hot and pointed it at my face.

"I burn you?" he threatened.

The sock prevented me from screaming. All I could manage was a pathetic moan.

Yasha lowered the cigarette so dangerously close to my eyes that I would feel its heat. He burst into laughter, positioning himself over me so he could touch my cheek with his hard cock.

"My dick cut, like Jesus. Not like Catholic man," Yasha said. "I've got a Jesus dick."

What was this, a demon sent to exact punishment on me for abandoning God?

Yasha laughed like a wolf baying over helpless prey. I clinched my teeth as Yasha pressed the cigarette into my ass.

"I baptize with fire, now I fuck you," Yasha said.

My throat tightened and I began to choke.

Yasha drove his cock through my seared sphincter, laughing at the pain it caused me. When I tried to lift my head from the pillow, Yasha smacked it down. I wondered if this would end with him snapping my neck.

Just rewards for a life of sin, sounded a taunting voice. It seemed fitting that I should die so far from home, at the hands of a sadist who compared his cock to the body of Jesus.

Yasha yelled into my ear every time I passed out. He wanted an attentive victim. He pumped harder as he tore into me. Yasha got what he wanted – the chance to ejaculate into a terrified body racked with pain. When he came, he lost interest. I watched Yasha dispassionately as he dressed himself, primping in the mirror, positioning his bowler hat from side to side until he was satisfied with the way it looked. He picked up my suit pants and fumbled around for my wallet.

"We spend your money," he said, turning the wallet upside down. I was sure he'd get angry and start tormenting me again, but he didn't seem to care. He took one of my business cards and said, "Maybe I see you in Hollywood."

I stared blankly as he untied my arms. I was cold, as if paralyzed. I couldn't feel my body.

Yasha kissed my forehead. Before leaving, he said, "You fuck good." Then he shut the door quietly behind him.

It felt as though a hot coal had been pressed into my ass. I went to the shower and doused myself with cold water. When I made it back to the bed, I collapsed, not waking until late the next day. My only thought was to get antibiotics. I managed to dress and made it to a pharmacy down the street. Applying ointment, I realized that my burn was not as severe as it felt. Yasha had been more threatening than truly torturous and had not actually inserted the ember. My imagination had been a willing participant to his sadism.

I stayed in bed the rest of the day, shivering more from disgust and fright than actual pain. Whenever I tried to sleep, I would awaken in a sweat, sure that Yasha was in the room. Once, I woke up repenting with a prayer I had learned as a member of the church: In the name of God and the True Parents, Amen.

MIFED was ending and I had to clear out the office. I arranged to have the remaining flyers and posters sent back to LA, and got in touch with a few buyers who still needed to sign letters of agreement.

It had been over three days since I last saw my traveling companions. I knocked on their door and was greeted by Gus, wearing nothing but a pair of sagging boxers. He looked skinnier without his clothes. The room smelled like a bathhouse, ripe with the odor of old sex.

"There's no more business to be done at the market," I said. "We may as well check out."

Kathy emerged from the bathroom, quickly pulling the strings at the front of her pink robe. She plopped on a chair, making a kind of nest out of the white towels collected on it.

"We can't leave yet," Kathy complained. "We haven't seen anything. What's the point of coming all this way if we don't see anything?" Her voice grew into a whine.

"Have you seen The Last Supper?" I asked.

"Yeah, that's good. Let's go see that," Gus said, perking up a little.

"How about it, Kathy?" I asked.

Kathy pulled her hair into a ponytail and picked up a rubber band from the side table to secure it. "Whatever Gus wants to do."

"Let's get the fuck going," Gus said. "My butt's about to stick to this goddamned bed."

While waiting in the lobby, I got a package of cookies from a vending machine. After my experience with Yasha, I had not felt like eating. Gus and Kathy exited the elevator dressed like tourists: Gus wearing plaid pants and a leather jacket with epaulets, Kathy in blue jeans with a rabbit fur coat.

We took a taxi took to the museum that housed the remnants of da Vinci's famous work. The original church had been destroyed by a bomb during World War II. The only thing that remained standing was the wall with The Last Supper painted on it. The fresco was so faded that the details were hard to make out. What impressed me were the photographs taken just after the World War II bombing. I pointed them out to Gus.

"That's as close to a miracle as it gets," I said.

"Yeah, fascinating," Gus said flatly. "Okay, I've seen it. Let's get the hell to a bar."

"Fine with me," I said.

On the way to the hotel, Kathy couldn't hold back the big question that had been nagging her.

"Why is it called The Last Supper?"

"Haven't you heard of Jesus having a last meal with his disciples?" I asked.

Kathy looked at me blankly.

"You don't have any idea what I'm talking about, do you?" I asked.

"No," Kathy said, clinging to Gus's arm. "Am I supposed to?"

"Not necessarily. Ask Gus about it."

Gus had fallen asleep.

"It doesn't matter. I don't care," Kathy said, ending the matter. "That place was boring anyway."

CHAPTER SIXTEEN

Gus and Kathy slept the entire flight back. Thad met us at the gate. Wally was with him.

"Have a good time?" Wally asked as our weary troupe shuffled toward baggage claim.

"Wonderful," I said without conviction.

Thad left to get my car as Wally retrieved Gus and Kathy's luggage from the carousel and rushed them outside where he had parked illegally. They were driving away when I spotted Thad.

"You wouldn't believe that pair," I told Thad on the way to Laurel Canyon. "It sure is good to see you." I took Thad's hand from the steering wheel but he quickly withdrew it.

"There's too much traffic," Thad said. "I have to drive."

I glanced at the odometer, noting that a lot of miles had been put on the car during my absence.

When I walked through the house after our arrival, my first thought was that it seemed too neat, as though Thad had not been there while I was away. While I unpacked, Thad rushed to clean the hot tub. I looked out the upstairs window and saw that it was full of debris. It looked as though the cover had been left off of it for some days.

I had hoped for a kiss, some kind of welcome. Thad didn't even ask how business went. After cleaning the patio, he offered to get Chinese food from a restaurant we both liked.

Thad ignored my advances in bed. It took some cajoling just to get him to cuddle.

"What's the matter, Thad?" I whispered in his ear. I tried to push my hand between his thighs, but he tightened his muscles to prevent me.

Thad was seeing someone else. I was sure of it.

The night with Yasha in Milan haunted my dreams. In the nightmares, I sometimes took his position and tortured myself.

I threw myself into work, trying desperately to forget the horror of my experience in Milan and to ignore the certainty that Thad was cheating on me. I should have been elated about the sales I had made, but Thad's affection was all I wanted. And that, it seemed, was out of reach.

Often, Thad would go on an errand and disappear for hours. I would call around trying to find him. Twiggy would say he hadn't seen Thad, but I'd unfairly accuse Twiggy of covering for him.

Sooner or later, Thad would return. He always had an excuse, and after a warm hug, I'd accept it. For fleeting moments, it would seem as though our relationship was back on track.

Thad would sense when I was at wits end, ready to end the relationship and kick him out. Thad would suggest we go to the Spotlight. We'd drink and play darts, and sing along when the jukebox played "Life is a Cabaret" and "That's Amoré". Thad would act as though I was the center of his life. People would whoop and holler when we kissed, commenting on what a romantic couple we made. Then Twiggy would announce last call, and we'd go home and jump in bed. My passions would be at fever pitch, but Thad would just roll over and go to sleep.

One afternoon as I was showing Thad how to move text between WordPerfect files, the phone rang. Thad answered.

"It's for you," he said, "Someone named Yasha."

My hand trembled as I took the phone.

"Yasha?"

"Simone? In Hollywood?" Yasha said. "This Yasha. Remember Yasha? I visit Switzerland. See mamma. I come to you? We have good sex?"

Beads of sweat began to form along my hairline. "No, Yasha. Absolutely not."

"Okay. You come soon? To Milano?"

"No, Yasha. I no come to Italy."
"Okay, bye-bye."
I dropped the receiver.
Thad took me by the shoulders. "Who was that?" he demanded. "Your Italian boyfriend?"
"You're the one who suggested I visit a hustler bar."
Thad stormed out the room.
"Hypocrite!" I yelled.
For a moment, I was glad Yasha had called.

My nerves were at a breaking point by the Christmas holidays. Vivian had been asking me to visit and I thought a drive across country might give Thad and me a chance to talk.

"You want me to meet your mom?" Thad said, lounging on the sofa one afternoon watching General Hospital.

"I used to go home every Christmas, but I haven't done that in years. I thought it might do us good to get away."

"Your mom doesn't know you're gay, does she? What will she think when I show up with you?"

"Vivian won't say anything. It might ruffle the feathers of my born-again sister, but that's a bonus as far as I'm concerned."

"Can I go in drag?"

I feared he might be serious and was glad the commercial ended and his focus returned to the soap opera.

We drove the southern route to Arkansas, passing through Phoenix and Tucson, then across the plains of Texas to reach the border city of Texarkana. Snow and hail dogged us during most of the drive. My plan to have a talk with Thad didn't amount to much. Whenever I started up a conversation, he put on headphones and disappeared into a Pet Shop Boys album.

We stayed one night in Tucson, and I hoped it might be romantic. Thad lay on his back and allowed me fondle him, but that was the extent of it.

Christmas Eve, just before noon, we rolled into Vivian's driveway. I had given her a brief description of my "traveling companion," so our arrival wasn't completely unexpected. Thad would stay in the guest bedroom. I would sleep in my old room.

In the middle of unpacking, I laid down for a minute. Suddenly, it was ten o'clock in the evening. I went to the refrigerator for a snack.

"I didn't want to disturb you," someone said. It was Vivian. Her voice startled me.

Thad was sitting next to Vivian at the dining room table.

"Thad here's been telling me about the ranch where he grew up in Idaho," Vivian said. "His family owns a lot of land up there. They graze cattle. I was just thinking, if we still had our horses, you two could go riding."

I felt sure Thad was making it all up.

"Did you know that Thad will inherit money when he turns thirty?" Vivian continued.

Thad did not so much as look at me while Vivian spoke. He got up from the table and walked past me on his way to the guestroom. At the bottom of the stairs, out of Vivian's sight, he wiggled his butt before sashaying away.

"Thad seems like a nice boy," Vivian said.

"Yeah, he does seem that way, doesn't he?"

Vivian looked away, not understanding what I meant.

Christmas had always been a miserable day for me. There was the time I got Bride, whose colt Lenny sold. Another was when I was nine and I received a four-inch reflecting telescope, ordered from Edmund Scientific Company. Lenny and his friends calibrated the latitude and longitude on the swivel dial to properly align it to the stars. I was forgotten as Lenny and his pals located Mars, expressed disappointment that Saturn's rings were barely visible, and commented about how the crescent moon looked like a banana pelted by gunshot. I wanted to see, too, but never got the chance.

After Thad went to bed, Vivian excused herself. "Connie will pick us up in the morning," she said. "You better get some sleep."

I made a snack of peanut butter and jelly and settled into the easy chair where Lenny had sat during the final months of his life. It fit my body perfectly. I stayed until the last movie of the night ended and a color test pattern filled the screen. I went to my room, avoiding the creaky spots on the stairs I knew so well.

Just before morning, I dreamed I was at the event in the church when Masako was chosen to be my wife. This time, a young man was tapped on the shoulder. The crowd gasped, but Reverend Moon reassured the young man that it was God's will. The young man and I looked deeply into each other's eyes. He held out his hand. We kissed. Suddenly, a loud noise woke me up.

"Simon, your sister's here."

Connie was with Vivian outside my door.

"I wanted to wish you Merry Christmas," Connie said. She sounded terribly chipper for it to be so early in the morning. It was still dark outside my window.

"Why don't you wake your friend," Connie said. "We're all going over to my place to open presents."

"Okay," I called out. "Thad and I will be downstairs in a minute."

When I heard Vivian and Connie walk away, I threw on some clothes and went downstairs. I tapped on the guestroom door and went inside. Thad was sound asleep on his stomach with the pillow pulled over his head. I yanked back the covers, marveling at the beauty of his baby-smooth ass.

"Hey, sexy," I said, leaning close to Thad's ear.

Thad turned over. He was stiff as a bat. I pretended it was a throttle as I said, playfully, "Ready for blastoff."

Thad shoved me aside as he got out of bed. "I gotta pee," he complained.

I picked up Thad's robe from the chair and handed it to him. "Merry Christmas."

"Yeah," Thad mumbled.

Vivian and Thad got into the back seat of Connie's car. I drove.

"This just doesn't seem like Christmas," Vivian said, gazing out the window at the soggy landscape. "I don't like it to rain on Christmas day."

We were having an Arkansas deluge that morning. I took a long route to Connie's house, trying to stay on roads that were above flood level. Even so, the last stretch to Connie's house was a ribbon of water.

"You'll have the cleanest fenders in town," I said as the tires churned the water.

Vivian started worrying out loud that a flash flood would catch us and we'd all be drowned.

"Calm down," I said. "I can see the road. Don't worry."

But water was rising along the shoulder and beginning to crash against the side of the car. The road was impossible to make out as I checked the rear-view mirror. I was glad that Vivian's attention was on the hill in front of us. Finally, we reached Connie's house.

For years, Connie had decorated an artificial Scotch pine using ornaments and lights she got from Vivian. Many were old bubble lights and antique Santa Claus bulbs that had adorned our trees when I was a child. I recognized the manger scene on Connie's coffee table as one of Vivian's favorite Christmas decorations.

My oldest niece, Cheryl, threw her arms around me, and then withdrew to look at Thad.

"Is this your friend?" she asked.

"This is Thad," I said.

Cheryl extended her hand and peered into Thad's eyes.

My niece was so grown up that it made me realize how long I had been away. Cheryl was now in high school. I was surprised when her boyfriend arrived at the house and I found out they were discussing marriage.

Everyone sat around Connie's phony tree as if it was something inspiring. Victoria, my youngest niece, opened her gifts of dolls, a play kitchen, and a plastic tree house filled with long-haired gnomes. Cheryl received gift certificates since no one felt confident to buy her things she wouldn't return to the store. Vivian got sweaters with open collars because we knew she thought anything touching her neck would cause goiters.

Edwin, Cheryl's boyfriend, a husky young man who was far too cute for me to feel comfortable around, stayed at Cheryl's side, keeping a wary eye on Thad and me.

As the day wore on, Thad made friends with Connie the same way he wooed Vivian. He helped Connie in the kitchen and was quick to provide helpful hints to spice up the taste of foods. He even followed Derek into the yard to smoke a cigarette. I saw out the window that they were engaged in a serious discussion.

The one time Edwin left Cheryl alone was when he went out for his own smoke.

"I like your boyfriend," I said to Cheryl. "He's a bit tough-looking, but that lisp gives him an endearing quality."

Cheryl studied me for a moment. "He's really self-conscious about his voice. I hope you don't bring it up."

"He shouldn't be ashamed. Even Moses had a lisp. It's a strange little detail in the Bible."

Derek, who had barely said a thing until then, perked up at the Bible reference. "God would have healed Moses if he had kept faith."

No one said a word.

Following hours of skirting around sensitive issues that might cause conflict, we gathered for the evening meal. Derek took Lenny's seat at the head of the table.

"Let's hold hands and thank Jesus for the food," Derek said, bowing his head and grasping the hands of those beside him.

Connie dutifully sat on his left side. I was on the right. Derek squeezed my hand as if trying to pump spiritual energy into my soul.

"Oh, Jesus," he began, "we thank you for bringing our brother Simon and his friend Thad from California."

I fought to keep from bursting out in laughter.

Platitudes followed – bless the food, bless the nation, bless the children, etc. – ending with, "We thank you, in the name of Jesus."

Derek had a weirdly serene look on his face that turned to indignation as the family began to compete for the bowls of food the moment he said, "Amen."

"Now you know our tribal rituals," I told Thad.

Connie passed the bowl of mashed potatoes to Vivian after she piled some on her own plate. "You have such a strange view of our family," Connie said to me.

Thad jumped to Connie's defense. "He's got unusual views about a lot of things."

"Well, I'm just glad he got away from that crazy religion," Connie said. "Joining that group was the strangest thing he's ever done."

"And believing that two thousand years ago, a dead Nazarene stood up and walked around Israel for forty days and not a single Roman historian thought to mention it is somehow more credible?" I asked.

"Simon!" Vivian shouted, slapping her spoon on the plate with a loud clack. "I can't believe you would say a thing like that."

"Please, everyone," Derek said, seizing the opportunity to display magnanimity. "Let's enjoy Christmas."

I thought about the manger scene in the other room, and the plastic image of the jolly man in the red suit that sat on the coffee table. Christians don't recognize what a drab day it would be if they didn't keep alive at least some of the pagan customs. Silent night, and jingle bells.

Two days later, when the weather finally cleared, I asked Thad to go with me to a favorite place in the Ouachita mountain foothills. We got up early and drove to Morrilton, the city closest to the Petit Jean plateau where I had taken LSD and Psilocybin with friends. We stopped for breakfast at a Denny's restaurant just off the freeway.

"My buddies and I used to come here to get high," I said, making sure none of the locals eating their Grand Slam breakfasts could hear.

"Another hippie story?" Thad asked impatiently.

"What hippie stories have I told you?" I protested. "I might go on too much about my days in the church. But I don't even think that much about my acid trips. Some were scary. Not when I was at Petit Jean, though."

"Keep it short," Thad pleaded, flashing his blue eyes as he brushed hair from his forehead.

"Can I at least tell you about the magic symbol I created at Petit Jean?"

Thad remained expressionless.

"Remember the sandstone rock on my dresser?"

Thad took a cigarette from his box of Marlboros and tapped it on the table.

"I carved it during an acid trip while hiking the Seven Hollows trail at Petit Jean. When I held it in my hand, I saw a kind of geometry. I found a piece of granite and scratched the pattern. It was a cross with pits at the cardinal endpoints. A couple of weeks later, I heard the church lectures, which talked about a "four position foundation" as the primary structure of the universe. I thought I was chosen, and that the rock had revealed a secret given to me by God."

"Yeah," Thad said, "and copping a feel under the sleeping bag of the guy next to you was an omen that you really were queer."

"I forgot I told you about that," I said, finishing my cup of coffee. "Let's go on the Seven Hollows trail. How about it?"

Thad looked out the window to view the sky. "Oh, darn. Look at those clouds. I'd say it's about to start raining again."

"Okay. We'll just go to the waterfall."

Thad enjoyed the drive to the top of the plateaus and had to admit that the waterfall was pretty. The serenity of the place seemed to affect him. I found the sounds of water echoing against the canyon walls irresistible. I took Thad's hand, half expecting him to pull away, but he didn't.

"Remember how it was when we first met?" I said. "We held hands like it meant something."

"It still does," Thad admitted.

I picked up a piece of sandstone and carved our initials into it with a piece of granite. Then I threw it over the falls.

CHAPTER SEVENTEEN

For Christmas, I gave Thad a Walkman CD player, which probably wasn't a good idea. He disappeared into his music and said almost nothing during the return trip to LA.

Out of the blue one day, he asked me how much cocaine I had done and why I had stopped using.

"Cocaine is the one lover a person never forgets," I said.

"Scott and Jerry offered me some," Thad confessed.

I'd only recently learned about Scott's new boyfriend, Jerry. He was a porn star that Scott had met him through the Gay Film Makers Association, a group he represented behind Maury's back. Jerry was brawny, muscular, stupid, and sexy – Thad's preferred type. Until his question, I didn't realize that Thad knew Scott.

"When did you meet Scott?" I asked.

"He came by the house while you were in Italy, and I–" he paused mid-sentence. "I went to the beach with them."

"Thad, promise me you won't try cocaine."

"Forget I asked you about it," he replied.

Every time I came home to an empty house, I was afraid Thad had gone to Scott's. When I called to find out, Jerry always answered. He'd say Scott wasn't there and then add, "Thad ain't here, neither."

Thad kept coming home in the middle of the night, dropped off by friends. As tortured a relationship as we had, it was still the closest I had come to having a lover, and I wouldn't press him on it. But I knew the friends were Scott and Jerry.

Before long, Thad began exhibiting the nervous behavior of a cocaine addict. I didn't want to think about what was happening, so I threw myself into work. There was plenty to keep me busy.

The lease on my Laurel Canyon house was expiring and I decided to find a less expensive place. The house had been fun, but I didn't need so much space. Thad was furious. He used my decision as an excuse to make his big announcement.

"I'm moving in with Scott and Jerry," he said.

"Fine," I said, storming to the closet and throwing Thad's clothes on the floor. "Go ahead. Get out!"

Thad folded his belongings neatly into paper sacks. Emotionlessly, he called Scott's house.

I carried Thad's belongings down the stairs and threw the sacks into the yard. Thad walked out with as much nonchalance as he could muster. I slammed the door behind him.

From my bedroom window, I had a good view of the street. Thad stood at the end of the driveway for over forty-five minutes, chain-smoking cigarettes. Not once did he glance toward the house.

When Scott drove up, I hid behind the curtain. Jerry put Thad's things in the trunk. Scott never got out of the car, but I could see him through the windshield.

I watched until they drove away and then stayed at the window. I couldn't bring myself to turn around and face an empty house.

Over the next few days, I put my things in storage and searched for temporary lodging. I wasn't ready to settle down in another house just yet. I went to a complex in Beverly Hills where I had rented a small bungalow during my last few months in the church. Lyle lived with me there. It was the place we were sharing when I left him, thinking that I was returning to the group. Scott and Sandra had dubbed it The Little Bungalow.

The manager didn't remember me, but then, there wasn't any reason he should. I was just another strung out druggie at the time, as far as he knew. He showed me a one-bedroom apartment on the ground floor within sight of the place where a fellow lived who used to buy cocaine from me, and through whom I met bands that played at the Roxxy and

Whiskey-a-Go-Go. Sandra used to score coke from one of the clients she befriended and then bring it to me after work so I could sell it at the clubs later in the evening.

Alone in the small abode, I set up my computer and made preparations to attend the American Film Market, which would be held that year at the Beverly Hilton.

My office was on the same floor as Nicolò's. I noticed that he had gotten a new salesperson – a short fellow in his twenties who kept walking by my office to see how much business I was doing. Rumor had it that Nicolò was telling people I had stolen from him. Quite the irony since it was the licensing rights Nicolò's claimed to own that were questionable.

Despite my doldrums, the market went well. Clients that I met at MIFED came by to finalize contracts. Some new deals materialized.

After AFM shut down for the day, I spent the evening with clients. A few of them were openly gay, and those I took to West Hollywood bars where eventually they forgot about me as they cruised the real and wannabe models who frequented those places. I kept up, but it wasn't my scene.

Near the close of the market, the president of the American Film Marketing Association came by to congratulate me on establishing a successful company. But I knew what was behind his seeming compliment. Now that I was gaining success, I had better become an AFM member. The Hollywood Reporter interviewed me and planned an article about the spirit of entrepreneurship that had taken hold as new media such as home video revived interest in older films.

The first night after the market ended, I went to the Spotlight. I needed to be among some real people for a change. Walking in the door, it struck me how the crudest of the hustlers had more heart than the entire lot of pretty boys who frequented Motherload. They might be drug addicts making a living through sex, but it was more honest than the snobs who went to West Hollywood bars and who probably carved notches into their bedposts to record another conquest, only to go to work the next day to rip someone off in a gold futures scam. At least the marketing of one's own body is direct. A Spotlight hustler does what he does and calls it what it is.

Don and Twiggy were sympathetic when I told them about Thad.

"You'll find another love," Twiggy said with a knowing smile. "You always do."

Of course, to Don and Twiggy, the definition of a lover was someone you kept around instead of tossing out the next morning.

It felt strange sitting at the bar without Thad. I must have looked glum. Twiggy kept the Boodles flowing in hopes of pulling me out of it.

"Cheers," Twiggy said, throwing back his own poison, straight tequila – to kill ya, as he called it.

Cheerfulness didn't materialize. If anything, I became increasingly maudlin. My self-pity centered not only on Thad, but also on the magnitude of the loss I had felt when I left the church. How could anyone, my gloominess told me, understand how much prestige and friendship I had possessed? God's Kingdom – lost. The possibility of having a family with Masako – gone. To be replaced with what – hustler sex and snorting coke? Twiggy patted my face with a bar towel as I began to sob.

"Simon," Twiggy said, shaking me, "you can't sleep at the bar. Don will get both of us. Come on. Wake up."

I almost fell off the barstool as I tried to right myself.

"Drinks for everyone!" I shouted, rearing back precipitously.

Twiggy set up the bar. Half of the patrons reciprocated. I had a dozen shot glasses in front of me. Twiggy and I knocked them back. But no amount of alcohol was going to relieve the pain. I missed Thad more than ever.

Twiggy leaned over the bar to whisper in my ear. "See that drag queen playing pool? Her name is Patricia – I think she's from Peru or someplace. She knows where to get some great shit. The stuff's better than anything I've seen in a long time."

"You are the devil, aren't you?" I said, halfway meaning it.

Twiggy grinned.

To some degree, cocaine was the reason I had lost Thad. If I'd offered to do it with him, to score as soon as he'd mentioned it, we might be together. Nevertheless, there I was, ready to start using again – as a way to forget him.

I took my drink to the pool table and watched Patricia flirt with an over-the-hill hustler as they finished their game.

"You no hit the eight ball unless ju say eight ball," Patricia called out.

When she realized I was studying her, the drag queen pranced toward me.

"I know ju," Patricia said, running a bony finger under my chin.

She made a convincing woman in her leather skirt and long black hair cascading over a fluffy white blouse. Heavy mascara accentuated large expressive eyes.

"Ju Scott's friend, *sí?*"

"You know Scott?"

"I see him in Venice, at the Rooster Fish. I see you there one time."

"You've got a good memory."

"You like what Scott likes, no? Even more than beautiful boy."

"You mean Jerry?"

"*Sí*, Sherry," Patricia grinned.

"Did you see a guy named Thad with Scott?"

Patricia pushed me away. "Ju ask too many questions."

I slipped my arm around Patricia's waist and pinched her butt through the leather skirt. She wagged a finger at me and smiled.

"Not on our first date," Patricia said as she sashayed toward the door, glancing over her shoulder and motioning me to follow.

We drove to a neighborhood on North Broadway near downtown.

"Is this where you live?" I asked.

"Oh no. I live in Echo Park. But my friend, his name is Jesús, he lives here." Patricia pointed to a white stucco apartment building and told me to park around back.

"I want a quarter ounce, okay?" I explained as we walked toward the building.

"Ju pretend to be my boyfriend," Patricia said, taking my hand and pressing it to her padded chest.

Jesús opened the door. He was a large man in loose cotton pants and a ratty tee shirt. He smelled of cigarettes and beer. Patricia clung tightly to me as she conversed in Spanish. The man finally allowed us to come inside. Patricia sat close with her arms around my neck.

A woman sat on the couch watching television with a young boy. They paid no attention to us.

Jesús went into a back room and returned with a baggy of cocaine.

"Ju try it before we buy," Patricia said, taking the baggy from Jesús and handing it to me. She and Jesús disappeared into the bedroom.

I was uncomfortable doing drugs in front of the child and his mother, but they never even glanced in my direction. I pinched out a hit and snorted it. My eyes filled with water. The room brightened as if sunlight had begun to stream through the window. A wash of euphoria swept over me.

Patricia and Jesús reappeared. Jesús had changed into Bermuda shorts. He took a seat on the couch between the woman and the boy.

"Are we set to go?" I asked.

"*Sí*. If you like," Patricia said.

I secured the baggy inside my pants and motioned toward the door.

The worst part of scoring drugs is getting to the car from the dealer's place without succumbing to paranoia. During the trip back to Hollywood, I was sure that the police were following us. Patricia wanted me to take her home, but I pulled to the curb in front of the Spotlight.

"Patricia, there's someone waiting for me at home," I lied. "Maybe another time."

"It's okay. Have fun with jure boy," Patricia said. She stormed toward the bar. I watched as she whipped back the curtain to dramatize her entrance.

On the way home, I kept thinking about Thad. I longed for him as much as I craved another hit of cocaine. Suddenly, as if someone else were driving, I found myself on the freeway headed to Scott's new condominium near the beach in Marina del Rey.

Scott answered my knock. He was drunk; he must have started right after getting off work since he was still in office clothes. He flashed a devilish smirk as he let me in.

Thad sat cross-legged on the couch wearing nothing but skimpy shorts. Jerry sat nearby, dressed in green sweat pants and a yellow tank top. A mirror sat on the coffee table in front of Thad and Jerry, nearly hidden by a forest of empty beer bottles.

"Looks like I'm just in time," I said, walking over and running my finger across the mirror to pick up the crumbs of cocaine. "Seems the party is running on empty."

I was trying to play it cool, and so was Thad. Jerry, on the other hand, leaped to his feet when he caught my meaning. The oversized sweat pants slid down his hips. His nipples hardened into little beads as I stared at him. I knew from his films just what rested beneath his loose pants. I even recognized the trail of hair fanning out from his navel.

Jerry rubbed his stomach with the flat of his hand, and then grasped my neck. Thad stared as he kissed me, but he didn't protest. There was no telling what had been going on between the three of them before I knocked on the door. Thad wasn't about to play innocent.

I sat beside Thad and took out the baggy of coke.

"Good ole Simon," Scott crowed. "And here I thought you had become a straight-laced entrepreneur."

"Don't be snide," I said. "Unless you want me to take my toys and go home."

"You can play here any time you want," Scott said.

"Then let's party."

Thad scooted closer. He tried to say something, but his throat was hoarse from coke drainage. He placed my hand on his thigh.

"I thought you weren't going to do drugs anymore," Thad whispered in my ear.

"You know what they say, better living through chemicals." It was the only thing that came to mind. I didn't want to start using coke again, but it seemed like I had to if I wanted to get Thad back.

Thad and I went into Scott's bedroom while Scott and Jerry snorted lines that I left behind. We frolicked in bed as if nothing had happened, as if we had never split up.

Cocaine is a jealous god. We became gripped by the idea that some of our drugs had fallen on the carpet. Suddenly, we were on our knees sorting through the rug fibers. Exhausted by the effort as the obsessive thought wore off, we returned to the bed and lay side by side. As cars passed along the road, my eyes followed every shadow thrown by the headlights. At some point, we fell asleep and didn't stir for a full day. I found Scott asleep on the couch. Jerry was curled up on a chair. A syringe had fallen on the floor beside him and a rubber tourniquet rested in his lap.

There was no point trying to rouse anyone; they were dead to the world. But I had to get home and check on business. Money was supposed to be wired to my account. Letters of credit should have cleared.

Thad was snoring loudly. I stood beside the bed for few minutes, wondering if I should try to wake him. In the end, I let him sleep.

A dense mist had rolled off the ocean. The drive was slow until I got out of Marina del Rey. I had left my watch in Scott's bathroom. It would give me an excuse to return after completing the day's work. I dared to hope that my new willingness to get high with Thad would bring him back to me.

CHAPTER EIGHTEEN

The quiet whir of my computer greeted me as I arrived at the temporary lodging. Several faxes waited. A Spanish client made excuses for not sending money. The German company who bought Bel Air Babes was concerned about a clause in the contract. The only good news came from Korea. A wire had been sent to settle the down payment on a new contract for five films.

By noon, I had taken care of business. With no more work to do, I began to experience a familiar craving. Experience told me it was a matter of time before I gave in to the urge.

I bought a newspaper and looked for rentals. Several places in Silverlake looked promising. One was located at 6000 Silverwood Terrace; I liked the sound of the address. The advertisement said the house overlooked the reservoir. I called for an appointment and was pleased that the owner could meet me right away.

The prospective landlord, a fellow named Henry, asked all the necessary questions. When I said I worked from home, he insisted that foot traffic was not allowed. I assured him that I only saw clients at the film markets. When asked if I lived alone, I said, cryptically, "Most of the time."

"What do you mean?" Henry asked.

"Well, I'm gay. Lovers don't seem to stick around very long."

Henry chuckled, "Then, we're family. You'll be a fine tenant, Mr. Powell, and you'll enjoy living in Silverlake. I'll meet you there in thirty minutes."

A narrow, winding road led from Silverlake Boulevard up a steep hill through a neighborhood of quaint houses. Henry stood on a sliver of ground that served as the front yard to a house that seemed to be constructed mostly of opaque glass. Above the front door was a sign that announced in cursive script: Six Thousand Silverwood Terrace. An Asian man stood with Henry. I presumed it was his lover. They appeared to be in their early thirty's. Henry wore a gray business suit and Italian shoes. The Asian lover was dressed more casually in jeans.

As I introduced myself, Henry scrutinized me carefully, checking my haircut (neat, trim), my clothes (not new, but well-pressed), and my shoes (expensive, I'd bought them in Milan).

Fong, the boyfriend, was no less observant of my appearance and demeanor.

"Fong and I lived here for eight years," Henry told me nostalgically. "It's special to us. We bought it together."

"Did you meet in Los Angeles?"

Fong spoke for the first time. "In San Francisco. I was waiting tables at a restaurant on Geary Street at twenty-second. Henry was attending a lawyer's conference. He asked me out. One date, and we were in love."

"That's romantic," I said with a smile.

Henry and Fong exchanged glances. There had to be more to their story, but they didn't elaborate.

We went into the house. A metal staircase spiraled to the second floor just to the left of the front door. The kitchen was straight ahead and to the right. Beyond the entrance was a common area, perfect for a small dining room table. A little further was the living room. The Hollywood sign was visible in the distance when standing on the balcony. Off to the right was Silverlake reservoir.

"Henry, I love this! How much do you want?"

"You haven't even seen upstairs yet, or the basement," Henry said.

"There's a basement?"

"Under the garage." Henry opened a door behind the staircase at the front entrance. Steep wooden stairs led to a carpeted room with sliding doors that opened onto the space below the house. Steel beams crossed by cables supported the entire structure. I slid open the door and went outside. Growing on the hillside, gnarled vines wound through patches of century plants that looked like sheaves of swords.

"Did you live here during an earthquake?" I asked.

Fong laughed. "It's quite a ride, but the structure is built to allow play."

"Play?" I repeated.

"A solid structure would fall down the hill onto the neighbors," Henry said. "The house has been here since the nineteen fifties. There's been no damage."

"Oh well, this is LA," I said. "The future will take care of itself, right?"

Henry and Fong smiled at the Hollywood truism.

"How much, Henry?" I asked again after a tour of the second floor where the main bedroom loft overlooked the living room and opened onto its own balcony

"Fifteen hundred a month. First and last as a deposit."

"You've got a deal," I said, smiling.

Henry gave me the keys in exchange for a check.

I went to a pay phone and called Scott's house to see if Thad was awake. I wanted to tell him about the house.

Scott was surprised to hear my voice. "When did you leave? I thought you were in the bedroom with Thad."

"I left early this morning. You and Jerry were pretty far gone."

Scott made a pathetic attempt to laugh. "You want me to get Thad?"

"Please."

Scott went away from the phone. I could hear him calling Thad's name, knocking on the bedroom door.

"He's not here. Looks like some of his things are gone, too."

"What do you mean, gone?"

"Gone. Out of here. Not in this place."

"Where'd he go?

"I don't know, Simon. I can't talk anymore. I can't even think."

Jerry yelled at Scott to stop chattering, saying that he had a headache.

I hung up, perplexed. Where would Thad have gone? Was I wrong about everything? I went to the Beverly Hills apartment, loaded my belongings, and took them to Silverlake. I wanted relief from loneliness. I'd thought I'd be doing drugs with Thad, but now I didn't care. I wanted some, with him or without him. I went to the Spotlight hoping to find Patricia.

Twiggy knew something was wrong as soon as I sat down. "Whatever it is," he said while pouring a shot of Boodles, "this will help take care of it."

An hour later, I was so drunk that I had forgotten about drugs. Twiggy and I gossiped until last call. When I got in my car, I set out for Scott's, as if that had been my plan all along, and somehow navigated the route, though I got lost after exiting the freeway at Marina del Rey. I stopped to call Scott's house. Jerry answered.

"Where's Thad?" I slurred.

"Simon?"

"Where's Thad? I want to talk to him."

"He's not here."

"You're lying. I want Thad. Now!"

"You're drunk."

"Fuckin-a!"

"Sober up and get a life," Jerry said.

I smashed down the receiver and staggered toward Scott's condominium, but instead of knocking on the door, I peeked in the kitchen window.

Scott and Jerry were at the sink. If they hadn't been so engrossed, they would have seen me. Jerry had a needle in his hand. I strained to see deeper into the room. Thad was on the couch kissing a guy I didn't recognize.

I ran to the front door and pounded on it with my fist. "Let me in, you tramp!"

No one came to the door. I went back to the kitchen window, but the couch was empty. Scott was heading to the front door. I ran to get there first.

"What's the fuss?" Scott said, failing to invite me inside.

"Thad's here, I saw him through the window."

"You're hallucinating."

"Liar!"

"Okay, look around for yourself." Scott stood aside to allow me to pass.

I raced to the bedroom. Thad's clothes were in the closet. "See? He's still here."

"I said he took some of his things. Not everything."

"You let him get out the back door, didn't you?"

Before Scott could respond, Jerry came into the room. "You need drugs," he said, dangling a syringe in my face.

"I can't believe you're shooting up," I said, staring at Scott with indignation.

"It's not that big a deal," Scott smirked.

"You're going to kill yourself."

Scott put his hands on my shoulders and said, "You need to do a line."

"You didn't say, Simon says," I shot back, idiotically.

"Okay," Scott said, humoring me, "Simon says, do a line. Now, chill out."

"Thad doesn't want to see you, Simon," Jerry said. "Isn't that obvious? Deal with it." He was feeling particularly confident with cocaine in his bloodstream.

Scott laid out lines on a mirror. He put a brass straw in my hand and said, "You go first."

The narcotic quickly overpowered the alcohol intoxication, draining the gin right out of my blood. My brain now functioned with focus and clarity. The future will take care of itself. I knew instantly. Why should I be upset?

Scott and Jerry snorted lines, and then we all began talking nonstop, carrying on multiple conversations at once. I told Scott and Jerry about my new place, raving about the view and how it was owned by a gay couple, a premonition that Thad and I could make it a love nest.

Jerry slipped into the kitchen. When he returned, he was panting as if he'd run a mile. He winked at Scott, motioning toward the kitchen with a tilt of the head.

"You can join me if you want," Scott said.

"Not on your life," I said. Needles had frightened me ever since I was a teenager and found Ernie passed out at a party with a needle hanging from his arm. I preferred to keep Ernie alive in my memories and not follow him into the grave. "I need to get home, to my new house."

"Here's something to tide you over," Scott said, scooping some powder into a folded paper.

On the way out, I glanced in the kitchen and saw Jerry stab a needle in Scott's arm. As he pressed on the plunger, Scott's knees buckled. I turned away.

I searched all over the neighborhood, trying to remember where I'd parked the car, only to find it a block from Scott's.

Thad was sitting on the hood. His expression was hard to read.

"Why did you come here?" he said when I was within earshot. "You said you didn't want to do drugs again. Did I drive you to it?"

"I came down here because I miss you."

Thad scooted off the hood and came toward me. We stared at each other in silence.

"I love you, Thad."

"I know you do."

"Want to do a line?"

Thad grinned. "I thought you'd never ask."

"Tell me one thing," I said. "Are you shooting up?"

"Look for yourself." Thad held out his arms.

"Who was that boy I saw you with at Scott's?"

"Just some kid I met on the beach. He had drugs. That's all it was."

"I got a new place today. It's on a hill in Silverlake. I want us to live there."

"I'm glad you came," Thad said. "I was afraid when you pounded on the door, but I'm glad now. If I had stayed here another day, Jerry would've convinced me to shoot up."

I wished that he wanted me more than he feared Jerry's needle.

"Let me get a few things," Thad said, rushing toward Scott's.

While he was gone, I got in the car and snorted a couple of lines. Thad returned before the initial rush had worn off. He threw his bags into the backseat and then spooned some coke up his nose.

I had wished for a romantic homecoming. This would have to do.

CHAPTER NINETEEN

If Thad wasn't a lover, at least I had a dope buddy. During the fleeting moments when we weren't doing drugs, I tried to get some work done. But the effort would come to little value when Thad went to see Patricia to score drugs from Jesús. I had hoped Thad and Patricia wouldn't get along, but they quickly became friends.

At first, I thought it was exhaustion from the drugs, but eventually, I didn't even have the strength to get up in the mornings. Over a two-week period, I lost ten pounds. My face became a gaunt mask.

When I couldn't muster the strength to lift myself off the toilet, and found that my stools were white and chalky, I really began to worry. My skin had a yellow sheen and felt clammy to the touch. I called out for Thad – who was passed out on the couch – but with such a weak voice that it didn't rouse him.

"Take me to a clinic," I said, shaking Thad, after finally managing to get out of the bathroom. "There's one on La Brea."

"Let me sleep," Thad complained.

"Thad!" I cried, pulling up my shirt and rubbing my yellow skin.

That got his attention. He quickly showered and drove me to the doctor.

At the clinic, they were sure I had hepatitis but weren't sure which type. A staff physician drew blood and told me I'd have to wait a week for the results. Meanwhile, all I could do was rest. The doctor warned that symptoms would get worse, but the worse the better; then, if I developed enough antibodies, my condition wouldn't become chronic. The information was small comfort as I lay on a pallet in front of the television, too weak to lift the remote and change the channels.

Soup was all I could keep down, but the stove was downstairs. No matter how much I pleaded with Thad, he barely helped me. And the sicker I became, the more frequently he disappeared with the car, leaving me to fend for myself. He would say that he was going for drinks at the bar and would be back in a few hours, but sometimes days went by before he returned.

I became sure I was going to die and telephoned Vivian. I needed to hear the voice of someone who truly loved me. She became frantic with worry and began calling every few hours. Sometimes, I didn't have the strength to answer and the machine picked up. Vivian would cry, begging me to return her call.

Business clients left messages asking about shipments waiting for release by customs brokers and wondering if letters of credit had been executed. I couldn't find the wherewithal to answer anyone. I wished that Thad would help me, but after a while, I nearly forgot that he had the car, and had no idea how long he'd been gone.

About a month into the ordeal, Thad brought Patricia by the house. He hadn't told her I was sick.

"*Bebé!*" Patricia exclaimed when she found me shivering on the couch under the blanket I had pulled around me. "Ju look like death. What's the matter with ju?"

Before I could answer, she went into the bathroom and returned with a wet rag, wiping my brow and feeling for fever.

"What happened?" Patricia asked.

My voice was faint as I said, "I have hepatitis B."

"Are you going to die?"

"I don't know," I said.

"Oh, baby," Patricia took my hands and washed them with the rag. Then an idea occurred to her. "It is contagious?"

"Not unless I fuck you."

"Oh-h-h," Patricia giggled, "No no no. I don't think ju fuck anyone right now. But who fucked ju?" Patricia leaned close to my ear, "Thad?"

"Some guy in Italy," I managed to say. "A hustler named Yasha."

Patricia crossed herself and prayed in Spanish.

Thad appeared at the top of the stairs.

"Ju don't love this man!" Patricia said angrily. "Ju should take care of him."

Thad went into the bedroom and shut the door.

"The other night, I did a line with Thad," I said. "I thought it might keep him here. But I became delirious."

"Ju don't need drugs. Ju need rest. If Thad won't take care of ju, I take care of you. Every day I come, even if I must take the bus."

Patricia proved every bit as good as her word. She came by every chance she got. Each time, she fixed some soup and then spooned it into my mouth. She helped me to the toilet too, supporting me as I hobbled to the seat.

Thad took advantage of the situation and disappeared for days with my car. It made me heartsick.

Weeks went by. I got worse. By the end of May, it felt as though my life had drained away. Then I began a slow process of physical recovery. I found the strength to get onto the couch instead of lying prostrate on the floor. A couple of weeks later, I managed to venture downstairs, though the trip back up nearly wore me out.

When he was around, Thad would become gruff with Patricia. She grew so angry that she told me she wouldn't come back unless I broke up with him. I couldn't do it.

The clinic doctor was pleased with my progress.

"You have to be careful not to get another strain of the virus," he said, "and if you get HIV, it may progress faster because of this."

The doctor went to a drawer and retrieved a pack of condoms. "Use these from now on," he said.

I couldn't bring myself to tell him that I had been raped.

After regaining my health, I had little desire to use drugs, even when Thad snorted lines right in front of me. Common sense demanded that I break off our relationship. Instead, I became increasingly foolish, willing to do anything to keep him from leaving. Thad loved gold, so I bought him a bracelet. He wanted a ring. Before his twenty-first birthday arrived, I went to a jeweler and ordered rings to be engraved, Simon and Thad 6-15-88. My plan was to take Thad back to Petit Jean and present our rings at the waterfall.

Thad refused to go.

"Your mother's a dear," he said, "but one visit to Arkansas is enough."

I went to my desk drawer and got the rings.

"I was going to give this to you in a more romantic setting, but here, take it."

Thad opened the velvet-lined case and put on his ring. I could tell he was pleased, but he fought to keep from showing it. I put on my ring and saw Thad's eyes dart between the two, making sure that his had a larger diamond. There was no point in mentioning the engraving. It would have meant nothing to him. I had to be satisfied with the knowledge that he would carry my name with him wherever he went.

I had promised Vivian that I would visit when my health improved. Before leaving, I got Thad a credit card and opened a bank account for him. The night before my flight, Thad was sitting upstairs watching television. I sat beside him and slipped the credit card into his shirt pocket.

"A credit card?" he said, reading his name. "Aren't you leaving me cash?"

"I opened a bank account," I said, handing him a debit card and giving him the code to get cash. "I deposited a thousand dollars."

Thad pocketed the card and then returned to his television show without another word. He had become little more than a kept boy, and I was merely fulfilling my obligations.

Sitting beside Thad, I felt as lonely as if I were actually alone in the house. I took his hand. "Can't we at least hold each other?"

"Maybe, if you do a line with me," Thad said, taking a mirror from the side table. It was prepared with four lines.

"I have to get up early," I protested.

"You can sleep on the plane," Thad said, taking the straw and snorting two of the lines. Then he gave me the mirror.

My hand trembled as I lifted the straw. I sensed that this was it – I would not be able to abstain again. Thad placed his hand on my knee. After two lines, all that mattered was getting more drugs into my system.

"Maybe you should call Patricia," Thad encouraged.

"Yeah. I guess she's still taking to me."

"Well, I know she's talking to me," Thad said. "The drugs we just did came from her."

Thad called Patricia and set things up. I gave him money and he took off with the car. It seemed as though he was gone for hours. When he finally returned, he was too high to talk.

"Good shit, man," he finally managed to say as he handed me a baggie.

"This looks like Peruvian flake," I said, relishing the aroma.

The first line made me amorous, but Thad scurried into the bedroom and shut me out.

I sat naked on the couch and put in a video. Hours went by watching a platoon of army guys fucking each other silly.

Before catching the shuttle to the airport, I found the bedroom door unlocked and went in, placing my face close to Thad's. He sensed my presence and covered his head with the sheet.

If I do this, if I go to Arkansas, I told myself, Thad might not be here when I return.

When the shuttle arrived, I stashed some drugs in my carry-on bag and rushed out the door.

CHAPTER TWENTY

At roughly twenty-minute intervals, I slipped into the plane's lavatory and snorted a line. By the time I changed planes in Dallas, I was frazzled. People on the concourse glared at me disdainfully, or so it seemed. I had just run out of drugs when we touched down in Little Rock. It occurred to me to turn around and head back to LA, but after a few shots of gin at the airport lounge, the craving for drugs temporarily subsided and I wasn't so bothered by the idea of seeing family.

When I met Vivian at baggage claim, she was unable to hide her alarm.

"Sorry," I said, "I must look like a wreck. I didn't have much time to sleep before getting on the plane."

Vivian took my hand. "You are my son," she said. "It's good to have you home."

The Arkansas humidity hit me hard as we walked through the parking lot toward for Vivian's Pontiac. My suitcase felt like a lead weight. When we finally arrived at the car and I opened the door, a blast of hot air bombarded me. I stumbled forward.

Vivian came around to my side of the car. "Bubby!" she shouted.

I struggled to remain conscious as Vivian helped me into the car.

Vivian started the engine. The air conditioner had been left on full-blast. After an initial bombardment of what felt like steam, cooler air followed as the compressor kicked in. I put my face against the vent.

"I'll be all right," I said. "Once I get some sleep."

By the time we arrived in Sibley, I was delirious. I barely made it to the front door.

Vivian pursed her lips the way she did when I was a little boy and she disapproved of something. "You should let me take you to the doctor," she said firmly.

"It's simply exhaustion, and this overbearing heat. I'm not used to it. I'll be fine after I take a nap."

"Your sister wants to see you," Vivian said. "She and Derek are coming over for dinner."

They were the last people I wanted to see. Connie would offer unwelcome judgment, with her eyes if not her words. Derek would lie in wait for the right moment to offer up Christ as the solution to whatever troubled me.

I collapsed onto the bed in my old room, but realized I was so dehydrated that I had to drink something. I went to the kitchen for a glass of iced tea, the Southern elixir for neutralizing the effects of summer. Vivian was on the phone.

"It's Connie," she said, handing me the receiver.

"Hi Connie." I tried to sound even weaker than I felt. "Vivian told you I'm not feeling well, right?"

"She did."

"Let's have dinner tomorrow, how about it?"

"Vivian told me that you almost passed out getting in the car. That sounds serious."

"We don't have humidity in Los Angeles. I forgot what it's like in Arkansas this time of year."

"You gave Vivian quite a scare," Connie said.

Vivian asked for the phone. I told her I was going back to my room as I handed it to her. On the way upstairs, I could hear her retelling the airport story. In this version, I collapsed face down on the asphalt.

As the morning sun began to filter through the curtains, Vivian was rattling dishes in the kitchen. I must have gone back to sleep because it seemed an instant later that a knock startled me.

"Simon, are you awake?" It was Vivian's voice. "Your sister's here. Can you come out?"

"Yeah! Give me a minute," I said.

Connie was at the door. "Hi, Simon," she said, attempting to sound chipper. "Dinner's almost ready."

"Dinner?" I called out. "What time is it?"

"Six in the evening," Connie responded. "Are you going to sleep through the whole visit?"

"Let me take a shower. I'll be down in a little bit."

I opened the curtains, hoping the daylight would get me going. I made out features of the familiar landscape. There was Ernie's house, and the pool, now derelict, with shrubs hanging over the edges. "Poor Ernie", I said aloud, but without emotion. I felt hollow inside, as though I'd only read about Ernie and didn't really remember the smell of his body as we fooled around during our sleepovers.

I drew the curtains and sat on the bed, wondering how I could possibly join the others for dinner. My entire body ached. I took a long shower, hoping that cold water might help wake me up. It didn't.

Connie hugged me as I entered the kitchen, a pretext for examining my bony shoulders.

"That illness really wore you down," Connie observed. "There's no meat on those bones."

"I was very ill," I said flatly. I wondered if she'd have been happier if I'd come home in a casket with an AIDS quarantine label on it. That way, she could start another career condemning the sins of her wayward brother who chose to be homosexual — and see where it got him.

We sat down and filled our plates with roast beef, carrots, peas, and heaps of red skin mashed potatoes.

Before anyone touched their food, Vivian offered a prayer. I acquiesced and bowed my head, not wanting to worry her about the fate of my soul when she was so concerned about my body. The moment she said, Amen, she looked in my direction, her face a roadmap of pain, each line etched by the sharp point of Lenny's belittling remarks and the endless condemnations of his mother, Mandy, who never failed to catch an opportunity to tell Vivian how lucky she was to be married to her son. Hearing Mandy talk, one would think Vivian grew up in abject poverty, picking tomatoes for market as soon as she could stand on two feet. I'd seen the ruins of the house where Vivian was raised; it was as large as the Sibley mansion. At least Vivian's family knew when to give up the past. They left that old house during the Depression and moved closer to town. The Powells never left sight of the family cemetery.

"It's been difficult," Vivian said, looking in my direction. "If Lenny had just put something away, but he made sure I wouldn't have much to live on."

"I had hoped Lenny was just being mean when he said that," I consoled. "I didn't think he really meant it."

"Oh, he meant it all right," Vivian said, pursing her lips.

Connie took my hand. "Our mother's had a rough time these last few years. She just didn't want you to know about it."

"I could have sent money," I said. "I didn't know you were hurting."

"You don't need to be thinking about me," Vivian said, shooting Connie a look of disapproval. Connie was almost visibly biting her tongue. "You have your own life to live."

I wondered what Vivian imagined my life to be like.

"Let me at least pay the property taxes," I offered. "How much is it?"

"Two thousand dollars. We've still got a lot of acreage back there." Vivian waved her hand toward the window.

"From now on, the taxes are my responsibility, okay?"

Vivian was about to protest that she'd be all right, but Connie spoke up. "That will be a big help, Simon. Vivian doesn't want you to know how hard it's been keeping up the property. After all, you'll be the one to inherit it someday."

It must have galled Connie to acknowledge that, since, according to the historical papers still governing the estate, the first son always inherited. The property could only be sold if every descendant of the Arkansas patriarch agreed.

After dinner, I went upstairs and wrote a check. Everyone was still sitting around the table drinking coffee when I set it down. Connie looked it over. Her eyes widened as she realized that I had made it out for twice the amount.

"What kind of money are you making out there in California?" Connie wondered. "How can you afford this?"

"My boy's always done well," Vivian said, "smart as he is."

"It's not that much," I said, taking the check from Connie's hand and placing it in Vivian's. "I'll do what I can from now on."

"Come home more often," Vivian said. "Having you here makes me feel better than anything."

There was no way to buy myself out of it. Vivian cared more about seeing me than keeping up payments on the property. My degree of self-worth was so low that I couldn't comprehend how or why she felt that way.

While I was at Vivian's, I frequently telephoned LA. The machine always picked up and I left a message each time. Thad never returned the calls. Finally, when I was about ready to have the police go to the house, he answered.

His voice was hoarse. I knew something was up.

"How are things?" I said.

When Thad recognized my voice, I heard scrambling, scuffs against the receiver, raucous background noises. "I was asleep," Thad said, his voice a little stronger, as if he'd drunk some water to clear his throat.

"Where are you? I heard a click before you picked up, like call-forwarding was on. Are you at Scott's?"

"No, no. I'm here. When are you coming back?"

"Today. I'll be there tonight. Can you pick me up?"

"Uh, well, the, uh, car isn't running so great. Maybe you should take a taxi."

"Be there when I get home," I said.

"Okay. Sure. Yeah," Thad said in a faltering voice. I knew he was high. I wanted to know where he was, and who he was with. I was sure about the call-forwarding.

I had promised Vivian I would drive her to Magnolia to visit relatives, most of whom I'd not seen since I was a kid, but I insisted that my business demanded that I return right away.

Vivian accepted the announcement courageously, until she came to my room and found me packing.

"Oh, hun," Vivian said, struggling not to cry. "I'm going to miss you so much."

If only I could have explained that I was afraid my lover was cheating on me. She would recognize the theme from the words of the country songs she knew. But it wouldn't make sense that a man could experience something like jealousy over another man. Anyway, I wasn't willing to give her the chance to understand.

"I wish I could stay," I said, not quite sure I was lying, "but a sale might be in jeopardy. I have to go back."

The next plane didn't depart until late evening. Connie, Derek, Cheryl, and Victoria came over for a final dinner. Connie brought a tub of Kentucky Fried Chicken with buckets of mashed potatoes and coleslaw.

After the meal, Vivian turned off the lights. Connie slipped out of the room, reappearing from around the corner with an extravagant devil's food cake decorated with thirty-five lit candles. Spelled out in icing were the words, Happy Birthday Bubby.

I'd completely forgotten what day it was.

I blew out the candles following an off-key rendition of the inevitable birthday song. When the applause faded, I opened my presents. Cheryl gave me a pen and pencil set. I acknowledged it by giving her a hug.

"It's not too practical, is it?" Cheryl asked.

"Not at all. Every time I use it, I'll think of you. That makes it special."

Little Victoria gave me a piggybank, telling me I needed to save money. That was her Sesame Street lesson of the day and she wanted to share it with me.

Vivian gave me a card with twenty dollars inside, saying sheepishly, "I didn't know what you would like."

I called a taxi to come from Little Rock. Vivian stood behind the screen door as the driver made his way across the gravel to the main road. She had already gotten ready for bed. Her hair, dyed black, was coiled into bundles and secured with bobby pins. Her face was covered with Jergens lotion. She clutched her bathrobe tight and waved goodbye.

CHAPTER TWENTY-ONE

During the Braniff Airlines flight, I pulled up the armrests in my nearly empty row of seats and stretched out to take a nap. But sleep was out of the question. Tumultuous thoughts bombarded my mind, ranging from anger at Thad and nearly unbearable craving for drugs to utter fear that I was about to lose the business I had worked so hard to establish.

Approaching the runway at Los Angeles International, we encountered wind shears that made the wings bounce up and down. The plane lurched forward. Passengers yelped in fear, but I was calm. If only the plane would burst into flames, I thought, my troubles would be over.

The sun was just breaking over the reservoir as the airport shuttle neared Silverwood Terrace. When we rounded the final corner, I spotted my car in the driveway. I paid the driver and carried my things to the front door, not knowing what to expect. The furniture was there, and I laughed with relief at that simple fact. I stuck my finger in the soil at the base of the twenty-foot fichus I had bought for the window at the patio. The dampness told me that it had been watered recently. The stereo, tape deck, and computer equipment were all in place. The bedroom was neat and tidy. There was no sign that Thad had ever lived in the house. The picture of us I kept on the dresser was gone. Thad's clothes were missing from the closet.

Computer logs indicated that files had not been accessed since I left. I picked up the phone and heard a beeping sound that told me call-forwarding was re-directing to my answering service. Thad must have come in after our phone call and reset it.

I called my bank and punched in the credit card number. In the last three days, there were charges that totaled a thousand dollars.

An idea struck me. I went to the telephone downstairs and pressed redial. After a couple of rings, I recognized Jerry's voice.

"Yeah, who is it?" he said.

I didn't respond.

"Who the fuck's there?"

"Can I talk to Scott?" I asked, trying to disguise my voice to sound as though I was calling from the office.

Jerry set down the receiver. I heard him trying to rouse Scott. Groggy and irritated, Scott answered.

"Hi Scott. I'm back."

"Simon?"

"Where's Thad?" I demanded.

Scott must have held the phone against his chest. I heard a muffled question asked of Jerry, Should I tell him? And Jerry responding, Who the fuck cares?

"Thad didn't want me to say anything," Scott teased. "He made me swear."

"You asshole! If you don't tell me what's going on, you can forget about our friendship."

"Let me think about this," Scott said.

"You son of a bitch, Scott!" I shouted, then calming down, "Excuse me, dear friend, here I was thinking you'd want to share in the ounce I'm about to buy. Guess not."

"You mean you really didn't know? Thad's in San Diego."

"Tell me the whole story, all of it."

Scott took a deep breath. "When do you think you'll be over with the drugs?"

"It's sounding like never."

"All right, all right. It started months ago, when you got sick. Thad came down here almost every day. He and Jerry would go to San Diego and hang out at Black's Beach."

"Didn't that bother you? My Thad and your Jerry traipsing around on a nude beach?"

"Get real, Simon. They'll do what they want whether we know about it or not. Look, do you want the story or don't you?"

"Go on."

"Thad met a marine. His name is Marvin. Thad turned him on to coke for the first time. That was it, instant love."

"Where's Thad now?"

"He told me he had forwarded your calls to Marvin's. When you said you were coming back, he drove up and forwarded the calls to the answering service. Then he came by here and put some of his stuff in the guest room."

Just as I suspected.

"Do you have an address? Do you know Marvin's last name?"

Once again, Scott hesitated. "When are you bringing the drugs?"

"Tell you what. Give me the information, then you can meet me tonight at the Spotlight, around nine."

Scott groaned at the long wait he'd have to endure. He gave me Marvin's last name as well as an address. Getting the phone number was a simple matter of calling information at the marine base.

When I heard Thad's voice, I froze.

"Hello?" Thad questioned, then a little louder, "Hello?"

"It's me, Thad."

I could hear him gasp. "How'd you get this number?"

"If you want to keep a secret, Scott is the last person to tell. He's been my friend a lot longer than he's been yours." Thad was silent. "Why'd you do it, Thad? Don't you understand that I love you?"

"I'm sorry, Simon," Thad's voice was cold and without remorse. "I don't want to live with you anymore. What do you want me to say?"

"What about the credit card? That's just plain stealing, Thad."

"Don't say that," Thad shot back with indignation. "You never gave me shit for staying around, so I helped myself."

"Staying around?! Is that what it was?"

Thad again remained quiet.

"Put your trick on the phone," I said, snidely. "I should warn him to keep his credit cards in his wallet."

"You're fucked up, Simon. I bought jewelry with your card. I'll send it to you. Just leave me the fuck alone. Okay?"

"And stay out of my life!" I shouted.

I went to the stereo, put on Schubert's C-minor quintet, and tried to relax, but instead of providing comfort, Schubert's somber melodies drove me deeper into despair. Only when the sun began to set and the amber light began streaming through the patio windows did I shake off the stupor and call Patricia.

"Simone!" she squealed. "Ju left without saying goodbye. Ju should have asked me to baby-sit jure Thad."

She obviously knew the story.

"And now ju call Patricia to cry about Thad, no?" Patricia giggled. "Ju want happy powder?"

"I'll come pick you up," I said, getting down to business. "Can we score an ounce?"

"*No problema, Señor* Simon," Patricia said, affecting a manly voice.

Patricia and I scored from Jesús. In the time since we'd first started dealing with him, he had moved into a gang-tagged neighborhood near MacArthur Park. The police had begun staking out his old apartment, forcing him to leave.

Jesús was alone. I wondered if his wife and kids had left him, or if they actually had been his wife and kids. Patricia held my hand and made a big to do, explaining how I had "come back to her." Jesús appeared more strung-out since the last time I saw him, and more paranoid. As we were leaving, he rushed to the blinds to peek outside.

Safely back in the car, Patricia dipped into the package, setting out a line on a small compact mirror she took from her purse. I bent over to snort it before starting the car. The drug was pure. My hands shook as waves of nervous energy tore through my system. In an instant, life was the way it was meant to be. Everything had happened for a reason.

After a few more lines, I wasn't sure I could make it to the Spotlight.

"We better go while I can still drive," I said.

"Okay, we go see Scott, and that juicy man, Jerry," Patricia said.

"You are one unique lady," I said.

Patricia smiled.

"I have to give Scott an eightball," I said. "That's what it took to find out what happened to Thad."

"Patricia would have told you about Thad." She clearly was disappointed that I had not called her first. "Ju treat me like drug whore."

"You're special, Patricia. I'm sorry. I didn't think you would know what happened. That's all."

"Okay, my love." Patricia kissed me on the cheek.

I parked along Selma Street and put the drugs I would give Scott in a folded piece of paper torn from the car's owner's manual, and packaged a few gram papers. Patricia took some for her own use. Lastly, I filled an ounce bottle that had a gizmo on top that delivered a hit by turning a valve. The contraption made it possible to sneak a clandestine snort while sitting at the bar.

Scott and Jerry were drunk. Rudy was playing liar's poker with Don. Twiggy was tending the bar.

Patricia glided toward Jerry and placed a well-manicured finger under his chin. She lifted his face and kissed him on the lips.

When I approached, Scott said, "Did that mean old Thad hurt your feelings?" He scrunched his face into a pout.

"Don't push your luck," I said. "I may go back on my promise."

Twiggy set up the bar upon my request as I set down a hundred dollar bill. I reached out to shake his hand, concealing a gram paper in my palm. Twiggy bent his middle finger to grasp it – a method we had perfected. He picked up a napkin and pretended to wipe his nose, wrapping the packet within it so he could put the drugs under the counter. Later he would pick up the napkin and head to the bathroom.

I slipped Scott his drugs under the bar and then shared my coke-snorting contraption. Scott and Jerry got so horny they started to make out. When Scott's head dipped into Jerry's lap, I worried that Don would see what was going on and throw us out. But Twiggy was on the ball. He told Scott and Jerry to leave on his own. The Spotlight couldn't risk an infraction called in by a vice cop.

Rudy bowed out of the card game, coming over to join Patricia and me as Scott and Jerry staggered through the curtain and out the door. Rudy didn't think much of Scott and kept his distance whenever he was around.

Someone had told me that Rudy was on a diet, but it didn't seem as though he'd lost any weight.

"Simon, my god, have I got something to tell you," Rudy began. "I thought that friend of yours would never leave." He took a deep breath. "You have got to meet this boy I found. He has the face of a cherub."

"Tell me more," I said.

Patricia leaned close to hear what Rudy was saying.

"If that cheating Miss Thad still lived with you," Rudy gushed, "you'd kick her out for this one."

Did everyone know about Thad?

Rudy explained how a young man had come into the bar earlier that day. Don wanted to let him stay, but he was obviously under twenty-one.

"Where is he now?" I asked.

"At my apartment with Charlotte and Lane. Have you met Charlotte?"

"I don't think so. Who's she?"

"Charlotte's an old friend from Miami. She's staying with me for a while. There isn't room for everyone in my apartment, and the minute Lane laid eyes on the kid, he put his foot down and said he can't stay. I didn't want to put him back out on the street. Simon, this kid is tailor-made for you."

"And Lane?"

"Honey!" Rudy seemed surprised. "He's been my boyfriend for weeks. Where have you been?"

"You make the kid sound like a lost puppy."

"Oh darling, no puppy's as cute as this one."

"Sounds like jailbait."

Rudy sighed. "Will you stop? This is destiny. The boy's name is Axl. I'm sure it's not his real name, probably thinks he's Axl Rose. But who cares about that. Oh, Simon, you're just going to die!"

"Destiny, huh?"

Rudy looked at me blankly.

"Never mind."

"Let's go to my apartment right now," Rudy insisted.

Patricia, despairing that she could not compete with Rudy's description of Axl, had gone into the back room to flirt with the pool players. She held out her hand as I approached, the overhead light reflecting in the glittered nail polish.

"I have to go, Patricia. But I wanted to thank you for helping me."

"Ju have a new trick?" she asked with a touch of melancholy.

"Rudy wants me to meet some kid that's staying at his apartment. Take care of yourself."

"I want him to take care of me," Patricia said, swinging her legs around and waving at a biker in a black leather jacket. He shifted his cigarette in his mouth and screwed his face into a grimace as he propped his cue stick on the edge of the table to prepare for a difficult shot.

Rudy's apartment was in a new building that had a sterile feel about it. The smell of sawdust still permeated the hallways. It was the first time I'd visited since giving Rudy the security deposit.

On the elevator, it struck me how badly I needed a line. Since telling me about his cocaine problem in Miami, I never mentioned drugs around Rudy and never did them in front of him.

"Are you jonesing?" Rudy asked.

"Yeah, Rudy. I am."

"And you have drugs on you?"

"You know I do. Nothing gets by you at the Spotlight."

"Please don't mention it to Lane. Axl will go gaga when he finds out you're holding, but I don't want Lane getting horny for it."

"I promise."

Rudy opened the apartment door and led me inside. At first, I only saw a woman who I presumed to be Charlotte. She was in the kitchen standing at the stove. She had the look of an ingénue from a 1920s Coca-Cola advertisement. Her red hair was thick, with curls that cascaded down her back. She smiled and said, "I'm making soup. Anybody want some?"

Before deciding, Rudy sniffed the pot. He might have appeared to be someone who would eat anything, but he was a connoisseur.

I looked around to catch a glimpse of the mythic youth, but didn't see him anywhere. Lane, who was on the couch hidden by a blanket, kicked it off to see who Rudy had brought home. He was a bit stocky for my tastes, but had a cute face and soft brown hair that swept over his forehead.

Charlotte stopped stirring the soup for a moment in order to shake my hand. "Hello, Simon. You're a wonderful friend to help Rudy get this place."

"Well, I didn't want to see him leave town right after I met him. Anyway, I could afford it."

Charlotte smiled, perhaps a bit too knowingly, before saying to Rudy, "Go in there and introduce Simon to Wonder Boy."

Rudy's eyes gleamed with mischief as he led me into the bedroom. Axl was strumming a guitar.

My heart stopped, not because the boy was so beautiful, which he was, but because he looked like Ernie – the same round eyes, the same long eyelashes. Axl's white-blond hair covered his ears and fell lightly across the nape of his neck, exactly like Ernie's. He wore only a pair of jogging shorts. The image of Ernie coming straight from a swim, crossing the field and climbing up the trellis to my bedroom window, flashed through my thoughts.

Axl rested his guitar against the wall and rose to his feet. He was thin but with taut muscles.

"Hey dude," Axl said with Ernie's voice. "Have we met?"

"Not in this life," I said, trying to remember the date Ernie had overdosed. Was it before this kid was born? Was Ernie looking at me from behind those eyes?

"How old are you?" I asked.

Axl shyly cast his gaze downward and said, "Seventeen."

Close, but it couldn't be – Axl was a baby when Ernie died.

Rudy put a chubby hand on my shoulder and said, "This boy needs a daddy." With that, he left the room, shutting the door behind him.

"Want to do some coke?" I asked, seeing no point in small talk.

When Axl grinned, dimples appeared beside his curling lips. If he wasn't Ernie, he was a Greek kouros.

"Rudy didn't say you were into drugs," Axl said, barely able to contain his glee. "I figured he was fixing me up with one of those trolls at the bar. You're cool, man. You're all right."

I handed Axl a paper of drugs.

"Damn man! You are all right," he gushed.

"Here, I have some ready to go." I took out my bottle and loaded the chamber.

"You come prepared, don't you?" Axl snorted the hit, then loaded the chamber and did another. "Wow. This is pure!"

"As pure as anyone gets in Hollywood," I said. Axl's eyes filled with instant devotion. He gathered his belongings while I helped myself to a few hits. Setting a gym bag on the bed, he took out a spoon, a lighter, and a short glass stem that I had seen hustlers use to smoke coke.

"You don't care if I rock it up, do you?"

I didn't know much about the process, but I knew it required baking soda. "You don't have everything you need, do you?"

"You're right." Axl considered the problem for a moment. "Can you go to the kitchen and get some baking soda? There's a box in the refrigerator. Say you want a beer or something. Bring back a pinch, like about this much." He used his index finger as a measure.

Rudy and Charlotte were sitting on the couch with Lane, watching a rented video. "You got a couple of beers that I can bum?"

"In the fridge," Rudy said, his eyes on the TV. "Getting some action in there?"

"Something like that," I answered. I went into the kitchen, took two cans of beer from the fridge, and poured a pile of baking soda into the palm of my hand.

Axl sat on the edge of the bed holding his spoon. He had also taken off his gym shorts and covered himself with the sheet. On the side table was a glass of water from the bathroom.

"Put the rest on the dresser," Axl said as he took some baking soda from my hand.

Axl mixed the ingredients in the spoon. I watched intently as he heated it with his cigarette lighter. After a few moments, Axl set down the lighter and tapped the spoon with his finger. The mixture coalesced into rock.

"Not much of a chemistry set, but it works," Axl said, grinning at his success. He sifted the excess water from the spoon using his finger as a sieve. Then he dumped the rock onto the sheet to dry it off.

"I used too much baking soda," Axl said as the rock broke into crumbs. "It'll be harsh on the throat, but it'll get us high. You want to join me, don't you?"

"No thanks," I said. "Snorting does me just fine."

"Doesn't it make your nose bleed?"

"Every once in a while. But I like the drainage when it pours down the back of my throat."

"I know what you mean," Axl said.

Axl was so young that the fuzz on his cheeks was like dust covering his deep tan. His chest was hairless. His entire torso was without blemish.

Aware of my examination, Axl's nipples grew hard. Goose pimples popped up around the edges.

I did a line while Axl prepared his pipe. I'd seen hustlers do it before, using a length of coat hanger wire to push a wad of metal scouring pad back and forth through the tube to clear off any residue that had built up.

The drugs hit me hard. Sweat dripped from my forehead.

"Hey man, take off some of your clothes and cool off."

I didn't need any more encouragement than that. I stripped to my briefs.

"You got a nice body," Axl said.

"Not really. Look at this." I pinched some flesh off my stomach.

"Ah, that's just because you're sitting down," Axl said. "Stand up."

I stood up, facing Axl.

"Yeah, see, you're trim." Axl pinched the front of my briefs. "What's this?" he asked playfully, pulling the elastic band forward and hooking it under my balls.

"At attention, sir," Axl commanded, leaning forward to gobble me up.

His mouth made a loud pop as he pulled away. "How'd that feel?"

Delirious, I couldn't answer.

Axl propped himself against the headboard and held the pipe to his lips. The rock transformed into what seemed like a form of liquid smoke. Axl held his breath so long I was afraid he had forgotten to exhale. I touched his leg. The smoke poured loosely from his slack-jawed mouth. Axl was in a hypnotic stupor.

"Must be pretty good," I said, anxious for him to say something. I couldn't tell if he was conscious.

Axl turned his head sideways and grinned. Stretching out at length on the bed, his lips formed the word, wow.

I took the opportunity to study the work of art between his legs, kissing the tip and cupping the perfectly formed testicles in my hand as I tasted each one. Our eyes met in a kind of animal glare and we burst out laughing.

"Simon! It's late," Rudy hollered, knocking on the door. "It's after midnight."

"Sorry, Rudy. Give us a minute."

The simple act of dressing required more coordination than Axl or I could muster. Axl struggled with his sneakers until I laced them for him.

Then I helped him into his gym shorts and slipped a jersey over his upstretched arms.

I carried Axl's belongings, all stuffed into a duffle bag. He lugged the acoustic guitar he'd been playing when I arrived. Rudy said nothing as we passed through the front room. Charlotte was asleep on the couch. Lane, on the other hand, watched our every move. I was about to pull away from the curb when Lane appeared at the driver's side window.

"Here man, you left this behind." Lane placed the crack pipe in my hand.

"I don't do the stuff. That belongs to Axl."

"Whatever," Lane said. "Rudy doesn't like me to do it. Let me come over sometime and smoke with you guys. Rudy doesn't need to know. Please?"

"We'll see." Images of a three-way flashed through my narcotic-addled brain. "What if you come now? Would Rudy throw you out?"

Lane slapped the side of car. "Aw-right." He looked up as if expecting to find Rudy looking out the apartment window. "Give me a minute," he said. "Don't drive away, okay?"

I wasn't at all sure I would be able drive, high as I was.

Minutes later, Lane hopped in the back seat. "Rudy thinks I'm going to the bar. I said you'd drop me off." Then he let out yelp, "Let's party!"

"Okay with you, Axl?" I asked.

"Whatever dude. Let's get rocking."

CHAPTER TWENTY-TWO

Wally and the other producers whose films I sold were content with my efforts as long as I periodically sent a check. Sometimes I sent money to make them believe I was making sales. The reality was that I had slipped up on a number of deliveries and a few clients had cancelled their contracts. My resources were fast depleting.

Instead of focusing on getting my business affairs in order, I began spending most of my time doing drugs with Axl. Rudy telephoned occasionally. He didn't seem to know that Lane sometimes came over to my place. Scott was barely a part of my life, and only occasionally did I speak with Sandra. Because of Axl, I rarely thought about Thad.

The basement lair began to look like an alchemist's shop, filled with an array of glass pipes, hand torches, and special baking sodas that I bought at a store in Hollywood. A darkly magical transformation came over Axl when he smoked crack. He wasn't used to drugs as potent as mine, and for the first time in his drug career, he began to have bouts of paranoia. Often, I would return home to find the front door barricaded with bar stools and sofa cushions. Once, he became convinced that the police were raiding the house. He thought he would escape by jumping off the balcony. The dagger-like fronds of the century plants would have impaled him had I not caught his belt in the nick of time.

Axl never ate and was becoming a veritable wraith. In the weeks he had lived with me, he had lost his tan and was pale, as if drained of blood. I joked that I should examine his neck for puncture wounds.

My own physical condition wasn't much better. I decided that we needed to escape for a while, perhaps vacation at the Ritz-Carlton in Laguna-Niguel. I'd gone there before when I needed a break. Sitting on the patio that came with the rooms and looking over the Pacific Ocean was invigorating. The day Axl and I were to head out, he was feverish and didn't want to get out of bed. I thought we should cancel the trip, but Axl insisted that he would be all right.

"My throat's just raw from smoking," he said.

I felt under his jaw. "Your glands are swollen. You should see a doctor."

Axl pushed my hand away.

"Look at yourself!" I said, sitting him up so he could see his reflection in the dresser mirror. "You're as red as a cranberry."

"No doctors!" Axl said. He struggled from the covers and locked himself in the bathroom.

"I can wait out here as long as it takes," I told him as I leaned against the door.

A few moments later he let me in. Axl had been throwing up in the toilet.

"That's it, man. You're going to a doctor."

I put a wet towel around Axl's neck and got him into the shower. Axl could not stand without support.

Hours passed before the emergency room personnel at County Hospital called Axl's name. Axl foolishly told the woman at the admissions desk that he was seventeen and that I was not his guardian. The woman glared at me and said, "Without the permission of a legal guardian, we cannot admit this boy."

"So, what does that mean? He collapses in your waiting room and you let him die?"

"You're being melodramatic," the woman said. "I suggest you get in touch with his family and let them deal with the matter."

Axl was nearly unconscious when I asked him to give me a phone number.

"That's my mother," he said, handing me a card from his wallet. "She lives in Maryland."

I rushed to the pay phones and made the call. A commanding voice answered.

"Is this Axl's mother?"

"Axl is my son. Who is this?"

So it was his real name.

"I'm a friend. Axl is with me at a hospital in California."

Before I could continue, the woman interrupted, "Hospital? Has Axl overdosed again?"

"Nothing like that. I think he may have tonsillitis or something. I brought him to an emergency room. But, well, Axl's under eighteen, so I can't get him admitted. He didn't want me to call, but I managed to get your number from him."

"And who are you?"

"A friend. My name is . . ." I hesitated, "Mr. Powell."

"Well, Mr. Powell, I don't know what you are doing with my underage son, but I will get him admitted."

I motioned for the desk attendant to come to the phone. As she spoke to Axl's mother, all I heard was "Um" and "Oh" and "I see."

"We'll admit the boy," she bellowed after she hung up. "He's covered on insurance through his mother."

So, that was the issue: who'd be responsible to pay.

Axl's mother had not asked to speak to him, and Axl didn't ask what she had said. Soon, a nurse escorted Axl in to see a doctor.

"Are you sure you don't want to admit yourself?" the nurse asked me.

"What do you mean?"

"You don't look well."

"I'm fine, I just need some rest. I was about to go on vacation."

The nurse took that for an answer, but not without a warning that I should take better care of myself.

As I suspected, Axl had tonsillitis. The doctor prescribed antibiotics and rest. When I got Axl home, he collapsed in bed and only woke up when I came with medicine or a bowl of soup.

Without Axl as a distraction, I kept thinking about Thad – one minute wondering if he was happy with his Marine boyfriend and in the next minute hoping a shark had bitten off his penis.

I grew tired of doing drugs alone and was bored without Axl's companionship. I decided to go shopping at the Beverly Center. A barking dog at a pet store caught my attention. At first, I thought it was a flashback to age thirteen. That was when Ernie and I had our falling out. Around the same time, I almost got a new pet dog. Somehow, the breakup and the dog were coupled in my memory of that time. Our neighbors down the road in Sibley had Boston terrier puppies for sale. By the time I saw them, all were taken except the runt. I thought he was the cutest animal I'd ever seen and begged Lenny to get him for me. I promised to take care of the puppy, saying that if I had to, I'd sell potholders door to door (I'd gotten a toy loom for my birthday that year). Lenny wouldn't budge. He didn't want another "good for nothing dog" around the yard.

"If you want a dog, we can get a coon hound," Lenny said. "Then we could hunt."

As if he had ever taken me hunting.

Two weeks went by. One morning as I ate a quick bowl of Sugar Pops before rushing to catch the school bus, Lenny told me he'd get the dog. Vivian had interceded on my behalf. I shouted with delight and ran down the street to tell the puppy I'd see him after school. He was at the fence and only stopped crying when I reached through and let him lick my fingers.

When school ended, I ran home and rushed toward the fence to see my new dog. He wasn't there. I ran home thinking Lenny had picked him up already.

"Where's my dog? Did you get him?"

Lenny looked at me solemnly. "Before I got there, someone else had bought him."

I figured this was Lenny's way of getting back at Vivian for going against his will. He probably got one of his friends to call about the dog.

Now, so many years later, I heard the same bark coming from a pet shop window. The Boston terrier puppy had the same markings, down to the identical white socks and shiny black coat, as the one I remembered from childhood.

"I want that dog," I told the clerk, a schoolboy with orange-spiked hair.

"You're taking Monroe?" The clerk seemed surprised. "That little fellow has been here for five months. Don't know why no one's wanted him."

"It must be destiny. I came to save him from a life of being called Monroe."

The clerk nodded. "Wasn't my choice. That's what his tag said when he arrived. Anyway, we've all wanted to take Monroe home, but no one could afford him."

The name Cicero popped in my head, and that's what I decided to call him.

Cicero, liberated from the three-foot square cage, explored every corner of the house and sniffed each piece of furniture. When he discovered Axl in the upstairs bedroom, it seemed as though Cicero had found his purpose in life. He stationed himself at Axl's side. At first, Axl was irritated, but it didn't take long for Cicero to win him over.

When he got better, Axl went immediately back to the pipe. Having Cicero as company had helped me stay away from the drugs, but now I started up again. Cicero sensed that Axl and I were harming ourselves. If I laid out a line or Axl picked up his pipe, Cicero dashed under the bed.

I sometimes wondered what life might have been like if Ernie and I had become lovers. Would I still have joined a cult? Would we have joined together? Or would I have gotten into heroin with Ernie and died young also? Perhaps I would have met Tony, anyway, and been rejected by him, leading to the same place I was now. Is the plan already laid out and is there nothing we can do about it?

"Don't ever leave me," I said to Axl one afternoon.

He banged out a minor chord on his guitar. "Long as there's drugs, man."

CHAPTER TWENTY-THREE

Patricia wasn't picking up her phone. I left messages until her answering machine tape filled up, and finally went to the Spotlight to see if she might be there. Twiggy had a drink ready by the time I took my place at the bar. He wanted to chat, but I had only one thing on my mind.

"You don't know?" Twiggy said. "Patricia got deported. That silly señorita put an ad in *Frontier Magazine* and a vice cop answered it. She's back in Peru. But I'll wager a bottle of gin she'll be back in a month. That girl is resourceful."

Twiggy set down a shot of Boodles. "Are you all right? You seem distracted."

The jukebox was playing something by Judas Priest and it reminded me of some of the hustlers I'd picked up over the years. They loved that kind of music.

"Sure, I'm okay," I said as my memories turned to one trick that had pulled a knife on me when I told him to leave. "Except that I really need to see Patricia. You know."

Twiggy cast a glance around the bar. He nonchalantly wrote something on a napkin.

"That's a mobile phone number," Twiggy said. "The guy who'll answer goes by different names. Recently, it's been Valentino. When you call, say you got the number from me. He'll ask how many 'cassettes' you want. If you want an ounce, tell him a box set. If you only want a gram, tell him you want a single."

I put a hundred-dollar bill on the counter and slipped Valentino's number into my shirt pocket. Twiggy picked up the bill and stuffed it into his pants pocket. "Don't be a stranger, you sexy man," he said, calling after me as I headed for the door.

"I won't, Twiggy. Thanks."

On my way out, Don motioned for me to come over. He grabbed my arms and looked straight into my eyes. "I see your future, Simon, and it's not good. Listen to a pro. I've been kicking around for sixty years now. No hustler is worth your life. You know what I'm saying."

For Don to rise from his stupor to prophesy on my behalf, I must have looked pretty bad. I knew what he was saying, but I didn't want to listen.

I called Valentino from a pay phone on Hollywood Boulevard. He was suspicious at first, but when I identified Twiggy as "the fat bartender at the Spotlight," he changed his tone.

"I'd like a box set of cassettes."

"Good first order," Valentino said. "Where are you?"

"Corner of Sunset and Cahuenga."

"In thirty minutes," Valentino instructed, "be at the Jack-in-the-Box. Look for a black Mercedes. It has tinted windows. When the door opens, hop in."

Thirty minutes later, to the second, the sedan appeared and the door opened. The driver was terribly handsome – dark-haired and swarthy. I was sure I'd seen him in a gay video. The moment I shut the door, he pulled out of the parking lot.

Unlike the handsome driver, Valentino was short and plump. His long hair, pulled into a coiled ponytail, crawled across his bright yellow shirt and ended at his alligator skin belt. Pancake makeup covered his face, which was heavily cratered with pockmarks.

The transaction was no nonsense. Valentino's schedule allowed for a few minutes per stop, coordinated by the dictates of the portable phone he answered every few minutes.

Valentino showed me the goods. I tasted a pinch and knew right away it was high-quality. I handed Valentino the money. When he had counted it, he said something in Spanish to the driver. The car stopped.

"We'll let you out here," Valentino said. He flicked a switch that unlocked my door. We were five blocks from the Spotlight.

I stuffed the cocaine into my underwear and stood on the sidewalk as the car sped off so quickly that my door shut on its own. A police car circled the block as I made my way back to the bar.

Valentino, Val as he told me to call him, warmed up when he realized how much, and how frequently, I would be placing orders. Axl and I easily consumed an ounce a week. Before long, Val started delivering to the house. We set up a schedule so he wouldn't show up at the same time or on the same day of the week. He would come alone, without the chauffeur, and would demand that Axl remain upstairs while we did business.

Rudy invited himself to the house one afternoon. He didn't have enough money to buy drugs and Lane was going crazy. Val had just dropped by and I had plenty to share. Rudy and Lane started coming by every day. Axl would smoke while Lane and I snorted. Rudy kept a close eye on the proceedings in case Lane should try to slip away with the pipe. Rudy stayed with alcohol only.

Sometimes, Charlotte came along. While we were all partying one evening, Rudy took me aside.

"I hate to bring this up, Simon. But I don't know who else to ask."

"Ask away," I said.

"I feel really bad bringing it up. And I'm sure it would only be temporary."

"Just blurt it out, Rudy."

"I'm getting evicted. I haven't paid the rent in two months. No matter what I've tried, chef jobs haven't lasted. I have somewhere to go with Lane. That's not the problem. It's...well, it's that Charlotte doesn't have any place to go."

"Where are you moving?"

"I got a live-in manager job at the Oban Hotel. You know, that crack haven on Yucca."

"That place is about as crummy as it gets, Rudy."

"Yeah, I know, but you can't beat free rent. And I'll get a small salary. So, do you think Charlotte can stay with you for a while?"

"How long?"

"Probably just a few weeks."

"I'm going to Italy soon. Can she do office work?"

"She managed a dance club in Miami. That's how we met. I was promoting a drag show and she booked the act."

"You in drag?" I scoffed.

Rudy covered his face demurely. "You should've seen me dressed like a ballerina."

I imagined the hippopotamus in Fantasia. "How many yards of cloth made up your tutu?"

Rudy did a pirouette with his finger poised on top of his head.

"Cute," I said. "All right, all right. Charlotte can stay, at least until I get back from Italy."

"Oh Simon, I love you," Rudy said, smothering me with a hug.

Not to be left out, Cicero came charging down the stairs to join Rudy and me in the basement.

"You know," I said, looking around the claustrophobic space, "I can make this into a bedroom. Charlotte can stay in the small bedroom upstairs. I've been meaning to make the loft bedroom into an office. Guess now's the time."

Rudy and I went upstairs. Charlotte, Axl, and Lane were standing in the kitchen laughing hysterically.

"Let me join the fun," Rudy said.

"It's a private joke," Charlotte grinned. Lane and Axl turned away, unable to hold back their giggles.

Rudy gave Charlotte a bear hug. "Simon agreed to be your new landlord."

Charlotte broke free and threw her arms around my neck. "You're so sweet, Simon! I won't stay long. I promise."

"Rudy said you managed a club. I was hoping you could help me with my business."

Charlotte shimmied while holding her thick red hair off her shoulders. "I'll be the best little secretary you ever had."

"On second thought, Rudy," I joked.

Charlotte took a seat on a barstool and crossed her legs demurely. "Or, I can be Ms. Proper, if that's what you want."

"That's okay. I like you just the way you are."

"A perfect match," Rudy said. "Two sex fiends sharing a house."

Cicero leaped into Charlotte's lap. "Hi, little fellow," she said, scratching behind his ears. "I'm your new mommy."

Cicero gave her a tentative lick on the chin.

I followed Rudy and Charlotte onto the balcony. On clear nights such as that, the Capitol Records building rose like a stack of silver pie plates on the horizon. The Hollywood sign glowed in a wash of floodlights.

"You've really done well for yourself," Charlotte said. "Rudy's told me about your background. I suppose that church group taught you a thing or two about business. I read that the guy who started it is a billionaire."

"It was perfect training for Hollywood, learning how to fool people into giving away their money. There's a lot of similarities between licensing a bad movie and marketing a religion. You've got to convince people that they're getting more than they see in front of them."

Charlotte laughed.

"What?" I asked.

"Lap dancing is like that. You let people think they're getting something, but they never see it. You're a trip, Simon. We're going to have fun."

Axl and Lane had disappeared into the basement while Rudy, Charlotte, and I were talking. A whiff of crack smoke drifted through the air, something akin to burning rubber and wood shavings. Rudy didn't seem to notice, but I was concerned about getting blamed. I went to the basement door and called down, "They're leaving in a minute, Axl. You guys better come upstairs."

"They'll be up in a minute," I said, as I returned to the balcony.

Rudy gave me a suspicious look, which grew into alarm when the basement door opened and Lane rushed out the front door.

"I guess he's ready to go," I said.

"Please keep that pipe away from Lane," Rudy said. "I'll lose him for sure if he starts that again."

Rudy motioned for Charlotte to follow him and they went to the car. Axl came stealing up from the basement. The wild look in his eyes told the story.

CHAPTER TWENTY-FOUR

Charlotte was especially adept at making excuses when producers called looking for their money. I kept meaning to explain more about what my business was about so she could help me with the contracts and deliverables, but I would lock myself in the basement with Axl for days on end.

"You're becoming a mole-person," Charlotte said, banging on the basement door one evening. "You've got to get out of that dungeon."

I pulled myself together and went with her to the Spotlight. And each day after that, Charlotte and I went out. Axl would remain at home indulging his paranoid delusions, often propping pieces of furniture against the door at the top of the basement stairs. Cicero's sniffing at the threshold probably made him think a monster was out to get him. It could take as much as an hour to convince Axl to remove the barricades so I could get into the basement.

The only time Axl ate was when I dragged him upstairs and sat him down in front of a plate of food. I'd have to watch him or else he'd scurry off downstairs at the first chance. Nourishment meant nothing. All he wanted was his pipe.

We never had sex anymore. Often, I slept on the couch in the living room to keep away from Axl's constant peering out the windows, sure that the police were outside.

Charlotte was a wonderful bar companion. The hustlers loved her. Super-tight jeans, spiked heels, loose blouse opened halfway down. She had the same style as Sandra. I also started taking tricks to the Oban for a quickie. The hotel was a couple of blocks from the Spotlight and Rudy always had an empty room to give me.

I lost all sense of the passage of time. Days were measured by the frequency of Charlotte's knock on the door to rouse me for the nightly excursion to the Spotlight. Weeks were marked by the empty baggie and the visits from Val. Wasn't I supposed to go to Italy? I put the question to myself upon awakening from a twenty-four hour sleep. I had no idea what day it was, much less the month. Axl lay beside me in a death sleep. I felt his face to check his breathing.

I ventured upstairs. Cicero came crashing down the steps to greet me.

"Good boy, Cicero," I said, sitting on the bottom step and cuddling him in my lap.

"Simon!" Charlotte came to the landing where she could see me. "My god, you're upstairs – and it's daylight!"

"Don't fuck with me, Charlotte. I feel like shit."

Charlotte went into the kitchen and poured a glass of orange juice. "Drink this," she said, pressing beside me on the stair.

"I'm sick of the drugs," I confessed. "But I can't stop."

Charlotte took my hand. "Are you still going to Italy? You're supposed to leave tomorrow, you know."

"My clients are going to kill me."

"There have been a lot of calls from overseas. I'm asked why you aren't responding to telexes."

I'd long ago bought my plane ticket and paid for the office at MIFED. Charlotte had faithfully followed my instructions and sent out promotional materials. Clients would be coming by the office there, expecting to make deals.

I might have pulled myself together and gone, even at that late date. But I knew I couldn't make it for two weeks without cocaine, and there was no way I would try to smuggle some with me. The Italian police had dogs sniffing every suitcase.

Charlotte put her hand on my shoulder. "We'll get by, honey."

I didn't want to think about it anymore. I went back to the basement and snuggled against Axl's unresponsive body.

The next day, when I should have been on a plane to Milan, I awoke to find the house empty. Axl wasn't there and the car was gone.

"It's no big deal," I said to Cicero, who'd come from upstairs the moment I opened the basement door. "They're probably shopping."

Yet a vague memory lingered, of Axl stirring about while I was passed out, and the faint image of him stuffing clothes into a bag. I rushed upstairs to the bedroom closet. Axl's guitar was gone.

Where was Charlotte? Had she gone with him?

A car drove into the garage. I opened the front door to find Charlotte carrying bags of groceries.

"Where's Axl?" I asked.

Cicero burst out the door behind me. I grabbed him before he made it to the street and put him in the house. I helped Charlotte with a bag that was starting to slip from her arms.

"I haven't seen Axl."

"Would Rudy know anything?"

"Rudy would call me if he'd gone to the Oban."

"I can't lose Axl," I said. "I just can't."

Charlotte began putting away the groceries as I went to the basement to look for clues. There was no note. He hadn't taken the remaining cocaine. I found his pipe in the garbage.

I went back upstairs.

"Charlotte, have you used the phone today?"

"No. It's been ringing, but I let the machine pick up. This is one day I can't face your clients."

I went to the office phone and dialed the Oban. Rudy picked up.

"Rudy, have you heard from Axl?"

"Hello to you too, Simon. Good to hear from you."

"I'm sorry, Rudy. You know how it is."

"All too well," Rudy said.

"I can't find Axl. I thought you might have heard something."

"Nothing, dearest. Not a word."

"Then, I'm afraid Axl has taken off."

Rudy called out to Lane and asked if he knew anything.

"Lane says that Axl mentioned something about going to see his dad if things didn't work out."

"I've spoken to his mother before," I said, "but he never mentioned his father. Anyway, thanks for the lead."

If Axl made a call before leaving, he would have used the kitchen phone. I hit redial. An eleven-digit long distance tone sounded. After several rings, a man answered.

"Hello?" I said. "I'm calling from Los Angeles. I'm trying to find information on Axl. Is this a number where he can be reached?"

"Who is this?" the man demanded.

"I'm a friend. Axl's been staying at my house, but he seems to have left without a note."

"So! You're the one."

"I'm concerned about Axl," I said, ignoring the accusatory tone of voice. "He didn't say he was leaving."

"I told him not to," the man said. "I wanted him to get away from Hollywood as fast as he could. My boy has been trying to recover from drugs since he was eleven years old. He's coming here and I'm putting him back in rehab. You ought to be thrown in jail for encouraging him! Don't bother my son again!"

A loud clack shot into my ear as the man slammed down the receiver.

I went to the bathroom and splashed cold water on my face. A haggard, weary reflection stared back at me from the mirror. I hardly recognized myself. The eyes were glazed and unfocused, like Lenny's were on the day he lay quivering in the throes of death.

"He's gone Charlotte," I said, helping her put away the remaining groceries. "My Axl's gone. They all betray me. They die, they turn to Jesus, or they just steal away in the night."

Charlotte tried to hug me, but I turned away and went to the balcony. Leaning over the edge and looking down, the century plants were green soldiers waiting to impale me on their swords.

CHAPTER TWENTY-FIVE

"Where is he?" a voice demanded.

I could hear the anger in Wally's voice as I pressed my ear against the basement door. He had sent people to my office in MIFED. When they found it empty and told Wally about it, he'd come by the house. Charlotte said that I had become ill and hadn't been able to attend.

"He's out of town," Charlotte insisted. "He went away to rest. What do you want me to do? He'll call you when he gets back."

"I don't believe it anymore," Wally said. "This is the end. Simon is no longer authorized to sell my films. Understand? I'm going to notify the labs and have his access revoked. You tell him that."

When Wally drove away, Charlotte and Cicero sat on the stairs near the basement door. Cicero whimpered as Charlotte tried to console him.

"It's okay, boy. Everything's going to be okay. I'll talk to Wally after he's calmed down."

I heard water running in the kitchen sink, then scratching at the basement door. Cicero had caught my scent. He placed his pug nose on the threshold and sniffed. He began to whine and Charlotte called him to come to her.

Craving demanded that I return to the tray of cocaine. The internal voices, which grew stronger with each line, told me never to open the basement door lest my soul be damned to eternal fire. Even so, bouts of hunger drove me out during the night to scavenge for food. I cut eyeholes in a towel to create a mask and wrapped myself in a sheet hoping the spirits would be fooled by the disguise.

Most of my clients accepted the excuse that illness had kept me away from MIFED, though Charlotte wasn't able to change Wally's mind about his library of films. He no longer wanted me to license them, but I had a long-term contract with him to sell the videos he produced. I still had deliveries to make on "Bel Aire Babes". Those proceeds would pay my rent and keep me supplied with drugs. Wally was a prolific videographer, concocting a new angle every couple of months – whipped cream boxing, even tossed salad wrestling. My Japanese client would take whatever he produced as long as the women were buxom.

Charlotte roused me from a half-coma sleep and demanded that I come out of the basement. She needed me to sign checks. We were going through invoices when the phone rang. Charlotte handed me the receiver.
I mouthed, "I can't talk to anyone."
"Take it," Charlotte said. "It's not a client."
"Hello?" I said, tentatively.
"Simon?"
It was Thad.
"I called to tell you that it's over."
"That's hardly news, Thad."
"No. I mean, it's really over. I'm going to die."
"What do you mean?" I smelled a ruse.
"I wanted you to know that I love you. You and my mother are the only people I'm contacting. Goodbye Simon. Don't be mad at me."
"Thad, wait!"
My plea was greeted by a dial tone.
I slumped forward in the chair.
"What's the matter?" Charlotte asked.
"I think Thad's going to kill himself!"
Charlotte laughed. "He's just trying to upset you. Suicide threats are a game people play. Forget he called."
"I believe him, Charlotte. I think he's going to go through with it."
"Okay, so what if you're right? What then?"
Her patronizing made me angry.

"Do you know where he is? Is there anything you can do?" she pressed.

"He's probably with his marine in San Diego. Although, that was a while ago. He's probably found someone new by now."

"Then there's nothing you can do."

"Thad said something about calling his mother. I've got her phone number. Maybe she knows something."

Charlotte sighed. "If it will make you feel better, give her a call."

"I'll bet Thad still wears the ring I gave him on his twenty-first birthday. He said he still loves me."

Charlotte said *ring* under her breath, shaking her head in disbelief.

I went to my computer and found the information – an address and phone number in Priest River, Idaho.

"Hello?" a woman answered.

"Is this Thad's mother?"

"Yes."

"Has Thad called you today?"

"Just a few moments ago. Are you Simon?"

"Thad has mentioned me?"

"I've heard all about you, dear. Thad called quite often when he was living with you. I suppose he told you he's going to kill himself."

Her matter-of-fact tone surprised me. "Yes! That's what he said."

"Don't get too worried, Simon. That's just his way. Been doing it since he was twelve. He even cut himself a few times, nothing beyond skin-deep, of course."

"You don't sound worried."

"After a while, you learn," the woman said. "Thad's always had a flare for drama."

"He told me you sent him to boarding school."

"I'm sorry," she said, apologizing for her laughter, "but I've heard the same story from other people. Boarding school – not exactly what I'd call juvenile detention."

"Thad said he had a trust fund waiting for him when he turns thirty."

"Not an ounce of truth in any of it," his mother said. "Too bad we couldn't have talked before you took him in. I'm surprised he even gave you my number."

"He never imagined I'd use it."

"I'll bet on that. We don't have any money," the woman said. "We're just a poor family. Thad was adopted. He had some crazy notion that we had stolen him from his parents. My husband and I adopted both Thad and his sister. Their parents were part of those religious-type folks who live around here. The police were called out to their farm one night and found the father beating both children. The court took them away. Thad's got a scar over his eye from before he was two. Maybe you've seen that?"

"Thad said he didn't remember how it happened."

"Well, that's probably true, but he was told how he got it."

If Thad's mother had been good enough to adopt abused kids, why was she so indifferent now? I wondered. It didn't make sense. I was about to challenge her when she continued her tale.

"My husband and I did our best. We gave Thad all the love we could. But when he got older, he'd say terrible things to us. He took money from my purse when he was as young as seven. He got caught stealing from the neighbors when he was nine. When he was a young teenager, the judge made us send him to reform school in Boise. I don't think he'll ever forgive us for that."

"It explains a lot," I said.

"Thad wouldn't want me telling you the truth about him. He lives by his fantasies. Thad said he worked for you, is that right? He said you'd given him a place to stay. Well, I can imagine what it's been like. Thad will say anything to make you care about him. Then he'll hurt you. That's his way."

I didn't want to hear any more, but the woman kept going.

"Thad won't kill himself. He just wants to make you feel powerless."

"Well, thanks for the information," I said. "If you hear from Thad, will you call me?"

"All right," the woman said. She took my number and we hung up.

I still worried that Thad would go through with his threat. I felt somehow responsible. My old beliefs told me that a person's actions affected everyone around them. Sin made it possible for evil to take control. If only I had given up drugs, if only I had been a better influence on Thad, maybe he wouldn't have thought about killing himself.

The shock following Thad's phone call got me to quit snorting coke, but I wasn't going to give up alcohol. Charlotte and I again started going regularly to the Spotlight. Hustlers substituted for the oblivion I found through cocaine. Sometimes I took a trick to the Oban early in the evening and found a different one to take home after the bar closed. But the more sex I had with affectionless strangers, the more I longed for Thad.

Scott had often accused me of falling in love with everyone I fucked. I was thinking about how wrong he had been as I sat at the bar one night, knocking back shots with Twiggy.

"Simon," Twiggy said, grabbing my hand. "I think I see a ghost."

The ghost took a seat at the far end of the bar. After ordering a drink, it waved as if acknowledging a casual acquaintance.

"Pour him a drink," I told Twiggy. "A Sloe-Comfortable-Screw-Against-The-Wall, isn't it?" I asked, loudly, to the whole crowd. "In fact, Twiggy," I shouted, "since we are witnessing the Resurrection of the Dead, set up the whole bar."

Thad paid no attention to my sarcasm. He finished his syrupy drink and then stood behind my barstool, leaning forward to place his soft lips on my ear.

I was lost.

Charlotte, who had been in the back room, raced to my side. Twiggy had sent a friend to alert her of the developing drama.

"Charlotte," I said, "I'd like you to meet Thad."

Thad held out his hand. Charlotte refused it, saying, "You look well for a dead person."

"Who are you?" Thad asked.

"This is my savior. If not for Charlotte, my business would have gone to hell a long time ago."

Thad wheeled me around on the barstool. "What's been going on?"

"I fell apart when you left! Like you didn't know that's what would happen?"

"I wasn't thinking about you, Simon. I never did."

"So why did you call me? Wasn't it enough to break my heart once? Did you have to drive the stake all the way through?"

Thad lowered his head. His silky hair fell forward and hid his face. "It's not what you think, Simon." When he looked up, there were tears in his eyes. "The guy I was living with found out he has AIDS. When I tested negative, he wouldn't have sex with me. He said he'd never have sex again. I was so torn up that I swallowed every pill in his medicine cabinet. He found me about an hour after I called you and rushed me to the hospital. I had to go through a live-in program for thirty days. I was going to ask Twiggy about you. I didn't know you'd be here."

Charlotte sipped her drink as she listened to Thad's story. She rolled her eyes until I pierced her with a sharp look. Then she pressed her lips against my ear and said, "I don't understand the rules of this game. I'm going to play pool."

Thad strained to catch her words.

"Charlotte said you were cute," I lied. "She lives at the house. I gave her the upstairs bedroom. I'm staying in the basement."

"Can I stay there too?" Thad asked.

Every fiber of my being screamed, don't do it, but I said, "Of course you can. I wish you'd never gone away."

Twiggy brought over shots of Schnapps to celebrate. The jukebox played "Cabaret". I looked at Thad and said, "Just like old times."

"To better times," Thad toasted.

Twiggy clinked his glass against ours. "I'll drink to that."

CHAPTER TWENTY-SIX

Thad and I picked up right where we left off, with me pawing him, horny as hell, and Thad scooting to the edge of the bed, ignoring my advances. A sensible person would not have taken him back. But I was in love with the Thad of my imagination, not the real person lying next to me. His mother's warnings echoed in my ear as I lay awake looking at Thad's face.

After a month, Thad said he felt "recovered." Neither of us had used drugs since he returned and had only gone with Charlotte to the Spotlight a couple of times. I hoped that Thad and I would finally start acting like lovers, but then a friend began dropping by the house to pick him up in the evenings. Thad told me it was someone he met during group therapy at the hospital. I convinced myself they were going to meetings, refusing to believe Thad was interested in the guy. The only way to endure the emotional turmoil was to throw myself into work. My associates, especially Wally, were overjoyed that I had resurfaced.

One morning, Charlotte found me sipping coffee on the balcony. Thad was in bed. I had already checked telexes and responded to an urgent fax from my customs broker. A light breeze rose from the hazy valley. Charlotte went to the kitchen to pour a cup of coffee for herself. She clutched it tightly to warm up her hands as she sat next to me.

"Why are you letting him stay?" Charlotte asked.

"It's simple. I love him. When I see Thad, there's a longing that rises inside me. It's hard to explain."

Charlotte shivered. "Let's go inside. It's cold out here."

We went to the loft and sat in swivel chairs around the office desk. Cicero raced back and forth between us as we teased him by throwing a tennis ball.

"I admit it's crazy," I confessed. "But it's no crazier than picking up a different trick every night."

"At least with a trick, you know what you're getting. And you know the rules of the game."

"But there's no love involved."

Charlotte sipped her coffee. "Love is highly overrated."

Scott called as we finished breakfast. He had just heard that Thad was living with me.

"And you were so sure he killed himself," Scott said.

"I should have called you before now," I admitted. Actually, I had not forgiven Scott for allowing Thad to stay at his place when he left me.

"Let me take you guys out to celebrate your reunion."

I suspected there was more to his motive than a simple celebration, but since getting relatively free of drugs, I was beginning to miss my friends. Scott and I had been through worse. He knew I would ultimately forgive him, whatever the infraction.

We arranged to rendezvous at a restaurant in Marina Del Rey. Charlotte was excited; she'd gotten an earful about Scott from Rudy. Scott had come to the Spotlight one night, horribly drunk, looking for me. Don didn't want to let him in, but Rudy, realizing that Scott was my friend, vouched for him. Scott ended up throwing a beer bottle at someone and the police showed up. Don held Rudy responsible. I ended up paying for the broken wall mirror.

At the last minute, as we were walking out the door to head to Marina Del Rey, Cicero looked up with pleading eyes. "You don't want to be here all alone, do you?" I said.

Cicero twirled on his back legs. He raced outside and jumped against the passenger-side door.

"You can sit in the back with me," Charlotte said.

Thad, who didn't like Cicero, grimaced. "Don't you think he'll bite the valet when we park the car?"

"Not my little Cicero," I said. "He loves everyone."

Thad rolled down the window. "It smells like dog in here."

Charlotte thumped Thad on the head. "Be nice!"

Cicero made fast friends with the valet, which seemed to upset Thad. He scowled at the boy as I handed him twenty dollars and told him to let Cicero out on his leash after an hour or so. The valet was happy for the tip and said he'd be glad to walk Cicero.

Scott had gotten us a table. Thad smiled when he saw Jerry, who looked as though he'd just woken up. Charlotte and Scott hit it off right away. Seeing them together, talking and laughing, I thought about my final days in the church — I was letting loose for the first time in a decade and the "the three S's," Sandra, Scott, and Simon, roared through Hollywood. That seemed like such a long time ago, though it had only been a few years.

After dinner, Jerry and Thad left the table and went to the bar. They laughed the way people do when they're flirting. Charlotte and Scott were so engrossed in conversation, comparing notes about their various conquests, that they forgot I was there. A couple of hours went by as I nursed a gin and tonic, followed by another, and then another. I staggered toward Thad. With all the drunken venom I could muster, I blurted out, "You don't seem to have a problem getting it up when Jerry's around!"

Rage welled up in Thad's eyes.

"You fucking hustler," I said, throwing my drink in his face.

A unison gasp rose from the assorted diners as Thad escaped out the door.

"Good fucking riddance!" I yelled.

Charlotte and Scott burst out laughing.

"You think it's funny?" I challenged.

"No, Simon. It's not funny," Charlotte said. "It's about time!"

Scott let out a whoop, "Go Simon!"

Jerry had disappeared into the men's room to avoid the scene. Suddenly, everyone turned toward the door. Thad stood there holding Cicero in his arms. When I ran toward the door, Thad slipped out.

I heard Cicero yelping in the distance and ran in the direction of the sound. It seemed as though dogs had started barking all over the neighborhood.

"Simon, get in the car!" I heard. It was Charlotte. She'd been driving around with Scott and Jerry looking for me.

"Where is Cicero?" I asked, desperately.

"Get in. Thad can't have gone far."

A few people on the street said they had seen a young man carrying a dog, but none of the leads panned out.

After an hour, Charlotte drove Scott and Jerry to their car.

"Call us if Thad shows up at your place," Charlotte told Scott as he got out. "I mean it."

Scott, stone sober by then, nodded. "Thad's not welcome there anymore. Not after this."

I couldn't sleep. Charlotte was even more frantic. We paced the floor, each casting furtive glances at the telephone every few minutes, hoping that Thad would come to his senses and call us.

"We could drive back to that neighborhood," I suggested.

"What if Thad calls?" Charlotte said. "He doesn't want Cicero. He just wants to hurt you."

"He's the one who's going to get hurt. He won't have to worry about suicide. I'll kill him myself!"

Charlotte shook her head. "How could anyone just take a dog like that? I keep seeing those eyes – those Cicero eyes!" She burst into sobs.

When the phone finally rang, Charlotte rushed to pick it up, dabbing her eyes with a tissue. She held out the phone so we both could here.

"I've got Cicero," said Thad's cold voice.

"You monster!" I yelled.

Charlotte shushed me.

"Let me come home," Thad said.

"Home!" I yelled. "This may be Cicero's home, but it's never going to be yours again!"

Charlotte cupped her hand over the receiver. "Calm down, Simon. Think of Cicero."

"Where are you?" I demanded.

Thad hung up.

Charlotte was furious, but when I too burst into tears, she tried to console me. I broke away and locked myself in the basement. I had kicked out a crazy trick one night who'd left behind several bits of rock cocaine. I still had one of Axl's crack pipes.

I knew the procedure, having watched Axl a thousand times. I dropped a few crumbs on the pipe and flicked a cigarette lighter, slowly drawing the smoke into my lungs. There was no time to put out the lighter or set down the fragile pipe before the narcotic hit my brain. It was like an out-of-body experience. My head became an echo chamber; my heartbeat, a drum roll.

When the room settled, ceasing to expand and contract with each breath, I glanced at the clock and saw that only twenty minutes had passed. It had seemed like hours.

I smoked for a full day before running out of the hustler's rock. By that time, I was crawling around the floor looking for crumbs I might have dropped.

Charlotte knocked on the door.

"Just a minute," I said. My voice was so hoarse I could barely speak. I got dressed and combed my hair before venturing to the top of the stairs.

Charlotte seemed startled at my gaunt appearance.

"A friend of mine called from The Pub," she told me. "He said a blond guy was there with a black and white dog."

The look on my face frightened her.

"What are you going to do?"

I had already gone to the kitchen and gotten a meat cleaver. I grabbed the car keys from the counter before Charlotte could intervene. She watched helplessly as I drove away.

With the meat cleaver in one hand and the steering wheel in the other, I thrashed the air, chopping Thad to bits in my mind. So what if I went to prison for the rest of my life? It would be worth it.

The Hollywood Freeway became a ribbon of blood. I ran the stoplight at Cahuenga and sped across Hollywood Boulevard. I made a right on Santa Monica and then drove on the wrong side of the street to get past traffic. When The Pub came into view, I double-parked and rushed inside.

"Someone's going to die!" I yelled, plowing through the saloon-style swinging doors.

Everyone froze. A few people scrambled toward the back door. An old man and his trick locked themselves in the bathroom. The bartender reached under the counter for a baseball bat that he used for defense against rowdy drunks.

"Put down the weapon, Simon!" the bartender said. "I've got your dog. Thad left him with me. Put down the knife before someone gets hurt."

I barely comprehended what he was saying. The bartender jumped over the counter and stood directly in front of my face.

"Do you want your dog or not?"

"Where is he?" I demanded. "Hand him over!"

The bartender cautiously lowered his bat. "Give me the blade and then we'll talk."

Suddenly, I recognized the bartender. It was Sweet Peter. I handed over the weapon. When I saw that the edge was bloody, I thought for a moment that I might have struck someone, but the blood was from my own hand.

Once he had possession of the meat cleaver, Peter turned me around and pushed me through the swinging doors. My car was still double-parked with the motor running.

"That yours?" Peter asked. He shoved me into the driver's seat and shut the door. "Hang on and I'll get your dog from the back room." Peter quickly returned with a confused and frightened Cicero. Peter stuffed him through the open window and said, "Go home."

Cicero pressed his head against my leg, shivering uncontrollably.

"It's okay," I said. "You're with me now."

Heading home on the freeway, I kept veering onto the shoulder, and once nearly careened off an overpass. By the time I arrived at home, Charlotte had already heard the story from Sweet Peter. He had mentioned to her that I cut myself and was bleeding.

"Nothing serious," I told Charlotte, but she led me to the kitchen and checked it out for herself.

"Are you kidding? It looks like you tried to hack off your fingers!"

"I don't remember doing it," I said.

Charlotte poured peroxide over the gaping wound. When I let out a yelp, Cicero began to howl.

"It's okay, little one," Charlotte said. "Daddy's okay."

Cicero wasn't convinced. He jumped against my leg until I picked him up so he could lick my face. Satisfied, Cicero went to find his drinking bowl. He didn't stop until all the water was gone.

While Charlotte wrapped my hand in gauze, Cicero climbed the spiral staircase. Before returning to the basement, I checked on him. He had collapsed on the couch and was snoring like an old man.

CHAPTER TWENTY-SEVEN

"He just lays there and watches videos," someone said. "He hasn't left the house for weeks."

"Should we call the police?"

Hearing such things being said about me, I would press my ear against the wall thinking that a neighbor had smelled the smoke from the crack pipe. I'd go about plugging every nook and cranny with bathroom tissue hoping to contain the smell, and then tack blankets over the door to make sure no one could peer inside.

The narcotic tide would soon crest and I'd drift back into consciousness, finding it hard to imagine what I'd just been doing, or why. Nevertheless, I would fire up the pipe again. The cycle of insanity would repeat itself.

Upstairs, beyond the basement, was a parallel universe that intersected mine only when sounds crept beneath the threshold or when I cautiously ventured out during the night in search of food and water. My old routines had returned, but with a vengeance.

Val started bringing along hustlers with his delivery of drugs. He knew my preferences and made excellent choices. He even primed them to know what I wanted. They never asked for money, so I knew Val was compensating them from his own profits.

I was an easy trick. It was enough just to have a naked boy with me as I smoked crack. The most difficult part for the hustlers was staying patient as I doled out the drugs instead of letting them have their own stash.

Episodes of lucidity would grip me, generally following a week of total collapse. At those times, Charlotte would take charge.

"If you don't start taking care of yourself," she said, "you're going to shrivel up and die. Look at you! Your belt is as tight as it will go, and still, your pants are barely hanging on your waist."

It was true. I looked like an unwrapped mummy. I had lost thirty pounds and my eyes were sunk deep into their sockets. My skin had the texture of wax paper.

"What about my long-delayed vacation?" I suggested. "Remember when I was going to take Axl to the Ritz? No time like the present. But there's no one to go with me. Val won't be able to find a trick on short notice."

"We'll go to the Spotlight and find someone," Charlotte said. "Go take a shower and put on some clean clothes."

It was Saturday night. The Spotlight was packed. I had hoped to see Rudy, but Charlotte said he didn't come around much anymore. The Oban had been busted by the police a couple of times and the owner wanted Rudy to stay in the hotel office in the evenings to watch out for trouble.

Don was in his usual spot playing liar's poker, intently studying the numbers on his folded dollar bill.

Twiggy couldn't believe his eyes. "Now I know I'm seeing ghosts," he said, happily turning to get a bottle of Boodles from inside a cabinet. "I've been guarding this for you. No one else drinks it, and Don stopped buying supplies."

I knocked back a shot. Twiggy kept them coming. As thin as I was, the gin hit me hard. Within thirty minutes, I was whooping and hollering, singing along with every tune that roared from the jukebox.

"Cabaret!" I shouted as Liza Minnelli's voice filled the smoky room.

A hustler turned toward me and winked. I returned the come-on with a sneer. Disappointed, he tossed back the last of his Budweiser and bounded toward the door. I was the last rejection he was willing to endure.

"Now you," I said to a hustler who caught my eye, "you're a cutie-pie. Want to join me for a trip to Laguna?"

The kid, a shirtless ruffian with a gallery of tattoos, glared fiercely and said, "Fuck off, faggot."

"God damn hustlers!" I screamed. I slammed my glass on the bar and rushed toward the door. As I pulled back the curtain, I turned and slurred, "I've had enough of this rotten place!"

Delirious with unfocused rage, I chased the passing cars and screamed, "God damn it! I deserve better!"

I stumbled down the middle of the road. Cars zoomed by, missing me by a hair's breath, as I ran toward Hollywood Boulevard.

Charlotte had been in the back, hanging on the arm of a cowboy fresh from Nebraska, who I had also rejected. She found me at Hollywood and Vine about to crash through the doors of The Derby restaurant.

"Simon, get your ass back to the bar," she said. "I've found someone for you and I reserved a room at the Ritz."

"What a girl!" I praised.

Charlotte led me back down Cahuenga, holding my hand as she steered me from the street. She sat me down across a table from a guy named Kevin. I'd almost taken him home once before, but decided against it when I realized there were track marks on his arm.

When I started to protest, Charlotte bent close to my ear and said, "I know Kevin. You'll enjoy yourself. Now relax."

We drove by the house so I could get some clothes. Without letting Charlotte know, since she was so intent that I take the vacation to chill out, I swiped a box of baking soda from the kitchen and made an emergency call to Val. This trip he came to the downstairs door to deliver the goods.

Cicero cried so pitifully when I appeared upstairs with my travel bag in tow that I didn't have the heart to leave him behind. "Okay, boy," I said, "you can go with us." He went straight for the car and jumped in the second I unlocked the door. He had ignored Kevin inside the house. Now that we were in the car, he eyed him suspiciously.

On the way to Laguna-Niguel, Kevin and I passed out. Cicero went to sleep on the floor under my feet. When we arrived at the hotel, Charlotte went inside to settle the arrangements. She returned after a few minutes, mad as a kite.

"They gave your room to another guest because we weren't here by midnight!"

"How dare they!" I growled.

Charlotte decided not to take the defeat lying down. She stormed back inside, returning moments later with the night manager. The man remained calm in the face of my verbal assaults, patiently explaining the hotel's policy concerning reservations. I hurled obscenities, getting out of the car and standing with him eye to eye.

Charlotte pleaded for a room. "You have no idea who you're dealing with," she said. "Mr. Powell is in the motion picture business."

The night manager was unmoved, determined to follow the rules.

Cicero shot out of the car just then, barking furiously and running circles around the manager. Charlotte tried to restrain him, but I egged him on.

"Piss on him Cicero. Hike your leg."

The night manager took a walkie-talkie from under his suit coat and pressed it to his lips, then to his ear. After receiving a message, he said politely, "Will you and your dog wait in the car? I'll make arrangements with your secretary."

I picked up Cicero and got back into the car, half-expecting to start hearing police sirens.

"You're not going to believe this," Charlotte said, getting into the driver's seat. "They had a file on you from past visits. When that idiot realized how much money you've spent, a room miraculously appeared. They're giving you a luxury suite for as many days as you want to stay. And get this – you'll be charged at the regular room rate."

My scowl didn't go away.

"You're going to take this and like it," Charlotte demanded.

"Did I say anything?"

Charlotte wanted to get us safely behind closed doors before Kevin did something stupid like pull out a syringe. Meth heads rarely thought about appearances. The bellhop came with a cart, but left when he saw that we only had shoulder bags.

"Everything all right?" Charlotte asked quietly as we approached the elevator.

"I'm fine," I said. All I wanted was to get settled so I could rock up the coke and do a blast.

The manager escorted Kevin and me to the suite with Charlotte following close behind. I apologized for my rash behavior and thanked the man for his patience. "The film industry is rough," I said, "and well, I just couldn't stand the idea of driving all the way back to Hollywood."

The manager assured me that I would have no more trouble. "You'll be given the royal treatment," he said. "Call me personally if there is anything that doesn't meet your standards." The man couldn't help but cast a suspicious eye toward Kevin as he said the word standards.

When he was gone, Charlotte opened the French doors and walked onto the balcony. The suit was on a corner of the building and the balcony stretched the entire length on both side. Every angle provided a view of the Pacific Ocean. The flecks of starlight highlighting the waves close to shore disappeared into the immense blanket of darkness that reached to a dim horizon, marked only by the lights of commercial ships and the occasional buoy.

"Amazing!" Charlotte said. "I've only seen rooms like this in the movies." With a sigh, she said she better go. "No telling what trouble Cicero has gotten himself into by now."

The suite had several rooms, including a formal dining area and living room with a fireplace. The bedroom was as large as most suites in expensive hotels. Kevin was fascinated by the bed, which was fit for a seventeenth century monarch. The walk-in closet had more space than my bedroom at the Sibley mansion.

After putting four logs in the fireplace and igniting them with an electric starter, we put on flannel bathrobes that we found hanging in the closet. I ordered a bottle of Dom Pérignon from room service and offered a toast to good times. After two unsatisfying glasses, I went into the kitchen and cooked up the powder I had gotten from Val. Kevin came to life when I returned with two crack pipes and a load of rock.

Until then, I hadn't paid much attention to Kevin's body. I lowered his robe and kissed him on the neck, expecting to continue exploring his muscular body, but he shook me off and scurried toward a small bathroom near the front door. Frustrated, I pounded on the door, but Kevin didn't respond. I went to the couch in front of the fireplace and loaded my pipe.

Paranoia like I had never known soon gripped me. I was sure that searchlights were sweeping the room and that any minute, the police would break through the door. I crawled across the carpet and pulled the drawstrings on all the curtains.

When the moment passed, I couldn't quite fathom what I was doing on my hands and knees. I went to the couch and stared at the fireplace. The glass pipe reflected the fire's glow as I did another blast. This time, my brain turned inward toward the comfort of past rituals. In the church, it was customary to set up a shrine whenever moving into a new place. Wasn't cocaine my new god? I left drugs on the coffee table for Kevin and locked myself in the bedroom, fashioning an altar on the nightstand with obsessive precision. I measured the spaces between the pipe, the butane cub torch, and the pellets of rock. In the middle of it all, I set a pornographic magazine opened to its centerfold.

I turned the bed into a nest, piling covers on either side of my body. The levees of bedding made a wall where I placed other magazines I had brought with me. With the next hit off the pipe, I intended to focus on the delectable male models. Instead, voices outside the window began whispering my name. It was a choral fugue.

"Simon, come forth." the voices summoned. I went the balcony. The ocean was barely perceptible under a covering of dark mist.

For two days, I rode the chemical rollercoaster, rising to sanity one moment and descending upon fantastic horrors the next. Kevin knocked on the third day. Only then did I remember that I had left him alone.

"I'm out of drugs," Kevin said, his face gaunt and desperate as I opened the door just enough to see him. "What are you doing in there?"

"Never mind, just leave me alone." I closed the door and went to get some drugs for him. When I handed them through the door, I said, "Don't bother me again."

Kevin's intrusion had brought back memories of my grandmother pecking on my bedroom door with the persistence of Poe's raven, Nevermore. Why wouldn't people just leave me alone?

"I'm sorry about the other night," Kevin said. "I got stomach cramps. It was the speed, man. I was coming down."

I barely remembered the incident. "Just go away," I said.

Another three days passed. I became so weak from not eating that it took all my strength to load the pipe. The vivid fantasies had faded into shadow plays. Barely audible voices told me that my life was over. "This is the end," they said.

Kevin's voice penetrated the fog.

"I banged on the door, but you didn't answer," he said. "I got into the bedroom through the balcony."

"I must have passed out," I said, trying to focus my eyes.

"Yeah, I think so. You looked like the Statue of Liberty holding that torch the way you were when I found you. I'm surprised you didn't set the bed on fire."

Kevin sat on the bed. "About a year ago," he began, "I was living with a guy named Bob. He survived off an inheritance from his mother. We shot up meth together. We didn't realize how weak we were getting. One morning, I woke up and found Bob's arm locked across my chest. When I picked it up, his whole body moved. He was dead. It scared the hell out of me."

Kevin took my head in his hands and looked me in the eyes.

"You're one blast from taking Bob's place."

"I don't want to die," I said.

Kevin rested my head in his lap and stroked my hair. "Go to sleep, Simon. I'll watch over you."

CHAPTER TWENTY-EIGHT

In a variation of a recurring dream, I thought that Reverend Moon had released me from my vows to Masako and matched me to a beautiful young man. I asked him, "Are you willing to have my children?" The youth began laughing. His body morphed to become a giant lizard. I froze as the creature fixed its mesmerizing gaze and plunged a slimy tongue down my throat. I gasped for breath, waking facedown in Kevin's lap.

"Guess that was worth cradling you all night," Kevin said, pulling away from me and going into the bathroom to take a shower.

I picked up the pipe and was about to ignite a piece of rock, but realized I better get something to eat. I propped myself against the headboard and called room service. Kevin finished his shower and went onto the balcony to dry off in the sunlight. He leaned back in the patio chair, propped his feet on the railing, and placed an arm over his forehead to shade his eyes.

It seemed an eternity before the doorbell rang and a cute server rolled in a cart of fruits and cheeses, along with the pitcher of Bloody Mary I had ordered. Kevin and I gorged ourselves as we sat on the Olympian perch while watching the surfers, each one a beauty to make Ganymede envious. Off in another direction, white-haired men played golf on a lawn that stretched as far as the eye could see. The retired gods of mythology, I mused.

Nourishment brought sensation back to our bodies. It seemed safe to get high again.

I motioned Kevin to follow me inside.

Throughout the meal, Kevin had been clasping and unclasping his fist. The glasses of weak Bloody Mary, following days of smoking crack, had not helped his withdrawal from speed. I order a bottle of Chateau Margaux, thinking the rich red wine might soothe his nerves. We got naked and took hits off the pipes. The combination of drugs and alcohol made us horny rather than paranoid. Kevin gave me a coy look as he drank straight from the bottle and dove onto me. I squirmed against the erotic sting of the alcohol he held in his mouth.

"I want to marry you," Kevin said.

The proclamation took me by surprise and I almost laughed, but stopped myself as I recalled the dream. I took a hit from the crack pipe. Deafened by the ringing in my ears, I read on Kevin's lips: Let's marry.

Kevin guided me into the bathroom and had me stoop in the tub. Ripe yellow fluid trickled down my face. Pagan magic, like the rituals Ernie and I used to perform when we swore to be blood-brothers for life, joined my spirit to Kevin's. I led him to the bed and positioned him in the manner of Leonardo's diagram of Man as the Measure of All Things.

"God is in me," I announced. "Ask me something. Ask me where the first humans came from. Ask me the meaning of life. I know, Kevin." Blood pounded my temples as adrenalin rushed through my system. "We are not Divine vessels," I proclaimed. "We are God's prison!"

Kevin watched expressionless as I danced about the room, a veritable Delphic Sybil. He grew bored and hit the pipe until our stash was gone. When the energy left me, I crouched beside the bed and gathered myself into a ball.

What was it, a day that went by? The next thing I knew, my eyes cleared and I found Kevin asleep. The empty drug container sat on the nightstand.

I telephoned Charlotte. She said she would come get us.

"Stay put," Charlotte said. "It will take me about an hour to get there."

I woke Kevin and told him we were leaving. He dragged himself from the bed and went into the bathroom while I contended with a new round of voices. No drugs had been needed to summon them. The chorus arose from within my head but reverberated against the walls:

Seven years, seven years. Abandoned by your God for seven years. You were given to the devil, you are master of the heavens, you were given to the void for seven years.

It had been seven years since I left the church and yet I was still haunted by notions of spiritual destruction. The voices diminished into a drone. One entity took prominence. It was my grandmother, Mandy. Buh-bee, she muttered. You'll remember when I'm gone.

I was a disappointment to my family, an apostate to my former church. And what was I to myself? I had no answer.

The voices subsided when Charlotte arrived and took charge. She gathered our things and led Kevin and me through the maze of corridors to the front entrance. Wealthy guests cast harsh glances as our troupe passed through the lobby.

The valet retrieved the car. I got in the back and lay down on the seat. Kevin sat beside Charlotte. As I drifted out of consciousness, I heard Kevin explaining to Charlotte that we had gotten married.

The voices were again pressing on my sanity as we arrived in Silverlake. I was sure my old messiah had sent avenging angels to torment me.

"Fuck them all," I said, rushing into the house. Cicero was so happy to see me that he went into conniptions. I picked him up so he could lick my face.

"He really missed you," Charlotte said.

"Where's my room?" Kevin asked.

The voices told me that Kevin was my spouse, that I must honor the sanctity of our union.

"Sorry, there's no room in the inn," I said. "You're going back to the Spotlight."

"You said you loved me!" Kevin insisted. "I saved your fucking life! You'd be dead if I hadn't been with you."

Kevin is Satan, the voices told me. He is Natas si Nivek, the enemy of God.

I covered my ears, but the voices grew louder. I took my pipe from the travel bag and balanced it on my palm.

"Into the bottle, you evil genies."

Kevin laughed. "You lousy crack head. I'm not going anywhere."

"Oh yeah?" I reached into the bag again and found the butane torch, flicking the button that ignited it. "Get out of my house!"

"You said you loved me," Kevin repeated. "Why are you doing this?"

I picked up a wicker basket that sat by the door. "One way or another, you're leaving. Go, or I'll burn down the house."

Charlotte flew down the stairs and extinguished the torch. She dragged me outside.

"What in the hell's wrong with you?"

I looked at the ground.

"Do you have any money?"

I took out my wallet. "About three hundred dollars."

"Give me a hundred. Go to Hollywood. I'll take care of Kevin. Get out of here before you do something stupid."

Charlotte followed me to the car, put my travel bag in the back seat, and stood watching as I drove away.

Go to Hollywood. You have passed the test of Moses and not struck the rock twice. You are Joshua who stands beside the Jordan. Your destiny waits.

CHAPTER TWENTY-NINE

Drug dealers kept a watchful eye as I drove down Yucca Street toward the Oban Hotel. When I didn't signal for drugs, they scurried into apartment buildings or dipped into alleyways.

"Rudy!" I hollered at the front desk. "I need a room."

Rudy came into the office from his living area. "Simon! Hey, want some beef stew? It's fresh from the stove." Rudy opened the iron mesh door that secured the office. He wiped his hands on a dish towel and gave me a hug.

"I'll pass on the food," I said. "Been to the bar lately?"

"Lately!" Rudy exclaimed. "Hun, I've been there every day this week. My boss is out of town. And, well, the beat-cop is a hunk. I fixed him up and gave him a special room. He's turned a blind eye ever since."

"Have you been naughty?" I teased.

Rudy giggled, covering his face with his fleshy hands. "Oh dear, have I." He rolled his eyes heavenward. "And from what I hear, so have you. Don said you got awfully drunk the other night."

"Yeah. Guess I did."

"Running through the streets like a madwoman is what I heard."

"You got a room, Rudy, or what?"

"Don't be sore. I was just saying," Rudy raised his eyebrows as he scanned the guest register.

"Something with water pressure, if you have it."

"How about the third floor? But the room isn't clean. Diana hasn't gotten to it yet."

Diana was the resident drug dealer who cleaned rooms in lieu of rent.

"Third floor's okay. Hand me some towels and toilet paper. Got clean sheets? And, uh, is Diana around?"

Her drugs were just as good as Val's, and I couldn't wait any longer.

"Oh dear. Should I contribute to your delinquency?" Rudy grinned, then said, "Only if you share."

"Of course."

Rudy disappeared down the hall and came back moments later with Diana, a short skinny girl barely twenty years old. She took me into Rudy's bedroom so I could test her product. It was well worth the two hundred dollars I gave her.

I left some on Rudy's dresser and returned to the office. Rudy handed me toiletries and linens along with a room key, then twirled on his tip-toes and pranced toward the bedroom. "Have fun!" he said. "I know I will."

Rudy had kicked Lane out a while back, after he started smoking crack right in front of him. Rudy might snort drugs like a four-hundred-pound vacuum cleaner, but he still resisted the pipe.

I picked up my bag and dragged myself up the steep stairs toward the third floor. On each landing, a drag queen called out, hoping to score a trick.

"Hey honey, want some tonight?" asked a Judy Garland look-a-like.

"My name's Crystal," said another, dressed like Loretta Lynn.

A striking seductress leaned against the wall beside the door to my room. "I'm Aphrodite," she said, affecting a sultry pose.

"Nighty Aphrodite," I said to the pouting goddess.

The room was the best the Oban had to offer, which wasn't saying much. At least it had a television, the kind that hangs from the wall suspended on a metal arm. The bed was nothing more than a spongy mattress laid down on a dingy shag carpet. Dirty sheets and towels from the previous inhabitants lay in a heap in the corner of the room. I put the clean sheets on the mattress and hung my towel on a corroded rod jutting from the bathroom wall.

Then I got to work cooking up the cocaine in a spoon. I put the bulk of the rocks in a pill-box, then plopped a sizeable chunk onto my pipe. Newly minted rock cocaine sizzles like bacon when it's ignited. When a critical temperature is attained, the solid material becomes a viscous smoke that slides into the lungs. Then it has you.

Voices rose from the street, policemen on walkie-talkies. A battering ram crashed against the door. I grabbed the pillbox and tried to find a place to hide it, but my hand was shaking so hard that when I tried to screw on the top, some of the drugs scattered into the carpet.

Paranoia gave way to desperation. I dove to the floor with my face inches above the rug and sifted through the fibers. At the end of an hour, I had made piles on the mattress of what I hoped were drugs. Examination of the contents revealed nothing but balls of lint, desiccated bugs, and moldy bread crumbs.

Tears formed as the drug's intense grip released me from its hold. I was so shaken that I hesitated to fire up again before getting some nourishment into my system. It was almost midnight, which also was good time to cruise Santa Monica Boulevard.

I stopped off at the Jack-in-the-Box and devoured a couple of burgers. Then I drove to the meat-rack, an area on Santa Monica between La Brea and Highland. I rolled down the passenger side window so I could call out if I saw someone who struck my fancy. I turned the heater on full blast to balance out the chilly night air.

At first, none of the street boys seemed promising, but then I spotted a fellow leaning against the concrete wall of a storage building striking a James Dean pose. His curly blond hair, cute face, and slim body was just what I had in mind. I circled several times. On each pass, the boy moved a little closer to the light. By the third go round, he had taken off his shirt and undone the top button on his jeans.

I slowed to a stop down a side street.

The boy poked his head through the passenger side window. "You're not a cop, are you?"

I reached into my shirt pocket and showed him my drugs.

"Man, I've been looking for you all day," the boy said, pulling open the door.

Even before I put the car in drive, the boy brought out a glass stem. "Give me some of that rock, man. I want to get high now."

"We'll be at my room soon."

The boy fidgeted in his seat.

"What's your name?" I asked.

"Name's Sean. Now, come on, man, give me a few crumbs at least. I'll wait before I light up. I promise."

"Patience. We're almost there." We were just about to turn onto Yucca Street.

"If you're not a cop," Sean blurted out, "put your hand over here." He undid his pants.

I rested my hand on his velvety stomach and slid down into his shorts. Sean pulled my hand away before I reached the prize.

"Okay, but none of that. Not until we're at your place. I want a blast first." With that he pulled up his pants, then shoved his hand under his belt to position himself.

Rudy was asleep on the office couch. I had to bang on the window to rouse him so we could be buzzed in. Rudy watched Sean and me as we started up the stairs. "Cradle robber," he called out.

"You're just jealous," I shot back, but Rudy already had turned away.

When we reached the third floor, Sean rushed into the room. "What a crappy place," he said, slamming the door with such force that bits of plaster fell from the ceiling. "How come you got so much cocaine and such a shitty room?"

I held out my crack pipe. "The room doesn't matter."

Sean sat beside me on the mattress and dropped a chuck of rock on his pipe. His hazel-green eyes narrowed and he fell backward onto the mattress. Smoke crept from the corners of his mouth like fog flowing from a container of dry ice.

"That's some intense shit," Sean said as consciousness returned. He propped himself on his elbows. "You must have some good connections."

I had just done a hit and was busy sifting through the shag looking for the drugs I had spilled earlier.

"Help yourself," I managed to say. Then, in a moment of self-awareness, I admitted, "I'll be at this for a while."

Sean and I fell into a routine. Sean would sit motionless on the mattress with his hands cupped over his ears. I would either dig through the shag fibers or stand sentinel at the door, peering through the peephole, sure the police were outside. When the drugs ran out, we collapsed beside each other. Unbearable horniness sets in during that twilight period after the last hit but before the moment exhaustion overtakes the body..

I took off Sean's tennis shoes, pulled off his socks, undid his jeans, and in a single motion slipped them off with his under shorts. We lay facing each other. I stroked Sean's baby-soft hair as we pressed together.

"You were lucky to find me tonight," Sean whispered, just before diving onto me with such enthusiasm that I gasped.

Then it was over. Sean started to dress.

"I can get more drugs," I said. "You don't need to go." I couldn't bear the thought of being left alone to contemplate the disaster my life had become.

The enticement worked. Sean slipped out of his clothes and snuggled next to me on the mattress. Judging from how quickly we fell asleep, I wasn't sure Sean could have made it to the street if he had left.

When we woke, our first thought was about getting drugs. I called Val, ensuring a much better deal than Diana offered, and after stopping at the teller machine, met him down the street at the Jack-in-the-Box. He didn't like to come anywhere near the Oban.

Back at the room, after cooking the drugs, I gave some to Sean, and then I loaded my pipe with three times what I normally smoked. A wire-like matrix superimposed itself on the world. I remembered the lines of energy described in Carlos Casteñada's books about his apprenticeship with the Indian sorcerer, Don Juan. I went to the window and exhaled the cocaine smoke into the alley. That's when I saw narcotic agents crouching behind cars parked on Yucca Street. A uniformed policeman stood in an alley cocking his rifle. Helicopter searchlights swept the neighborhood as drug dealers crawled under cars to hide.

Then the matrix disappeared. I had actually witnessed gang members harassing a freelance drug dealer. A junkie was sitting inside a dumpster where before I had seen a leg dangling over the edge and thought it was a corpse. The junkie jabbed a needle into his arm as I watched. Cars stopped without incident at the intersection of Yucca and Cahuenga. A police helicopter was shining a light into an alley, but that was nothing unusual for a Hollywood backstreet.

Rudy knocked loudly on my door.

"Give me a minute," I said, unsure who I was, much less the day of the week.

"You've been in there nearly five days. Are you okay?"

"Yeah, everything's fine."

"Just wanted to make sure you hadn't conked out on me."

I was beginning to think a little more clearly. "We're okay, Rudy. Are you going to the bar?"

"Girlfriend, you are so out of it. It's only nine in the morning!"

"Morning?" I muttered.

"Keep the room as long as you want. Long as you're okay."

"Thanks for checking, Rudy."

I felt disgusted with myself as I looked around the scrofulous room. I wondered if Charlotte had successfully dealt with Kevin, but I didn't want to go back to Silverlake. Home reverberated with a sense of guilt over unattended responsibilities. I just couldn't think about how I was squandering my good fortune in the film business.

Sean grumbled bitterly when I tried to wake him up. "God damn fuckin' shit," he spewed, rising to his feet and disappearing into the bathroom to take a shower. When he came out, shaking his head to dry out his long blond hair, I marveled at what a sexy guy I had picked up.

"Tell you what," I said. "I'll get more drugs and we can keep going in a nicer room. How about it?"

"Sure. Whatever," Sean agreed.

On the way out, Rudy shot me a look of concern and called me to the window.

"Be careful with that kid," he warned.

Before I could ask what he meant, Sean pulled me away.

"Aren't we gonna score some coke?" Sean asked when I pulled into the Sunset Hilton's parking garage.

"Don't worry. I'll call my dealer when we get a room."

"Your dealer delivers?" Sean asked, clearly impressed. He started to say something more, but stopped himself.

I gave the desk clerk my American Express card and told him that I wanted a suite on the top floor.

"You're in luck, Mr. Powell," then man said, reading my name off the card. "We had a cancellation and the luxury suite is available." He gave me the key, a plastic rectangle with holes in it. "Seventh floor, Suite 701. Just put the key card in the slot beside the door."

Even the hallway on the seventh floor was elegant, furnished with mahogany tables decorated with massive arrangements of pompom chrysanthemums and red gladiolas. The plush carpet muffled our footsteps as we approached the double doors to Suite 701. The door latch clicked open as if by magic when I inserted the card. Lights from the billboards along Sunset Boulevard flooded the room. I opened the glass door leading onto a narrow balcony to take in the panoramic view of Los Angeles.

Sean was uninterested in the accommodations. He plopped onto an oversized couch and glowered at me as I leaned over the balcony to gaze at the nightlife on the street below

Jump!

I leaned deep over the railing. Someone grabbed my belt.

"Get the fuck in here and call your dealer," Sean insisted.

I shook free of Sean's hold and sat in one of the balcony's metal chairs. "In a minute," I said. "Leave me alone." I felt disoriented, unsure where I was all of a sudden.

Sean went back to the couch and ordered a bottle of Jack Daniels from room service.

Voices began to chant, *Call Charlotte – sweet Charlotte.* Charlotte must be wondering what happened to me.

"Dude!" Sean shouted, jolting me. "Come on! You said you'd call."

Another week faded into a haze of paranoid delusions, with Sean rocking back and forth like a terrified child, and me glued to the peephole, watching every movement in the hallway with obsessive scrutiny.

Waking from a partial stupor, I forced myself to order food. I parted the curtains and opened the sliding door to allow some fresh air into the stale room. Sean opened the bottle of whiskey that he'd ordered on the first day and guzzled half of it. The shock on his system sent him to the bathroom with a queasy stomach.

Finally, I put in a call to Charlotte. The telephone rang until voicemail picked up, but I kept redialing. When Charlotte eventually answered, the hoarseness in her voice told me that she was just waking up. It was three in the afternoon.

"Where in the hell are you?" Charlotte rasped after clearing her throat.

"The Sunset Hilton. Can you come over?"

"Why don't you come home? Kevin's not here anymore."

"I don't know. I just need to be away for a while."

"You need to sign checks. And the lab needs your signature on some papers from the customs broker."

"Get your trick to drive you over here," I said. I was sure she had someone in bed with her.

"If I can wake him up. He's pretty far gone. We were up most of the night."

"I'm sure you were."

Charlotte sighed. "I'll be there soon. Don't go anywhere."

"I'm in a penthouse, Suite 701."

"You do know how to party, don't you. I'll be there soon."

Sean and I sat on the balcony, basking in the afternoon sun. Sean took off his shirt and leaned his chair against the wall as he propped his bare feet on the railing and rocked himself. He was so much sexier than Kevin had been in a similar pose.

"Where are you from?" I asked. There was something about Sean that made me want to know his story. I could imagine us staying together for awhile.

Sean opened one eye and squinted. He recited a truncated biography that, I got the impression, was well-rehearsed. "I'm twenty-one. I was born in San Diego. I went into foster care when I was eight." The mechanical recitation mellowed. "If the foster fathers didn't beat me, the mothers took baths with me. A judge gave me an emancipation letter when I was sixteen. I've been on my own ever since."

"Didn't you finish high school?"

"Naw," Sean said, pinching his left nipple so hard it became red. After a long silence, he took a black and white photograph from his wallet – an image of a chubby boy sitting on a woman's lap. "That's me and mom."

"She has a kind face," I said. "She's looking at you with a lot of tenderness."

Sean snatched the photo away and tucked it back into his wallet. He turned his chair to be more in line with the sunlight.

By the time Charlotte arrived, I had collapsed on the bed. I stumbled on my way to the door when I heard the bell, bruising my knee on the edge of the coffee table. Sean was still on the balcony.

Charlotte energetically pranced into the room wearing a billowy white blouse and squeaky-tight jeans. Her fiery red hair fell from the edges of a green scarf. She went straight for the bathroom mirror to check her face. Satisfied that everything was holding together, she gave me a juicy kiss on the forehead.

"Just what I need," I said, "lipstick imprints."

Charlotte led me into the light. "Darling, you look terrible. That lipstick's the only color you have."

I managed a faint smile as Charlotte got down to business, spreading out bills on the coffee table. Each one had a check clipped to it, ready for my signature.

"And here are checks post-dated for the next three months' rent," she said. "Just in case I can't find you."

"That's a pretty sad statement," I said, but I knew she was being realistic.

"Now for the home front," Charlotte said. "I had to call the police to get Kevin out of the house. I don't know what went on between the two of you, but he was convinced that you told him he could stay. I'd never seen him act like that before."

"How's Cicero?"

"He wakes up in the mornings and searches every room looking for you. We both miss you."

I didn't know what to say. I hardly understood what she was talking about.

"I've got to get going," Charlotte said. "My boyfriend is out front on his Harley."

As I looked into Charlotte's sympathetic eyes, the word *help* formed in my thoughts, but never made it out of my mouth.

"Take care of yourself, Simon. Cicero and I need you." At the door, Charlotte called toward Sean on the balcony, "Maybe I can meet you next time."

The door had barely closed before Sean was at my side. "Let's get high," he said, taking me by the hand into the bedroom. He squirmed out of his jeans and beckoned me to join him.

We leaned against the headboard, rubbing our legs together like two naked crickets, and loaded our pipes. Sean's hand shook so hard that an ember fell on the bed and burned a small hole in the sheet. He cupped his hands over his ears to fend off the voices of imagined tormentors.

On my first drag from the pipe, I thought an earthquake had struck, and the shaking bed seemed to confirm it. I jumped up and braced myself in the doorframe at the bathroom door. Sean stayed on the bed, unaware of the danger. I tried to tell him to lie down in the bathtub, but the roaring was so loud that I could barely hear my own voice.

Then everything settled. Whatever quaking there had been was in my own brain.

Sean tried to say something, but the words wouldn't form. He fell back and stared at the ceiling, finally managing to say, "Let's do that again."

CHAPTER THIRTY

Sean was removing the rag he always wrapped around his head to cover his eyes as he slept, when I said, "I'm going to be an artist."

The pronouncement was greeted by a blank stare.

I added to the fantasy by proclaiming, "We're going to New York."

"Aw, nuts," Sean replied. "You won't know where to score drugs in New York."

"A boy with his priorities in order," I said, but Sean was busy gobbling down a pile of scrambled eggs he had ordered from room service and paid no attention.

Watching Sean eat, I realized how famished I was. Room service brought up a plate of cheese and fruit, and though questioning the wisdom of ordering wine, I asked for a bottle of Bordeaux to go with it.

"We'll drive by my house in Silverlake and pick up some things," I said, functioning under delusions that made packing a bag and driving to New York to become a famous artist seem perfectly sensible.

"You're kidding, right?" Sean said, hardly believing it when I called the front desk to request the final bill.

Cicero leaped against the front door at the sound of my key in the lock and pressed through the second it was opened. He jumped against my leg until I picked him up. When he spotted Sean, Cicero stretched his stump of a neck over my shoulder and insisted that I hand him over.

"Hi, little fellow," Sean said, scratching Cicero behind the ears.

"If Cicero approves, then you're definitely okay," I said.

Sean held Cicero out from his body. "Hey man, your dog's into water sports!"

Cicero had peed on Sean's shirt.

"He does that when he gets excited."

I grabbed Cicero's leash from its hook and walked him down the block. Upon returning, I saw that Sean had taken off his shirt and draped it across a bush to hose it down. He stood in the doorway smoking a cigarette.

"I should have told you to make yourself at home," I said.

Inside, Sean walked onto the balcony, stripping the leaves from a branch of the fichus tree as he passed it. It was a clear day. The letters of the Hollywood Sign glowed white in the distance.

"Quite a place," Sean said, letting the fichus leaves drift into the breeze. He looked over his shoulder into the house. "Isn't Charlotte supposed to be here?"

"If she hasn't come down by now, she's probably in bed with someone."

I went upstairs and tapped on her door, with Sean following close behind.

"Wazzup?" a gruff voice responded.

"Hey buddy!" I shouted, banging on the door. "That's my wife you've got in there!"

The voice let out a desperate, "Oh shit!"

Through the door came the sound of someone scrambling for their clothes.

"You fucker!" Charlotte called out. "That's just my boss. Ignore him."

"Ain't funny!" the gruff voice shouted. A thrown shoe thudded against the door.

"I'm with Sean," I said. "You don't need to come out."

"Good," Charlotte said, adding, "Oh, Cicero needs a walk."

"Already done."

"Get lost," the gruff voice said.

Sean and I descended into the musty basement. It was dark as pitch with the bedspread I had hung over the sliding door blocking out the daylight. The king-sized futon on the floor and the entertainment center at its foot filled up most of the room. I stumbled around to find the overhead light and then went to the bureau. I opened a drawer to display my pipe collection – a veritable chemist's shop of Pyrex bulbs, test tubes, and glass stems. There were Cub torches of all sorts and canisters of butane refill. The torches were much better than using cigarette lighters on the crack pipes because they left no carbon residue.

Sean's face was like a child's on Christmas morning. He pressed against my back and reached under my shirt.

"Wouldn't it be great to try one of those right now?" he said. "Why don't you call Val?"

"Not this time," I said, to Sean's complaint, "Why not?"

"If I'm going to New York, I just can't."

"Then let me get high! Going to New York wasn't my idea."

"Okay," I relented, "but we have to leave tonight."

"Whatever," Sean said. "Just get the dope."

Val wanted me to meet him near the bar because he didn't have time to drive to Silverlake. He said to call again when I was in Hollywood. Sean stayed behind, watching television in the basement.

First, I went by the bank and got cash, not only for the drugs but also for the long drive across country. Despite my dereliction toward the business I had worked so hard to establish, I had enough money to get to New York and settle into a loft. I knew just where I wanted to live – in SoHo. Every nook and cranny of New York was familiar to me from my days selling flowers on the streets, fundraising for the church.

I tried to imagine what my future as an artist would be like, seeing myself in a bright loft, stretching canvases and applying tubes of paint, swirling the colors together on the surface with brushes and palette knives. With those weapons, I could fend off the worst of the Furies that plagued me.

The best place to meet Val was at the Oban. It would give me a chance to say goodbye to Rudy. Upon hearing the news, he wrapped me in a bear hug and began to cry. Yet he snapped out of the sentiment when I told him I needed to call Val. He raced into his bedroom and came back with a wad of cash.

"I've got such a trick in there, you just would not believe," Rudy said, "but he won't put out unless I get drugs. You could not have come at a better time." He had completely forgotten what I said about leaving, or perhaps hadn't believed it. Druggies often proclaim big plans, but rarely act on them after the high wears off.

Val had just made a run to San Pedro, he told me when I called to arrange the meeting. He added, "I have something very special, if you want it."

When I pressed for details, he told me he'd like it to be a surprise. I was dozing off on Rudy's couch when Val showed up, but jolted awake when he knocked loudly on the glass window. Val had untied his ponytail, allowing long dark hair to flow over his shoulders. He wore quarter-inch false nails, painted red, which gave his hands a claw-like appearance.

"What I've got in the car will cost extra," Val said, "but it's top quality." He took my hand, led me outside, and opened the back door of the limousine. Inside was a boy no older than twelve. He was naked except for loose fitting, cutoff jeans. The boy flashed an eager grin as he looked up at me. His dark complexion and raven hair told me that he was a freshly-smuggled refugee. I'd heard about such slave boys, but never met one before.

Val went to the other side of the car and got in. The boy scooted over to sit between us as the driver rushed toward the Hollywood freeway. I was terrified, but couldn't help looking at the child. He caught my glance and lifted his pants leg to reveal a hard-on. I thought about the sex games Ernie and I played when we were this boy's age. The memories gathered into a terrifying desire. I considered leaping from the car and taking my chances on the pavement rather than give into such a terrible temptation.

Val opened a briefcase and took out a baggie of white powder. The young boy's eyes grew wide with anticipation. He stroked himself leisurely, no doubt imitating what he'd seen his adult tricks do to themselves. Val put some powder on his palm and handed the boy a bronze straw. The child snorted the drugs like an expert, then stretched his torn pants leg down as far as it would go. An expression shadowed his face that can only be described as terror mixed with sadness and remorse. Beads of sweat poured from his hairline.

"Please, Señor Valentino," the boy said. "I go to home now, if please you."

"Take the kid home," I said. "This isn't something I want."

Val tapped the boy on the knee and spoke to him in Spanish. I understood most of it: This is a good client, and you obey, or I will not help your momma.

The drugs quickly wore off, and with the admonition, the boy again found his bearings. He rested a small hand on my thigh. Happily, right at that moment, the driver made his way onto Yucca off of Cahuenga.

"Here's the cash for the drugs," I said.

Val was disappointed that I didn't take him up on his special offer.

"You sure you don't want this?" Val asked, brushing back the boy's hair.

"I no get you trouble," the boy said, then plaintively added, "I make feel oh so good."

"There is someone waiting for me," I said, not able to flatly reject the come-on.

"I make him feel good too," the boy said.

The driver kept the motor idling while I hesitated, but he kept gunning it as he was nervous about sitting in an area with so many police cars roaming around.

"I can't, Val," I said, looking into the boy's disappointed eyes.

As the limousine sped away, I stood on the sidewalk watching until it rounded the corner. That I had considered Val's offer, even for a second, made me wonder where I would end up if I didn't leave Hollywood. Even if driving to New York to be an artist was a pipe dream, it might save me from utter damnation. I was sure that Val would try again. He saw that I was tempted, and he no doubt calculated that such opportunities frightened men when first presented to them.

I had to get out of Hollywood, and fast.

CHAPTER THIRTY-ONE

As good as her word, and Twiggy's prediction, Patricia had managed to get back to Hollywood from Peru. I wanted to say goodbye to her and to Twiggy and used Rudy's phone before going home to Silverlake, but Patricia's answering machine picked up, and Twiggy was nowhere to be found.

Gripped by an increasing sense of nostalgia, I tried to contact Scott. Perhaps I thought Thad would be there. I felt a sense of relief when no one answered. What if he had picked up the phone? I couldn't help loving Thad, still. He'd been crazy drunk and jealous when he took Cicero, and I had been equally out of control when I pursued him. But there didn't seem to be a way back to each other after that night.

I arrived home to find Charlotte heating up meals in the microwave. An old Steppenwolf song, "The Pusher", blared from the living room stereo. Cicero came to greet me, but with less enthusiasm than usual.

"Welcome home," Charlotte said, shouting down the stairs loudly enough to be heard over the stereo. "Sean must be in the basement. Haven't seen him since just after we got up."

I went to turn down the stereo and found Charlotte's trick sprawled on the couch. He opened a droopy eye when I touched the control. Not my type, but definitely a sexy guy, especially since he was wearing nothing but terrycloth gym shorts. A dark patch of hair covered his stomach, so thick it kept the shorts' waistband from touching his skin. He held out an apelike arm and grasped my hand.

"Name's Dan," the fellow said. It was the gruff voice I had heard through the door.

"Been in some fights, have you?" I said, brushing my index finger over a wide scar on his forehead.

"Had m'share," Dan said with a touch of pride.

"Simon! Get in here," Charlotte called.

Dan eyes locked with mine.

Charlotte motioned for me to come around the counter into the kitchen. "Hands off," she whispered sternly, wagging a finger in my face.

I smiled devilishly. "Are those big feet any indication?"

"You'll never know," she said. "Hands *off*."

"Okay, Charlotte. I'll be good."

"Yeah, right. Anyway, go check on your Sean. That guy looks like trouble. I hope your VCRs didn't walk out the back door."

I went into the small bathroom near the front door to divide the drugs before allowing Sean to see how much I had scored. While separating the ounce into smaller bags, crumbs fell on the counter. By reflex, I took out a credit card and made a line, then rolled up a dollar bill.

Val had come up with some incredibly potent cocaine. My eyes turned into a roadmap of red veins as the rush worked its way through my system. I splashed cold water on my face hoping to fend off a bout of paranoia. There were voices, but I refused to listen. I stashed the drugs down my pants and opened the door a crack.

"Get a grip," I said aloud, springing from the bathroom to make a beeline into the basement. Cicero tried to follow, but I closed the door too fast.

Sean was lying on the futon watching a bi-sexual video. My eyes fixed on the blanket stretched across the sliding door as a curtain. Shadow playing against it made me think that someone was outside. In a moment of panic, I stashed several baggies in a box under the stairs. Sean had been patiently waiting for the mania to subside. He watched eagerly as I set a baggy on a tray beside the mattress. I laid out several lines and handed Sean a straw. When the drugs barely gave him a buzz, he said, "Come on, man – rock it up. I didn't even think you liked to snort."

"As an appetizer, sometimes," I said, laying out a fat line and sucking it up. When I came down from a bout of mania, having fixated again on the curtains, my hands were shaking too much to try cooking the drugs. Sean didn't know how, so we continued with the lines. When we finally licked the last bits of dust from the inside of the baggy, I was glad. Sean grudgingly accepted that I didn't have any more. He wrapped his tee-shirt rag around his head and tried to go to sleep. I collapsed, lost in narcotic hallucinations.

New York! A dream creature shouted as if to awaken me so I'd hurry about my business and hit the road.

"New York," I repeated, sitting up. I had to leave. My life depended on it, and so did my art.

Art? Spoke a sarcastic voice. *When did you last paint?*

"All that matters is what I do from now on," I said.

The voice raised no argument.

"Come on, Sean," I said, trying to wake him up. "We need to leave."

Sean was lifeless under his blanket.

I let him rest and went upstairs to take a shower. I heard the water running, so I plopped down on my recliner to wait. Moments later, Dan opened the door.

"Howdy," he said, surprised to see me. He stopped drying his hair and wrapped the towel around his naked waist.

"Hope Charlotte is taking good care of that," I said. As I pointed at his waist, I saw the towel move.

"Charlotte's asleep," Dan said, backing into the bathroom and nodding for me to follow.

Dan placed his rough hands behind my head and pulled me forward as I knelt in front of him. He thrust hard and I started to choke, but his grip was too strong for me to break free. When he came, I threw up. Dan chuckled at the mess as he mopped the floor, pushing the towel around with his foot. He threw the dirty towel onto the shower floor and shoved me into the stall. With a smirk, he left the room, muttering to himself, "They always give the best head."

"Fucking Hollywood," I said, turning on the hot water to douse the tears that were streaming down my face.

I felt worthless and empty.

Cicero waited for me outside the bathroom door. When I saw the sadness in his expressive eyes, I said, "Do you want to come too?"

Pricked up ears told me he somehow understood. Wherever I was going, he wanted to be there too. Cicero sped down the stairs when I opened the basement door. He pounced on Sean.

"Your turn," I said. "Go take a shower. We'll leave as soon as you get ready."

Sean dragged himself up the stairs with a blanket wrapped as a toga.

While he was upstairs, I stuffed some clothes in a bag and then went into the office. I signed a few checks and hid them around the house. Later, I planned to call Charlotte and tell them where they were in case of emergency. Otherwise, I'd send her checks made out for the rent and other expenses. I collected my company checkbook and a folder of important contracts.

I wasn't sure how I would dispose of my business, or if I might keep it going at some level once I settled in New York. Charlotte could deal with the outstanding deliveries that needed to be made.

Even though I wanted to get out of Hollywood, I wasn't ready to burn all my bridges. What was it I heard in a low budget movie that I screened one time? Hollywood is a one-night stand that you stay with the rest of your life.

Charlotte was in the bedroom with Dan. I scrawled a note saying that I was heading to New York and that I'd be in touch. I left the note on the office chair where Charlotte would be sure to notice it.

I was retrieving the hidden stash of coke when Sean came downstairs. "Shit man. I thought we were out of drugs."

It was a lot easier to think about leaving Hollywood than to take the first step. As if it were as normal a thing to do as eating breakfast, I began cooking the powder into rock.

"Hell yeah," Sean said, watching me.

After drying the nuggets on a paper towel, I wrapped each one in aluminum foil and put them in a baggie. I handed Sean a piece, but managed to resist smoking one myself.

Sean took out his straight-shooter pipe and blasted off. He fell to his knees when the smoke hit his lungs, motioning for me to take the pipe before he lost his grip.

Cicero's ears drooped as Sean fell backwards onto the mattress.

Holding the pipe, smoke still pouring from the stem, I wanted more than anything to take a hit.

Think about your art, Simon. Think about the future.

When Sean regained consciousness, I insisted that we leave immediately. I grabbed a bag of dog food from the kitchen cupboard and took Cicero's leash from the hook. We got in the car and drove away. Cicero sat in Sean's lap and hung his head out the widow, keeping his eyes fixed on the house until it disappeared from sight.

CHAPTER THIRTY-TWO

Just do it, urged my body.
Follow your dream, came the counter argument.
On and on, for miles and miles, the battle raged. By the time we reached Albuquerque, one side had conceded defeat.

Sean suggested a motel at the edge of town where a truck driver had once holed up with him to do drugs and have sex. The motel owner came to the window wearing a dirty T-shirt that didn't cover the lower half of his beer belly. A spider web of veins covered the end of his nose.

"Keep the tab open until we check out," I told the man.

"Plannin' to stay awhile, are ya?"

"Need to rest up. Got a long drive ahead."

"It's goin' t'be extra for the dog," the man said, a Mr. Lynch, according to the motel license posted on the window.

"Add it to the charge."

"You stayin' here 'cause of the sign out front? The one that says A'Merican owned?"

"Just seemed like a convenient place."

"Y'know them damn fereners, 'specially them Indians, you know, from India, they're buyin' up all these places. Why hell, we're the only A'Mericans on the strip these days."

Before the surly man could continue, I urged him to get the credit card approved because I needed to walk the dog.

"Been drivin' awhile then, a'ya?" Mr. Lynch asked as he had me sign the credit slip.

"Yep, that's it. Dog's about to burst."

Once we settled into the room, Sean turned the television to an X-rated channel. The picture was wavy and unfocused, the performers more like pallid zombies than flesh and blood human. Sean couldn't get out of his clothes fast enough. Seeing the naked women, however faintly, made him as frantic as a starving man at a banquet.

After some food and water, Cicero curled up in a bed of towels that I placed on the bathroom floor. I joined Sean and brought out the drugs. The only time I saw daylight was when I forced myself to take Cicero for a walk. He was not used to being confined to a small room behind a closed door. He endured by sleeping most of the time. Otherwise, he gnawed on a rubber toy I'd brought along. The gnawing fed my delusions, conjuring images of a giant rodent eating through the walls.

The television mostly served as our lighting since the overhead bulb hurt our dilated eyes. Sean's gaunt face, illuminated by the greenish glow, took on the appearance of a death mask. His eyes began to drift independently, as if they were decomposing and falling away. His mouth locked to form a sardonic grin. I stumbled into the bathroom, suddenly remembering Cicero and realizing that I couldn't remember the last time I fed him. I found him stretched out on the bathmat. He was bored, but surviving.

Under the bathroom's florescent light, my flesh looked bleached and puckered as if I'd been in the tub too long. My chest and forearms were dotted with what looked like bruises, but I couldn't recall bumping into anything. My physical appearance should have raised an alarm, but I felt dispassionate, as if I were looking at someone else's body.

You can't live like this, I heard a voice say.

I stumbled toward the bed and loaded the crack pipe. On the television came a special announcement: Found dead in an Albuquerque motel room, one Hollywood film distributor and an unidentified drifter, both of cardiac arrest brought on by prolonged use of crack cocaine.

Cicero threw himself against the bathroom door with enough force to wake me up. I struggled to find the doorknob. A powerful stench flooded the room. Cicero pushed past me, desperate to escape the smell of the rotting excrement that littered the floor. I dressed, dragged a comb though my tangled hair, and fastened Cicero's leash onto his collar.

Before going outside, I felt Sean's jugular, just to make sure. The slow thump of a heartbeat reassured me that he was alive.

Taking in the clean desert air revived my senses somewhat. I took Cicero across the street to a convenience store, tied him to a pole, and went inside to purchase a quart of milk and a package of cupcakes.

The date on the newspaper by the checkout stand caught my attention. It was Saturday – more than a week after Thanksgiving.

Cicero tugged his leash as we exited, pulling me toward a sandy lot beside the store.

"I've never let a Thanksgiving pass without calling the family," I said, looking into Cicero's bulging eyes.

Cicero woofed.

I went to a payphone near the sandy lot so I could call Vivian while Cicero did his business. I rehearsed an apology, but gave up on the idea by the time Vivian answered.

"It's me," I stammered, and before Vivian could respond, I blurted out, "I'm sorry I haven't called."

"We've been sick with worry!" Vivian said. "I called your house on Thanksgiving and some girl answered. She said you'd left town – that you were driving across country. I was sure..." Vivian paused, likely to fight back tears, "...you'd been in an accident. You're all right, then?"

"I'm okay. I wanted to get away from Los Angeles. I thought that going out to the desert would do me some good. There weren't phones around."

The lies came as fast as I could think them up.

Vivian, expressing her worst fear, said, "You're not going back to that church, are you?"

"No, nothing like that! What would make you ask such a question?"

"That girl, what's her name – Charlotte? She said you were heading to New York. It's where we came to see you get married in that strange ceremony."

Telling her that I was heading to New York to be an artist was about as nonsensical as saying I was going back to the church, but I gave it a try.

"You remember how I love art," I began. "I want to check out the possibilities. See if I can get a career going. I know New York well, after all."

"Who's taking care of your business?" Vivian asked, always practical.

"Charlotte's my personal assistant. I trust her to keep things going while I'm away."

"Well, if you trust her. Are you coming through Sibley? I miss seeing you, Bubby."

"I'm traveling with a friend," I said, "and my dog. I told you about Cicero."

"He's a Boston terrier, right?"

"That's right. I'm out walking him now. He's here beside the payphone, straining on his leash. I better go."

"I love you, son. I hope you come through Sibley"

"We'll see."

Police cars had been speeding past while I was on the phone. Their presence shook me and, even though sober, I fought a bout of paranoia, convinced that the officers were radioing each other as they monitored my movements. I took a meandering route back to the motel. Once inside, I quickly threw the deadbolt and took up sentinel at the peephole.

Cicero jumped on the bed and snuggled against Sean.

"What are you doing?" Sean asked, starting awake. "What's that smell?"

The odor that drifted from the bathroom, to call up one of Lenny's favorite phrases, was bad enough to gag a maggot.

I went to shut the door when, suddenly, a loud bang shook the room. Someone was demanding to be let in.

"Police!" a voice shouted. "Open up!"

Sean and I jumped into action, stashing the drugs and the paraphernalia. Cicero barked furiously at all the commotion.

"Just a minute," I said. "I'm getting dressed."

I ran to the door just as one of the officers was about to shoulder his way through by using the passkey. Sean grabbed Cicero's collar and held him back as several policemen barged into the room.

"Whew!" each officer groaned as the odor of dog shit bombarded their noses.

"It smells like death in here!" the captain bellowed, a huge fellow with sagging jowls whose face had contorted into a mask of disgust.

One of the cops peered into the bathroom as he covered his nose with a handkerchief. When he pulled the door to shut it, the bottom scraped across a pile of feces. The freshly released odor pushed him over the edge. He barely caught the edge of the sink before vomiting.

"The manager said you haven't paid for the last few days," the captain explained. "He was afraid there might be something wrong, so he called us."

"I'm sorry officer. I was exhausted from driving, got this room, and collapsed. I just woke up and took the dog out. I was going to clean up that mess." I pointed toward the bathroom.

My voice was surprisingly steady given the circumstances. The policemen were easy to convince. All they wanted was to escape the horrid smell. One by one, they left the room. I heard a policeman retch as soon as he reached his patrol car.

"I'm terribly sorry, officer," I said, walking outside with the captain. "The manager has my credit card number. He was supposed to charge by the day until I checked out. I'll clean up the room and be on my way."

"That would be wise," the captain said. "Your story seems to check out. We watched you when you left your room and went to the phone."

"I was calling my mother. She was expecting me in Arkansas by now."

"You best get in there and work things out with that manager. There'll be trouble if he has to call us again. Now go on."

I stepped inside the room as the captain got into his car. I had soiled my underwear when the police entered the room. The smell must have been unnoticeable compared to the stench coming from the bathroom.

Sean eyes were wide with terror. He had been catatonic as he held Cicero.

"It's okay, Sean," I consoled. "Finish getting dressed. I'm jumping in the shower and then we'll leave. I don't intend to clean up the room. That fat bastard at the front desk can put the expense on the credit card."

Sean nodded absently as Cicero bounded from his arms and took up vigil at the door.

"Good boy, Cicero," I praised. "That horrible smell drove the cops away before they even thought about searching the room."

Cicero looked at me plaintively, happy to be out of his prison, whatever it took.

CHAPTER THIRTY-THREE

No Renaissance painter ever imagined the single-point perspective that is formed by the roads leading into Amarillo, Texas. As I drove, it seemed that the converging lines would go on forever.

Upon reaching the city, I couldn't stop thinking about the fundraising teams I lead there when I was in the church. How strange, a decade later, to be riding into town looking for a place to do drugs with my sex partner.

I pulled into a Holiday Inn downtown, just off the freeway, and asked for a quiet room, saying I was in town on business and didn't want to be disturbed. The polite Asian woman at the front desk gave me a room facing the back parking lot.

Once we settled in, I told Sean I was going to wash out his shirt and jeans in the bathtub.

"Aw, come on," Sean said. "When we get high, it won't matter." He examined the remains of our stash. "This won't last long. Why don't you get something sent from Los Angeles?" Then he paused before continuing. "Or, we could go back."

I saw myself at the bar threatening Thad with the meat cleaver. I thought of Kevin and how, in anger, I'd almost set my house on fire. I quaked at the memory of the young boy in the back of Val's limousine. The ladder of descent in Hollywood had no bottom rung.

On the other hand, I'd started with nothing but my wits and built up a company in the impossible business of film distribution. Could I really give it all up?

Before joining Sean, who'd already smoked enough crack to be glued to the peephole, I placed a call to Charlotte, telling myself that I wanted to see if there were any emergencies.

Charlotte picked up on the first ring and broke into tears when she recognized my voice. "Simon! Thank god you called! There's so much going on. Where are you?" Then she said more calmly, "How are you?"

"I'm fine. Sean and I are traveling. What's up? You sound frantic."

"I am. The landlord's been calling. He got upset that I kept picking up the phone and saying that you weren't here. He came by the other day and wants to know what's going on. He demanded to know if I was living here. I said I was house-sitting while you were in Europe. He said the neighbors have complained about strangers coming by at odd hours."

"He and his lover lived there for years. They are friends with most of the neighbors. I guess they didn't like seeing Val's car pulling up."

"You didn't leave a rent check. I didn't know what I was supposed to do!"

"I meant to send checks for the bills. I'm sorry, Charlotte."

"What should I do about the rent?"

"Are you on the portable phone? Go to the bookcase. Look up the word money in the encyclopedia Britannica. You'll find a signed check between the pages. Use it to pay the rent."

"I've got it," Charlotte said with relief. "The landlord should calm down when he gets his money. But you ought to call him. Do you have his number?"

"Yeah, I do. I'll call after he's gotten the rent check. In a few days. What else is going on?"

"Oh god, Simon. I don't know where to begin. There's a chance to make a deal with one of your Spanish clients. They want thirty films that were listed in the brochure you handed out at the American Film Market. You should contact them."

"Which films?"

"They're all part of Wally's library. All the masters are at the lab. I don't know how Wally is feeling about you these days. He hasn't called in a long time."

"Doesn't matter. My representation agreement is in effect still. I don't need his permission to make a sale."

Sean wrapped his legs around my waist. A puff of crack smoke filtered through my hair as Sean exhaled on the back of my neck.

"Fax the Spanish clients for me," I told Charlotte. "They'll need to issue an irrevocable letter of credit. Then we can order a set of video masters from the lab. I did a deal with another Spanish company about a year ago. Use that contract as a guide. Can you do that?"

"Sure," Charlotte said. "I know the contract you're talking about. I looked at it the other day to see when their next payment was due."

"Tell them the price is fifty thousand per title on a five year deal. Okay?"

"You realize that I'll get over eighteen thousand dollars if it goes through?"

"You'll have earned your five percent, Charlotte."

"But Simon! How will I get a hold of you? You know they'll want to negotiate. They'll need to hear from you."

"I'm in Amarillo."

"Texas?"

"Longhorns and all. I'll stay put until the deal is complete."

The drugs were almost gone by the time Charlotte called back. "There's good news," she reported, "and not so good news. The Spanish clients agreed to the price and everything, but they want to check the quality of the video masters before they'll release the money."

I hardly understood what she was saying.

"Are you still there?" Charlotte asked after a long silence.

"Yeah, I'm here." Slowly, an idea took shape. "Here's what we'll do. Tell the clients that I'll deliver the tapes myself. We can screen them together at a lab of their choice. After they accept the quality and release the funds, I'll give them possession."

"Are you sure you can go to Spain?" Charlotte wondered. "I mean, in the shape you're in?"

"What are you saying?"

"You're a great negotiator, Simon, I've seen it. But is this a good time for you to leave the country? Perhaps you should come back to Los Angeles first. Sean can stay here with me while you're away."

"Fax the clients. That's the first step. If they agree, then I'll figure out the rest. Okay?"

"I'll do it right now," Charlotte said. "We'll probably get an answer by tomorrow. Will you still be there in the same room?"

I set down the receiver without answering, picked up the crack pipe, and loaded a bowlful of rock.

Sean wrapped his arms around me. As soon as the drugs hit my brain, I broke free of his embrace because I heard noises that made me think the police were outside. I would have flushed the rest of the drugs down the toilet if I could have found them, but Sean had anticipated my paranoia and hidden the stash.

I strained through the peephole to see down the hall. Not able to discern any movement, I fell to the floor and laid my head sideways so I could peer under that door.

Sean came over and pulled me to the bed.

CHAPTER THIRTY-FOUR

Sean was grumpy as a troll when I tried to wake him up.

"Come on Sean, get showered. Then let's get something to eat. I'm starving."

I was energized by the news about my Spanish clients, and even though I didn't like the conditions of the letter of credit, I was happy to have the chance to visit Spain.

Sean couldn't understand my chipper mood. He was angry because I hadn't asked Charlotte to send us drugs. He offered to hit the streets and find a dealer, but I said no, that we were driving to Arkansas.

I put our belongings in the trunk, and in case we should get pulled over, wrapped the pipes in a paper bag and stored them in the tire well.

Cicero, always eager to travel, perched on Sean's knee and stationed himself at the window. When downtown Amarillo sank below the horizon, Cicero climbed into the back seat to curl up in a patch of sunlight.

The landscape had been monotonous and boring for hundreds of miles, but as we came to eastern Oklahoma, the flat prairie gave way to groves of mesquite and pine. The first of the Ozark foothills appeared around us and I began to get sense of home.

When night came, I stopped on the roadside to gaze at the sky. I had forgotten the stunning glory of this majestical roof fretted with golden fire, so aptly described by Hamlet. We might be the only creatures capable of pondering the universe. If so, life has meaning due to that very possibility.

My reverie crashed on the shoals of hard reality when flashing lights appeared out of nowhere. I'd not seen a car for miles, but there it was – a police car rising over the low hill we had just crossed.

Sean was sleeping in the back seat. I started him awake with a shout.

"What the fuck?!" Sean complained.

"We are fucked! A cop is pulling up. Sean, what's your real name? Your *whole* name."

"Where the fuck are we?"

"What's your full name, Sean? He's liable to ask me. I don't want it to seem like I just picked you up!"

"Sean Everett Lange, okay? Where are we?"

"Somewhere in Oklahoma. Just be cool. We don't have any drugs. We should be okay."

"Oklahoma," Sean repeated. "Maybe we will be okay."

Before I could ask what he meant, the cop was at the car asking for my registration and proof of insurance.

"Where are you headed?" the man asked. "You're a long way from California."

"Just passing through, officer. On the way to visit family."

"Y'all sure are in a hurry to get there."

"Was I speeding? It's so dark, and there weren't any cars on the road. I didn't realize."

"Step away from the car," the officer commanded.

"Why?" Always the wrong question to ask in such a situation.

"Face the car," the officer insisted. "Hands on the roof. Spread your legs."

The policeman at first told Sean to follow suit, but then said, "Hold on to that dog, son."

Cicero was barking ferociously, straining his neck out the window. Sean held him firmly by the collar.

The policeman, a Sergeant Stacey, took the car keys from the ignition before frisking me. Then he put on handcuffs and marched me to the patrol car where he told me to get into the back seat. Sean and Cicero remained beside the Topaz.

Sergeant Stacey read my information to a dispatcher and got back word that I had no outstanding warrants.

Having taken off his coat before he got in the driver's seat, his short sleeve shirt showed off his bulging biceps. Sergeant Stacey's dark hair and olive skin indicated American Indian heritage.

"I need to search your car," Sergeant Stacey said.

That seemed odd, given the report he had received, but I wasn't going to make the same mistake twice and ask why.

"There's two ways we can go about this," Sergeant Stacey began. "You can give me permission to open your trunk, or I can bring in the K-9 unit. If those dogs smell anything, we got cause to search."

"I'd rather you not go through my things," I said.

"The dogs can be here in an hour, but I'll have to take you to the station while we wait."

Cicero's eyes gleamed pink in the bright headlights of the patrol car as he stared in our direction. I was afraid Sean would panic and try to run into the brambles. There was no telling what his information would turn up if Sergeant Stacey called it in.

"What are you expecting to find?" I asked, with as much innocence in my voice as I could muster.

"You were weaving all over the freeway, but you don't appear to be drunk. I figure you been doing drugs. I'm always suspicious of California boys passing through these parts."

Sergeant Stacey's words reminded me of Lenny's description of California as the place where all the loose ends fell when you tipped America on its end.

"I just don't like people touching my things," I said. "That's all."

Sergeant Stacey radioed for the K-9 unit.

"Okay," I said. "Have it your way."

"I have your permission to search the car?"

"Yeah. I guess so."

Sergeant Stacey left me in the patrol car and walked toward the Topaz. Sean had gotten out of the car, holding Cicero on the leash. He had unbuttoned his shirt, despite the chilly night air. He had also loosened the top button of his jeans.

I saw the light from the glove box as Sergeant Stacey rifled through the car. Then he shone a flashlight over the back seat. Not finding anything, he spoke to Sean.

"You and the dog get in," the officer said, motioning Sean toward the back seat.

The officer walked me back to the car and removed the handcuffs. "Open the trunk," he said, handing me the keys.

"See? Just a bag of clothes and a lot of junk."

I hoped he would be satisfied, but it wasn't enough. The sergeant unzipped each compartment of my travel bag. Only then did I remember my magazines. Sergeant Stacey studied one of the cover images. He laid my travel bag on the ground and leaned deeper into the trunk. I thought he was reaching for the tire well, but he was opening the magazine to the centerfold. A moment later, he took the stack of magazines to his patrol car.

When he returned, I watched in horror as he shined his flashlight over the spare tire.

"You said you didn't have no drugs," he said.

"I left Los Angeles because I'm trying to quit," I made up on the spot. "That's why I'm in such a hurry to get home to Arkansas. There's no drugs in there, just my pipes. I know it was stupid to hang on to them, but—" I paused for effect, "they just won't let go."

"You really trying to give up drugs?" the officer asked.

"Yes, sir," I said, squeezing a tear from the corner of my eye.

The sergeant handed me one of the pipes.

"Break this on the gravel and ask the Lord's forgiveness."

I obeyed, and crushed the pipe under my heel.

"The Lord will help you," Sergeant Stacey said.

"Yes, sir. I'm sure of it."

"Are you gay, son? Is that kid gay?"

"Yes, sir."

"That why you didn't want me to go through your things, so I wouldn't find out?"

"Yes, sir. You never know how someone's going to react."

"Sit here in your car," Sergeant Stacey instructed. "I'll talk to that boy and see if your stories match up."

First, I saw Sergeant Stacy and Sean in the front seat, then I couldn't see Sean. About twenty minutes later, Sean came walking toward the car.

"Here's your keys," he said.

"Should I ask?"

"Ask what?" Sean grinned.

The patrol car sped onto the freeway and shot off into the distance.

"The fucker kept my magazines," I said.

"And you crushed our pipes, except these." Sean dug into the seat cushion and retrieved a couple of stems.

"It could have been worse," I said.

Sean scratched Cicero under his chin, and sighed, "Yeah, the guy just wanted a blow job. Something about Oklahoma. Every cop I've met here goes for that."

CHAPTER THIRTY-FIVE

My idea was for Sean and Cicero to stay with Dean while I was doing business in Barcelona. Dean and I had kept in touch since our meeting shortly after Lenny's death. Twice he had come to Los Angeles to visit. He'd arrive before Christmas, spend a few days, and then we'd drive together back to Arkansas.

Dean enjoyed the Spotlight with its never-ending drama. It was a problem that he didn't use drugs, even if he compensated for that by drinking lots of alcohol. The last time he came to Los Angeles, he never suspected that I was high on cocaine the entire time.

I had one reservation about leaving Sean at Dean's house. I didn't know if Dean would keep his hands to himself. For that matter, I had no reason to trust Sean. I didn't mind the episode with Sergeant Stacey; it probably kept us out of worse trouble. But if he had sex with a friend, that would be different.

Dean still sold insurance, working at home making cold calls from the phonebook.

"Guess who?" I said when he finally answered.

"I'd know that voice anywhere. Are you calling about Christmas? I'm still planning to come out there."

"Plans have changed," I said. "I'm on my way to Little Rock, and I have a favor to ask."

"Anything."

"Someone is with me. We're, well, we're sort of like lovers. I just found out that I need to travel to Europe on business, and I can't let him stay with Vivian. What do you think? Could he stay there?"

Dean laughed, "Sort of like a lover? Let's see, does that mean you met him at the Spotlight?"

"Try Santa Monica Boulevard."

"Say no more. I get it."

"It's okay then?"

"Sure. There was someone living with me, but he flew the coop the other day."

"Sorry about the person leaving, but I'd glad you can help. I'll be there around noon. Okay?"

"Can't wait to see you, and this lover of yours."

Cicero ambled to my side of the bed and nudged my hand to be petted. He sensed something was up. Sean finished his shower and when he came naked from the bathroom, I tried to get affectionate and dry him off, but he would have none of it.

"Fuck off," he growled, shaking out his long locks. "What the fuck're we gonna do for drugs?"

I wanted to say something like, we don't need drugs, we have each other, but I would not have sounded convincing.

"We have to talk," I said. "We're stopping in Little Rock."

"What about New York?"

"I still plan to go, but I need to take care of some business first. It's important, especially if we're going to stay in the money."

"What about me?" Sean said, softening his tone.

"I was hoping you would stay with a friend of mine until I get back."

"What about drugs? What about money?" Sean's mind raced through a list of anticipated hardships.

"I can leave some money with you. But my friend Dean is pretty straight when it comes to drugs."

"Nah. I'm not going to be tied down. You give me some money. I'll show up when you get back." Sean tucked himself into his jeans as if preparing a weapon for battle. Then his tough hustler face wilted and the neglected little boy surfaced. "You'll come back for me, won't you?"

I gave him a hug. Sean wrapped his arms around me and squeezed. He took me to the bed, shucked off his jeans, and then took off my clothes.

"You will come back, won't you?" Sean asked again.

"And what about you?" I countered.

"You're funny," he said with a grin. "I'll come back. We're a team, aren't we?"

"There's a truck stop in Russellville," Sean said as we crossed the border into Arkansas. "I've been there before."

My heart sank. I hated the idea of him going back to hustling. At Van Buren, I exited the freeway and took out money from a teller machine. Sean crammed the cash into his pants pocket.

"Those jeans are filthy, Sean. Let me buy you a new pair. And don't you want to take a toothbrush and a change of underwear?"

"I'm not heading to summer camp," Sean laughed.

Already, a change had come over him. His eyes were set purposefully.

"You'll need this," I said, wishing that Sean had asked for Dean's number without my offering it.

He put the piece of paper in his wallet. At least he checked to make sure he could read the writing.

At the truck stop, Sean strutted away without even patting Cicero on the head.

"It's okay," I comforted him. Cicero had his nose pressed against the window. "Sean's in survival mode. He'll come back to us."

Cicero pawed the window when a bearded trucker offered to light the cigarette Sean was holding. It took about thirty seconds to close the deal. Sean stepped on the side rail and swung into the cab. Cicero curled into a ball on the seat and looked up at me with a whimper.

"You really like Sean, don't you buddy?"

A confirming woof told me that Cicero understood.

When crossing the Arkansas River into Little Rock, I decided to go straight to Sibley to see if Vivian would take care of Cicero. The weather-worn mansion, home to five generations of Powells, appeared like a ghostly fortress as I rounded the final curve. Across the street, the tombstones of my ancestors glowed white under recently installed streetlights.

Connie's car was in the driveway. Vivian might refrain from asking questions, but not Connie. She'd wonder if I had AIDS, though I didn't believe the family had cause to suspect I was gay. They'd met Masako, after all. The story they accepted was that, living outside the church, we just couldn't make it as a couple.

The house disappeared in the rearview mirror as I headed to the bluehole bauxite pit where Ernie and I so often stripped naked, rubbed red clay and bauxite chalk on each other's bodies, and pretended to be Indians on the warpath. One of us always received a mortal injury in these make-believe games, requiring the application of a magic potion. All our games ended up being an excuse to touch each other.

I laughed at the innocent simplicity of those boyhood days as I threw a rock into the aquamarine waters. There was nothing simple about my adult feelings for Thad or Sean. I believed my affections for Thad were real. Sean was a hustler. But did that make it all right for me to treat him as little more than a sex pacifier? Was Thad truly more than a hustler? He genuinely seemed to love me. Perhaps he was just too emotionally damaged to form a real relationship.

I drove back to Little Rock trying not to think about it.

Dean heard the car pull up and came outside. The second I opened the car door, Cicero dashed toward a shrub.

"Where's Sean?" Dean asked.

"Come here, Cicero," I called. I caught Dean staring at me. "What?"

"Just looking you over. Is your hepatitis flaring up again?"

"No, I'm okay," I said, considering that Dean had given me something to say when Vivian eventually asked about my sickly appearance.

"You don't look well," Dean said.

"I'm just tired. You know how I burn the candle at both ends."

"I'd say the candle is running out of wax."

"Really, Dean. I'm okay."

We went inside and sat on a sofa that was turned toward the front window.

"Sean got nervous about staying with someone he didn't know," I said. "I left him at a truck stop. He's going to ride his thumb while I'm gone."

"Sounds like it won't be the only thing he'll be riding," Dean chuckled. "So, have you been to Sibley? I'm sure your mother's looking forward to seeing you."

"You're the only one who knows I'm in town."

Dean lit a cigarette as an excuse to consider why I was acting so coy. He would never go to his hometown and not let his mother know.

"Relax here for a few days," Dean offered. "I don't have a thing in the fridge. Let me take you out to eat, and we can pick up a few things."

"Would it be okay if I took a nap first? I'm really exhausted."

Dean went to prepare the bedroom. By the time he returned, I was falling asleep on the couch with Cicero at my side. Dean covered us with a blanket.

When I awoke, Dean was teasing Cicero, trying to get him to jump in the air for a piece of bacon. My mouth felt as though I'd swallowed desert sand and my eyes were nearly matted shut. Every muscle ached. I was an old man at thirty-six.

"Where am I?" I said.

"You poor thing," Dean said.

I extended my arm like a starving man seeing a vision of banquet food. "That bacon smells like heaven. And coffee! God, do I need caffeine." I poured a cup and took a seat at the table.

"Cream?" Dean offered.

"No. I take it black."

"Cicero and I made friends," Dean said, patting his thighs. Cicero jumped into his lap. "He slept with me last night."

"How long have I been out?"

"More than a day. I figured you needed it.

"Damn. I'm supposed to be in Spain."

"I was wondering about that," Dean said. "I didn't know if I should try to wake you."

"Do you mind keeping Cicero while I'm away? And could you drive me to the airport? I'll need to leave my car."

Dean reached across the table to touch my hand. "I'm happy to help out, Simon."

"Cicero won't be any trouble," I said. "But he does like to go exploring. He'll run away if he's not on a leash."

Dean scratched Cicero behind the ears. "We'll be fine, won't we boy?"

"I need to call Los Angeles," I said. "I've got a girl living at my house."

"A girl!" Dean exclaimed.

"Don't get excited. She's helping me with the business. There's so much to tell you, but I have to get to the airport."

"Why don't you take a hot shower and then make your calls. Okay?"

Clean, and refreshed by a generous breakfast, I called Charlotte. She had found a lab in Barcelona and gotten all the paperwork done. I jotted down the pertinent information.

"Please don't mess this up," Charlotte said.

"I'll be on a plane today," I promised.

Charlotte read off a list of the checks she needed and made me swear to put them in the mail before I left.

"When you get back," Dean said, sitting next to me in the lounge at the departure gate, "I hope you'll stay at my house for a while. You need to regain your health."

"I'm fine. That long sleep did wonders."

"I know this isn't the best time to ask," Dean said, "but I'm going ask anyway. Do you have AIDS?"

"How can you ask such a thing?"

"Don't be upset. I've just never seen you so thin. What's the word I'm looking for? Sanguine. You look sanguine. I thought maybe . . ."

"Well, stop thinking so much. I'm fine. You try running a business in Hollywood. You'll look worn out, too."

"I'm sorry, Simon. Anyway, I better get going."

"Yeah, you better," I shot back. Then, regretting it, I said, "Thanks for keeping Cicero."

"He'll be fine," Dean said.

Dean kept looking at me, until I said, "Don't worry. So will I."

CHAPTER THIRTY-SIX

The Spanish clients were at the gate to greet me the moment I passed through customs in Barcelona. David Rodriguez, the company president, was a middle-aged man, undistinguished except for his impeccable attire. His interpreter, Emilio Ruiz, offered stark contrast as an older gentleman whose suit hung on his large frame like a sack. Emilio was somewhat simian in appearance as I considered his round head and jutting jaw. I was captivated by his slushy Catalonian accent.

If it had been up to David, we would have gone directly from the airport to the lab, but Emilio intervened.

"Your secretary informed us that you had been on vacation," Emilio said, taking my suitcase before I could pick it up myself.

"Well, yes, I was, but our business is important. That is why I'm wearing casual clothes. I didn't have a suit with me."

Emilio said something to David, who gave me a sympathetic look.

As we passed from the terminal into the late autumn air, an elegantly dressed woman greeted us. She was waiting beside a black limousine.

"This is David's wife, Irene," Emilio said.

"Enchanted," I said, taking Irene's hand. She began speaking to David in an animated tone.

"Irene insists we get you to the hotel so you can rest after your long flight," Emilio told me.

"Thanks, Emilio. That sounds like a good idea. I am tired."

We drove to a charming hotel in downtown Barcelona. Emilio said they had planned on dining with me in the hotel's restaurant, which was highly regarded, but I convinced them that I had eaten on the plane.

Emilio made sure I understood that they had paid for the room, and that I should order anything I needed from room service. He promised that the next day, before conducting any business, they would treat me to a tour of the city.

Even though I knew I should sleep, my fingers involuntarily fidgeted with the bedspread. I found myself wondering if I could find cocaine in Barcelona.

"Fuck!" I shouted. "What am I thinking?"

I took a shower and went downstairs, hoping that a few drinks would calm me down. The hotel's bar was a dimly lit room with a chamber ensemble playing popular music in a bandstand. I found a seat in an empty, semi-circular booth upholstered in red leather. Couples occupied all the other booths. The women were well dressed in satin and lace. The men were more casual in gray or black sport coats. Everyone had a cigarette dangling from their fingers.

In my jeans and plaid shirt, with my stringy hair raked to one side, I was woefully uncoifed and underdressed. Maybe, I hoped, they would consider me an eccentric Brit come to Barcelona on his way to the Costa Brava.

The waiter, a young man with sexy eyes and a melodic voice, spoke a little English. He took my order for gin and tonic, and I managed in Spanish to ask him for bread and cheese. Just then, I heard a familiar voice. Emilio was speaking to the bartender and pointing in my direction. The ill-fitting suit was gone. Emilio now wore a blousy shirt and a plaid jacket. A wool overcoat was draped across his arm.

"Mr. Powell, may I join you?" he asked, approaching my booth.

Emilio was the last person I wanted to see, but what was I to do? "Of course," I said. "What a surprise to see you. But please, call me Simon."

"Señor Simon, I was concerned because we abandoned you so soon upon your arrival in Cataluña."

Emilio slid into the booth. I'd noticed when I first met him at MIFED that he tended to trespass on one's personal space.

"I couldn't relax," I said, hoping that would explain why I was not resting as advised.

The waiter had returned and was patiently standing a few feet from the booth. Emilio asked him several questions, and then addressed me, "Would you like wine? A good Spanish wine?"

"Sounds nice," I said.

A few commands from Emilio and the waiter dashed off without setting down my gin and tonic or the cheese.

"Barcelona is a wonderful city," Emilio effused. "You must get to know it."

"I can't stay long," I said. "After you view the master tapes, I must return home."

The waiter came back with the wine in half the time it had taken to get my gin. He handed Emilio the cork.

"Some of our finest," Emilio said. He sloshed a sip around his mouth and then spit into an empty glass.

I couldn't translate much of what was printed on the label, but the date was clear. The wine was bottled in 1934. It was delicious. Prodded by the gregarious Emilio, I drank the entire bottle. Emilio ordered another.

"God's blood," Emilio slurred as he raised his glass in a drunken toast.

When the band started up a saucy tango, the older couples began dancing. Even the overweight clientele undulated on the floor with remarkable grace. The music seemed to offer them the ability to contradict gravity. To my drunken eyes, I was in the midst of a Fernando Botero painting.

Emilio tugged my sleeve. "Let's go," he said. "I take you where the people are younger." He called for the waiter to settle the bill.

I held Emilio's arm to steady myself as he whisked me to his Mercedes. The car sped through Barcelona's wide boulevards. We passed Antonio Gaudi's famous apartment building, its façade appearing as if it had been melted by a flamethrower. Emilio drove on, ever faster and with more recklessness, eventually veering down a side road and screeching to a halt in front of a discotheque. A long line of people waited to enter the establishment, which was clearly a Barcelona hotspot. A majority of the men wore leather jackets and American designer jeans. Most of the women sported puffy down coats and colorful Spandex pants. First appearances proved deceptive. Not all the women were what they seemed, and the tight jeans on many of the men didn't have the requisite bulges to prove the manhood of the wearers.

Despite the long queue, Emilio took me straight to the front of the line. The bouncer lifted a velvet rope and let us pass. The club was illuminated by multi-colored squares on the dance floor, alternately flashing and then going dark. Elaborate contraptions hung from the ceiling, shooting laser beams in syncopation with the music. A coterie of people greeted Emilio the moment we settled into a booth. They all referred to him as *Tío Emi*. Emilio basked in the attention, laying sloppy kisses on everyone who approached. He made quite a show of fawning over the youngest guys.

The waiter brought Emilio a special drink called a sunset something, and indeed, the alcohol changed colors from blue to russet as I watched, emulating the effect of a sunset. The waiter asked me in Spanish what I wanted to drink. Emilio told him to bring a gin and tonic.

One by one, sexy young men flowed from the dance floor to squeeze in close to Emilio. On one occasion, I saw a cute brunette give Emilio money. Emilio reached inside his overcoat and gave the boy a foil packet.

My heart stopped. Emilio had drugs!

An overwhelmingly handsome man came and sat beside me. He spoke clear, if broken, English and minced no words in regard to his intention.

"Smoke hash with me?" he asked.

Emilio whispered in my ear, "It is okay. I sold it to him."

I followed the attractive Spaniard through a set of doors that opened onto a hallway of administrative offices. The fellow wrapped an arm around my shoulders. I felt the flexing of his bulging biceps as the muscles pressed through his silk shirt. He opened an office door and pulled me inside.

"What's your name?" I asked.

The young man closed the door behind us and locked it. "Felipe," he said, producing a hash pipe from his shirt pocket. "You are *Americano*?"

"From Los Angeles."

Felipe unwrapped a piece of foil. Inside was a yellowish-black substance that looked like a wad of tar mixed with honey.

"*Tío Emi* wants me to turn you on," Felipe said.

"I'm already turned on," I said, grinning foolishly.

Felipe pressed his leg against mine, lit the hash with a cigarette lighter, and offered me a drag.

The pungently fragrant hash made for a potent aphrodisiac. I unbuttoned Felipe's shirt. He undid my belt, let my pants drop, and pushed me against the wall. After exhausting my desires, Felipe kissed me on the cheek and disappeared. I found my way back in time to see Emilio hand Felipe money just before he slipped into the crush of dancers on the disco floor.

I guzzled several gin and tonics in rapid succession, but I was so high on hashish that it didn't seem to affect me. The hallucinogenic nature of the narcotic sparked a bout of paranoia. I was sure I saw Masako under one of the flashing lights. And that cute ass on the dance floor, didn't it belong to Thad? Wasn't that Axl's face on the boy walking by?

Pat Benatar's latest song blared over the ceiling-mounted speakers. The aroma of salt-tinged sweat and poppers wafted through the room. The laser beams altered perception such that the dancers became a series of tableaux.

"You look sleepy, amigo," Emilio said.

"Jet lag," I managed as an excuse.

Emilio reached under the table and placed something in my hand. His scraggly mustache tickled my ear as he whispered, "This will wake you up."

A glass vial rested in my palm. I looked down and realized it was a gram bottle of coke.

When Emilio began flirting with a lithe Scandinavian boy, I found a bathroom near the office where Felipe had taken me and went into a stall. In my excitement, I nearly dropped the bottle onto the tile floor.

My nose hungrily absorbed the friendly narcotic. Emilio had given me some potent drugs, laced with something more than cocaine, perhaps. My lungs constricted with asthma, and my throat was as tight as if a snake had coiled itself around my neck. Paralysis gripped my legs and I collapsed against the wall. It took all my concentration keep from passing out.

A knock on the door brought me around. "*Americano*, are you there?" It was Felipe.

I forced my arm to reach for the lock.

"We go to Emilio," Felipe said.

Emilio had landed the Scandinavian boy, who now was sitting in Emilio's lap.

"Perhaps we should go to your hotel," Emilio said, seeing that I was with Felipe.

We snorted from the glass vial as we drove across town in Emilio's Mercedes. As soon as we got to the room, Emilio laid the Scandinavian boy on my bed and undressed himself. Then he sat upright on the mattress. His hairy stomach rested on his haunches, hiding his genitalia under a barrel of flesh.

Sören, the Scandinavian boy, crouched behind Emilio and rested his cock on his shoulder. Felipe tried to excite me, but the strong drugs had made me impotent. The drugs were what interested me, far more than the proposed orgy.

Emilio and Sören rolled onto the bed like a porno version of Yogi Bear and Boo Boo.

Felipe laid out lines, snorted two, and left three for me. After inhaling them, I propped myself against the shaking bed. Felipe positioned himself for the taking if I wanted it. I stared at him, stupidly. I was so high, my brain felt like a block of ice.

Somehow, all of us ended up on the bed. Emilio and I snorted lines off the boys' chests. I kept wishing I had the means to cook the powder into rock.

During a lull in the sex play, Emilio asked if everything was satisfactory – as if this had been the arrangement of a gracious host.

"Well, I'd rather be smoking this than snorting it."

Emilio smiled, rolled off the bed, and found his overcoat. He reached inside the lining and took out a vial of rocks.

"Emilio! You are a satyr!" I said, patting his naked stomach.

Sören and Felipe stared at the rock with something akin to horror.

"You can use my hash pipe," Felipe said, reluctantly.

I placed a chunk of rock on the bowl. The mixture of rock cocaine and hash resin produced a narcotic effect more potent than anything I'd ever experienced. I was sure I heard someone knock on the door and sought refuge under the bed. The carpet fibers caught my attention and I began sifting through them, sure we'd dropped some of the rock.

Emilio laughed at my mania. "You should limit yourself to snorting, my American friend."

As the intoxication crested, I pulled myself onto a chair and I stared into the distance. It took some time, but eventually the crack released its grip. Emilio was again having sex with Sören.

Felipe looked glum when I picked up the pipe. "Must you smoke more, *señor?*"

I smiled. "Sure you don't want to join me?"

"Very sure," Felipe said.

With the next hit, not only did I see searchlights at the window, I heard footsteps marching down the hallway. It sounded like an army battalion. I hurriedly dressed and waited for the inevitable arrest.

Around four in the morning, Emilio decided to leave. He motioned for Sören and Felipe to follow.

"We have much to do tomorrow," Emilio said, addressing me.

Felipe asked to stay, which I appreciated. I felt anxious about being left alone. Emilio spoke in stern Spanish to Felipe, admonishing him not to steal anything – and to be kind.

CHAPTER THIRTY-SEVEN

I felt like Schrödinger's cat, both dead and alive. Better I had not formed the thought because, the moment I did, I found myself facing a new day and no quantum ambiguity could protect me from it.

"What was that club called?" I asked Felipe as we got dressed.

"*Muchachos*. It is biggest disco in Barcelona."

"And Emilio. He goes there often?"

Felipe walked into the bathroom to survey his face, popping a couple of pimples before responding. "It is Emilio's club."

"Really." That explained the way the bouncer treated Emilio, not to mention the access Felipe had to the administrative offices.

"But, you know Emilio," Felipe said, implying a question.

"I thought he was just a translator. I license video. He came along with one of my clients. Do you know David, Emilio's friend?"

Felipe seemed surprised by my ignorance. "What kind of video you sell?"

"Mostly horror pictures and low-budget action films."

Felipe laughed. "You sell the films that are not porno?"

"You're right. I don't sell porno."

"But Emilio makes porno." Felipe was genuinely confused. "David Rodriguez is partner. He, how do you say, takes the money and cleans it."

"Money laundering?"

"*Sí*. That is the word, laundering. Maybe I shouldn't tell you. Emilio said before he left that I should not say too much."

"Don't worry. I won't get you in trouble."

Felipe sat up. "I am in many films by Emilio."

"Perhaps I can see them someday."

Felipe smiled. "I think you have the real Felipe. No need a movie."

I placed my arm around Felipe's shoulder. "Thanks for staying with me."

"You smoke *coca*. I know what this does. I was afraid for you."

"Thank you, Felipe." I kissed him on the cheek.

"You should be careful, *señor*."

"Careful of what, Felipe?"

"Señor Ruiz, Señor Rodriguez, they are dangerous men. Do what you must do, and go home."

"You're serious, aren't you?"

"*Muy*, very."

"You saw how Emilio treated me. He was generous."

"Because he needs you," Felipe cautioned. "When you finish business, you must go home to America."

Felipe's warning sent a chill through me. The realization struck me that I was on foreign soil, at the mercy of people I knew nothing about.

A loud knock came at the door. Through the peephole, I recognized Emilio.

"You're dressed!" Emilio said as I allowed him to come in.

"And ready for business," I said.

Felipe remained seated on the bed. He and Emilio carried on a lengthy conversation in Spanish. Whatever they spoke about, it put Felipe in a cheerful mood.

"Must be good news," I said.

"*Sí*. Soon I start new film for Emilio." Felipe immediately realized that I was not supposed to know about Emilio's business, but having already said too much, he continued, "Sören too. We are the stars."

"Bound to be a hit," I said, winking at Emilio. "Felipe explained that you make movies."

Emilio smiled. "I will wait for you in the lobby," he said to Felipe, and then to me, "Is the lab ready for us to view the videos?"

Felipe gave me a prolonged kiss, keeping one eye on Emilio as he whispered, "Do not stay long, *señor*."

I made a call to the lab that Charlotte had arranged through the customs broker. They said they could accommodate us, but complained about the short notice. When I mentioned that I had clients pressuring me, and that it was David Rodriguez, the woman changed her tune. A screening room would be reserved for the entire afternoon.

David and Emilio were sitting in the foyer by a window overlooking the bustling boulevard. It was a sunny day. I was relieved to see David in casual attire. I didn't feel as underdressed as I had before.

Emilio interpreted for David.

"Irene sends her greetings. She might join us later. Will the lab receive us?"

"Everything's set," I confirmed. "We have a screening room starting at one o'clock."

"Well, it's eleven now," Emilio said. "Why don't we eat?"

Food had meant so little to me for such a long time that considering a meal as something important seemed strange. Dean probably wasn't the only person wondering about the cause of my skeletal physique.

We arrived at a restaurant specializing in Andalusian cuisine – smoked shellfish appetizers and unfamiliar varieties of seafood stuffed, steamed, baked, and fried, all served with generous portions of spicy couscous. The waiters all knew David and Emilio. We were given a table in a private room that was designed like a Spanish galleon with fishing nets stretched from ceiling to floor, and strewn with plasticized ocean fauna. The walls were decorated with rope moorings and life preservers.

"David isn't worried about the videotapes," Emilio said as our conversation turned to business. "We're sure they'll be fine." Emilio looked at David. "What interests us is the fact that you can arrange so many titles. Your catalog has dozens of films, yes? Over the years, we have noticed that you continually find new films."

I was struck by the fact that David and Emilio had been tracking my career.

"Are these truly your films?" Emilio challenged.

"I have contracts with the owners."

"Yes. The owners. And who owns the films? The original producers?"

These were thorny issues dealing with the legality of what constituted non-theatrical rights.

"There's a long chain-of-title on most of them," I said, trying to steer clear of specifics.

"Chain-of-title," Emilio repeated. "You can document the chain-of-title?"

I took a sip from my water glass with a determinedly steady hand. "I can provide whatever documentation you need."

Emilio reared back in his chair, gently stroking his mustache. "The titles you are able to acquire, such a thing is not possible for us," he said. "We need many films."

"How many films do you need?" I asked.

David smiled as Emilio asked, "How many can you find?"

I raced through a mental Rolodex. Many people had stopped talking to me, but I had no doubt they'd return if I came with cash in hand. Nothing engendered forgiveness quicker than a fat check. "Hundreds," I finally said, "if you make a firm commitment."

"*Sí, bueno,*" Emilio said, rising to his feet.

David touched Emilio's arm to ask what was being said. As Emilio filled him in, David's face wrinkled in a worried expression. "We must show the Spanish authorities that you have the right to sell the films," Emilio translated. "Documentation is important. We trust you on quality."

"Definitely not a problem," I said. "But the video stores will care about the tapes; you should view the masters to be sure."

Emilio chocked on an open-throated laugh. "You still do not understand, my friend. No one knows what an old film is worth. We license a film from you and make contracts with many companies around Spain. Money goes into circulation."

"I think I get the picture," I said, slapping my forehead, and risking to say, "You want to launder money."

"Make the money legitimate," Emilio corrected.

"Money from your films?" I asked.

Emilio frowned. "This does not concern you."

I recalled Felipe's warning and figured I better not ask any more questions.

"My films have limited value," Emilio said. "We need to report more money than my films can make."

Emilio was telling me it was drug money that needed laundering. It suddenly struck me that I was joining illegal activities on an international scale.

Both Emilio and David studied my reaction to all that had been said.

"None of this is a problem for me," I said with a smile. The danger in Emilio's proposal was oddly alluring.

"*Bueno!*" Emilio exclaimed.

"*Bueno*," David repeated.

Emilio took my hand in a vigorous handshake. "Trust no one," he said sternly, pulling me close. "No one must know about this arrangement."

Despite their professed lack of interest in the quality of the video master, David and Emilio studied the films closely as we sat in a screening room at the lab.

"Send us quality this good," Emilio said after viewing the last video. "Then, we never have a problem."

"Of course," I said.

"About the price," Emilio began. "You will need money to negotiate with your Hollywood contacts. Our lawyer will write up an agreement."

I was sure the document would record more money than they would put into my account.

"Here's what we propose," Emilio said. "You manage your contracts. For the Spanish authorities, to authorize the transfer of American dollars, we will make new contracts showing fifty thousand dollars for each film."

Emilio was talking about millions.

"At first, we will give you two hundred thousand dollars."

"With capital like that," I suggested, "we could purchase the Spanish rights to independent films. Movies that could make millions."

Emilio thought for a moment and then said, "Such films would arouse attention. The Spanish government would ask many questions. Fifty thousand a title on paper, this will not be noticed. The contract will say the money is an advance against royalties. Acquire as many titles as possible."

"This I can do," I said with confidence.

"Keep your finances in order," Emilio said. "Otherwise, you stop being useful."

Again I recalled Felipe's warnings. "Don't worry," I said. "You can depend on me."

We prepared contracts at David's office – one set for me, one for the Spanish authorities. I signed them all. Everyone was happy.

"Now I show you Barcelona," Emilio said. "Or we can go to my villa on the Costa Brava, a few hundred kilometers from here. Perhaps you like to gamble in Monte Carlo?"

"Your offer is tempting," I said, "but Christmas is near. I should get back to the United States. I promised my family I would come home for the holidays."

"Good to be with *su familia*," Emilio said. "And yes, I should tend to my own children, Felipe and Sören. We start filming after Christmas."

"Felipe is a sweet fellow," I said. "Take good care of him."

"Of course," Emilio said. "He is one of my boys."

CHAPTER THIRTY-EIGHT

Dean met me at the airport. The first thing he told me was that Sean had been calling. "He phoned last night," Dean said. "He gave me a number for a motel somewhere in Texas."

As soon as we arrived at Dean's house, I rushed to the phone. Sean answered after what seemed like a thousand rings.

"Sean, I'm back," I said enthusiastically, to no response. "Sean?"

"Yeah," said a barely audible voice.

"Should I come get you?"

Another moment of silence, and then, "Where are you?"

"Little Rock."

"I'll be there tomorrow."

"You'll call when you get into town?"

"Yeah," Sean said, abruptly ending the conversation.

Dean scurried about the house vacuuming while I unpacked.

"Aren't you curious about my trip?" I asked Dean, later, as we sat in his parlor. Cicero went to Dean's chair for a scratch behind the ears.

"Sure, but I've been waiting for the chance to tell you that your sister called. Charlotte gave her my number. Your mother is ill. Connie said to make sure I told you. But I knew you'd want to hear about Sean first."

"Shows you where my head is at, doesn't it," I confessed.

No one answered when I telephoned Connie, so I tried Vivian's number.

Connie picked up the phone.

"How's Vivian?" I asked.

Connie had her own question. "Where are you?"

"Dean told me you called," I said, avoiding a direct answer.

"We had no idea how to reach you. It's like your family doesn't even exist to you."

"What's wrong with our mother?" I asked, trying my best to avoid getting into a spat.

"She had a stroke."

"Is it bad?"

"Bad enough. She can barely talk, and there's stiffness in her left arm. Are you coming to see her?"

"Of course I am, Connie."

"I heard that some boy was traveling with you. That woman at your house mentioned something about it."

"Did Charlotte also tell you about my dog?"

"Your mother's here. Do you want to say hello?"

"Yes, Connie."

The receiver banged against a hard surface.

Vivian's stroke had made it a chore simply to articulate a hello. It came out something like, A-ee-o.

"Don't try to talk," I said. "Put Connie back on. I'll see you soon."

Vivian was trying to communicate something when Connie came on the line.

"Are you staying with Vivian?" I asked.

"Someone has to. I'll tell you more when I see you. When are you coming by?"

"As soon as I can."

"Vivian keeps asking for you."

I had never forgotten the shame I experienced when Vivian warned that I might grow up to be homicidal, intending to say homosexual, even if, through the years, I'd been able to laugh it off because of her linguistic faux pas. I wanted to rush home and assure Vivian that she had raised a successful son. But it wasn't that easy. As a child, if I brought home straight A's on my report card, Vivian warned that my friends might shun me if I flaunted my intelligence. For Vivian, the only safe way to live was to be anonymous, to appreciate whatever scraps life provided. She feared success even more than failure. Failure she understood.

When I explained Vivian's condition, Dean started to ask me something, but instead went to the kitchen and brought us cups of coffee. We sat in his living room and watched the blinking lights on his Christmas tree. The gaudy angel on top reminded me of one of those Sumerian statues with the huge eyes. Its gaze would not let me go. When smoke from Dean's cigarette entered my nose, it summoned Lenny's ghost along with thoughts about Christmases past. I could not recall a single one that I wanted to remember.

"See you later," I said, abruptly rising from my seat. "I'm going out for a while." I needed to find drugs.

Cicero's ears stood at attention.

"Let me give you a key," Dean said, finding a spare in a kitchen drawer.

"I don't know when I'll be back," I said, "but I'd like to stay here when I return. If that's all right."

"That's why I'm giving you a key, silly. Go work things out. See your mom. Take care of yourself." Dean placed his hand on my arm. "Simon, I'm here for you."

Cicero sprang to his feet.

"You be good, Cicero. Stay with Dean."

As I walked out the door, Cicero's crying nearly broke my heart.

I set out for Sibley and drove around the old neighborhoods. Memories began flooding my thoughts. I passed the house of my high school friend, Jake, where I had first experienced LSD and had visions of heaven that led me to believe the messiah had returned and that I was destined to be a new disciple.

My twelfth grade art teacher, who seduced me during a moment of weakness following an attempted suicide, still lived in the same apartment. It was there that I made love to Tony, who rejected me for Jesus. When he broke off our affair, saying I was going to hell for being gay, it was the first time I realized just how hateful religion was towards homosexuality. Seemingly overnight, Tony had lost his ability to love.

I left Sibley and drove toward Little Rock, following the same route I had taken the night Tony broke up with me. Feeling betrayed by everyone and everything in my life, I thought I might go through with it this time – drive off the cliff as I had meant to do so many years ago.

But I never made it to Overlook Drive. As if guided by a force beyond my control, I found myself near Highland Court – Little Rock's largest housing project. It was dusk and a dense fog had risen. Cars driving down Twelfth Street pierced the night with an eerie blend of low-beam headlights and slow speed. Parka-hooded men stood in front of a Church's Chicken adjacent to the Delta Express convenience store.

I pulled in to fill the tank, trying to make eye contact with one of the young men lurking about. They were being especially cautious since I was a white guy in a black neighborhood. I hoped that the California license plates would make it clear that I couldn't possibly be a cop.

One of the hooded figures walked up as I was returning to the car after paying the attendant. The boy wore a camouflage military jacket open at the chest. Dog tags jangled against his white-ribbed undershirt.

"Want a piece?" the boy said, holding out the box of chicken.

I took a greasy wing.

"Chicken what you looking for around here?" the boy asked.

"Actually, I was hoping to find something to put in a pipe. Trouble is, I haven't got one of those either."

"How much you spending?"

"Whatever it takes."

"You willing to drive into the projects?" he asked, nodding toward Highland Court.

"Let's do it," I said.

When he got into the car, a few of the other lurkers called out warnings: "You goin' to get ripped off!" and "Don't go with him! I'll show you some action."

"Let's get outa here," the boy urged. "We're attracting too much attention. Lots o' cops 'round here."

The fellow pointed toward a street heading into the heart of the projects.

"Is there someplace to buy a pipe? What's your name, anyway?"

"They call me Snake," he said. "And yeah, they's pipes up on Twelfth Street. Let's go there first."

Snake led me to a record store called Big Man Blues. "I'll have to go in with you," he said. "Big Man won't sell to white folk."

Snake purchased a glass pipe with a three-inch globe that I selected. He just wanted a simple stem.

"Easier to hide," he said, putting the stem inside his jacket.

Getting dope wasn't as easy as buying the pipes. Snake ran from the car several times to talk to men hiding in the shadows. The first few told him they had run out earlier in the day.

"If you drive through this place alone," Snake cautioned, "you might not get out."

"I'll be sure to come and find you," I assured him, "that is, if you really can find something."

Snake ground his teeth in response.

The streets were a maze. Some of the roads ended in cul-de-sacs while others went around apartment buildings, widening to become parking lots. It took knowledge of the layout to stay on the main road. The small row houses were nearly all covered in graffiti. The garbage bins overflowed with trash that reeked of rotted meat and rancid vegetables.

Snake finally gave up trying to score anything in Highland Court. He guided me to Rice Street, near the site of what had been Little Rock High School when Vivian and Lenny went there. Our bad luck followed us.

Next we went to College Street, once a middle-class neighborhood until people abandoned the area during the white flight of the late 1950s. Now it was a neighborhood of crack houses and slumlords. Snake returned from each effort with a familiar tale. I began to grow suspicious. I had given Snake forty-dollars when we first started. I wondered if he had been making deals during our various stops. I decided to call him on it.

"Snake, man, I can't believe there's nothing out there. What's going on?"

"They got dope, but nothin' you want," Snake said, reaching into a shirt pocket and taking out a small rock. "You don't want this yellow shit. Nothin' good about it."

"But you bought it with my money, right?"

"Been tryin' to get the money back every since. It ain't no good, though, man. I'm tellin' ya. Let's go to the East End."

Snake's lampblack skin, coupled with his alluring green eyes, gave him an aura that fit his nickname. His mesmerizing, lyrical voice made his statements believable even when it was clear he was lying. I wanted to put my hands to his cheeks and run my hands around his neck. I bet he kissed like a little cupid. Try that, I knew, and if I were lucky, I'd wake up in the hospital with a knife wound in my gut. Snake asked me what I was chuckling about. I told him that I couldn't believe I was driving around such dangerous areas of Little Rock. He just shrugged. They were his neighborhoods. He had always lived there.

We drove down Ninth Street, past an industrial park with scaffolding lit by unearthly searchlights. We went beneath an underpass and paralleled a Missouri-Pacific train yard. Bonfires flared from the tops of rusted barrels where homeless men were trying to keep warm.

The East End was laid out on a grid with rows of evenly spaced, depression-style houses. Each had a small yard but there were few trees. The community was built on Arkansas River bottomland. After the Civil War, it had been a refugee camp for former slaves. I supposed that some of the current inhabitants were their descendants.

A crowd of people was gathered at Harrington and Tenth Street in front of a blues club called Dante's. The building was painted with dancing figures in silhouette.

"Park here," Snake said, instructing me to pull into a self-service car wash. "You better give me whatever you want to spend."

I took five twenties from my wallet. "You get me a hundred and keep the forty I gave you earlier."

Snake tried to act cool, but I could almost see his brain cooking up a scheme.

The moment Snake took off toward the club, someone knocked on the window. I nearly swallowed my tongue with fright. The man peering in the window had a round, clean-shaven face. One of his front teeth was missing. The remaining one was capped in gold.

"Don't be scared of BT," the man said. "I ain't goin' to shoot you or nothin'. Roll down the window."

If he was going to shoot me, I figured the glass wouldn't do much good anyway.

"You give that crazy dude your money?" BT asked.

I didn't answer.

"Oh, man. That's Snake. Why do you think people calls him that? Snake-In-The-Grass. That's his full name. He'd take your time if you give it to him. Got you to drive him around town, didn't he?"

"Yeah," I said, "something like that."

"What you trying to get?"

I showed him the pipe I had tucked between my thighs so I could throw it out the window if the police showed up.

"Got what you want right here," BT said, reaching into his bulky jacket and taking out five rocks. "Go ahead. Taste one."

I rolled one around my tongue. The numbing effect told me it was the real thing.

"Hundred bucks. All five."

As I reached for the cash, BT asked me if I'd drop him off down the street.

"I really ought to wait for Snake," I said.

"Man, you gotta deal with it. Snake ain't comin' back. Next time you see him, he'll be all about them excuses. 'Oh, I got robbed and I didn't want to face you.'" BT laughed heartily as he thought about what Snake would say. "Ol' BT won't do that, man. I'm going to show you where I live. When you want something, you come to BT."

BT lived in projects that I had never seen before, a community of one-story, red-brick buildings not far from the airport.

"Come off the freeway at the airport exit and keep going. You'll find this place next time," BT told me.

Two doors from the end of the first building, BT told me to pull over.

"Come on inside and try out a piece."

"You don't mind?" I asked.

"I ain't prejudiced. I let white folks in my house," he laughed.

"Why do they call you BT?" I asked on the way in.

BT grinned. "Because folks were always saying it's 'bout time I showed up. I ain't never in no hurry."

The walls of BT's apartment were made of unpainted cinder blocks. The floor was concrete. A woman in a nurse's outfit sat on a couch with three children, a girl and two boys, snuggling close. The sole light source was the television set.

"This is my wife, Violet," BT said. "And them's my chillun."

The little girl rushed toward BT and clung to his neck as he carried her back to the couch. The boys stared at me like they'd never seen a white man before. Violet barely raised her head as she greeted me with a tentative, "Hello."

"Violet works down at Baptist Hospital," BT said. "Just got off work. She walks from the freeway."

"That's probably three miles," I noted.

"That's why I ain't getting up," Violet said. "I don't mean nothing rude. My dogs is tired."

BT led me to a small bedroom. We sat on a rolled out sleeping bag that reeked of sweat.

"I'm sorry the place ain't so clean, or me neither," BT said with an embarrassed chuckle. "Ain't had no hot water for a week. But I gots fire." BT took a pipe from a stack of shoeboxes that served as a chest-of-drawers, and dropped on a sliver of rock. The flame from his lighter illuminated his face from below, turning it into a carnival mask. Letting out the smoke, BT yelled, "Boo-yah!"

Curious word, from bouillabaisse I supposed. People often used the word base instead of rock. I guessed that boo-yah-base made sense in the odd logic of drug abuse.

"Bouilla!" I repeated, placing a crumb on my new pipe. The sweet smoke was as pure as evaporated milk.

The next instant, I had no idea where I was or who the man was sitting beside me. Why was I in a room of cinder block walls and no windows? Had I landed in jail? Were guards about to show up because I'd just done drugs with my cellmate? I stared at the door without blinking until tears began to drip down my cheeks. I focused on the aluminum doorknob, finding a universe in the reflections cast upon it.

BT lit up a second piece of rock and motioned me to try another hit.

"I can't," I said, rising to consciousness. "I need to get going."

BT slowly exhaled. The smoke crept up the sides of his mouth and covered his face so densely that I was reminded of the doctored séance photos that show ectoplasm flowing from the heads of the mediums.

"If I come back and you're not here, should I drive around to look for you?" I asked.

"Naw, Holmes. You wait in your car out front. If Violet or one of the kids are here, they'll let you in. Don't go driving around. You'll end up getting shot."

BT walked me to the door and made sure Violet and the kids knew it would be okay if I came back without him. Heading for the car, I noticed two men in trench coats standing on the curb down the street. BT whistled from the apartment door and they left. I made a U-turn in the middle of the street and drove toward the airport, following the route BT had described.

I drove mindlessly, unsure where I was going. I vaguely recalled the money from Spain that, by then, should have been deposited into my account. I gripped the steering wheel so hard my hands began to hurt, and I couldn't stop grinding my teeth. I desperately wanted to fire up a rock.

By midnight, I found myself circling through the back roads around Sibley. I kept passing the mansion, trying to convince myself to pull into the drive, run to the door, and confess everything. I'd throw the damned drugs into the swamp.

Instead, I drove back to Dean's house.

CHAPTER THIRTY-NINE

Dean had fallen asleep on the couch with one leg dangling over the back and a socked foot propped on the armrest. I startled him when I turned the lock and unexpectedly burst into the room. He quickly realized it was me, as did Cicero, who crawled out from under the sofa.

"Cicero's been pining away since you left," Dean said.

I picked up and got a tongue bath. "There anything to eat?" I asked, taking a seat beside Dean, who had sat up and put on his shoes.

"Spaghetti. Let me heat a plate in the microwave. There's a present for you," Dean pointed to a red box tied up with a green ribbon. "I was going to mail it to Los Angeles – then, voila, you came to town."

The aroma from the microwave made my stomach growl, and I devoured the warmed up pasta. The tiredness that had been pursuing me caught up with a vengeance. My eyes would hardly stay open.

"There are clean sheets on the bed," Dean said, realizing that I was falling asleep. "Maybe you should lie down."

"I'm so tired, I could sleep for a couple of days," I said, but that wasn't my plan.

Dean led me to the bedroom with Cicero following close behind. I waited a couple minutes until I heard Dean go into his room at the other end of the hall. It was an old house. Every footstep made the floorboards creak. I'd have to be careful not to make any noise that would betray the fact I was not, in fact, sleeping.

When he saw me take out a pipe, Cicero pinned his ears back and nuzzled the covers until I lifted the bedspread to let him scoot under the blankets.

Inhaling the first blast, panic struck me as I imagined the smoke seeping under the door into the hallway. Stars flashed in my field of vision as I held my breath and tried to make it to the window. The latch wouldn't cooperate, and then, with the window finally unlocked, I could only manage to lift if three inches because of the heavily painted frames. I stuck my mouth in the opening and blew the smoke outside. Ghostly faces formed in the mist, each with a countenance that mocked and accused.

The aroma of frying bacon aroused my senses and enticed Cicero from beneath the covers. I opened the door and let him into the hallway.

"You want to go outside?" Dean asked, listening to the castanet clicking of Cicero's toenails on the hardwood floor.

By the time Dean and Cicero returned, I was lying on the bed with my eyes glued to a hole in the ceiling, convinced that someone was watching me through the tiny opening. The phone rang and I went to listen at the door.

"Simon," Dean called softly, tapping on the door. "Sean is on the phone. Can you take the phone? It'll reach inside."

I snuck back to the bed and made sounds as if I were just waking up, and then went to the door and took the phone.

"Sean?" I said, hugging the receiver to my ear.

"Yeah, what's up?" he responded in a droll voice. "We going to New York or what?"

My frazzled brain didn't recall the plan.

"Come home," I managed to say in a faltering voice.

"You going back to LA?"

"No, I mean, home to me, here in Little Rock."

The deafening roar of an eighteen-wheeler revving its engine nearly drowned out Sean's voice, but I caught the words, "Be there tonight."

I placed the phone on the floor outside the bedroom door. Cicero started to push his way through, but Dean called to him. Then I remembered that I needed to call Charlotte and took the phone back inside. I punched in the correct digits after getting numbers wrong on several attempts. The phone rang and rang. Charlotte never picked up.

Next I called the bank, slowly and deliberately punching in numbers I had written down on a card in my wallet. My balance would tell me if the Spaniards had come through with the money.

"Your current balance is five dollars."

I swallowed hard, and punched in a few more codes to get a list of recent activity. Three hundred and sixty thousand had arrived by bank wire. The same day, four checks were cashed totaling all but the remaining five dollars.

"God damn it!" I screamed. Charlotte must have found the signed checks and stolen my money.

"Are you okay?" Dean asked, gently knocking on the door.

"Not really," I said. "I'll be out in a minute."

I hid the pipes and stashed the remaining cocaine under a pile of junk in the closet. I got dressed and ran a brush through my hair. Unsteady on my feet, I bruised my thigh stumbling against the edge of the dresser. I went to the window for a dose of cold air so I wouldn't pass out from the pain. Just beyond the window, an oak tree's bare limbs grew into monstrous claws that seemed to scratch against the sky.

"You don't look well," Dean said when I emerged from the room.

"I don't feel well."

"How can I help?" Dean offered.

"Charlotte stole money from my bank account. I'm broke."

"How much did she take?"

"It's embarrassing," I said. "Some clients in Spain had recently wired money. Let's just say it was enough for her to stay hidden for quite a while."

"You met her at the Spotlight, right?"

"Through someone I knew from there."

Dean sipped his coffee. He didn't need to say what he was thinking. While he tried to hide his concern by reading the paper, I made some phone calls. My first was to the Oban.

An unfamiliar voice picked up the phone. "Is Rudy there?" I asked.

"He don't work here no more," the woman said.

"Know where I can reach him?"

"Ain't around. Took off a few days ago. Said he didn't have a forwarding address when I asked him."

I told Dean the story about Rudy, and how he had introduced me to Charlotte. "Rudy's part of it," I said. "What am I going to do now?"

"You should call the police," Dean suggested.

I turned pale at the suggestion. There would be plenty of evidence in my house that could land me in jail instead of Charlotte. A K-9 unit would surely find cocaine residue. Charlotte may even have planted a gram or two, hoping they'd be more interested in me than in her larceny.

"It's my fault," I said. "I left signed checks stashed in the apartment. I wasn't thinking straight."

Dean clearly wanted to give me advice but knew that I had to decide for myself what to do next.

"I'll be there for you," Dean said.

CHAPTER FORTY

That night, I actually slept, even though my mind was chaotic with worry, and the cocaine stash beckoned each time I happened to stir. Dean fixed me a fine breakfast waffle and sat with me until I had finished eating a bowl of various fruits.

"It's Christmas Eve," Dean reminded. "Maybe you should go see your mother."

"I'm going to," I said, sounding as though it had been my plan all along. The drugs hidden in the closet were like a siren calling to me and I didn't want to spend the holiday in the grips of that particular demon.

"If Sean calls, will you go pick him up?"

"I'd be glad to go get him, Simon. Don't worry about that. Spend time with your family."

At four years old, I raced into the living room on Christmas morning to find a Lionel Train set mounted on a board with little houses, a terminal station, plastic trees, and a bridge that crossed a river made of blue putty. Lenny had resented not getting a train set when he was boy. Through my Christmas present, he now had one.

Don't think about Lenny, I told myself as I neared the mansion. But it was Christmas – how could I avoid remembering? Lenny may as well have been sitting in the passenger seat beside me.

By the time I pulled into the driveway and parked behind Connie's Buick, Ernie had taken over from the melancholy about Lenny. I recalled the last time I saw him alive, knowing that drugs would kill him, as they finally did. Now it was my turn.

Victoria was sitting in the tire swing attached to the limb of the oak tree where marauders hanged the family patriarch, an act remembered on Halloweens past with an effigy dangling where the tire now swayed.

The other recent times I had driven by the house, I had not noticed how badly weathered it had become, now more grey timbers than whitewash. The yard was in ruin. Dandelion husks had replaced the thick St. Augustine grass that once carpeted the front yard. Dried up Kudzu vines hung from the trellises. The gardens were full of dead Johnson grass that had smothered the remains of once glorious dahlia beds. The gardens had been Vivian's pride, her escape from a multi-year sentence as dutiful and adoring wife.

As I walked toward the porch, I noticed our ragged manger scene – hand-crafted of tiger oak, the roof made of wax moss – sitting beside the door where we'd always displayed it at Christmas. The figurines were made of plaster-of-Paris that Connie and I had painted with Testor's enamel, left over from coloring the models of Frankenstein and Werewolf that crowded my dresser. The baby Jesus figure had disappeared long ago, gnawed into dust by a raccoon that took up residence in the attic one year. I laughed out loud when I saw that someone had replaced the baby Jesus with a rubber piglet because it fit nicely in the cradle.

"Hello, Simon," Connie said. She was standing akimbo in the doorway. "You should have called."

Sharp at first, Connie's tone mellowed when she got a better look at me. "Are you sick?" she asked.

"Homesick, perhaps," I responded. "I've been driving around the area. The place sure has changed."

"If you're sick, you shouldn't come in," Connie said, the hint of compassion having had its moment. "We can't risk Vivian being exposed to something."

Connie's makeup and jet-black dyed hair made her look like the bust of Nefertiti. She slipped a finger into her blouse and hooked it under the wire at the bottom of her bra, a reflex action whenever something made her nervous.

Vivian appeared in the doorway wearing a sky-blue robe with satin trim. Her hair was tucked under a pink sleeping bonnet. She tried to smile, but her stricken face muscles could only manage a slight grin.

"Mother!" Connie exclaimed, catching Vivian's arm as she tilted to one side. "You're not supposed to be up."

Vivian made an awkward attempt to step onto the porch, pulling her arm from Connie's grasp.

"I'm going to hug my son," Vivian said with determination.

I met her at the threshold. "Mother, I'm so sorry," I said, overcome by remorse.

"It's not your fault," Vivian said. "This old body is just wearing out."

Connie squeezed past us and stormed off in the direction of the kitchen. I helped Vivian onto the sofa in the den. She squeezed my hand as she raised her right shoulder to help get her immobile arm into her lap.

"My right side is funny," Vivian said. "The doctor said I shouldn't be alone, not until I learn to walk better."

Connie, who'd been listening at the door, chimed in, "Derek's finding out just how much I do around the house since I've been staying here."

The situation was about Connie, not Vivian's predicament. Hoping to change the subject, I said, "Victoria was so preoccupied on the swing, she didn't even see me drive up," but I could tell by Connie's grin that she liked the idea that my arrival had not been anything special to her daughter.

"I just hate that I'm putting everyone out," Vivian struggled to articulate.

"What did she say?" Connie probed, finding it difficult to make out Vivian's words.

"Mom thinks she's being a burden."

Connie came over and hugged Vivian. "You know that *I'm* here when you need me." She stared at me as she spoke.

"Do you need me to stay in Little Rock?" I asked, returning her gaze.

"I thought you were on your way to New York to become a famous artist or something," Connie said, sarcastically. "And where is that traveling companion, by the way?"

"My business consumes most of my time," I said, "but yes, I would like to live in New York. It would nice to find out if people would respond to my art. As for my companion, he's visiting friends right now."

"Oh, that's right," Connie continued. "You were in Europe or something. Did you make a lot of money? We sure could use. . . ."

Vivian grabbed Connie's arm. "Simon's got his own life," she said. "He's had a long way to go since he left that group."

Connie harrumphed and stood to go into the kitchen, saying that she had to check on the roast. As she opened the oven door, the aroma of the spiced meat flooded the house.

"Derek will be here around six," Connie hollered. "Are you going to eat with us?"

"I'd love too. But I've got tons of stuff I need to get done."

"You'll be at Connie's house tomorrow morning, won't you?" Vivian asked, pressing my hand. "It just hasn't felt like Christmas this year." She waved her hand in the direction of the bay window. "I don't even have a tree."

Vivian had always decorated for Christmas, at least putting up an artificial tree.

"I'll try," I said, but I knew I wouldn't.

Vivian lifted her foot and pulled up the heel of her slipper. Laughing, she said, "I thought something felt odd. I must have been walking on that all day."

Vivian depended on mundane details in order to avoid painful situations. Connie on the other hand relished the chance to dig into a wound.

"I don't believe that," she said, entering the room. "Can't you do better than try?"

"My concerns have nothing to do with you," I shot back, then excused myself to the upstairs bathroom. Connie sat beside Vivian, making a show of comforting her.

One of the paintings I had done in high school hung in the hallway. It had been among the few to escape the bonfire I set when I joined the Unification Church and was told to sacrifice the thing I loved the most. It wasn't half-bad.

Vivian struggled to her feet when I came downstairs and announced I was leaving. "Take care of yourself," she said, reaching out with her good arm as I raced toward my car.

I drove to the blue hole. This time, my thoughts went to my first girlfriend, Virginia. I sat on exactly the same spot where she offered herself to me. My lack of interest had undone any hope that something would change and I'd mysteriously start liking girls.

Surrounded by the white mounds of chemically saturated clay, with the winter darkness coming on fast, a severe sense of dread came over me. I realized how I had practically begged Charlotte to rip me off. How purposely naïve I had been. What was I going to say to Emilio when asked to send more videos? Could I finagle something with Wally or one of the other producers who might be willing to talk to me?

As the sun began to set, it got colder. The wind whipped through the leafless trees. I scurried up one of the white mounds and looked straight down into the water. The white light of a full moon had taken over where the sun left off. Its reflection in the rippling pit of water invited ominously.

Jump! commanded a familiar voice. My feet moved closer to the edge. Pebbles splashed into the blue-black water. My feet slipped forward as the hill began to collapse. At the last second, I caught a tree limb and pulled myself to safety. Tears streamed down my cheeks as I lay back and gazed up at the starless sky.

I hoped that Sean would be at Dean's, but no one was at the house. Dean's car was gone. I seized the moment of privacy and went to the bedroom. The pipe practically leaped into my hand of its own accord.

Though I am the fallen angel, a voice echoed in my head, *I will see God before you have the chance.*

"It's a lie!" I protested. "Reverend Moon was a fraud, and what you say is from the Father of Lies."

You think a woman named Charlotte took your money. But she is my handmaiden, Lilith.

"Liar. She is Charlotte, and I forgive her."

Ha! Satan screamed. *You have no power to forgive. I am, and always was, the Angel of Light.*

Satan's drool fell across my shirt. I ran to the bathroom to scrape off the putrid mess.

"Is that how you killed Ernie?" I demanded. "Strangling him on your vomit?"

You want to see Ernie? Satan responded. *He now sucks my horned cock. Do you want it, Damned One?* I felt a hand on my fly. *Here it is!*

"You are Lies and the Father of Lies!" I yelled.

And the Father of Truth? Is that the messiah who fooled you for ten long years?
"Stop talking!" I demanded,
You betrayed Christ and will be forever damned!
I ran to the car and raced toward the East End. Satan hounded me the entire way.
Twelve times twelve and thirty-six times ten times ten. That is how much I took from you. Do you know what it signifies?
"Leave me alone!" I screamed. "Why did you take my money?"
I will hound you for the remainder of your existence.
The voice grew dim the faster I drove. Yet the devil's stench remained. Undigested food soaked my beard and dampened the seat between my legs. I pulled over, and even though it was ice cold, took off my shirt and used it to rake vomit from the car. I checked my watch. It was just after midnight.
"Christmas Day," I said aloud.

If I hadn't smelled like a vagrant, I might have considered going to Connie's. Instead, I made my way back to Dean's rather than continuing on to BT's house. When I walked in the door, Dean could barely contain his disapproval. "You've been drinking, haven't you?" he asked.
Drinking was a good excuse for the way I looked. "I fell asleep in my car."
"At least you pulled over and didn't try to drive."
"What about Sean?" I asked. "And where's Cicero?"
"They're both in the bedroom. Sean's been asleep since I picked him up earlier. Cicero sure was glad to see him."
"Yeah. They're pals."
"I was hoping you'd return soon. I need to spend the day in Texarkana with my mother. I won't be back until tomorrow night. You're welcome to stay, but . . ."
"What?"
"Well, just that I don't want you to leave Sean here alone."
"I won't."
Dean sighed with relief.
"Thanks for picking up my little hustler," I said.
"Cute as a rat's ass, isn't he?" Dean said.
"As tight as one, too," I added.
Dean disappeared into his room to finish getting ready for his trip.

Cicero stirred under the covers when I entered the guest room, but I was out of my clothes and in bed before he found an escape.

If I reeked of puke, Sean smelled of gasoline and cigarette smoke. It didn't matter. We were together. I pressed myself against Sean's body and buried my face in his hair. Sean took my hand and kissed my knuckles as Cicero snuggled close behind my knees. I fell asleep, contented in the warmth of my little family.

CHAPTER FORTY-ONE

The lights were off at BT's house. Then I realized that the entire area was pitch-black. My guess was that a transformer had blown – or someone had shot it out. Undaunted, I drove deeper into the neighborhood until I saw a faint reddish glow as if someone were cloaking a flashlight by covering it with their hand. Just then, someone pointed a beam of light in front of the car. I pulled alongside a group of shadowy figures.

"What's up, white boy?" one of the men asked. "What'chu doin' around here?"

Sean squirmed in his seat and said, "Get the hell out of here!" as several men surrounded the car.

I wasn't going to leave the East End without drugs, no matter how dangerous the situation.

"Hey! That's my home boy," someone shouted.

Snake emerged from the crowd and pushed next to the fellow with the flashlight. "Where'd you go the other night?" he asked. "I came back, but you wasn't there."

"Don't say another word," I said, firmly. "Not unless you have my money."

Snake had been squatting at the window. He rose so he could talk into my ear without the others hearing. "Let me get in. I'll make it up to you."

I motioned for Snake to get in the backseat, even as Sean hit my leg to warn that I was making a mistake. Snake signaled for his compatriots to disperse, and directed me toward the other side of the projects. I parked at the end of an alley.

"How much you wanting?" Snake asked.

"Can you get a hundred bucks worth?"

"Holmes," Snake said, straining his voice to a high pitch, "you know I ain't got that money now. You give me what you wants and Snake'll do you right this time. Ain't no one else around here gonna get you nothin'."

Sean tried his best to stop me, but I took out two twenties and told Snake, "You bring me back a good deal, and we'll see about doing more."

"Oh man," Snake said. "You ain't going to get nothin' for this. You got to do at least a hundred."

"That's it for now."

Snake begrudgingly got out of the car, saying, "Don't leave before I get back."

"Forget about him," Sean said after Snake disappeared behind a building. "If he does come back, it'll be to shoot us in the head." Sean held onto the door handle, ready to bolt in case of trouble.

A group of slender boys came out of an apartment and went behind the same building where Snake had gone. A few moments later, they headed toward the car. I was ready to back out of the alley and make a break for it, but Snake ran toward us. The others scattered in different directions.

"Take this, Holmes," Snake said, appearing at the window. "It's one hell of a boulder."

He placed a marble-sized rock in my hand. I rolled it around my tongue. "Taste's fine," I said.

"They ain't got no more," Snake said. "Might have some in an hour or so. You want to come back?"

"Where will you be?"

"That corner over there, by the tree."

I told Snake I'd cruise by in an hour, and made my way onto the road to the airport. A twelve-foot fence topped with barbed wire separated the poorest part of Little Rock from the taxiing airplanes. I remembered a bank at Ninth Street and College Ave and went to the drive-through automated teller.

Sean seemed nervous. Instead of firing up his pipe, he put the rock in his pocket.

"Go ahead and smoke it," I said.

"Let's go to Dean's. We can come back during the day."

"We're already at the bank," I said. "Let's get some money." Sean didn't know that I was getting advances from my credit cards, since I had no cash in my checking account.

I keyed in my personal identification number and withdrew the limit – three hundred and fifty dollars. Crisp twenty-dollar bills slipped into a pile. I put the money in my wallet and started to drive away.

Then I saw him – a man wrapped in a black overcoat was standing in front of the car, pointing a shotgun directly between my eyes.

Sean sank to the floor, blathering as if he'd lost his mind. I hit the gas pedal and leaned over to avoid the line of fire. I heard a thump as if I had run over something. The car lurched forward. When I saw the overhang of the bank drive-through, I sat up and peeked over the dashboard. An explosion echoed through the night. Shards of glass rained onto the back seat. Another boom and sparks flew over the trunk. Two more gun blasts sounded like shots from a revolver. I sped down College Street to escape the gunfire.

Just before reaching the freeway, I looked in the rearview mirror but didn't see anyone pursuing us – only porch lights coming on as people opened their doors to see what was happening.

I felt a trickle of blood on my face. A salty taste dripped over my lips into my mouth. Sean was balled up on the floor in the front seat.

"Are you okay?" I asked, maneuvering a sharp turn.

"Yeah," Sean said, uncoiling himself to peek out the back window. He noticed the blood. "Are you shot?"

The steering wheel was slippery with blood. "I don't know," I said. "I don't feel any pain. Maybe the glass cut me."

Sean looked into the back seat. "There's glass everywhere."

"Do you think Snake set me up? I mean, I did mention the bank."

"Didn't you see him? He was right there, pointing a gun at your head!"

"All I saw was the gun."

"Well, that was Snake, ready to blow your brains out."

My ankle became so weak from fear that I had to push on my knee to keep pressure on the gas pedal. Cold air swirled the broken glass into a hurricane of shattered fragments.

I managed to drive to Dean's house. The neighborhood was quiet except for a few dogs warning about the approach of a car so late at night. After parking, I realized that the blood was from a gash above my left ear, caused by a shard of glass. The back window was entirely gone, exploded over the backseat.

Sean patted me down, looking for another wound, finally satisfied that I only had the one injury.

"There was so much glass," Sean said. "I'm surprised my eyes weren't put out. Dean's car isn't here. We have the place ourselves, right? Let's go in and get high."

The police were probably swarming all over College Street by that time. I hoped that no one had written down my license plate number. Even so, they wouldn't know where I was staying, and I was sure we hadn't been followed.

"Did I run over someone?" I asked as I unlocked the door, greeted by a jubilant Cicero.

"I didn't see shit," Sean said. "And none of those guys are going to say anything, even if you did."

I placed a note on the door so Dean would see it as soon as he came home: I'll explain about the car tomorrow. No one is hurt. Everything's fine.

CHAPTER FORTY-TWO

Cicero wanted to go to the door when he heard Dean's key in the lock, but I forced him to stay under the covers. Luckily, Dean went right to bed, though his curiosity about the car must have been killing him. After smoking what was left or our rock, my paranoia was at fever pitch.

The next morning, Dean began knocking on the door. Sean and I were in a nether land of half-sleep, a kind of pretend sleep, which is the best one can manage for many hours after smoking cocaine. I knew I wouldn't be able to carry on much of a conversation, but I had to try. I threw on some clothes and let Cicero out of the room.

"Will you take him for a walk?" I called out. "I need to get cleaned up."

As soon Dean and Cicero went outside, I scurried to the bathroom, took a cold shower, and then worked as many tangles out of my hair as I could.

"You're damn lucky you didn't get yourself killed," Dean said as I joined him at my car.

He had discovered a couple of holes in the front windshield. Two bullets had whizzed right past my head.

"Where were you?" Dean's voice was a blend of concern and consternation.

"At a drive-thru bank."

"People have been robbed at drive-thru banks all over town. It's been in the news. How did they get you?"

"A gang of hoodlums surrounded the car as soon I reached for the cash. I had just pulled off the freeway, somewhere around Sixth Street."

"Sixth Street, huh? So, you were near the East End. That's a dangerous area even during the day. Sean's okay, I suppose?"

"He's shaken up."

"You need to call the insurance company," Dean said.

"I'll call today."

Dean fought to hold back his questions. He knew I wasn't telling him the whole story.

We spent the next hour sweeping broken glass from the seat and floorboards. We plugged the rear window with cardboard, securing it with duct tape.

"This is the ugliest thing I've ever seen," Dean said, stepping back to examine our repairs.

"Maybe I can tell people it's the car that Bonnie and Clyde were driving."

We both laughed.

"What are you going to do?" Dean asked when we were back inside the house.

"I'm thinking I might spend some time at Vivian's. No one's upstairs anymore since she set up her bedroom on the first floor."

Dean grasped my hand as I reached for my coffee cup. "If you need to talk, you can call me any time, day or night. All right?"

I gave Dean a look as though I didn't know what he meant. "Of course," I said. "I know that."

The insurance company had a million questions. In the end, they demanded that I file a police report. Fortunately, that didn't require a trip to the station. An officer took my report over the phone. He was polite enough. When I mentioned where the incident took place, I was afraid there might have been reports about the car that I'd have to explain. But nothing was said.

Later, Sean and I drove to the Mercury dealer where Lenny and I got the car. They took possession of the badly damaged vehicle and gave me a loaner. Until I settled the insurance claim, I couldn't get a replacement. We drove off the lot in a bright red Cougar. Sean thought it much jazzier than the gray Topaz, but I missed the old jewel. We'd been through a lot together.

Before heading off toward Sibley, I telephoned. Connie was there.

"Vivian's gotten used to her privacy since Lenny died," Connie said. "It's going to be an adjustment if you stay here. And that boy."

"Sean's not a boy, Connie."

"I just don't want you to put stress on Vivian."

"I'm not trying to cause trouble," I said. "I need to recharge for a while, that's all."

Connie choked back her comments.

I was dismayed to find Vivian sweeping the upstairs hallway with Connie nowhere to be found. She worked the broom with one arm as she steadied herself with her cane in the other. I couldn't imagine how she had managed to climb the stairs.

"You don't need to worry about cleaning," I said, wrapping Vivian's arm in mine.

"But it's so musty up here," Vivian said. "I didn't want you to come home to this."

"Sean and I will take care of it. Let me get you downstairs." Vivian had not even acknowledged that Sean was standing behind me.

"I can manage," Vivian said resolutely. She shuffled down the hallway to the landing. Upon reaching the stairs, she looked back, sheepishly. I was right behind her. We took the steps one at a time. I got her positioned into her favorite chair, the old Lay-Z-Boy that had been Lenny's. Then I went back upstairs.

"Is this where we're going to stay?" Sean said, examining my old bedroom.

"Beats the cab of an eighteen wheeler, doesn't it?"

Sean shot me a wicked glance. "At least I'd have drugs in an eighteen wheeler."

"You've got a point. Let's go back to the East End. BT might be home by now. At least we'll be in a car that Snake won't recognize."

"Yeah? And then what, smoke here at your mother's house?"

"We'll hear her on the stairs if she tries to come up. I know every creak those stairs make."

"What about your sister, and that Derek guy?"

"That's her husband, silly. Look, unless she gets wind of trouble, Connie will appreciate getting a break from tending to Vivian."

"Whatever. Let's go."

"Do you mind walking Cicero while I make a phone call?" We had left him in the Cougar.

"Okay, but hurry up."

Vivian managed to get up from there chair and make it into the kitchen where she was drinking a glass of milk.

"What are you thinking about?" I asked, noting a look of melancholy.

"I haven't been upstairs in a while. It brought back memories. Having you here makes me think about Lenny."

Lenny's ghost tapped me on the shoulder.

"I'm going to have my stuff brought from Los Angeles," I said.

"Then, you're really leaving that place?"

I laughed, "'That place' is a pretty good description of Hollywood."

"Sibley will always be your home," Vivian said.

I hugged her, but in my shredded emotional state, it was a hollow gesture.

Vivian steadied herself on her cane and shuffled toward her room. "Come and go as you please, Bubby," she said. "I'm glad you've come home."

I needed to get someone to me help me settle my affairs in California. All my belongings would have to be put in storage, or possibly trucked to Arkansas. I hoped I could arrange it before my credit cards dried up.

Though I had lived in Los Angeles for eight years, I had few people I could truly count on. Scott and Sandra were the only ones who'd been there since the start. They knew my sins and loved me anyway.

I held the receiver for several minutes before dialing Scott. I knew he'd help me. A slurred voice answered.

"Scott? Is that you?"

"Simon?" Scott's voice became instantly coherent. "Where in the hell are you?"

"I'm in Little Rock."

Then I heard a familiar voice in the background say, "Who is it?"

"It's Simon," Scott responded to the person.

There was shuffling against the receiver as Scott handed off the phone.

"Is that really you?" a voice asked.

I wanted desperately to hang up, but I couldn't make myself do it. In a barely audible voice, I responded, "Hello Thad."

"It *is* you!" Thad exclaimed.

The sound of Thad's voice struck a deep sense of longing in my heart.

"I've been trying to find you," Thad said. "I heard about what happened."

"What do you mean? What did you hear?"

"Charlotte took all your money, right?"

"Who told you that?" I asked.

"I heard it from Patricia. When you left the message on her machine that you were leaving, she called your house and spoke to Charlotte. Charlotte was so rude that Patricia became suspicious. She went to the Spotlight and warmed up to Rudy."

"So Patricia's part of it, too?"

"Calm down and listen," Thad insisted. "Patricia wanted to find out what was going on. Rudy asked about any places in the Silverlake house where you might have hidden cash. Patricia and Rudy went there. She was surprised that Rudy had a key. Charlotte wasn't there. Patricia pretended to know where you hid things, but of course there wasn't any cash in the places she showed Rudy."

"She didn't know my hiding places."

"It was just an excuse to win Rudy's confidence," Thad said. "Patricia found some of the faxes from Spain and saw those big numbers. You must have done a hell of a deal."

"A lot of good it did me."

"Patricia called me later that night. She thought Rudy and Charlotte might be planning to rip you off. By the time I got to Hollywood, and we went to Silverlake, Rudy and Charlotte were gone."

"Is the house okay? Did they take my things?"

"Everything's there. I called the bank and pretended to be you. I gave them your mother's maiden name for identification. Don't be angry with me. I just wanted to know. I looked through the phone bills for numbers where Charlotte called you, but I couldn't find you. Did your mother tell you I called, or your sister?"

"Neither one."

"I left messages with both of them. They were supposed to tell you to call Scott."

"You mean, Scott knows all this?"

"Scott and Sandra both."

"You had no right to tell them, Thad."

"Scott may be fucked up, Simon, but he's your friend. So is Sandra. Patricia's forgiven me for leaving you alone when you were sick. We're friends now," he assured me.

"Some group of friends," I said sarcastically.

"I was an asshole," Thad said. "I admit it."

My mind reeled at the idea he would admit to any of his faults. "What do you want, Thad? I'm penniless."

"That's the drugs talking," Thad said.

"No dear, that's me – speaking from experience."

"Drugs screwed me up, too, Simon. I even tried to kill myself."

"I've seen how you try to kill yourself. Then you show up the next day with a smug grin."

"That was the drugs, Simon. Not me."

"Don't hand me a load of crap!" I shot back.

"I stopped using," Thad confessed. "I got help."

"I feel sorry for you. I truly do."

"Listen to me," Thad said sternly. "I came here to see if Scott knew where I could find you. And then you called. That means something."

"It means you don't know how to mind your own business."

As we spoke, I thought perhaps I could turn the nonsense to my advantage. "Look," I said, "I need someone to get my things out of Silverlake. I can't afford the rent and I don't want to go back to Los Angeles."

"I'll bring everything to you," Thad offered. "I owe you that much."

Now we were getting somewhere.

"Do you realize how much furniture I have?"

"I helped you pick out most of it. It'll fit into a rental truck. Could you pay for a truck at your end? Then I could drive it there."

"You'd do that?" I said, trying to sound as appreciative as possible.

"I need to make amends."

The word amends clued me in. He'd become a 12-stepper. I'd heard enough of that babble from Axl to recognize the lingo. The only thing that would get Axl to stop talking that way was to put a pipe in his hand.

"I'll go by a rental place tomorrow."

"Do it tonight, Simon. It's a long time until tomorrow."

I knew what he was thinking – that I'd get high and forget we'd ever spoken.

"Here's a thought, Simon. What if I wait for your call at the Silverlake house? I already took the spare key from the hiding place in the century plant frond."

"Alright. See if there are any faxes, and check my telexes. Maybe some other deals have come through."

I couldn't believe I was allowing myself to trust Thad, but what choice did I have?

"If there's anything urgent," Thad said, "I'll let you know. I promise."

After we hung up, I leafed through the phone book and made calls until I found a company with a truck available in Los Angeles. I'd have to go to the local office at a truck stop near the East End to pay. Cicero was getting agitated. I thought about leaving him at Vivian's but decided against it, picking him up and heading outside.

"What the shit took you so long?" Sean demanded when I got into the car after completing the rental company's paperwork. Fortunately, my credit card had gone through.

"Things take time," I said. "What do you want?"

"Drugs. That guy over there's been eyeballing me ever since you went inside. He looks like he's on speed. Shit dude, I could've turned a trick in the time you were in there."

A skinny guy in a Peterbilt hat and shaggy beard sat in the cab of the largest truck on the lot. He seemed to be working on his own paperwork under the cab-light. From time to time, he revved his engine, a mating call to Sean's ears.

I threw the car in gear and raced deeper into the East End. Mercury vapor lamps flickered with the approach of evening. Whatever had caused the earlier blackout must have been fixed. The area took on an eerie yellowish glow against the russet sky in the west.

BT's wife, Violet, peeked out of the window before letting me in when I knocked. The only light in the room came from the glow of her old black and white television set. "BT ain't here," she said, speaking softly. The children were leaning against each other, asleep on the tattered couch. A nest of blankets marked Violet's spot beside them. Canned foods, each with a Christmas ribbon tied around it, covered the dining room table. "Don't know when BT will be back," Violet said, picking up a can of peaches and turning the handle of a hand opener.

I thought about roaming the projects or chancing a run by Dante's Club, but the idea sent a shudder up my spine.

Violet pulled her terrycloth robe close around her neck. "What if I tell you where to find BT? You do something for me?"

"Anything," I said.

"BT don't like me smoking none of that crack, but I been wanting some. What if, when you get yours, you put a little piece for me right here behind this lamp? Would you do that for Violet?"

"Of course."

"BT will bring you back here. He's out hustling a deal, but no one's got money after Christmas."

Violet slipped into a pair of well-worn slippers and walked me to the car. Cicero jumped to the window when he saw us. Violet shrieked.

"He won't hurt you," I said.

"I don't like them white dogs."

Cicero tried to nose his way through the partially opened window, always anxious to meet a new person.

"See? He's trying to get at me," Violet said.

I let Cicero lick my hand. "He won't hurt you, Violet."

"Keep it away from me anyways."

Violet pointed down the street. "You see that row of apartments there? My brother lives in the one on the end. BT should be there."

Violet hurried inside as I told Sean I'd be right back. I walked the short distance, guided by the incandescent light over the brother's door.

I could hear BT's voice as I got near.

"BT?" I called out, knocking gently.

BT greeted me with an enthusiastic, "Homeboy!" and let me in.

The layout of the apartment was identical to BT and Violet's. Some folding chairs, with flattened pillows for cushions, and a flimsy card table sufficed as the only furniture. Someone with a flair for design had nailed crushed Budweiser cans into an arrangement on the wall.

"I was just saying how I wished someone would show up wanting something, and here you come," BT placed his hand on my shoulder and introduced me to Violet's brother, a chubby man missing his bottom front teeth. His matted hair was speckled with bits of dead leaves as if he had been sleeping outside. BT didn't introduce the two women and two men also in the room, simply waving his hand in their direction and saying they were folks from Memphis.

One of the men appeared to be gripping a revolver under the heavy coat draped across his lap. The whole crew dressed fashionably. The women had on short dresses that emphasized the sexiness of their fishnet stockings. Their sleek shoes had high pointed heels. The material of the men's suits glistened in the light.

BT took me into a back room. His voice betrayed a certain urgency as he said, "Holmes, this is your chance to score big. I was just trying to tell these folks about my connections in these parts. If you can do big business right now, we gonna have a supply for the next year. I'm tellin' ya."

My heart beat faster as I anticipated having that much again.

"Damn, BT. I've only got a couple hundred bucks on me, and for a while it's going to be tough getting cash."

BT's expression sank. "Just a couple hundred, huh?" Then he broke into a smile. "What 'bout the credit cards? You got credit cards, right? American Express?"

"Yeah."

BT shared his idea. "They want to rent a van for a couple of days. Says they got some things to move to Little Rock. I reckon you could rent them a van and they'd give us a good stash."

I agreed to try. BT went into the front to work out a deal, leaving me alone. With him gone, I noticed the rank odor of dirty laundry choking the windowless space. I thought I heard something in the corner under a pile of trash. I was ready to run if I saw a rat, but just then BT returned.

"These folks is pretty nervous," he said. "But they say if you rent a van, they'll give us a half ounce right now."

"How do we make it work?"

"You go and pay for a van. Put down this name as the person who'll pick it up tomorrow."

BT gave me a piece of paper with the name Joyce Briggs written on it. He told me to make sure the rental company asked for extended approval on the card, in case the move took more than a couple of days.

"We get the drugs now?" I asked.

"Soon as you return," BT said.

Sean was suspicious, but the prospect of getting drugs, no matter what the risk, kept him from voicing more than a general warning. I parked and told Sean to sit tight as I went into the airport to make arrangements. The rental companies were flush with vehicles. The clerk quickly did the paperwork and got the approval from my bank.

Back at the projects, I parked in front of Violet's, then walked to her brother's place. One of the well-dressed men took the rental papers from me and checked over the agreement. There was the name, Joyce Briggs, as an authorized driver, and an open-ended approval, as requested. They could use up a thousand dollars, but I didn't see how they could run up that much just going to Memphis and back. BT asked me to wait again in the smelly back room, but only moments later, he came and got me, saying to follow him to his place.

The Memphis group had left. "Did everything work out? Did you get the drugs?" I asked.

"Bouilla!" BT smiled.

Sean got out of the car when he saw us approaching. Cicero barked until we disappeared into BT's apartment. Violet and the kids were no longer on the couch. Gone to bed, I presumed. BT led us into the small room where I'd first smoked with him. When we were settled on the floor, knee to knee in a circle, I introduced Sean, saying, "This is a friend of mine from LA."

BT produced a baggy from the inside of his greatcoat and placed it on the floor between us.

"At least a half ounce," I said, picking up a small rock and rolling it around my tongue.

BT took out a pipe and fired up a piece. His eyes went from narrow slits to bulging golf balls. When Sean did a blast, he held his hands over his ears to fend off the familiar noise that always hounded him when he got high. Before I fired up, and while my friends were too high to notice, I took a chunk into the front room and placed it behind Violet's lamp. I returned to the circle and did a blast. The room transformed into a whirling carnival ride as the walls began to spin around me. Sparks ignited in the air, as if matter and its opposite had met within my own mind and begun to self-annihilate. Shapes began to materialize – first BT reappeared, then Sean took form.

BT's eyes went back to normal. He summed up the experience pretty well, exclaiming with a laugh, "Da-yum!"

CHAPTER FORTY-THREE

Sean and I checked into a cheap hotel on the outskirts of Little Rock and finished up our drugs. Before crashing, I decided to use my last ounce of energy and try to make it to Sibley. It was the middle of the night when we crept into the house. I taped a note to the refrigerator saying that Sean and I were upstairs in my room, that we'd come down with something and needed to rest. I locked Cicero out of the room, knowing that once I fell asleep, I might be out for days, and that Connie would surely take care of him. Sometimes he'd scratch at the door. I'd think about The Giant Rat of Sumatra from Sherlock Holmes and remember the phrase: it is a story for which the world is not prepared.

"Simon! Simon!" someone called out as they banged on the door.

I opened it just enough to see who it was. A hand shot through and grabbed my arm.

"You look like shit," Thad said, taking me by the shoulders.

"Yeah, I get that a lot."

I went to sit on the bed next to the Sean, still asleep, with his head bound in a tee-shirt.

"Connie was about to call the police to come check on you."

"God forbid she should just knock on my door."

"She said she's been knocking on it all day. Derek even tried to climb up the trellis, but he was too heavy for it."

Thad followed me down the hall to the bathroom. I was so weak, he had to help me onto the toilet.

"Thad," I said, mortified by my condition, "why are you coming back into my life? Why now?"

"It's simple. I love you."

All manner of protest entered my thoughts. But then, here I was, a derelict, not the successful businessman living in fabulous houses. And yet, Thad had used the word *love*. *I love you.*

Thad got the shower started and slipped out of his clothes before helping me inside. He wrapped a strong arm about my waist and soaped me up. When I was clean, Thad found an electric razor in a drawer that must have belonged to Lenny and supervised a shave.

"Your hair is so silky," Thad said as he ran a comb through after getting out the tangles with a brush. "I never noticed how baby fine it is."

"You never noticed a lot of things."

"I know. I should have been more attentive."

"What does Vivian think is going on?" I asked as we left the bathroom. "Is she okay?"

"I called her just before I was ready to leave LA in the truck, and again when I was on the way. She said you had come in during the night and holed up in your room. I tried to cover for you, saying that we had spoken and that you and Sean had the flu, and that you were worried about her catching it. She went to Connie's house with Cicero. I drove by there first and picked up the house key. Connie is really upset that you would come into Vivian's house with a virus. Then, when she couldn't get you to answer the door, she was afraid you'd lapsed into a coma or something."

"Glad you got here before Connie called the police."

Sean appeared in the hallway. He'd slipped into his jeans but was shirtless and shoeless. He glared at Thad.

"Fucker!" Sean screamed. "Who the hell's that?" Then, switching tactics, affected a pout, and said, "The two of you pushing me aside?"

I approached and pulled his head to my chest. "Thad brought my things from LA. He's not here to push you out."

"You better go now, Thad," I said, pointing my chin toward the stairwell.

"Your things are in the basement," Thad said, pausing to consider his next words. "I love you, Simon. I always will."

"How will we get more drugs?" Sean asked the moment that Thad closed the front door.

If I was torn between chasing after Thad and doing drugs with Sean, the conflict was short lived – I chose to get high. "Let's go see what's in the basement," I said, "then we'll head to the East End."

Sean followed me downstairs through the strangely deserted house. I was shocked to see my furniture. Derek must have helped Thad haul the stuff in through the storm doors.

"Weird," Sean said, plopping onto the futon couch. "Like day-jaw-view, or whatever the hell."

"Déjà vu," I laughed.

The furniture was arranged something like it had been in Silverlake. I opened one of the boxes stacked along the wall and found several of the video recorders I used for copying promotional tapes.

"This equipment should get us something," I said. "Let's find a pawnshop."

"Will we be coming back to that house?" Sean asked as we drove toward Little Rock. "It's old and creepy. I don't like it."

"I don't know. Maybe we'll go on to New York," I said.

What Sean really wanted to know, of course, was whether I planned to dump him for Thad.

We stopped at a pawnshop near the Highland Court projects where I had met Snake. The name, Big Dude's, was blazoned in neon lights across the façade. Situated so near the drug zone, I figured they would be accustomed to seeing motley characters like Sean and me. Big Dude, the owner, wore a seventies afro with blue jean overalls and a red vest. First off, the man called in the serial numbers to see if they were stolen. Satisfied they were clean, he checked the quality, taking off the covers to examine the heads for wear. The video recorders were professional models. Each would be worth several hundred dollars, retail.

"Two hundred," Big Dude offered. "But I can only take four machines."

I was in no frame of mind to haggle. The amount seemed reasonable. I'd sell some of the furniture later on and redeem the equipment. That is, if none of my business prospects came through. I'd not asked Thad if he had news from any of my clients. Thad's proclamation of love, and Sean's sudden appearance in the hallway, had gotten me completely flustered. I probably would not have had the wherewithal to ask, anyway.

Sean turned pale when I drove into Highland Court. "What are you doing?" he said. "Let's go to BT's."

"I want drugs now," I said. "Someone around here's bound to have a twenty dollar piece."

"Yeah, and a gun in their pocket."

Dusk had fallen. The buildings cast long shadows, providing cover for the drug dealers. But no one would come near the car.

"They probably think we're police," I said.

"There's two cop cars behind that building." Sean said, sitting up and motioning toward an alley.

When I came over a rise in the road, flashing lights filled the rearview mirror as the cars raced toward me.

Sean shrieked, "Get the fuck out of here!"

I hit the accelerator. Now sirens blared in syncopation with the flashing lights.

"They're following us," I said, nervously.

"Ditch the pipes," Sean said.

As we crossed a bridge, I reached under the seat and tossed the pipes into the stream. Only then did I begin to slow down.

"We haven't done anything to worry about," I said, but my thumping heart betrayed the seeming confidence.

I turned onto a side street just beyond the projects. One police car parked behind me. The other pulled alongside. A voice came over a loudspeaker, "Turn off the engine and get out of the car."

Sean and I stood on opposite sides of the car. The voice said to put our hands on the hood of the car. We obeyed. One of the cops took my wallet.

"What are you stopping us for?" I asked.

"Shut up," the officer said.

One of the policemen took the keys from the ignition and opened the trunk. "Looks like these two stole some video equipment," he said to his compatriots.

"They're mine," I protested. "I hocked some at Big Dude's pawnshop. He didn't want them all. Look in my shirt pocket. There's a receipt. The fat guy at the store ran a check on everything. Come on, call Big Dude's. They'll confirm it."

The policeman closed the trunk, took the receipt out of my pocket, and went to his car. A few minutes later, he returned. "Looks like Old Grissom at Big Dude's checked out the machines. None of 'em stolen." The man gave me a stern look. "But I know you fellows are up to something. Stay in position while I run a check on your license plate."

I probably seemed like a fool who'd accidentally driven into a dangerous housing project. I was sure the ordeal would be over soon and that Sean and I would be on our way to BT's.

Suddenly, the policemen got out of their cars with pistols drawn.

"What now?" I asked.

One of policemen forced me to the ground.

"Mr. Powell, you are under arrest for grand theft auto," the office said. Then he recited the Miranda warning.

"This is my car. It's on loan from the dealership."

"This isn't the stolen vehicle," the officer said. "You stole a van."

I tried to piece together what must have happened. Those Memphis people did it, I started to say, but figured I better keep my mouth shut.

One of the policemen called for a tow truck.

"Let my friend take the car," I said.

"It would save us some paperwork," one of the policemen acknowledged.

"Fine. Let him take it," the other replied.

"Take it to Dean's," I told an ashen-faced Sean. "Tell him I'm in jail."

The officers shoved me into a patrol car. As we drove away, I could see Sean sitting behind the wheel seat. I wasn't even sure he knew how to drive.

CHAPTER FORTY-FOUR

During the summer that I turned seventeen, I was at the apartment of a co-worker from my job at Burger Chef. He was a little older than me, probably in his early twenties. We weren't friends, exactly, but on occasion he had invited me to drop by his place to smoke pot. He assumed I was cool because of my long hair and the fact that he saw me reading *The Greening of America* during breaks.

I took him up on the offer and went by one evening after dropping off a date at her house. The girl had wanted to kiss me, and I just couldn't do it. I was in love with a guy and had only gone on the date as cover. The girl's disappointment and the knowledge of my own hypocrisy made me want to escape myself.

At my co-worker's apartment, five people were sitting in a circle on the floor. Incense perfumed the air as sitar music drifted from the stereo. The group stood up, nervously, when I came into the room. Two of them had just robbed a drugstore. On the coffee table in the middle of the circle were dozens of red, yellow, and black pills arranged in piles on a handkerchief.

"The guy's okay," my co-worker vouched. "Everyone relax." The group didn't look convinced, but they sat back down.

"Take one," a skinny fellow told me. I figured he wanted to confirm that I wasn't a narc by watching me take a pill. "Wha'cha want? Yellow jacket? Black mollies?"

I said "red" because it was my favorite color. I had no idea what the pill would do to me.

The skinny fellow placed a couple in my hand. "Better take a couple of jackets with you, 'case you want to wake up later on."

Someone handed me a bottle of beer. I washed down two of the reds.

The next thing I knew, I was being pulled over by a policeman. I didn't remember going to my car, much less leaving the apartment. When I didn't respond to the policeman's commands, he pulled open the driver's side door. I collapsed onto the pavement like a scarecrow removed from its scaffolding.

I regained some composure as I sat in the back seat of the patrol car. I felt in my pocket and found the yellow pills, pretending to cough so I could inconspicuously swallow them. By the time we arrived at the police station, I was alert.

The desk officer put a rotary phone on the desk and told me I could make one call. I dialed home. When Vivian answered, I told her that I'd been picked up on my way home. She and Lenny would be there right away, she said. Since I was only seventeen, the police allowed me to wait on a bench in the hallway rather than throw me in the drunk-tank.

"What are you on?" a policemen asked me. "Uppers or downers?" Then he laughed, making his multiple chins squeeze out of his shirt. He walked away, running a finger around his collar to tuck in the folds of flesh.

The mirror opposite my seat showed me what I looked like to the policemen – a hippie with embroidered jeans, and a brightly colored sweatshirt with green trim around the sleeves and a strawberry printed on the front.

By the time Vivian and Lenny came marching down the hallway, I was stone sober.

"Why is my son here?" Lenny demanded of the double-chinned policeman.

"We done pulled him over," the man said, "else he would've killed someone weaving all over the road like he was." When he finished speaking, the man rolled his tongue around the inside his cheeks and then picked up a Styrofoam cup to spit out tobacco juice.

"It was my contact lenses," I said quietly as a private message for Lenny and Vivian. "My eyes were hurting."

"Did you do a breath test?" Lenny asked. "My son don't drink."

"We will if you want," the cop said. He ordered one of his subordinates to administer the test.

I passed with flying colors; the one beer didn't even register.

The desk sergeant reached in a drawer and found a syringe. "We found this in the back seat of the patrol car that brought in your son," he said to Lenny.

"Get that out of my face," I said as the policemen waved it at me.

"My boy don't do nothing like that," Lenny protested.

The fat policeman grabbed my arm and pulled it taut so he could see the fold at my elbow. He was sure there would be track marks.

"You see? My boy ain't done nothing!" Lenny said, madder than I'd ever seen him. "I want to speak to the captain."

The double-chinned policeman and his cohorts decided to let me go. They apologized to Lenny, but when they looked at me, I could hear their thoughts: Your day will come.

Now, twenty years later, I found myself in the same dingy hallway sitting on the same uncomfortable bench.

"Why am I here? I haven't done anything," I said to the booking clerk. "What's this about a rental car?"

"You'll find out at the arraignment," the man said without sympathy or emotion.

The Little Rock jail was notorious for being overcrowded. It was equally well-known for its dangers. The evening news often carried reports of inmates being stabbed in their cells. I thought about that as the guard led me down a dimly lit corridor and thrust me into a cage with at least twenty other men. When the door slid shut, I held onto the bars, afraid to look around for fear of making eye contact.

"Look at that tight ass," someone said.

"Give me a piece of that action!" another hooted.

"Aw, leave him alone," said an older voice. "Probably got a disease to be that skinny."

A high-pitched call came from the back of the cell: "Hey, Holmes. We got rock back here. You want some?" And when I didn't turn around, "Hey crack-head! We're talking to you."

I wanted a blast so desperately that I almost believed them. I stayed at the cell door and kept my eye on the guard leisurely strolling up and down the hallway.

"Hey, homeboy," called out a muscular black fellow with hair done up in pigtails. He grabbed my shoulder, leaned close, and said, "You suck dick?"

Sweat poured from my hairline. If I said yes, I'd be beaten up as a queer. If I said no, they'd condemn me as worthless and beat me up anyway.

The pigtailed fellow, shirtless, and wearing loose blue jeans that fell just below the band of his under shorts, pushed me against the wall. "Well?"

"Sometimes," I said faintly, my heart rising to my throat.

"Follow me," the dude said. He must have had seniority. Everyone else scurried onto their bunks as we passed. A few murmured to themselves, but the catcalls stopped.

Only a few inmates were as skinny as me. Many were obese. Everyone stank of body odor. A shower stood in one corner, but it had no curtain and didn't appear to have been used recently. The toilet, a stainless steel seat jutting from the floor, was in constant use, adding to the rank odors that made it hard to breath.

Pigtails escorted me to his bottom bunk opposite the dry shower. The bunk was draped by faded blankets that hung from the upper frame. Several men had obviously given this guy their bedding.

"Just a sec," I said, excusing myself. "I've really got to pee."

While I was relieving myself, a young, dark-haired fellow came up behind me. "That's the Boss, dude. You better do what he says. For a nickel, he'll get you killed."

I went back to the pigtailed Boss's bunk. From inside, sitting up on his knees, he pulled back the corner of a blanket and motioned me to join him. As I was crawling in, Boss whipped out his hard ten-incher and wagged it in my face. I dreaded what it might taste like, and wondering how I was going to manage the size, took it in my fist and stroked, hoping to delay the inevitable as long as possible.

Suddenly, the curtains parted. Every criminal in the cell stood around gawking at the scene. They laughed with hideous glee.

"I told you we'd get the next one," the Boss said, tucking his deflating cock into his loose jeans.

"Got an honest-to-god cocksucker here!" one of the cellmates jeered.

The Boss knocked me on the mouth and shoved me out of his bunk. I tumbled onto the concrete floor.

"Goddamn queer," he taunted.

Humiliated, and frightened that one of the other inmates would take over where the Boss left off, I ran to the bars at the cell door and wrapped my arms through them. A bloodcurdling scream rose from my lungs. Guards rushed over to see what was happening.

"Get me out of here!" I screamed.

When a guard opened the door, I fell forward, blathering incoherently. The Boss had busted my lip. Saliva and blood soaked the front of my shirt. The guard probably thought I'd been shanked.

"What did they do to him?" one of the two guards asked the other as they escorted me down the hall.

"They were fuckin' around. Hell, he ain't hurt. That's just spit and blood on him."

"That guy in the pigtails probably put him through the initiation," one of the guards said.

They laughed so hard they almost lost their grip on me.

Next, I was dragged inside a room with no furniture except a metal cot bolted to the floor. The guards told me to strip. They sat me on the cot and left. Streams of water surged from spigots on the wall, so cold it felt like a spray of angry bees digging into my skin.

When the shower ended, someone opened the steel door and tossed me a towel. Then a different guard appeared.

"Put this on," the man said, handing me an orange jumpsuit. He watched as I struggled to get into it.

"It doesn't fit," I complained. The garment was a least two sizes too small, and I wasn't given underwear. I nearly maimed myself trying to zip it up.

"It'll have to do," the guard said. "Ain't another one come out of the laundry yet."

"I can't go back to that cell," I said as we entered the hallway.

"Then we'll have to put you with that murderin' Riddle," the man said, opening the door of a small cell near the guard station.

Inside, two platforms that served as beds jutted from the wall one above the other. A shower stall in the corner was defined by a mildewed curtain that hung from three hooks fastened to a rusted metal bar. A toilet and sink took up the opposite corner. The place reminded me of isolation tanks such as one might see in an old movie. Instead of bars, the cell door was solid except for a six-inch window with a sliding strip of metal that could only be opened from the outside.

Murderin' Riddle was a young man. He wore the same type of jumpsuit I'd been given, but his was yellow, and it fit. He sat on the bottom bunk looking up sympathetically as the cop shoved me through the door and slammed it shut.

"Don't worry," Riddle said, extending a rough, weathered hand. "I ain't like them other guys. That was you screaming earlier, wudn't it?"

I nodded.

"They sez I'm a murderer. But I ain't murdered no one."

Murderer or not, the friendly look on Riddle's face put me at ease, despite the scars on his face and forearms that told of a violent life. I leaped onto the top bunk and was confronted by chips of plaster that had fallen from the ceiling. One corner of the mattress was damp from a leak. I swept off the ceiling dust and covered myself with the scratchy blanket, keeping my feet to one side to avoid the wet spot.

Riddle lay on his bunk and began narrating his story, as if he'd been waiting for the opportunity to tell someone.

"They can't pin it on me," Riddle began. "I don't care how hard they try. They say I left the party and went home for my gun. Weren't true. I had that gun right there in my pocket. He drew a knife and I shot him. That's the way it happened. Weren't pre-medicated – think that's what they tried to call it – but I hadn't done no drugs. You understand what I'm saying?"

A quiet groan gave Riddle confirmation that I was listening. Actually, I wanted Riddle to be quiet and leave me alone, but I dared not say anything. He continued for what must have been an hour, finally ending his tale with, "Riddle's not in here for long. Not the Riddle man."

Satisfied that he had fully explained himself, Riddle fell asleep. Then I almost wished he were still talking. His droning had at least made me drowsy. Now I was kept awake by the relentless murmur of voices coming from the other cells and by guards talking loudly to each other outside the metal door. At some point, though, I passed out.

At six o'clock the next morning, a guard set paper plates on the floor. I was sure he set the food near the toilet deliberately, out of spite.

Riddle lurched for the breakfast. "Better get yours before the mice beat you to it."

I rolled off the bed just in time to see what Riddle meant. A rodent came out of a hole near the shower and made its way along the wall under Riddle's bunk.

"My God!" I exclaimed. "What kind of place is this?"

"The Little Rock Ritz," Riddle said with a twisted smile.

I swallowed some of the grits-like substance on the plate. The slice of toast had the consistency of sandstone. Chalky powdered milk was all we were given to try to wash it down.

When Riddle finished his food, he leaned against the door, shifting his position one way and then another to afford himself various views of the hallway. When he spotted a guard, he begged for food, affecting in a little boy's voice. "I'll have more, sir," he said, probably not realizing who he sounded like. I was sure he'd never read Dickens.

"Aw man," Riddle called out plaintively. "You're not goin' to sit there eating donuts right in front of me."

Half of a donut came through the metal window. Riddle received it as if it were steak.

"Thank you, sir," Riddle said in mock-gracious tones. "I sho' does thank ya mas. . ." He stopped short of saying massuh.

"Shut up, ya ungrateful niggah," the guard shouted. Riddle smirked. He didn't seem to mind the slur as long as he got his sweets.

"How long have you been in this cell?" I asked.

Riddle stayed at the door as he answered. "About six months." He put his mouth to the window. "Hey Legion!" he called out. "Legion!"

A gurgling sound rose from down the hallway. The strange noise grew in intensity, expanding from froglike croak to a banshee howl. I heard a man's and a woman's voice, but they appeared to be arising from a single individual.

"Legion! Speak to me," Riddle again called out.

A disturbing cacophony of sounds blended with the sexually ambiguous howl.

"What the hell is that?" I asked, putting my face next to Riddle's so I could hear what was happening.

"That's Legion," Riddle said.

Riddle backed away to allow me to have a look. The sounds came from a nearby cell with a solid door like ours, but with an even smaller window. Behind the open slit peered two bloodshot, animalistic eyes.

"Legion gets disturbed when I call it out," Riddle explained. He went back to the window and shouted, "I know who you are, Legion."

Riddle sat on his bunk and took a Gideon Bible from under the mattress. He began reading loudly.

"'He had his dwelling among tombs. Unclean spirit! No one could bind him, not even with chains. He saw Jesus from afar and worshiped him. Cried out, 'What have I to do with You, Jesus, Son of the Most High God? Do not torment me.'"

Riddle shook the Bible at the window.

I recalled reading that part of the Bible once, and feeling sympathy for the suffering, rebellious creature it described.

Legion's screaming resumed more violently than before. I wondered how anyone could sustain such a sound that without popping an artery.

"Shut up!" the guard yelled at Riddle. "Quit aggravating that girl."

"I's aggravatin' a demon, Massa," Riddle mocked.

With the harsh slamming of the window flap, we lost sight of the world beyond our cell. The space became claustrophobically smaller.

"Guess that's all the entertainment we get this morning," Riddle said, resigning himself to a long stretch of boredom.

Riddle and I were the same height and about the same weight, both skinny as rails. But Riddle was large-boned and in good shape. He was clean-shaven, while I had a scraggly beard. As I began to ponder how Riddle managed to maintain such a close shave, he took out a mirror and plastic razor from a box stored under his bunk.

"Time to clean up," Riddle said, placing a stopper in the sink. "Hardly any hot water," he noted, "but if you soak long enough, it don't hurt to shave."

With that, he unzipped the jumpsuit halfway and pulled it off his shoulders, rolling the material down to his waist. He wetted a washrag, lathered it with soap, and held it against his face. I took the opportunity to study his body. Riddle was solid muscle.

"How are old are you?" I asked.

"Eighteen," Riddle replied. "Why'd you want to know?"

"Might have been better if you shot the guy a year ago."

"They'd still a'tried me as an adult. Seventeen don't make no difference in Arkansas."

I sat on my bunk gazing down at Riddle's shoulders and watching his muscles flex as he positioned the razor. Riddle turned sideways to angle himself for a neck shave. When he shifted to the other foot, the jumpsuit slipped precariously low. I caught Riddle's eye in the mirror. He was watching me.

"You make me nervous sittin' up there like a cock-a-tiel," Riddle said, emphasizing the first part of the word. He finished shaving and dabbed his face with paper towels. "Shit man. I ain't had no partner in here for a long time. How am I supposed to get cleaned up?"

A hell of a long time, I repeated to myself. So, someone had shared the cell with him in the past. I started fantasizing about what they might have done together.

"Clean up like you usually do," I said. "Don't mind me."

Riddle sucked in his stomach and the jumpsuit fell to the floor. A large pole levitated from his body as the garment raked across it. "I usually do somethin' else in the mornings, if ya know what I mean."

Without weighing the consequences, I jumped to the floor and unzipped my tight-fitting jumpsuit. Riddle and I sword played with our cocks. The act was spontaneous, a game boys play with each other when they get horny.

"Riddle ain't used to this," my cellmate said. "But I ain't protesting. It's kinda fun."

I went to my knees and took in as much of Riddle as I could manage. He made pigtail Boss look small. Riddle's knees began to buckle and he fell back onto the bunk.

"Want to fuck me?" I whispered.

Riddle stepped from his jumpsuit, laid me on his bunk, and raised my feet so I could press them against the upper bunk.

"Soap it up," I said.

Riddle urgently lathered his finger and worked it inside me. Then he approached like a jousting knight.

"This ain't going to hurt, is it?" Riddle asked before going all the way.

"I want it to hurt," I said, bracing myself.

My words drove Riddle's passions as he pressed his weight against me. The air grew saturated with the pungent odor of bodies in heat. Luxurious pain consumed me.

Funny how religious experience and sexual release are so closely related. As the pain soared up my spine, I felt relief in believing it was payment for my sins. I was Legion getting his just deserts. The mix of emotions took over my judgment and I started to scream. Riddle stuffed the edge of his blanket into my mouth.

"Be quiet," he said. "The guards'll hear you and we'll both be damned."

Just then, Legion began to howl. The hysterical voice penetrated the metal doors as if it were a spirit gaining access to our cell.

"I am Legion! For we are many!" the ancient demon announced as the din become a ghostly chorale.

Legion! For we are many!

The voices merged to form a unison chant.

I aided Riddle by pushing up hard. His body jerked spasmodically.

Legion's wail softened and a familiar voice rose above the din. *I am the wife you betrayed.*

Riddle's passion raced into my body as liquid fire. He collapsed beside me and used the end of the sheet to wipe himself off.

"Blood of the Lamb," Riddle laughed, commenting the stains caused by my torn ass.

The voice of a lonely girl now came from down the hall. It was the whimpering of a woman trying to keep her demons at bay. She was speaking to a guard, insisting on her innocence.

"You ain't innocent," the guard responded. "You stabbed your boyfriend like he was a slab of meat.

"But I am innocent," the girl insisted. "He beat me to an inch of my life!"

The guard slammed shut the metal window on the girl's cell. The clack resounded through the hallway.

Riddle went to the shower to wash out the sheet and to clean himself better. "Damn," he said, "you're one crazy fuck."

I sat on the clammy concrete floor. The area around me grew red as the weight of my body forced blood from my anus. Riddle put on his jumpsuit. He reached out a hand to help me up.

"No," I said, pushing him away. "Pain is all I know of redemption."

"What the hell you talking about?" Riddle said, easily irritated now after his violent orgasm. "You need to get in the shower, too. I don't want no doctor at the infirmary accusin' me of raping you or somethin'. I got enough troubles."

I did as he asked, relishing the stab of pain caused by the lye-based soap.

When I came out of the shower, Riddle had curled up on his bunk facing the wall.

From the hallway, voices rose in unison: *I am Legion, for we are many.*

CHAPTER FORTY-FIVE

On Monday morning, the door to the cell opened and I felt a nightstick poke me in the back. "Get up," a guard demanded. "Arraignment time."

The man led me to the front desk to sign out. On the way, we passed Legion's cell. A chill ran up my spine as I looked at the closed metal shutter. I expected it to fly open at any second and for that strange pair of eyes to follow me down the hall.

I joined a train of men, handcuffed and shackled. Most were rough-looking characters with Bible-ink tattoos and scarred faces. Thirteen manacled men marched toward the courthouse. We weren't allowed to wear coats and the sharp wind blowing across the Arkansas River ripped through our flimsy jumpsuits. Upon our arrival, a guard herded us into the cramped quarters of a waiting room. Soon, a heavy-set man was unshackled and led away.

Hours passed as one by one, our numbers diminished. No one had returned, and I wondered if perhaps I would be seeing a lenient judge who had released them all. Finally, a guard loosened my handcuffs and led me into the courtroom where sunlight streaming through the windows momentarily blinded me. The guard took a seat at a mahogany table next to the public defender who had been assigned to me. I was startled to see familiar faces seated in the front row. Connie was there, her expression frozen in a mask of disapproval. Derek held onto the pew in front of him as if he might kneel at any moment and offer a prayer. Vivian stood up when our eyes met, but she quickly collapsed under the burden of her grief.

The judge listened to the charges. I was in such a fog that I barely comprehended what was going on. Was this an inquisition? Was I being charged with apostasy?

"How do you plead?" the judge asked.

"Innocent," I responded.

The public defender looked at me with alarm and began explaining to the judge that I had rented a van for another party, and though they kept the vehicle longer than originally intended, my credit card should have covered the additional expense. The problem was that the rental company entered the number incorrectly and the amount wasn't authorized. The clerk at the rental company reported the vehicle stolen.

The judge made no comment as he set a trial date. An officer led me back to jail. On the way across the street, I heard a slurred voice.

"Bubby!" the voice called. It was Vivian, walking arm-in-arm with Connie and Derek.

"Tell them you're guilty and you can come home, now," Vivian said. "That lawyer told us."

"Guilty?" I said. "Woman, what have you to do with me?"

Vivian pretended not to hear, looking quizzically at Connie, who said, "We'll try to get you out on bail until the court date."

The guard yanked my bound hands and thrust me into the street when the walk sign came on. He motioned for the family to keep their distance.

"You'll have to communicate with him through the lawyer," the guard said. "Ya'll just stay here until we get to the other side."

"Bubby!" Vivian called again.

I spent the next day in a stupor, barely nibbling the bland jailhouse food, and oblivious to the presence of Riddle, who wasn't interested in talking anyway. He had stopped needling Legion. All day, he retreated to his bunk and poured over his Gideon Bible, seeking atonement, I figured, for having had sex with me.

The monotony was interrupted by a guard pulling back the metal shutter and informing me that I had a visitor. I stood in front of the bunk until he unlatched the door and then I marched forward with my arms outstretched. The guard slipped handcuffs onto my wrists and shepherded me to a booth where inmates spoke to visitors sitting opposite a Plexiglas window.

Dean had come to visit. He held the receiver of the old phone to his ear while resting his elbow on the ledge. He motioned for me to pick up the phone on my side.

"Are you okay?" Dean asked. "Do you need anything?"

"Is Vivian all right?" I asked, ignoring his questions.

"She called," Dean said. "Well, Connie called for her. It's difficult for your mother, you know – you being in here and all, seeing you in court."

I'd never seen him so circumspect.

Dean continued, "Connie said you didn't recognize Vivian, that you said something cruel."

"That whole morning is a blur," I demurred.

"Simon," Dean said, "Do you even know why you were arrested?"

"Not really," I confessed.

"They say you rented a van and that it was impounded during a drug bust in Atlanta. The district attorney there wants to pursue charges, accusing you of being an accomplice. You should be glad that Arkansas doesn't cotton to extraditing one of its own."

The Memphis Mafioso, BT, Violet, Sean, Thad, my belongings – a flood of disjointed images flooded my thoughts.

"Atlanta?" I asked.

"Did you lose your credit card or something?"

"Someone paid me to rent them a van. I needed cash."

"You were conned," Dean reasoned. "Anyway, the public defender had it all worked out. You were supposed to plead guilty to a misdemeanor. But you spoke too quickly and claimed innocence. Now the lawyer isn't sure what to do."

I couldn't even remember the court appearance.

"Are they feeding you well enough in there? Should you see a doctor?"

"What happened to Sean?" I asked, changing the subject.

"He brought your car to my place. I held onto the keys and wouldn't let him drive it."

"Is he okay?"

"He stayed for a few days, but then he disappeared. I haven't heard anything since."

The phone slipped from my hand, but I caught it.

"Thanks for coming to see me," I said. I looked around at the stark walls and admitted to Dean that everything was a blur since the day I was arrested.

"I'll get you help," Dean promised as he stood up to leave.

"The judge wants to see you, boy," a mountain of a guard said as he opened the cell door and motioned for me to come out.

Sensing that this would be the end of my ordeal, I wanted to offer Riddle a few words of comfort. From what I knew of his case, he likely would be in prison for the rest of his life. He was asleep, though, and I dared not wake him, having made that mistake once before and nearly gotten a black eye for it.

The public defender was ready to argue my case, but the judge dismissed all charges before he even got started. All the judge cared about was the fact that no one appeared to represent the rental company and there were no formal charges stemming from any arrests in Atlanta.

Following the dismissal, I was taken back to the jail where the guard returned my street clothes and personal affects. I signed a form and stepped through a gate to freedom – and to friends and family.

"We're glad to have you back," Dean said as he gave me a hug.

Connie and Derek were with him. Connie's eyes virtually simmered with disdain. Derek wrapped an arm around her waist to pull her away before she said something hurtful, I supposed. At the car, released from Derek's grip, she could hold back no longer. "We went through all your things from Los Angeles."

Derek shot her a disapproving glance and said under his breath, "Not now."

"Not now?" Connie repeated. "He may be my brother, but he nearly killed our mother!" Her gaze locked on me. "We found your videos – and those magazines. Is that how you made your living out there? Selling trash?" Overcome with vengefulness, she ended her tirade, saying, "I can't believe you've sunk so low."

"And I can't believe you went through my things," I muttered.

Connie harrumphed and turned away.

"We were looking for the rental agreement on the van," Derek said. "We didn't mean to pry."

"But Vivian wanted me to be guilty," I said.

"No, Simon," Derek said. "You misunderstood. The public defender told us that under the circumstances, if you pleaded guilty, the judge would give you time served. But now, it's good you didn't do that since the charges were dropped."

"Is Thad still in town?" I asked.

"He's at our house," Derek said. "He didn't want to leave town until he knew you'd be all right. The night you were arrested, he called to talk to you. We had just gotten word from Dean that you were in jail."

"Tell Thad he can go back to Los Angeles. I'll stay at Dean's. I need to get my car, and all."

"*And all* means that Sean kid, right?" Connie spewed.

Derek grabbed her forearm.

"It might be best for Simon to stay with me for a few days," Dean said to Derek, almost imperceptibly tilting his head toward Connie.

Derek gave Dean a handshake and said, "Simon needs more friends like you." Then he put a hand on my shoulder. "We're praying for you, Simon."

The way I recoiled, he may as well have sprinkled holy water on a vampire. I ran to catch up with Dean who'd already started down the street toward his car.

I wanted to retrieve Cicero, find Sean, and be on my way to New York. It was the only dream I had left – to find a studio and paint. Religious fantasies had played enough of a part in my life and I had endured the numbing effects of drugs far too long. It was time to seize my destiny and become the artist I should have been.

"I put the video equipment in the bedroom," Dean said as we passed the Cougar parked in his yard. "You were trying to get drug money, weren't you?"

A rejoinder formed in my mind, but I kept silent.

"Let me get you help, Simon."

"I don't need any help," I said, trying to sound as though I had no idea what he meant. "I'll be leaving soon. You can have the VCRs if you want them."

"Putting the house in order?" Dean asked. I detected something close to alarm in his voice.

"Just getting rid of things I won't need," I said. "Take my computer if you want it. You can go to Vivian's and pick it up. I'll leave a letter saying it was a gift."

"You've been through a lot recently," Dean said. "Stay here for a few days and relax."

Without replying, I went to shower. I smelled like the jail – sweaty and fecal – and couldn't wait to get cleaned up.

Afterward, I quietly opened the door to listen as Dean spoke on the phone. What I heard infuriated me. I stormed into the bedroom, found my keys, and dashed out the front door.

He's displaying the classic signs, Dean had said. I was a counselor. I know when someone is contemplating suicide.

Dean stood helpless in the doorway as I drove off. Never again will I have to deal with this, I thought. Not Dean's dripping concern or Derek's egregious sympathy. I'd be free of Vivian's debilitating worry and oblivious to Connie's despicable schadenfreude.

I still had the two hundred dollars cash from the pawnshop. I went directly to BT's. Sean would be there. I was sure of it. I banged on the apartment door. My heart sank with each unanswered knock. When I finally accepted that no one was at home, I returned to my car, slumped toward the passenger seat, and began to sob, but only for a moment. I pulled myself upright and started the hunt anew.

Dante's Club was closed, but I spotted a group huddled around the barrel across the street. As I approached, BT waved. He pulled away from the group and approached the window.

"Where the hell you been?" he asked, evidently unaware of the trouble caused by the Memphis people. "That dude of yours been coming around here. He keeps trying to tell me you'll pay later if I give him something. He never did say where you was."

"Been in jail," I said without further explanation.

BT smiled. "I know what that's like."

"Got anything on you?" I asked.

"Nah. But I know where to get some. How much you spending?"

"I can part with a hundred."

"Tells you what. You and me, let's take a ride. They's a fellow comes and parks up the street about this time of day."

We drove up Sixth Street to a liquor store. A swarthy, handsome man sat in the driver's seat of a white pickup.

"Who's that guy?" I asked as BT was getting out of the car.

"That's Gabriel."

The voices broke their silence. *Blow Gabriel's horn*, they sang. *The end approaches.*

BT returned within moments. "The fellow I was lookin' for ain't around," he said. "But Gabriel's got a hundred hisself. If you two go in together, we got us some booyah."

I took out a hundred dollars and handed it to BT.

"We gots to drive a ways. Gabriel said we could go in his truck. Says he gets nervous riding around in other folks' cars. Not that he thinks you're a narc or nothin'."

"Guess that's okay," I said. "Let me park over here." I found a spot where I hoped no one would bother the car. The white truck pulled alongside.

"My name's Gabriel," the driver said. "Pleased to meet you."

"Same here," I said, grasping his soft hand.

Gabriel's hair fell in strands over his ears and brushed against his collar in the back. With his high cheekbones, aristocratic nose, and lips that invited kissing, he was a beguiling creature.

BT directed us to Highland Court. We stopped one block from where the police had pulled me over. Returning to the site of my arrest felt as though I were tempting fate. BT told Gabriel to back into a parking space between two vans. Then he disappeared with our money into one of the apartments. He said he would only be a few minutes, but a half hour later he had not returned. I kept trying to break the ice with Gabriel.

"Are you from Little Rock?" I asked, but because of his accent, I was sure he wasn't.

"Fort Worth, actually," Gabriel responded. "Just moved here."

Gabriel's voice was mesmerizing. I was thrilled when, at one point, he asked, "What are you doing after we get drugs?"

"Don't know," I said. "The friend I'm staying with doesn't do drugs."

The look on Gabriel's face made him look like a young boy who wants to ask for something but doesn't want to be disappointed, and therefore holds back. He turned toward me and stared directly into my eyes.

"I thought I'd get a room downtown. Want to join me? I have pipes and stuff."

"Yeah, sure," I said, stumbling over my words. "We can smoke together. That'd be great."

My fantasies about what might happen in the hotel had me sweating. I was happy when BT finally returned. He first came to my window and dropped ten rocks into my hand.

"I'm impressed, BT. These are big as marbles."

"Okay with you?" I asked Gabriel, showing him what I had.

"I'll be staying here," BT said. "Y'all go on about your business."

Gabriel started the engine and sped away.

"Thought I'd get a room at the Little Rock Hotel," Gabriel said once we were back on the main road.

A lump formed in my throat. He was planning to stay at Little Rock's gay hotel. I rolled the drugs around my palm.

"Careful with those," Gabriel said. "Reach under the seat. There's a bag with my stuff in it."

I felt under the seat and located a pouch. Inside were two crack pipes and a small container. I placed the rocks in it.

Gabriel rested his bronze hand on the seat beside me. He had on a ring of yellow and white gold in a weave pattern.

"Is that a wedding ring?" I asked, crestfallen.

Gabriel smiled, his lips widening to reveal perfectly straight, ivory-white teeth which shone against his dark skin and short-cropped goatee.

"I'm not married, and don't plan to be."

I found myself blathering. In the midst of chatter about Los Angeles and the film industry, I blurted out, "And you know I'm gay, don't you?"

Without skipping a beat, Gabriel said, "That's okay. I go both ways."

At the Little Rock Hotel, Gabriel left me in the truck while he went inside to get a room. I pulled down the visor and checked myself in the mirror. What a sad comparison I was to Gabriel. My hair was stringy beyond the help of a brush. My shirt stank with sweat. The cuffs of my jeans were frayed and dirty. I had often been aroused by hustlers just as unkempt, but never imagined I'd wind up in such a state myself.

Gabriel returned with the room key and parked in an alley behind the hotel. I carried a bag with the paraphernalia and drugs and followed him through the lobby. An antique elevator took us to the sixth floor where we found our room at the end of a long corridor.

"The guy at the desk said this is the quietest room they have," Gabriel told me as he slipped the key in the lock.

A voice whispered, *the sixth floor is where Satan lives*. I tried to ignore it. *When you blow Gabriel's horn, the end will come.*

Don't listen to it!

"What?" Gabriel asked, shutting the door behind us.

"Nothing at all," I said, not having realized I'd spoken aloud. "Let's fire up that pipe."

Gabriel sat on the bed, shucked off his shoes and socks, and leaned against the headboard.

"You dress well," I said, as I took a razorblade from the pouch Gabriel had set down and cut slices from one of the rocks.

"I go to college at Philander Smith," Gabriel said. "Everyone there dresses well – better than me, most of them. Mind if I get more comfortable?"

"Not at all," I said, trying to keep my voice at a steady pitch.

Gabriel rolled to the other side of the bed and took off his shirt and trousers. By the time he bounced back against the headboard, he wore only a pair of silk boxers. He plunged his toes under my thigh as I readied the drugs.

"Got cold feet," Gabriel laughed nervously.

I took off my shoes and socks, then my shirt and jeans. Naked to my jockeys, I sat on the edge of the bed and handed Gabriel one of the pipes, loaded with drugs.

"Want me to light it for you?" I asked.

"Sure," Gabriel said. He held the stem to his lips.

I waved a flame over the rock. Sparks sprayed the air as smoke swirled into the spherical chamber. Gabriel's body tensed and he sank into the pillows. I took the pipe from him and placed it on the table. Then, taking a chance, I pressed my lips against his. Gabriel exhaled into my mouth with a smoky wet kiss. The drug had an arousing affect, and there was no hint of paranoia in Gabriel's eyes. I ran my hands over his chest, catching his nipples and gently pinching. By the time I worked my way to the elastic band supporting his boxers, Gabriel's horn was peeking through the fly.

Just high enough from the secondhand smoke to feel ravenous, I pulled off the boxers, spread Gabriel's legs, and worshipped his body, kissing my way from his feet to his thighs. Gabriel moaned like Pentecostal speaking in tongues. I did a blast, mustering all my will not to get paranoid. Gabriel pushed me deeper between his legs, and I finally exhaled. Smoke rose up to surround Gabriel's erection.

"Lick it," Gabriel pleaded.

Gabriel has come for the end of time.

All became black, like the void of death. I heard laughter, cruel and harsh. From a tiny pinpoint of light, Gabriel's eyes emerged from the darkness, then a face with horns, and ears like swine. A hand reached from above us and broke off one of the horns. Someone commanded that I open my mouth and a chorus of voices blared forth, though I was sure my mouth was not moving.

Then the darkness melted away. I was wrapped tightly in a blanket on the floor beside the bed. I called out for Gabriel, but the room was empty. I wriggled free of my cocoon and quickly dressed. The drugs and the pipes were gone. There was no evidence that anyone else had occupied the room. From the walls sprang winged creatures. They wore luminescent robes hued in rainbow colors. I rose from my lowly position and soared among them. They sang, *You have met the joys of heaven and known the depths of hell. You are the dark soul seeking light.*

An insistent knocking caught my attention, and all of a sudden, an upright creature took form within the room. It attempted to communicate, but the primitive speech was unintelligible.

A species called human, said one of the bright beings hovering around me. *Pay no heed.*

The creature persisted in its desire to convey meaning. The angels led me to the door and soared into the night. I was ready to fly away with them, but the upright creature caught me by the shirt and pulled me back. The angels returned to lead me onward to the elevator. How primitive to use a machine, I thought, when I am borne on the wings of angels.

I was on the streets of an abandoned city. A new angel, a slender giant with a single bright eye, lit the way before me.

You must be cleansed, the angel said, *baptized in the river of your birth.*

The being led me to a muddy embankment near the Arkansas River, a point called La Petit Roche.

Upon this rock you must shed the torment of your flesh and rise anew.

I stripped bare for the baptism.

When I looked upon the surface of the gently flowing water, each painting that I had burned upon joining the church rose from the waves. I tried to grab them, but they dissolved upon touch.

The angels sang, *Art is Isaac in a dream, stop the heart and hear God scream.*

I lowered myself into the freezing water. The angels departed, spiraling through the sky in a scene straight from the pages of William Blake. Only one remained by the time I climbed, shivering, from the water. The being wrapped me in a linen shroud.

The sound of celestial trumpets merged with the blare of cars honking. Traffic rushed across the bridge above me. Commuters sped along the road just beyond the underbrush that concealed my body, naked but for a film of river mud.

Sick and coughing, only one thought stuck in my mind: how stupid could I be to let Gabriel make off with the drugs? I took a wad of dried leaves and scraped the mud from my body. Fortunately, I located my clothes without too much trouble. My underwear was in a half-frozen puddle in plain view of passing cars. My jeans hung in the branches of a shrub and my shirt was on the ground below it. I managed to get dressed without exposing myself to motorists – and before freezing to death.

CHAPTER FORTY-SIX

Overhead, cars zoomed across the Broadway Bridge carrying people to work. I was at the edge of a parking lot that was beginning to fill up with commuters. Occasional glances in my direction brought shrieks of horror. By all appearances, I was a homeless schizophrenic.

As I wandered toward downtown, I kept thinking about Sean, imagining where he might be. At the entrance to an office building, several people gathered in the lobby and peered at me through the glass windows. I scurried off before they called the police.

I remembered that Sean once referred to Kansas City as his hometown, and so I felt certain that was where I would find him. I tapped my pocket and was relieved that I still had my wallet and keys. I considered trying to find my car, but instead kept walking. Halfway across the Broadway Bridge, a chilling wind stopped me. I had not found my coat along the riverbank, and my shirt offered scant protection against the cold. I paused to watch a barge hauling canisters of some sort. Diving into the void seemed a viable option. No delusions of salvation. I just wanted to die.

I kept moving, though by the time I reached North Little Rock, my body was so numb from the cold I felt like I had died. A car slowed down and the driver asked me if I needed help. That is, until I turned toward the man and he saw my eyes. He sped away. I meandered my way to the bus station, dipping into alleys and hiding behind garbage cans.

"Kansas City," I told the woman at the ticket counter.

"Do you have money?" she asked.

Don't be afraid, I carry the scent of martyrdom.

When I didn't answer her, the woman probably figured I must be mute. I gave her two twenties. She handed me the ticket and change, and said, "The bus leaves in thirty minutes. Do you have baggage?"

I shook my head.

"They'll be boarding passengers shortly."

"FT. SMITH JOPLIN KANSAS CITY," came an announcement over the loudspeaker.

I shuffled toward the gate and watched my hand extend toward the bus driver to give him the ticket. Once on the bus, I shoved past the passengers to make it to the rear seat. I rested my forehead against the glass and watched the landscape pass in a dizzying blur. I suddenly wished that I had used the bus station facilities while I had the chance – my bowels, long neglected, felt as though they might explode. Luckily, I fell asleep.

When the bus arrived in Ft. Smith, the driver tried to wake me. I came to only enough to open my eyes.

"Do you want a doctor?" the driver asked. There was pity in his voice.

"Help me off the bus," I said in a barely audible voice.

I found the strength to stop by the men's room and then to get on the bus transferring to Joplin and Kansas City. Pulling myself up the steps, I heard the driver speaking to a policeman.

"At least get him across the border," the policeman said. "We'll let Missouri deal with this one."

When I opened my eyes again, I was reclining on a bench with someone prodding me to stand.

"Is Sean here?" I asked.

"Who's Sean?" the man, a Brink's Guard, asked impatiently. "You came alone on the bus. Go on now, and don't cause any trouble. Come on."

The guard pulled me to my feet.

"Okay, okay, give me a minute," I complained. "Where am I?"

"You're in the Kansas City bus station. We let you sleep for a few hours, but you can't stay any longer."

"I need something to eat."

The guard pointed to a row of vending machines.

The ticket counter was closing up, but they took a five-dollar bill and gave me coins. The guard followed me until I got a bag of potato chips, then escorted me to the sidewalk.

Compared with Little Rock and its miniature skyscrapers, Kansas City was the Emerald City. Wind roared down the byways with enough force to topple an adult. The cold air sliced through my clothes and bit my skin. Snow banked against the sidewalks and more snow pressed against the edges of the buildings. I darted from skyscraper to skyscraper, dipping for a moment into the lobbies to get warm. Guards kept sending me on my way.

At the headquarters of IBM, I paused to look at my reflection in the green-tinted windows. I lifted my arms above my head, and then slapped them at my side, repeating the action until I began to think I was a bird and that if I flapped hard enough, I could fly closer to the sun and get warm. I was on a trip as dramatic as the ones I experienced when dropping acid as a teenager. On Good Friday before I joined the church, I had seen the face of God in a swirling vortex. On the same trip, I had spoken to a pine tree about the sadness of God's Creation at having lost its Divine Gardeners. Through the cold of Kansas City, a juniper asked me to brush snow from its needles. I shook my fist at the corporate sign above the lobby entrance and cursed those oblivious to the suffering of nature. Someone in the doorway held a telephone to their ear. I was sure the police would be called.

I wove precariously through the traffic. Pushing away from the hood of a car that stopped just in time, I made it to the sidewalk and dashed into a phone booth. I scanned the White Pages for the last name that Sean had once given me. I made calls to strangers; most hung up before I finished asking my questions.

Far from home, cold to the point of hypothermia, nearly starved to death, I collapsed, having made my way to a public fountain where I could sit. Bronze horses, nostrils flaring, reared above me as their mythic riders struggled for control.

A kindly man approached. "There's a Mission nearby," he said. "You should get inside. "

"Where am I?"

"Kansas City."

"Where?"

"Let me show you."

The man helped me to my feet and pointed the way to a sign that read: Jesus Saves.

My legs wouldn't support my weight. The man helped me to the door of the refuge. The mission's caregivers sat me in front of a portable floor heater and began rubbing my hands to restore circulation. They fed me split-pea soup and a ham sandwich. They asked no questions.

Slowly, I gained my bearings.

"Your cheeks are starting to have some color," said a man with a heavily grooved face. He was bald except for rogue sprouts of hair. "Do you want a shower? You should get out of those clothes."

"I'll take him to the clothes rack," said another fellow who led me to a closet and found a pair of corduroy trousers and flannel shirt. He handed me a pair of wool socks, clean boxers, and an undershirt which he found in a goodwill box. He then directed me to the shower stalls.

I stayed in the shower for a long time, steaming my body with water as hot as I could stand. My bowels gave way. I pointed the water spigot at the mess and made sure it washed down the drain.

The two men who had helped me said I should attend evening service, but as I followed them toward the sanctuary, I stumbled and hit the floor. They led me to the dormitory and found a cot near the back of the room. "Rest here," said the bald man. "No one will bother you."

CHAPTER FORTY-SEVEN

I was awakened by the smelling salts of alcohol flatulence – a strong motivation for getting dressed and finding the cafeteria. A long table was stocked with piles of cold toast and buckets of lumpy oatmeal. Those who arrived early were treated to a dollop of creamed chipped beef. Everyone got a cup of what tasted like day old coffee. A man resembling Popeye the Sailor stared at me and said, cryptically, "Tomorrow could be too late."

"Yeah?" I replied, anxious to dive into my bowl of gruel. "I'll keep that in mind." I took a seat on a metal chair that ground into my bony rump.

Before leaving the Jesus Saves Mission, one of the workers gave me a coat, somewhat tattered, and a pair of lace-up boots. They were too big, but at least my feet would have protection from the snow and ice.

I still imagined that I would find Sean and figured the bus station would be a good place to watch for him. The search had become my reason to live. The guard who earlier had asked me to leave was nowhere around, so I sat at the end of a row of chairs and tried to seem as though I were waiting for someone to arrive. Buses loaded and unloaded, the station filled with people, then grew deserted. As dusk approached, I considered returning to the mission, but the thought of getting there through the snow kept me seated.

Around midnight, a wizened old man nudged me. "Here's something for you," he said, as he handed me a paper sack. Never had I been so pleased by the aroma of a Big Mac and fries.

"Don't have a home?" the man asked.

"I don't think so," I replied.

"Whatever is troubling you," the man said, "family can help."

Before I could respond, he dashed off to a sedan that was waiting outside the sliding glass doors. A middle aged woman opened the car door and helped the old man into his seat. Two ponytailed girls hugged him from the back seat. I watched the car until it disappeared from sight. He must have had the woman stop at McDonald's and then return to the bus station in order to give me the meal.

The word *family* haunted me as I heard an announcement for passengers to board the bus to New York. Family was the word I associated with the church, and New York was home to that family, home to the messiah. That decade in my young adult life seemed a utopia compared with the profligate years that followed. How ironic that I should end my journey in Kansas City – the home base of a church leader who was expelled for his acceptance of homosexuals.

I remained inside the station throughout the night, and by morning I was famished. The McDonald's food had not provided much nourishment. I wondered if I had any money left on my credit card. I found a bank near the bus station and tried the ATM. After three unsuccessful attempts, I finally remembered the PIN. Even so, the machine swallowed the card with a warning that it had been confiscated as a security measure.

"Guess this really is the end," I said to the machine. "Quite a life, wasn't it?"

Back at the bus station, I mulled over an option that wouldn't leave me alone. Could I, in fact, return to the church? I recalled happier times as a successful leader, admired by the membership for his self-sacrifice and dedication. In my current state of mind, I couldn't remember why I left. What had seemed like unpardonable sins at the time struck me now as minor infractions. Hadn't I believed in the mission to create an ideal world, to establish God's Kingdom? Hadn't I lived communally for ten years, sharing everything, even giving up my education and leaving my family? I had considered my life worth something back then.

I hardly knew what I was doing as I found a telephone and struggled to recall the numbers for church offices. Finally, I decided to try a number I knew I could get from information.

"Yes, operator, the New Yorker Hotel."

I called the church headquarters collect. A Japanese secretary accepted the charges.

"This is Simon Powell," I said. "Is Taicho there?"

After a long pause, the sister spoke, "Commander Simon? Left-the-church Simon?"

I smiled at the familiar style of broken English. How long it had been since anyone called me Commander, the term for regional leaders such as I had been. The sister's sweet voice caused me to burst into tears.

"Yes," I sobbed, "that Simon."

The Japanese sister also began to weep.

"I want to come home," I said.

"It so difficult come back," the sister said. "Much suffer and repent."

"But I have to come back," I pleaded.

"Who spiritual parent?" the sister asked.

The concept had become so alien that I almost failed to understand the question. She wanted to know who brought me to the church. A friend of mine had convinced me to hear the teachings, but he left the group years before me. I gave the sister the name of the man who I had chosen as my adopted spiritual parent.

"You must call him," the sister told me. "To come back, that up to him. I give number."

The sister went away from the phone. In the background I heard Japanese voices. *"Nan des ka?"*

"Thank you," I said when the sister gave me the number. *"Domo arigato."*

I took a deep breath and dialed. The phone rang and rang. Then someone lifted the receiver. It was the wife, a dour woman who I had not liked even as a member. To her, all Americans were barbaric and unclean.

"This is Simon," I said. "Remember me?"

No sympathy colored her tone as she said, "Eight years, you no call. Why call after so long time?"

"I want to come back," I said, battling resentment and yet desperate to be saved from my fate.

"Church different now. No anyone can join. People must have society position." She challenged, "You have good job? Or you just want Church take care of you?"

I started to respond, but she pressed on, "And what about sex problem? Are you repent?"

"Does God hate me, then?" I asked.

"It you hate God," she accused. "You are hate-God person."

I felt a stone roll across the entrance to my self-made tomb.

"Goodbye," I said. "Don't worry. You won't hear from me again. I'd rather die on the streets."

I slammed the receiver so hard that it shattered. One of the larger pieces flew past an elderly woman, clipping her cheek and drawing blood. People scattered, worried perhaps that a ricocheting bullet had caught the woman.

Two guards headed toward the pay phones. "You! Yeah, you! Stay where you are."

When I glanced over my shoulder, I saw them talking into their radios. I ran outside to put some distance between me and the station, slipping and sliding with every step.

Ice water found its way through cracks in my boots and soaked the cuffs of my secondhand trousers. Throughout the day, I tried to warm up in building lobbies, as I had earlier, but this time I barely made it past the revolving doors before someone chased me away. I dipped into a café where a friendly waitress with her hair done up in a bun served me vegetable soup and buttered rolls. The place was about to close. The proprietor, an eastern European man, sat next to me at the counter. I got the impression that he was in the habit of feeding the city's less privileged inhabitants. He asked me what I was doing on the streets, but his English was so heavily accented that I had a hard time understanding the question. When I did, I said simply that I had fallen on hard times. When I finished the meal, and needed to leave because they were locking up, I took a business card from a holder near the cash register thinking that I would send him money when my next deal came through. He must understand, I kept thinking, this is not who I am.

I left the café, thanking the waitress and the owner. As he locked up, a dowdy woman, who I assumed was his wife, came from the kitchen and kissed him adoringly on the cheek. I had been grateful for the charity as long as I was inside, in the warm café, but when the cold night air hit my face, I suddenly felt patronized. The meal felt like an act of condescension. I pounded my fists on the window with such force I almost broke it.

"You think you're better than me?" I yelled. "You have no idea who I am!"

The husband and wife looked at me with an air of sadness. I expected them to call the police, but the sympathy in their eyes told me they wouldn't. I stormed through the streets until I spotted a bar. The sign on the door read, Cock Pit.

Thinking of the down-and-out hustlers at the Spotlight, I never imagined how easily I could find myself in their place. The minute I set foot in the bar, a man in his mid-fifties offered to buy me a beer. After guzzling the bottle, he got me a gin and tonic. I bragged about my high-flying days in Hollywood while my patron listened with half-interest.

The man dragged me to the sawdust-covered dance floor, a roped off corner near the jukebox. My pants were so loose that I had to keep a finger through a belt loop to keep them from falling off. The man – Businessman as I began to call him after several failed attempts to remember his name – kept trying to raise my arms in the air so I couldn't hold on. He pulled off my shirt, and I tucked it into the back of my trousers.

The jukebox stopped playing. Businessman took me back to the bar. As I stood next to him, I felt his hand reaching into my pants. He grinned at the bartender, who gave him a smirk and set up a round.

"Do you have somewhere to go?" Businessman asked.

"Nowhere." I said.

"Stay with me." The man took his hand out of my pants threw back a shot of schnapps

"Better'n a belt," I slurred, shoving my hips forward to highlight the fact that a hard-on was preventing my pants from falling down.

Businessman licked his lips as he finished his last beer. "Let's go," he said.

We walked several blocks down the street.

"Where in the hell did you park?" I asked.

"I thought we might stop for a minute," the man said, leading me into an alley. A duct jutting from one of the buildings provided a flow of warm air. A large dumpster hid us from anyone passing on the street.

The man's experienced hands reanimated my now-flaccid cock as he leaned me against the brick wall. He stooped and took me into his mouth while unfastening his lizard skin belt and lowering his slacks. The sight of the man's puny dick, just visible within my line of sight over his bald head, made me chuckle. The man's mop of carefully sculpted hair had fallen to one side. I couldn't stop laughing. He was undaunted in his efforts. I felt something like the need for sexual release, but it was just that I had to urinate. The urge became uncontrollable and I let go. The man guided the stream over his face like a kid playing with a water hose on a summer day.

"You sick fucker," I said. "Go ahead, if that's what you're into. Drink it."

I grabbed the back of his head, ignoring his choking and gagging.

"Son of a bitch!" I yelled, kicking the man after he broke free and began to scurry off on his hands and knees.

I'd never seen such terror in a man's eyes as he coiled into a fetal position to protect himself. I stepped over his body and began walking up the street. As the cold air cleared my head, I began to worry about what I had done. I went back to the scene of the crime. A trail of blood led from the alley. I followed it to within a few yards of the bar.

At least he had made it back to his friends.

CHAPTER FORTY-EIGHT

Returning to the alley, I took garbage bags from the dumpster and made a bed by placing them beneath the warm air coming from the duct. Just as the sun was rising, a sanitation truck began rattling up the street, grinding its jaws like a scavenging tyrannosaur. I heard it from blocks away, but was too exhausted to move. Eventually, two workers approached the alley. They began tossing trash into the mighty machine until the removal of one bag exposed my blood-soaked legs.

"Yo!" the man yelled. "There's a body here."

"I'll radio the police," said his co-worker.

Startled by the exchange, I sat up, momentarily frightening the men out of their skins.

"Never mind," the first one said. "It's just a drunk."

The men allowed me to pass by without further comment. For them, it was just business as usual.

I was cold and miserable – and filthy. Aside from the dirt, I had blood on my pants leg. I went into a restaurant and ordered a coffee with the little bit of change I had left so I could use the restroom to at least relieve myself and wash my face. The owner soon asked me to leave.

"Where's the bus station?" I asked a woman in a fur coat. Instead of answering, she quickened her pace. Overhearing my question, another pedestrian said, "You'll see the station sign if you walk a few blocks that way."

I pushed against the icy wind toward the bus station and sneaked through the main doors unnoticed. I made a beeline to the men's room, cleaned up as best as I could, and when I didn't see any of the guards who might recognize me, took a seat near the payphones. I knew what I had to do, but it had been easier to make a call to the church than to reach out to my own family.

What did any of them have to do with me? Connie and Derek had criticized and condemned me over the years. Vivian was a vortex of need, her love selfish and consuming. Lenny and his cold indifference still haunted me.

The one person who might actually understand what I was going through was Thad, and I kept blocking him from my thoughts. Could he really have awakened from the haze of drug addiction and concluded that he truly loved me?

And then there was Dean, mostly clueless about who I was, really. But he had never betrayed me. He tried to help, even when it meant opening his home to Sean, who he knew was not to be trusted. *Classic signs*, Dean had said to Vivian – classic signs that someone is going to commit suicide.

You have to do it.

This time, the voice was my own inner self.

Ask for help.

I didn't want to call collect, so I searched every corner of the station looking for loose change. After an hour scouring the seats and asking for handouts, I dialed Vivian's number. My stomach tightened when a recorded voice asked for the money. I hung up. Still, I had to talk to someone. I made a collect call to Dean. When he accepted, I couldn't find the courage to say it was me.

"Simon?" Dean asked, hesitantly. "Is that you?"

"It's me," I said.

"Where are you?"

"I don't want to say."

"The police found your car in the East End and had it towed to the dealership. Thad has been calling me. I didn't know what to tell him. Are you okay?"

"I'm afraid, Dean." I thought about Businessman, and about the old woman who got hurt when I broke the pay phone. "I think I may be insane."

"Tell me where you are," Dean said. "I'll do whatever I can."

"Is Sean with you? Have you heard from him?"

"Not a word. He hasn't called." Dean paused to weigh his words. "You knew he would leave."

"What about Thad?"

"He didn't want to go back to California until we heard from you. Thad told me about your history together. I honestly believe he cares about you."

I started to argue. And yet, what else did I hope for except that Thad loved me? "I'm afraid, Dean. I need to be put somewhere." I stopped short of suggesting an insane asylum.

"Let me call Thad now and give him the number of the payphone you're calling from. He'll work out something with you."

Faint voices warned of a trap, but I ignored them. I read Dean the barely legible number for the payphone. Then I waited.

When the phone rang, I willed myself to answer.

"Simon?" Thad's voice seemed hesitant.

"I'm here."

"What is that area code? I don't recognize it. Must be far from here."

"Further than you might imagine," I said. "I went looking for Sean."

I instantly regretted mentioning his name. But Thad knew my feelings for Sean were not deep.

"Listen to me," Thad said, forcefully. "I love you." When I didn't respond, he added, "Do you hear me?"

"I hear you."

"Do you want me to come get you?"

After some commotion in the background, Vivian took the phone.

"We love you, Bubby. Don't you know that?" Before I could respond, she began sobbing, but still managed to say, "Thad explained about the drugs. Oh son," she continued, "I had no idea. Let us help you."

Evidently, everyone was there. Cheryl took the phone and explained that she had friends who got off drugs. "There are places that can help," she said. "We love you, Uncle Simon."

Derek came on next. "I'll come pick you up, if you want," he said, then paused. "Seems your sister wants to say something."

I braced myself for the onslaught, but Connie was contrite.

"Is it my fault?" she began. "Did I make you leave? Oh Simon, please come back. Can you forgive me?"

Poor Connie – she couldn't fathom what was going on with me. All she could imagine was that it had something to do with her.

Finally, Thad took back the phone. "What do you want me to do?"

"Send me a bus ticket. I'll come back to Arkansas if you put me in an asylum or something."

"I'll prepay a ticket, and I'll figure out someplace for you to go when you arrive, okay? Stay put until I call back."

"Not much choice there," I said. "I'm broke."

"Come on, Simon," Thad said, lifting me from the seat. I had slept the entire trip. Everyone else had left the bus.

"My, my," Thad said, propping me against the wall outside the bus station. "Look at those clothes. What a tramp!"

"I feel like a tramp."

"Okay. So listen up. I've got Vivian's car."

I looked around, expecting to be ambushed.

"It's just me," Thad promised. "Vivian wanted to come, but I convinced her I should see you first."

Even so, I kept waiting for Connie or Derek to appear from around a corner.

"Where are you taking me?" I asked as we got into the Pontiac.

"A place called Riverdell," Thad said. "It's the only facility that I could find on such short notice."

"Facility," I muttered.

"Are you sure about this?" Thad asked.

"Yes," I forced myself to say, knowing I had no idea what I was getting myself into. What I truly wanted, desperately, was a good blast. As we were driving, I considered asking Thad to drop by BT's apartment.

"It's going to be terrible, isn't it?" I said. "They'll lock me in a padded cell."

"I wouldn't let something like that happen to you. A few months ago, I went into rehab in San Diego. Things had gotten pretty bad for me, too."

"As bad as this?"

Thad laughed., which seemed new to me. He had always been guarded in the past, so I never really knew what he was feeling. "You are a sad sight," he said. "But everyone bottoms out sooner or later. You just took your sweet time."

"I almost killed someone last night," I confessed, "someone who wanted to trick with me in an alley."

Thad grinned. "You'll have a lot to talk about in group discussion."

After a short ten-minute drive from the bus station, we pulled into the parking lot of a two-story frame building. I noticed a badminton net on the lawn that stretched from the back patio to a line of cottonwoods. The Arkansas River flowed just across the street. Upstream, a train was crossing on an old railroad bridge.

"I can't do this," I said.

Thad touched my elbow. "You can't back out now. I'm taking you inside". Thad looked around to see if anyone was watching, then he kissed me. "That will have to last a while," he said.

I wanted him so badly, but couldn't bring myself to say it.

What was wrong with me?

I supposed I was at Riverdell to answer that very question.

CHAPTER FORTY-NINE

I sat on a small bench by the entrance, clutching a suitcase that Thad had packed for me, and kept my eyes glued to the door. I was ready to make a run for it if men in white suits showed up. Whatever I had said about getting myself committed, I didn't meant it!

"Are you going back to LA?" I asked Thad.

He put his hands on either side of my face. "I'll wait for you. That is, unless you want me to go back."

"No. Don't leave," I said.

"Vivian offered to let me stay at the mansion. I'm going to take her up on it."

"Vivian?"

"She doesn't care that you're gay, Simon. And she knows we have been lovers. Connie is the one with the problem, but I'm working on her."

Could Thad have changed so much? And was I ready to change, to finally accept that I was gay, and that there wasn't anything wrong with it?

A fellow named Harris came from one of the offices. He was tall and thin, with firm muscles that spoke of someone who worked out regularly. I liked his snappy, stylish clothes.

"I'll be your counselor," Harris said. "Let's go upstairs. I'll show you the dormitory."

I followed Harris up the stairs to a large room filled with bunk beds. "Looks like this top one is available," he said, patting a thin mattress. He opened the door of a wooden cabinet and said, "This is yours. The showers are over there. Why don't you get cleaned up and then come downstairs. We have a few formalities to go through."

Sponge bathing in the sink at the bus station had not removed all the dirt and dried blood. How had Thad tolerated the way I smelled! I peeled off my clothes, wrapped a towel around my waist, and headed for the showers.

For the first time in a long while, I felt safe.

Harris was waiting for me at the bottom of the steps. "You need to sign some forms," he said, "and then we should talk."

Harris and I went to an office where a rough looking guy was sitting behind a desk. He seemed to be sizing me up. I wondered if he was one of the success stories. As if reading my thoughts, the man said, "Been sober for twelve years. Everyone that works here has been through treatment."

The word *treatment* made me think of shock therapy. I wondered if they would bind me to a table and electrocute the personality out of my skull, or perhaps remove my thoughts with a needle to the temples. A weak smile formed as I thought about a song I had once heard on Dr. Demento, I'd rather have a bottle in front of me than have a frontal lobotomy.

At first, the paperwork seemed standard. I supplied the names of people to call in case of an emergency, and wrote down my address in Hollywood as my place of residence. But then I was asked to sign an affidavit admitting myself as a ward of the state. That would ensure that Riverdell received financial aid from the state.

Emilio will come through with more money. I just need to get a fax off to Spain and make an excuse. There's nothing wrong with me that a good blast from a crack pipe won't cure.

"Don't listen to it," Harris said, observing my demeanor. "You've made it this far."

"You can't know what's inside of me," I snapped. I signed the affidavit, but then threw the pencil across the room. "Happy now?"

"It's not as though you're under arrest. If you decide to leave, the door is open. Let's go outside and talk, all right?"

"Afraid I might start breaking things?" I asked, nodding toward a vase that, in fact, I *was* thinking about throwing against the wall.

"Partly," Harris said with a smile. "You wouldn't be the first."

"At least you're honest," I said, following him outside.

Harris took me to a bench near the grove of cottonwoods. It was late afternoon. Across the river, a demolition ball swung against a derelict office building.

"Why are you here?" Harris asked.

The simple question hit me hard.

"It's okay," Harris said. "We all have different reasons."

"I don't want to die." Before Harris could comment, I walked to one of the trees and leaned against it.

"It will be rough at first," Harris said when I returned to my seat.

Harris was thinking of drug addiction, but that didn't seem like my biggest problem. "Guilt is eating me up," I said. "I abandoned everything I believed in because I'm gay, a homosexual."

"And since God isn't punishing you, you do it to yourself."

There was truth in Harris's assessment.

"Let me ask you something," Harris said. "If you could do anything you wanted, what would it be?"

"You make things sound so simple," I laughed.

"They are, in a way."

"How did you answer that question?"

"After getting sober, nothing seemed more important than helping people. So I became a social worker. I grew up on Chicago's south side. When I was twenty, I joined the Nation of Islam, which at least got me out of the gang I was in. After a few years, though, I was back on the street. I started using. Before long, heroin was the only thing that mattered."

"Did you feel guilty? About leaving your religion, I mean?"

"I kept myself too stoned to know what I felt," Harris said. "Deep inside, yeah, I probably did feel guilty."

"How in the hell did you end up in Little Rock?" I asked.

"Came down here to do a big score. Arkansas has quite a drug trade, you know. While I was with friends in the East End, I shot up a paper of heroin. It turned out to be pure. I started foaming at the mouth and couldn't breathe. My buddies dumped me at the door of the Baptist Hospital emergency room."

"My childhood best friend died of a heroin overdose," I said, thinking about Ernie.

Harris nodded. "After I sobered up in the hospital, I realized that if I had died, it wouldn't have mattered to anyone. The hospital chaplain came to see me, and I asked for help. He told me to come here to Riverdell. That was seven years ago."

"I want to be an artist," I said.

"What's stopping you?"

Just then, an explosion sounded on the river. The demolition ball succeeded in knocking down the old building it had been hitting. Dust crawled along the surface of the river like a brown fog.

"Look at that," I said. "'Destroy the temple and I will raise it up.'"

"A good metaphor," Harris said. "Destroy the old life and build a new one on the remains."

CHAPTER FIFTY

At dinner, I sat at a table with men ranging in age from eighteen to fifty who all seemed to come from different walks of life.

"Yeah, the damn judge sentenced me to thirty days in this fart-smelling dump," one of them said.

Another fellow, whose bulbous nose was covered with red spider veins, said, "If the guy in the bunk below mine don't stop snoring every night, I'm puttin' a piller over his face."

The youngest, a boy of eighteen, said, "If they hadn't busted me robbing that drug store, I'd be high right now."

"I hate trying to sleep with one eye open. But if I don't, one' a them damn faggots is goin' t'get me," complained a man sitting at the far end of the table.

"Ain't no faggots around here," a tough man said. "If there was, I'd be gettin' me a piece of his ass." The guy looked directly at me. "You a faggot?"

"I'm not a faggot," I said, fortified after my talk with Harris. "I'm gay."

It felt good to say it out loud to strangers.

"Woo!" the man with the spider nose yelped. "We sure as hell got ourselves an asshole to fuck tonight."

Harris, catching wind of the conversation, raced to the table. Other counselors followed. Suddenly, one of the men at my table smacked me on the back of the head. I bolted for the door. My only thought was to get to the railroad bridge. I was worse than Satan, worse than the most despicable creature in the universe.

Few obstacles blocked my path to the bridge – just a few brambles to navigate, until I hit a patch of fire bushes. Thorns ripped through my socks and a branch scraped my arm. A tree limb caught me on the forehead and nearly poked out an eye.

I ran up an embankment and skipped every other railroad tie until I made it to the middle of the river. I lodged myself in a narrow space between the rails and the metal beams. Inches separated me from the edge as I gazed into the abyss.

"Simon!" a voice called out. Someone was at the Riverdell end of the bridge. It was Harris.

"Don't come any closer," I called out.

The heel of my shoe slipped off the edge. Reflexively, I wrapped my arms around the beams. The flowing river was dark and inviting. A gust of wind almost took me over. I looked toward Riverdell.

Police cars arrived, flashing their lights. The area became a surreal disco of alarming sights and sounds as people rushed to the scene from inside the recovery center.

"Simon!" Harris called again. He took a step onto the bridge. "Talk to me."

What was there to talk about?

Harris took two more steps onto the bridge.

A tugboat approached, bellowing its foghorn. The captain must have wondered what was going on. Once the boat passed, the water became blacker than ever – like death itself.

The bridge began to rattle.

Harris called out again. I couldn't see him, but his voice sounded close.

"Vivian is here. So are Connie and Derek. Can you see Thad? He's standing with me."

I didn't want to look.

"Let them love you, Simon."

Which was worse: death below or death inside? Love? That was the word Harris used.

The bridge began to vibrate. A train was definitely approaching. I struggled to keep my heels in place and tightened my grip on the beams.

A horn sounded like the last call of an avenging angel – the final blast of Gabriel's horn.

The locomotive heading my way, with its Cyclops eye, seemed like a devouring monster. The shaking made my heels slip, and my feet dangled from the bridge.

Harris arrived beside me.

Would he risk death to save me? The train entered from the west and roared onto the bridge. The vibrations nearly shook us loose.

"I'm sorry," I said, loudly to be heard above the roar of the boxcars passing just a few inches from our backs.

A Doppler melody played out as the last car sped into the distance. Harris pulled me toward him. Over his shoulder, I saw figures moving onto the bridge. Harris released me into Connie's arms. "Brother," she sobbed, burying her face in my chest.

"We better get off this bridge," Harris cautioned.

Vivian was there, unable to walk without Thad's support. Through a shield of tears, I watched my mother approach, arm in arm, with my lover.

Only then was I sure I could try living this life one more time.

ABOUT THE AUTHOR

William Poe was born in Little Rock, Arkansas, and currently resides in Silver Spring, Maryland. He is both a writer and artist. William earned a Bachelor's degree in art at the University of Arkansas at Little Rock and a Master's degree in anthropology from the University of Nebraska-Lincoln. He has written two books, collections of poetry, and several short stories.

Made in the USA
Charleston, SC
21 May 2012